# ALL OR NOTHING

## BY
## CATHERINE MANN

MILLS &
BOON

Published in Great Britain 2013
by Mills & Boon, an imprint of Harlequin (UK) Limited,
Eton House, 18-24 Paradise Road, Richmond, Surrey TW9 1SR

© Catherine Mann 2013

ISBN: 978 0 263 90466 6
ebook ISBN: 978 1 472 00584 7

51-0313

Harlequin (UK) policy is to use papers that are natural, renewable and recyclable products and made from wood grown in sustainable forests. The logging and manufacturing processes conform to the legal environmental regulations of the country of origin.

Printed and bound in Spain
by Blackprint CPI, Barcelona

*USA TODAY* bestselling author **Catherine Mann** lives on a sunny Florida beach with her flyboy husband and their four children. With more than forty books in print in over twenty countries, she has also celebrated wins for both a RITA® Award and a Booksellers' Best Award. Catherine enjoys chatting with readers online—thanks to the wonders of the internet, which allows her to network with her laptop by the water! Contact Catherine through her website, www.catherinemann.com, find her on Facebook and Twitter (@CatherineMann1) or reach her by snail mail at PO Box 6065, Navarre, FL 32566, USA.

To Shelley, welcome to the family! Love you much!

# One

*Monte Carlo, Casino de la Méditerranée*

It wasn't every day that a woman bet her five-carat, yellow-diamond engagement ring at a roulette table. But it was the only way Jayne Hughes could think of to get her pigheaded husband to take the rock back.

She'd left Conrad messages, telling him to contact her attorney. Conrad ignored them. Her lawyer had called his, to no avail. Divorce papers had been couriered, hand delivered to Conrad's personal secretary, who'd been told not to sign for them under any circumstances.

As Jayne angled through the crush of gamblers toward the roulette table, her fist closed around the engagement ring Conrad had given her seven years ago. Since he owned the *Casino de la Méditerranée,* if she lost the long-shot bet, the ring would be back in his possession. All or nothing, she had to lose to win. She just wanted a clean break and no more heartache.

Jayne plunked down the ring on the velvet square for 12 red. The anniversary of their breakup fell on January 12, next week. They'd spent three years of their seven years married apart. By now Conrad should have been able to accept that so they could move on with their lives.

Familiar sounds echoed up the domed ceiling, chimes and laughter, squeals of excitement mixed with the "ahhhh" of defeat. She'd called these walls full of frescoes home for the four years they'd lived together as man and wife. Even though she moved with ease here now, she'd grown up in a more down-to-earth home in Miami. Her father's dental practice had kept them very comfortable. Of course, they would have been a lot more comfortable had her father not been hiding away a second family.

Regardless, her parents' finances were nowhere close to touching the affluence of this social realm.

Her ring had been a Van Cleef & Arpels, one-of-a-kind design that had dazzled her back when she believed in fairy tales.

Cinderella had left the building. Jayne's glass slipper had been shattered right along with her heart. Prince Charming didn't exist. She made her own destiny and would take charge of her own life.

Nodding to the croupier in charge of spinning the wheel, she nudged her ring forward, centering it on the number 12 red. The casino employee tugged his tie and frowned, looking just past her shoulders and giving her only a second's warning before...

*Conrad.*

She could feel his presence behind her without looking. And how damn unfair was that? Even after three years apart, never once laying eyes on him the entire time, her body still knew him. Wanted him. Her skin tingled under the silky beige gown and her mind filled with memories of spending an entire weekend making love with the Mediterranean breeze blowing in through the balcony doors.

Conrad's breath caressed her ear an instant ahead of his voice. "Gaming plaques can be obtained to your left, *mon amour*."

My love.

Hardly. More like his possession. "And divorce papers can be picked up from my lawyer."

She was a hospice nurse. Not a freaking princess.

"Now why would I want to split up when you look hot enough to melt a man's soul?" A subtle shift of his feet brought him closer until his fire seared her back as tangibly as the desire—and anger—pumping through her veins.

She pivoted to face him, bracing for the impact of his good looks.

Simply seeing him sent her stomach into a predictable tumble. She resented the way her body reacted to him. Why, why, why couldn't her mind and her hormones synch up?

His jet-black hair gleamed under the massive crystal chandeliers and she remembered the thick texture well, surprisingly soft and totally luxurious. She'd spent many nights watching him sleep and stroking her fingers along his hair. With his eyes closed, the power of his espresso-brown gaze couldn't persuade her to go against her better judgment. He didn't sleep much, an insomniac, as if he couldn't surrender control to the world even for sleep. So she'd cherished those rare, unguarded moments to look at him.

Women stared and whispered whenever Conrad Hughes walked past. Even now they didn't try to hide open stares of appreciation. He was beyond handsome in his tuxedo—or just wearing jeans and a T-shirt—in a bold and brooding way. While one hundred percent an American from New York, he had the exotic look of some Italian or Russian aristocrat from another century.

He was also chock-full of arrogance.

Conrad scooped the five-carat diamond off the velvet, and she only had a second to celebrate her victory before he placed it in her palm, closing her fingers back over the ring. The cool stone warmed with his hand curling hers into a fist.

"Conrad," she snapped, tugging.

"Jayne," he rumbled right back, still clasping until the ring cut into her skin. Shifting, he tucked alongside her. "This is hardly the place for our reunion."

He started walking and since he still held her hand, she had no choice but to go along, past the murmuring patrons and thick carved pillars. Familiar faces broke up the mass of vacationers, but she couldn't pause to make idle chitchat, pretending to be happy around old friends and employees.

Her husband's casino provided a gathering place for the elite, even royalty. At last count, he owned a half dozen around the world, but the *Casino de la Méditerranée* had always been his favorite, as well as his primary residence. The old-world flair included antique machines and tables, even though their internal mechanisms were upgraded to state of the art.

People vacationed here to cling to tradition, dressed to the nines in Savile Row tuxedos and Christian Dior evening gowns. Diamonds and other jewels glittered, no doubt original settings from Cartier to Bvlgari. Her five-carat ring was impressive, no question, but nothing out of the ordinary at the *Casino de la Méditerranée*.

Her high heels clicked faster and faster against the marble tiles, her black metallic bag slipping down to her elbow in her haste. "Stop. It. Now."

"No. Thanks." He stopped in front of the gilded elevator, his private elevator, and thumbed the button.

"God, you're still such a sarcastic ass." She sighed under her breath.

"Well, damn." He hooked an arm around her shoulders. "I've never heard that before. Thanks for enlightening me. I'll take it under advisement."

Jayne shrugged off his arm and planted her heels. "I am not going up to your suite."

"Our penthouse apartment." He plucked the ring from her hand and dropped it into her black bag hanging from her shoulder. "Our home."

A home? Hardly. But she refused to argue with him here in the lobby where anyone could listen. "Fine, I need to talk to you. Alone."

The doors slid open. He waived the elevator attendant away and led her inside, sealing them in the mirrored cubicle. "Serving the papers won't make me sign them."

So she'd noticed, to her intense frustration. "You can't really intend to stay married and live apart forever."

"Maybe I just wanted you to have the guts to talk to me in person rather than through another emissary—" his deep brown eyes crinkled at the corners "—to tell me to my face that you're prepared to spend the rest of your life never again sharing the same bed."

Sharing a bed again?

Not a chance.

She couldn't trust him, and after what happened with her father? She refused to let any man fool her the way her mother had been duped—or to break her heart the way her mother had been heartbroken. "You mean sharing the same bed whenever you happen to be in town after disappearing for weeks on end. We've been over this a million times. I can't sleep with a man who keeps secrets."

He stopped the elevator with a quick jab and faced her, the first signs of frustration stealing the smile from him. "I've never lied to you."

"No. You just walk away when you don't want to answer the question."

He was a smart man. Too smart. He played with words as adeptly as he played with money. At only fifteen years old, he'd used his vast trust fund to manipulate the stock market. He'd put more than one crook out of business with short sales, and nearly landed himself in a juvenile detention center. His family's influence worked the system. He'd been sentenced by a judge to attend a military reform school instead, where he hadn't reformed in the least, only fine-tuned his ability to get his way.

God help her, she still wasn't immune to him, a large part of why she'd kept her distance and tried to instigate the divorce from overseas. The last straw in their relationship had come when she'd had a scare with a questionable mammogram. She'd desperately needed his support, but couldn't locate him for nearly a week, the longest seven days of her life.

Her health concerns turned out to be benign, but her fears for her marriage? One hundred percent malignant. Out of respect for what they'd shared, she'd waited for Conrad to come home. She'd given him one last chance to be honest with her. He'd fed her the same old tired line about conducting business and how she should trust him.

She'd walked out that night with only a carry-on piece of luggage. If only she'd thought to leave her rings behind then.

Standing here in the intimate confines of the elevator, with classical music piping through the sound system, she could only think of the time he'd pressed her to the mirrored wall and made love to her until she could barely think, much less remember to ask him where he'd been for the past two weeks.

And still he wasn't talking, damn him. "Well, Conrad? You don't have anything to say?"

"The real problem here is not me. It's that you don't know how to trust." He skimmed his finger along the chain strap of her black metallic shoulder bag and hitched it back in place. "I am not your father."

His words turned residual passion into anger—and pain. "That's a low blow."

"Am I wrong?"

He stood an inch away, so close they could lose themselves in a kiss instead of the ache of all this self-awareness. But she couldn't travel that path again. She stepped closer, drawn by the scent of him, the deep ache in her belly to have his lips on hers. The draw was so intense it took everything inside her to step back.

"If you're so committed to the truth, then how about proving *you're* not *your* father."

When Conrad had been arrested as a teen, the papers ran headlines, Like Father, Like Son. His embezzling dad had escaped conviction as well for his white-collar crimes thanks to that same high-priced lawyer.

In her heart she knew her husband wasn't like his

old man. Conrad had hacked into all those Wall Street companies to expose his father and others like him. She knew intellectually…but the evasiveness, the walls between them… She just couldn't live that way.

She reached into her large, dangling evening bag and pulled out the folded stack of papers. "Here. I'm saving you a trip to the lawyer's office."

She pushed them against Conrad's chest and hit the elevator button for her floor, a guest suite, because she couldn't stomach the notion of staying in their old quarters, which she'd once decorated with hope and love.

"Conrad, consider yourself officially served. Don't worry about the ring. I'll sell it and donate the money to charity. All I need from you is your signature."

The elevator doors slid open at her floor, not his, not their old penthouse, but a room she'd prearranged under a different name. Her head held high, she charged out and into the carpeted corridor.

She walked away from Conrad, almost managing to ignore the fact that he still had the power to break her heart all over again.

Conrad had made ten fortunes by thirty-two years old and had given away nine. But tonight, he'd finally hit the jackpot with his biggest win in three years. He had a chance for closure with Jayne so she wouldn't haunt his dreams every damn night for the rest of his life.

He stalked back into the lobby toward the casino to turn over control for the evening. Once he'd been alerted to Jayne's presence on the floor, he'd walked out on a Fortune 500 guest and a deposed royal heir, drawn by the gleam of his wife's light blond hair piled on top of her head, the familiar curve of her pale neck. Talking to Jayne had been his number-one priority.

Finding her thunking down her ring on 12 red hadn't been the highlight of his life, but the way she'd leaned into him, the flare of awareness in her sky-blue eyes? No, it wasn't over, in spite of the divorce papers she'd slapped against his chest.

She was back under his roof for tonight. He folded the papers again and slid them inside his tuxedo jacket. As he walked past the bar, the bartender nodded toward the last brass stool—and a familiar patron.

Damn it. He did not need this now. But there was no dodging Colonel John Salvatore, his former headmaster and current contact for his freelance work with Interpol, work that had pulled him away from Jayne, work that he preferred she not know about for her own safety. Conrad's wealthy lifestyle and influence gave him easy entrée into powerful circles. When Interpol needed an "in" they called on a select group of contract operatives, headed by John Salvatore, saving months creating an undercover persona for a regular agent. Salvatore usually only tapped into his services once or twice a year. If he used Conrad too often, he risked exposure of the whole setup.

The reason for the missing weeks that always had Jayne in such an uproar.

Part of him understood he should just tell her about his second "career." He'd been cleared to share the basics with his spouse, just not details. But another part of him wanted her to trust him, to believe in him rather than assume he was like his criminal father or a cheating bastard like her dad.

The colonel lifted his Scotch in toast. "Someone's in over his head."

Conrad sat on the bar stool next to the colonel in the private corner, not even bothering to deny Salvatore's implication. "Jayne could have seen you there."

And if the colonel was here, there had to be a work reason. The past three years in particular, Conrad had embraced the sporadic missions with Interpol to fill his empty life, but not now.

"Then she would think your old headmaster came to say hello since I'd already come to see another former student's concert at the Côte d'Azur." Salvatore wore his standard gray suit, red tie and total calm like a uniform.

"This is not a good time." Having Jayne show up unannounced had turned his world upside down.

"I'm just hand delivering some cleanup paperwork—" he passed over a disc, no doubt encrypted "—from our recent...endeavor."

Endeavor: aka the Zhutov counterfeit currency case, which had concluded a month ago.

If Conrad had been thinking with his brain instead of his Johnson, he would have realized the colonel would never risk bringing him into another operation this soon. Already, Jayne was messing with his head, and she hadn't even been back in his life for an hour.

"Everybody wants to give me documents today." He patted the tux jacket and the papers crackled a reminder that his marriage was a signature away from being over.

"You're a popular gentleman tonight."

"I'm sarcastic and arrogant." According to Jayne anyway, and Jayne was a smart woman.

"And incredibly self-aware." Colonel Salvatore finished off his drink, his intense eyes always scanning the room. "You always were, even at the academy. Most of the boys arrived in denial or with delusions about their own importance. You knew your strengths right from the start."

Thinking about those teenage years made Conrad uncomfortable, itchy, reminding him of the toxic time in his life when his father had toppled far and hard off the pedestal Conrad had placed him upon. "Are we reminiscing for the hell of it, sir, or is there a point here?"

"You knew your strengths, but you didn't know your weakness." He nudged aside the cut crystal glass and stood. "Jayne is your Achilles' heel, and you need to recognize that or you're going to self-destruct."

"I'll take that under advisement." The bitter truth of the whole Achilles' heel notion stung like hell since he'd told his buddy Troy much the same thing when the guy had fallen head over ass in love.

"You're definitely as stubborn as ever." Salvatore clapped Conrad on the shoulder. "I'll be in town for the weekend. So let's say we meet again for lunch, day after tomorrow, to wrap up Zhutov. Good night, Conrad."

The colonel tossed down a tip on the bar and tucked into the crowd, blending in, out of sight before Conrad could finish processing what the old guy had said. Although Salvatore was rarely wrong, and he'd been right about Jayne's effect.

But as far as having a *good* night?

A *good* night was highly unlikely. But he had hopes. Because the evening wasn't over by a long shot—as Jayne would soon discover when she went to her suite and found her luggage had been moved to their penthouse. All the more reason for him to turn over control of the casino to his second in command and hotfoot it back to the penthouse. Jayne would be fired up.

A magnificent sight not to be missed.

Steamed as hell over Conrad's latest arrogant move, Jayne rode the elevator to the penthouse level, her old home. The front-desk personnel had given her a key card without hesitation or questions. Conrad had no doubt told them to expect her since he'd moved her clothes from the room she'd chosen.

Damn him.

Coming here was tough enough, and she'd planned to give herself a little distance by staying in a different suite. In addition to the penthouse, the casino had limited quarters for the most elite guests. Conrad had built a larger hotel situated farther up the hillside. It wasn't like she'd snubbed him by staying at that other hotel. Besides, their separation wasn't a secret.

She curled her toes to crack out the tension and focused on finding Conrad.

And her clothes.

The gilded doors slid open to a cavernous entryway. She steeled herself for the familiar sight of the Louis VXI reproduction chairs and hall table she'd selected with such care only to find…

Conrad had changed *everything*. She hadn't expected the place to stay completely the same since she'd left—okay, maybe she had—but she couldn't possibly have anticipated such a radical overhaul.

She stepped into the ultimate man cave, full of massive leather furniture and a monstrous television screen halfway hidden behind an oil painting that slid to the side. Even the drapes had been replaced on the wall-wide window showcasing a moonlit view of the Mediterranean. Thick curtains had been pulled open, revealing yacht lights dotting the water like stars. There was still a sense of high-end style, like the rest of the casino, but without the least hint of feminine frills.

Apparently Conrad had stripped those away when they separated.

She'd spent years putting together the French provincial decor, a blend of old-world elegance with a warmth that every home should have. Had he torn the place apart in anger? Or had he simply not cared? She wasn't sure she even wanted to know what had happened to their old furnishings.

Right now, she only cared about confronting her soon-to-be ex-husband. She didn't have to search far.

Conrad sprawled in an oversize chair with a crystal glass in hand. A bottle of his favored Chivas Regal Royal Salute sat open on the mahogany table beside him. A sleek upholstered sofa had once rested there, an elegant but sturdy piece they'd made love on more than once.

On second thought, getting rid of the furniture seemed like a very wise move after all.

She hooked her purse on the antique wine rack lining the wall. Her heels sunk into the plush Moroccan rug with each angry step. "Where is my bag? I need my clothes."

"Your luggage is here in our penthouse, of course." He didn't move, barely blinked...just brooded. "Where else would it be?"

"In *my* suite. I checked into separate quarters on a different floor as you must know."

"I was informed the second you picked up your key."
He knocked back the last bit of his drink.

"And you had my things moved anyway." What did
he expect to gain with these games?

"I'm arrogant. Remember? You had to already know
what would happen when you checked in. No matter
what name you use, the staff would recognize my wife."

Maybe she had, subconsciously hoping to make a
prideful statement. "Silly me for hoping my request
would be honored—as your wife."

"And 'silly' me for thinking you wouldn't embar-
rass me in front of my own staff."

Contrition nipped at her heels. Regardless of what
had happened between them near the end of their marriage, she'd loved him deeply. She was so tired of hurting him, of the pain inside her, as well.

She sank into the chair beside him, weary to her
toes, needing to finish this and move on with her life,
to settle down with someone wonderfully boring and
uncomplicated. "I'm sorry. You're right. That was
thoughtless of me."

"Why did you do it?" He set aside his glass and leaned
closer. "You know there's plenty of space in the penthouse."

Even if he wouldn't offer total honesty, she could.
"Because I'm scared to be alone with you."

"God, Jayne." He reached out to her, clasping her
wrist with callused fingers. "I'm fifty different kinds
of a bastard, but never—never, damn it—would I hurt
you."

His careful touch attested to that, as well as years together where he'd always stayed in control, even during
their worst arguments. She wished she had his steely
rein over wayward emotions. She would give anything

to hold back the flood of feelings washing over her now, threatening to drown her.

Words—honesty—came pouring out of her. "I didn't mean that. I'm afraid I won't be able to resist sleeping with you."

# Two

With Jayne's agonized confession echoing in his ears and resonating deep in his gut, holding himself still was the toughest thing Conrad had ever done—other than letting Jayne go the day she'd walked out on their marriage. But he needed to think this through, and fast. One wrong move and this confrontation could blow up in his face.

Every cell in his body shouted for him to scoop her out of that leather chair, take her to his room and make love to her all night long. Hell, all weekend long. And he would have—if he believed she would actually follow through on that wish to have sex.

But he could read Jayne too clearly. While she desired him, she was still pissed off. She would change her mind about sleeping with him before he finished pulling the pins from her pale blond hair. He needed more time to wipe away her reservations and persuade her that sleeping together one last time was a good thing.

Pulling back his hand, he grabbed the bottle instead and poured another drink. "As I recall, I didn't ask you to have sex with me."

If she sat any straighter in that seat, her spine would snap. "You don't have to say the words. Your eyes seduce me with a look." Her chin quivered. "*My* eyes betray me, because when I look at you…I want you. So much."

Okay, maybe he could be persuaded not to wait after all. "Why is that a bad thing?"

A clear battle waged in her light blue eyes that he understood quite well. The past three years apart had been a unique kind of hell for him, but eventually he'd accepted that their marriage was over. He just refused to end it via a courier.

Call him stubborn, but he'd wanted Jayne to look him in the face when she called it quits. Well, he'd gotten his wish—only to have her throw him a serious curveball. She still wanted him every bit as much as he wanted her.

Granted, sex between them had always been more than good, even when they'd used it to distract them from their latest argument. One last weekend together would offer the ultimate distraction. They could cleanse away the gnawing hunger and move on. He just had to persuade her to his way of thinking

The battle continued in her eyes until, finally, she shook her head, a strand of blond hair sliding loose. "You're not going to win. Not this time." Standing, she demanded, "Give me my clothes back, and don't you dare tell me to go into our old bedroom to get them myself."

He'd been right to wait, to play it cool for now. "They're already in the guest room."

Her mouth dropped open in surprise. "Oh, I'm sorry for thinking the worst of you."

He shrugged. "Most of the time you would be right."

"Damn it, Conrad," she said softly, her shoulders lowering, her face softening, "I don't want to feel bad for you, not now. I just want your signature and peace."

"All *I* ever wanted was to make you happy." Tonight might not be the right time to indulge in tantric sex, but that didn't mean he couldn't start lobbying. He shoved to his feet, stepped closer and reached out to stroke that loose lock of hair. "Jayne, I didn't ask you to have sex, but make no mistake, I think about being with you and how damn great we were together."

Teasing the familiar texture of her hair between his fingers, he brushed back the strand, his knuckles grazing her shoulder as he tugged free the pin still hanging on. Her pupils went wide with awareness and a surge of victory pumped through him. He knew the unique swirl of her tousled updo so well he could pull the pins out of it blindfolded.

He stepped aside. "Sleep well, Jayne."

Her hands shook as she swept back the loose strand, but she didn't say a word. She spun away on her high heels and snagged her purse from the wine rack before making tracks toward the spare room. He had a feeling peace wasn't in the cards for either of them anytime soon.

Jayne closed the guest-room door behind her and sagged back, wrapping her arms around herself in a death grip to keep from throwing herself at Conrad. After three long years without him, she hadn't expected her need for him to be this strong. Her mind filled with fantasies of leaning over him as he sat in that monstrously big chair, of sliding her knees up on either side until she straddled his lap.

There was something intensely stirring about the times she'd taken charge of him, a scenario she'd half forgotten in their time apart. But she loved that feeling of sensual power. Sure, he could turn the tables in a heartbeat—a gleam in his eyes would make that clear—but then she would tug his tie free, unbutton his shirt, his pants…

She slid down the door to sit on the floor. A sigh burst free. This wasn't as easy as she'd expected.

At least she had a bed to herself without arguing, a minor victory. She looked around at the "tomato-red room" as Conrad had called it. He'd left this space unchanged and the relief she felt over such a minor point surprised her. Why did it mean so much to her that he hadn't tossed out everything from their old life?

Shoving back up to her feet, she tapped a vintage bench used as a luggage rack and skimmed her fingers along the carved footboard. He'd even kept the red toile spread and curtains. She'd wanted a comfortable space for their family to visit. Except Conrad and his older sister only exchanged birthday and Christmas cards. Since his parents and her mother had passed away, that didn't leave many relatives. Jayne definitely hadn't invited her father and his new wife…

Had she let some deep-seated "daddy issues" lead her to choose a man destined to break her heart? That was not the first time the thought had occurred to her—okay, how could she dodge the possibility when Conrad had tossed it in her face at least a dozen times? She'd forgotten how he had a knack for catching her unaware, like how he'd sent her clothes here rather than demanding she sleep in their old room.

Like the way he'd tugged the pin from her hair.

Her mind had been so full of images of them together, and she'd actually admitted how much she still wanted him. Yet, he'd turned her down even though it was clear from his eyes, from his touch—from his arousal—how much he wanted her, too. She knew his body as well as her own, but God, would she ever understand the man?

She tossed her purse on the bed and her cell phone slid out. She snatched it up only to find the screen showed three missed calls from the same number.

Guilt soured in her stomach, and how twisted was that? She wasn't actually dating Anthony Collins. She'd been careful to keep things in the "friend" realm since she'd begun Hospice care for his aged great-uncle who'd recently passed away from end stage lung cancer.

She'd seen a lot of death in her job, and it was never easy. But knowing she'd helped ease a person's final days, had helped their families as well, she could never go back to filling her time with buying furniture and planning meals. She didn't even want to return to working in an E.R.

She'd found her niche for her nursing degree.

While there were others who could cover her rounds at work, she wanted to resume the life she'd started building for herself in Miami. And to do that, she needed closure for her marriage.

She thumbed the voice mail feature and listened…

"Jayne, just checking in…" Anthony's familiar voice piped through with the sound of her French bulldog, Mimi, barking in the background since he'd agreed to dog sit for her. "How did your flight go? Call me when you get a chance."

*Beep.* Next message.

"I'm getting worried about you. Hope you're not stranded from a layover, at the mercy of overpriced airport food."

*Beep.* Next call from Anthony, he hung up without speaking.

She should phone him back. Should. But she couldn't listen to his voice, not with desire for Conrad still so hot and fresh in her veins. She took the coward's way out and opted for a text message instead.

Made it 2 Monte Carlo safely. Thanks 4 worrying. 2 tired to talk. Will call later. Give Mimi an extra treat from me.

More of that remorse still churning, she hit Send and turned off the power. Big-time coward. She pitched her phone back in her purse. The *clink* as her cell hit metal reminded her of the ring Conrad had slipped back inside. She'd won a battle by delivering the divorce papers, and she could think of plenty of charities that would benefit from a donation if—when—she sold the ring.

She may not have gotten to place her bet, but she'd won tonight. Right?

Wrong. She sagged onto the edge of the bed and stared at her monogrammed carry-on bag. Good thing she'd packed her ereader, because there wasn't a chance in hell she would be sleeping.

Parked on the glassed-in portion of his balcony, Conrad thumbed through the Zhutov document on his tablet computer.

Monte Carlo rarely slept at night anyhow, the perfect setting for a chronic insomniac like himself. Beyond the windows, yachts bobbed in the bay, lights glowing. No doubt the casino below him was still in full swing, but he'd soundproofed his quarters.

The divorce papers lay beside him on the twisted iron breakfast table. He'd already reviewed them and found them every bit as frustrating as when his lawyer had relayed the details. And yes, he knew the contents even though he'd led Jayne to believe otherwise.

She was insistent on walking away with next to nothing, just as she'd done the day she'd left. He'd already drawn up an addendum that created a trust for her, and she could do whatever the hell she wanted with the money. But he'd vowed in front of God and his peers to protect this woman for life, and he would follow through on that promise even beyond their divorce.

He hadn't made that commitment lightly.

Frustration simmered inside him, threatening his focus as he read the Zhutov report from Salvatore. He'd given up his marriage for cases like this, so he'd damn well better succeed or he would have lost Jayne for nothing.

The world was better off with that bastard behind bars. Zhutov had masterminded one of the largest counterfeiting organizations in Eurasia. He'd used that influence to shift the balance of power between countries by manipulating the strength of a country's currency. At a time when many regions were struggling for financial survival, the least dip in economics could be devastating.

And from all appearances, Zhutov had played his tricks out of an amoral need for power and a desire to advance his son's political aspirations by any means possible.

Helping Interpol stop crooks like that was more than a job. It was a road to redemption after what Conrad had done in high school. He'd committed a crime not all that different from Zhutov's and gotten off with a slap on the wrist. At the time he'd manipulated the stock market, he'd deluded himself into thinking he was some sort of dispenser of cosmic justice, stealing from the evil rich to give to the more deserving.

Utter crap.

At fifteen, he'd been old enough to know better. He'd understood the difference between right and wrong. But he'd been so caught up in his own selfish need to prove he was better than his crook of a father, he'd failed to take into account the workers and the families hurt in the process.

He might have avoided official prison time, but he still owed a debt. When Salvatore had retired as headmaster of North Carolina Military Prep and taken a job with Interpol, Conrad had been one of his first recruits. He'd worked a case cracking open an international insider trading scam.

The sound of the balcony door opening drew him back to the moment. He didn't have to turn around. Jayne's scent already drifted toward him. Her seabreeze freshness, a natural air, brought the outdoors inside. She'd told him once she'd gotten out of the practice of wearing perfume as a nurse because scents disturbed some patients. And yes, he remembered most everything about her, such as how she usually slept like a log regardless of the time zone.

That she was restless now equaled progress. It was already past 2:00 a.m.

He shut down the file and switched to a computer game, still keeping his back to her.

"Conrad?" Her husky voice stoked his frustration higher, hotter. "What are you doing up so late?"

"Business." The screen flashed with a burst of gunfire as his avatar fought back an ambush in Alpha Realms IV.

She laughed softly, stepping farther onto the balcony silently other than the swoosh of her silky robe against her legs. "So I see. New toy from your pal Troy Donavan?"

Conrad had the inside track on video games since a fellow felonious high school bud of his now ran a lucrative computer software corporation. "It's my downtime, and I don't even have to leave town. Did you need something?"

"I was getting a glass of water, and I saw you're still awake. You always were a night owl."

More than once she'd walked up behind him, slid her arms around his neck and offered to help him relax with a massage that always led to more.

"Feel free to have a seat." He guided his avatar around a corner in dystopian city ruins. "But I can't promise to be much of a conversationalist."

"Keep playing your game."

"Hmm…" Alpha Realms provided a safe distraction from the peripheral view of Jayne sliding onto the lounger. The way the silky robe clung to her shower-damp skin, she could have been naked.

Her legs crossed at the ankles, her fuzzy slippers dangling from her toes. "Why do you keep working when you could clearly retire?"

Because his fast-paced, wealthy lifestyle provided the perfect cover for him to move in the circles necessary to bring down crooks like Zhutov. "You knew I lived at the office when you married me."

"I was like any woman crazy in love." She cupped a water glass between her hands. "I deluded myself into believing I could change you."

He hadn't expected her to concede anything, much less that. He set aside his tablet, on top of those damn divorce papers. "I remember the first time I saw you."

The patio sconce highlighted her smile. "You were one of the crankiest, most uncooperative emergency room patients I'd ever met."

He'd been in Miami following up on a lead for Salvatore. Nothing hairy, just chasing a paper trail. He would have been back in Monte Carlo by morning, except a baggage handler at the airport dropped an overweight case on Conrad's foot. Unable to bear weight on it even when he'd tried to grit through the pain, he'd ended up in the E.R. rather than on his charter jet. And he'd still protested the entire way.

Although his mood had taken a turn for the better once the head nurse on the night shift stepped into the waiting room to find out why he'd sent everyone else running. "I'm surprised you spoke to me after what an uncooperative bastard I was."

"I still can't believe you insisted you just wanted a walking boot, that you had an important meeting you couldn't miss because of what you called a stubbed toe."

"Yeah, not my shining moment."

"Smart move sending flowers to the staff members you pissed off." She scratched the corner of her mouth with her pinky. "I don't believe I ever told you, but I thought they were for me when they arrived."

"I wanted to win you over. Apologizing to your coworkers seemed the wisest course to take." He'd extended his stay in Miami under the guise of looking into investment property.

They'd eloped three months later, in a simple ocean-side ceremony with a couple of his alumni buddies as witnesses.

Jayne sipped her water, her eyes unblinking as if she might be holding back tears. "So this is really it for us."

"Nice to know this isn't any easier for you than it is for me."

Her hand shook as she set aside her glass. "Of course this isn't easy for me. But I want it to be done. I want to move past this and be happy again."

Damn, it really got under his skin that he still hurt her even after all this time apart.

"I'm sorry you're unhappy." Back when, he would have moved heaven and earth to give her what she wanted. Now it appeared all he could give her was a divorce.

"Do you really mean that?" She swung her feet to the side, sitting on the edge of the lounger. "Or is that why you held off signing the papers for so long? So you could see me squirm?"

"Honest to God, Jayne, I just want both of us to be happy, and if that means moving on, then okay." Although she looked so damn right beside him, back in his life again. He would be haunted by the vision of her there for a long time to come. "But right now, neither of us seems to be having much luck with the concept of a clean break."

"What are you saying?"

Persuading her would take a lot more savvy than sending a few dozen roses to her friends. "I think we need to take a couple of days to find that middle ground, peace or closure or whatever the hell therapists are calling it lately."

"We've been married for seven years." She fished into the pocket of her robe and pulled out her engagement ring and wedding band set. "How do you expect to find closure in two days when we've been trying for the last three years?"

He did not want to see those damn rings again. Not unless they were sitting where he'd put them—on her finger.

"Has ignoring each other worked for you? Because even living an ocean apart hasn't gone so well for me."

"You'll get no argument from me." Her fingers closed around the rings. "What exactly do you have in mind?"

He sensed victory within his sights. She was coming around to his way of thinking. But he had to be sure because if he miscalculated and moved too soon he could risk sending her running.

"I suggest we spend a simple night out together, no pressure. My old high school buddy Malcolm Douglas is performing nearby—in the Côte d'Azur—tomorrow night. I have tickets. Go with me."

"What if I say no?"

Not an option. He played his trump card. "Do you want my signature on those divorce papers?"

She dropped her rings on top of the computer that just happened to be resting over the divorce papers. "Are you blackmailing me?"

"Call it a trade." He rested his hand over the five-carat diamond he'd chosen for her, only her. "You give me two days and I'll give you the divorce papers. Signed."

"Just two days?" She studied him through narrowed, suspicious eyes.

He gathered up the rings and pressed them to her palm, closing her fingers over them again. "Forty-eight hours."

Forty-eight hours to romance her back into his bed one last time.

# Three

Gasping, Jayne sat upright in bed, jolted out of a deep sleep by…sunlight?

Bold morning rays streamed through the part in the curtains. Late morning, not a sunrise. She looked at the bedside clock: *10:32 a.m.?* Shoving her tangled hair aside, she blinked and the time stayed the same.

Then changed to 10:33.

She never overslept and she never had trouble with jet lag, thanks to her early years in nursing working odd shifts in the emergency room. Except last night she'd had trouble falling asleep even after a long bubble bath. Restless, she'd been foolish enough to dance with temptation by talking to Conrad on a moonlit Mediterranean night.

He'd talked her into staying.

God, was she even ready to face him today with the memory of everything she'd said right there between

them? The thought of him out there, a simple door
away, had her so damn confused. She'd all but propo-
sitioned him, and he'd turned her down. She'd been so
sure she would have to keep him at arm's length she'd
checked into the room on another floor. That seemed
petty, and even egotistical, now.

He'd simply wanted the common courtesy of a face-
to-face goodbye and he'd been willing to wait three
years to get it. The least she could do was behave ma-
turely now. She just had to get through the next forty-
eight hours without making a fool of herself over this
man again.

Throwing aside the covers, she stood and came face-
to-face with her reflection in the mirror. A fright show
stared back at her, showcased by the gold-leaf frame.
With her tousled hair and dark circles under her eyes,
she looked worse than after pulling back-to-back shifts
in the E.R.

Pride demanded she shower and change before facing Conrad, who would undoubtedly look hot in whatever he wore. Even bed-head suited him quite well,
damn him.

A bracing shower later, she tugged on her favorite black skinny jeans and a poet's shirt belted at the
waist, the best she could do with what little she had in
her suitcase. But she'd expected to be traveling back to
the States today, divorce papers in hand. At least she'd
thought to change her flight and arrange for more time
off before going to bed last night.

Nerves went wild in her chest as she opened the
door. The sound of clanking silverware echoed down
the hallway, the scent of coffee teasing her nose. He'd
said they would spend two days finding peace with

each other, but as she thought about facing him over breakfast, she felt anything but peaceful.

Still, she'd made a deal with him and she refused to let him see her shake in her shoes—or all but beg him for sex again.

Trailing her fingers down the chair railing in the hall, she made her way through the "man cave" living room and into the dining area. And oh, God, he'd swapped her elegant dining room set for the equivalent of an Irish pub table with a throne at the head. *Really?*

And where was the barbarian of the hour?

The table had been set for two, but he was nowhere to be seen. A rattle from the kitchen gave her only a second's warning before a tea cart came rolling in, but not pushed by Conrad.

A strange woman she'd never met before pushed the cart containing a plate of pastries, a bowl of fruit and two steaming carafes. At the moment, food was the last thing on Jayne's mind. Instead, at the top of the list was discovering the identity of this stranger. This beautiful redheaded stranger who looked very at ease in Conrad's home, serving breakfast from a familiar tea cart that had somehow survived the "purge of Jayne" from the premises.

Jayne thrust out her hand. "Good morning. I'm Jayne Hughes, and you would be?"

Given the leggy redhead was wearing jeans and a silk blouse, she wasn't from housekeeping.

"I'm Hillary Donavan. I'm married to Conrad's friend."

"Troy Donavan, the computer mogul who went to high school with Conrad." The pieces fell into place and, good Lord, did she ever feel ridiculous. "I saw your engagement and wedding announcements in the tabloids. You're even lovelier in person."

Hillary crinkled her nose. "That's a very polite way of saying I'm not photogenic. I hate the cameras, and I'm afraid they reciprocate."

The photos hadn't done her justice, but by no means could Hillary Donavan ever look anything but lovely— and happy. The newlywed glow radiated from her, leaving Jayne feeling weary and more than a little sad over her own lost dreams.

She forced a smile on her face. "I assume that breakfast is for us?"

"Why yes, it is," Hillary answered, sweeping the glass cover from the pastries. "Cream cheese filled, which I understand is your favorite, along with chocolate mint tea for you and coffee for me."

And big fat strawberries. All of her favorites.

She couldn't help but dig to find out who'd thought to make that happen. "How lovely of the kitchen staff to remember my preferences."

"Um, actually…" Hillary parked the cart between two chairs and waved for Jayne to sit. "I'm a former event planner so nosy habits die hard. I asked Conrad, and he was wonderfully specific."

He remembered, all the way down to the flavor of hot tea, when he'd always preferred coffee, black, alongside mounds of food. As she stared at the radically different decor, she wondered how many other times he'd deferred to her wishes and she just hadn't known.

Jayne touched the gold band around a plate from her wedding china. "I didn't realize you and your husband live in Monte Carlo now."

"Actually we flew over for a little unofficial high school reunion to see Malcolm's charity concert tonight. Word is he's sold out, set to take the Côte d'Azur by storm."

They were all going in a group outing? She felt like a girl who thought she'd been asked to the movie only to find out the whole class was going along. How ironic when she'd so often wished they had more married friends.

"I have to confess to having a fan girl moment the first time I met Malcolm Douglas in person." Hillary poured coffee from the silver carafe, the java scent steaming up all the stronger with reminders of breakfasts with Conrad. "I mean, wow, to have drinks and shoot the breeze with the latest incarnation of Harry Connick, Jr. or Michael Bublé? Pretty cool. Oh, and I'm supposed to tell you that evening gowns are being sent up this afternoon for you to choose from, since you probably packed light and it's a black-tie charity event. But I'm rambling. Hope you don't mind that I'm barging in on you."

"I'm glad for the company. Not many of Conrad's friends are married." When Troy had come to visit, she'd wished for a gal pal to hang out with and now she finally had one…too late for it to matter. "And when we were together, none of his classmates had walked down the aisle yet."

"They're getting to that age now. Even Elliot Starc got engaged recently." She shook her head laughing. "Another bad boy with a heart of gold. Did you ever get to meet him?"

"The one who was sent to the military high school after too many arrests for joy riding." Although according to Conrad, the joy riding had been more like car theft, but Elliot had influential friends. "Now he races cars on the international circuit."

"That's the one. Nobody thought he would ever settle down." Hillary's farm fresh quality, her uncomplicated friendliness, was infectious. "But then who would have thought my husband, the Robin Hood Hacker, would become Mr. Domesticity?"

The Robin Hood Hacker had infiltrated the Department of Defense's system, exposing corruption. After which, he'd ended up at North Carolina Military Prep reform school with Conrad. Malcolm Douglas had joined them later, having landed a plea bargain in response to drug charges.

Taking their histories into account, maybe she'd been wrong to think she could tame the bad boy. Was Hillary Donavan in for the same heartbreak down the road?

Shaking her head, Jayne cut into the pastry, cream cheese filling oozing out. "You're not at all what I expected when I read Troy got married."

"What *did* you expect?"

"Someone less…normal." She'd always felt so alone in Conrad's billionaire world. She hadn't imagined finding a friend like the neighbors she'd grown up with. "I seem to be saying all the wrong things. I hope you didn't take that the wrong way."

"No offense taken, honestly. Troy is a bit eccentric, and I'm, well, not." She twisted her diamond and emerald wedding ring, smiling contentedly. "We balance each other."

Jayne had once thought the same thing about herself and Conrad. She was a romantic, and he was so brooding. Looking back now, she'd assumed because of his high school years he was some sort of tortured soul and her nurse's spirit yearned to heal him.

Silverware clinked on the china as they ate and the

silence stretched. She felt the weight of Hillary's curious stare and unspoken question.

Jayne lifted her cup of tea. "You can go ahead and ask."

"Sorry to be rude." Hillary set aside her fork, a strawberry still speared on the end. "I'm just surprised to see you and Conrad together. I hope this means you've patched things up."

"I'm afraid not. The divorce will be final soon." How much, if anything, had he shared with his friends about the breakup? "We had some final paperwork to attend to. And while I'm here, I guess we're both trying to prove we can be civil to each other. Which is crazy since our paths will never cross again."

"You never know."

"I do know. Once I leave here, my life and Conrad's will go in two very different directions." Jayne folded her napkin and placed it on the table, her appetite gone.

She couldn't even bring herself to be mad at Hillary for being nice and happy. And Jayne hoped deep in her heart that Troy would be the bad boy who'd changed for the woman he'd married.

She'd been certain Conrad had changed, too, but he'd been so evasive about his travels, refusing to be honest with her when she'd confronted him again and again about his mysterious absences. He didn't disappear often, but when he did, he didn't leave a note or contact her. His excuses when he returned were thin at best. She'd wanted to believe he wasn't like his father... or her father. She still wanted to believe that.

But she couldn't be a fool. He kept insisting she should trust him. Well, damn it, he should have trusted her. The fact that he didn't left her with only two conclusions.

He wasn't the man she'd hoped, and he'd very likely never really loved her at all.

This little fantasy two-day make-nice-a-thon was just that. A fantasy. Thank God, he'd turned her away last night, because had she fallen into bed with him, she would have regretted it fiercely come morning time. Her body and her brain had never been *simpatico* around her husband.

But she had a great big broken heart as a reminder to listen only to her common sense.

Common sense told him that keeping his distance today would give him an edge tonight. But staying away from Jayne now that she'd returned to Monte Carlo was driving him crazy.

Seeing her on the security camera feed from the solarium didn't help his restraint, either.

But the secure room offered the safest place for him to hang out with a couple of his high school buds—Donavan and Douglas—who'd also been recruited for Interpol by Colonel Salvatore. The colonel had his own little army of freelancers drafted from the ranks of his former students. Although God knows why he'd chosen them, the least conformist boys in the whole school. But they were tight with each other, bonded by their experiences trying to patch their lives back together.

They'd even dubbed themselves "The Alpha Brotherhood." They could damn well conquer anything.

Now, they shared a deeper bond in their work for Salvatore. For obvious reasons, they still couldn't talk freely out in public. But a vaulted security room in his casino offered a place of protected privacy so they could let their guards down.

The remains of their lunch lay scattered on the table.

Normally he would have enjoyed the hell out of this. Not today. His thoughts stayed too firmly on Jayne, and his hand gravitated toward her image on the screen.

Donavan tipped back his chair, spinning his signature fedora on one finger. "Hey, Conrad, I picked up some great Cuban smokes last week, but I wouldn't want to start Malcolm whining that his allergies are acting up."

Douglas scratched at the hole in the knees of his jeans. "I do not whine."

"Okay—" Donavan held up his hands "—if that's the story you want to go with, fine, I'm game."

"I am seriously going to kick the crap out of you—" Douglas had picked fights from day one "—just for fun."

"Bring it."

"I would, but I don't want to risk straining my vocal cords and disappoint the groupies." Douglas grinned just like he was posing for the cover of one of his CDs. "But then, you've been benched by marriage so you wouldn't understand."

Some things never changed. They could have all been in their barracks, seventeen years ago. Except today Conrad didn't feel much like joining in. His eyes stayed locked on the screen showing security feed from his place.

Or more precisely, his eyes stayed locked on Jayne at the indoor pool with Donavan's wife. He couldn't take his eyes off the image of her relaxed and happy. Jayne wore clothes instead of a swimsuit, not that it mattered when he could only think of her wearing nothing at all. She was basking in the sun through the solarium windows.

Donavan sailed his hat across the room, Frisbee

style, nailing Conrad in the shoulder. "Are you doing okay, brother?"

Conrad plucked the hat from the floor and tossed it on the table alongside his half-eaten bowl of ratatouille. "Why wouldn't I be?"

"Oh, I don't know…" Malcolm lowered his chair legs to the ground again. "Maybe because your ex-wife is in town and you haven't stopped looking at her on that video monitor since we got in here."

"She's not my ex-wife yet." He resisted the urge to snap and further put a damper on their lunch. "Anybody up for a quick game of cards?"

Donavan winced. "So you can clean me out again?"

Malcolm hauled his chair back to the table. "Now who's whining?"

Pulling his eyes if not his attention off Jayne, Conrad swept aside the dishes and reached for a deck of cards.

Between their freelance work for Interpol and their regular day jobs, there was little time left to hang out like they'd done during the old days. Damn unlucky for him one of those few occasions happened to be now, when they were all around to witness the final implosion of his marriage.

And what if he didn't get one last night with Jayne? What if he had to spend the rest of his life with this hunger gnawing at his gut every time a blonde woman walked by? Except no woman, regardless of her hair color, affected him the way Jayne did.

No matter what he told his brothers, he was not okay. But damn it, he would be tonight after the concert when he lay Jayne back on that sofa and made her his again.

Jayne hadn't been on a date in three years, not even to McDonald's with a friend. How ironic that her first post-separation outing with a man would be with her own estranged husband. And he'd taken her to a black-tie charity concert on the Côte d'Azur—the French Riviera.

Although she had to admit, his idea of finding a peaceful middle ground had merit—even if he'd all but blackmailed her to gain her cooperation.

At least seated in the historic opera house she could lose herself in the crowd, simply sit beside Conrad and enjoy the music, without worrying about temptation or messy conversations. Malcolm Douglas sang a revamp of some 1940s tune, accompanying his vocals on the grand piano. His smooth baritone voice washed over her as effortlessly as the glide of Conrad's fingers on her shoulder. So what if her husband had draped his arm along the back of her seat? No big deal.

In fact, she'd been surprised at how little pressure he'd put on her throughout the day, especially after their intense discussions, their potent attraction, the night before. Waking up alone was one thing. But then to have him spend the entire day away from her…

His amenability was good. Wasn't it?

That niggling question had grown during the rest of the afternoon without him. Lunchtime passed and she started to question if she'd heard his offer of a date correctly. Except Hillary had mentioned it, as well. Then the staff brought a selection of evening wear in her size. She'd chosen a silver gown with bared shoulders, the mild winter only requiring a black satin wrap.

By the time Conrad arrived at their suite to pick her up, her nerves had been strung so tightly, she was ready to jump out of her skin. The sight of him in a tuxedo, broad shoulders filling out the coat to mouthwatering perfection, had just been downright unfair. All the way to the limo, she'd thought he would make his move, only to find Troy and Hillary Donavan waiting in the limousine, ready to go out to dinner with them before the concert. But then hadn't Hillary said Troy and Conrad were having some kind of reunion?

The evening had been perfect.

And perfectly frustrating.

Conrad's thumb grazed the sensitive crook of her neck, along the throb of her pulse. Did he know her heart beat faster for him? Her breath hitched in her throat.

Hillary leaned toward her and whispered, "Are you all right?"

Wincing, Jayne resisted the urge to shove Conrad's arm away. "I'm fine, just savoring."

Savoring the feel of Conrad's hand on her bare skin.

Damn it.

He shifted in his seat, his fingers stroking along the top of her arm and sending shivers along her spine. She struggled not to squirm in her seat and draw Hillary's attention again. But that was getting tougher and tougher to manage by the second. He had to know what he was doing.

Still, if he'd been trying to seduce her, he could have been a lot more overt, starting with ditching the other couple. Her mind filled with vivid memories of the time he'd reserved a private opera box for a performance of *La Bohème* and made love to her with his hand under her dress.

Only one of the many times he'd diverted an argument with sex.

Yet now, he turned her down. Why?

The lights came up for intermission, and Conrad's

arm slid away as he applauded. She bit her lip to keep from groaning.

He stood then angled back down to her. "Do you and Hillary mind keeping each other company while Troy and I talk shop? He's developing some new software to prevent against hackers at the casino."

"Of course I don't mind." She'd given up the right to object when she'd walked out on him three years ago. Soon, their breakup would be official and legal.

"Thanks," he said, cupping her face in a warm palm for an instant before straightening. At the last second, he glanced back over his shoulder. "I didn't think it was possible, but you look even more beautiful than the night we saw *La Bohème*."

Her mouth fell open.

The reference to that incredible night had been no accident. Conrad had known exactly what he was doing. No doubt, her savvy husband had planned his every move all day with the express purpose of turning her inside out. The only question that remained?

Had he done so just for the satisfaction of turning her down again? Or did he want to ensure she wouldn't back away at the last second?

Either way, two could play that game.

# Four

Conrad downshifted his Jaguar as he took the curve on the coastal road, Jayne in the passenger seat.

After the concert ended, he'd sent Troy and Hillary off in the limo, his Jaguar already parked and waiting for the next part of his plan to entice Jayne. She'd always loved midnight rides along the shore and since neither of them seemed able to sleep much, this longer route home seemed the right idea for his campaign to win her over.

When he took her back to the penthouse, he wanted to make damn sure they were headed straight for bed. Or to the rug in front of the fireplace.

Hell, against the wine rack was fine by him as long as he had Jayne naked and in his arms. The day apart after the fireworks last night seemed to have worked the way he'd hoped, giving the passion time to simmer. Even after three years away from each other, he understood the sensual side of her at least.

He glanced over at her, moonlight casting a glow around her as she toyed with her loose blond hair brushing her shoulders. His fingers itched to comb through the silky strands. Soon, he promised himself, looking back at the winding cliff road. Very soon.

She touched his arm lightly. "Are you sure you wouldn't rather visit with Malcolm tonight?"

Instead of being with her?

Not a chance.

"And steal Malcolm away from his groupies?" He kept his hand on the gearshift, enjoying the feel of her touch on him. Too bad the dash lights shone on her empty ring finger. "Even I wouldn't be that selfish."

"If you're certain." Her hand trailed away, searing him with a ghostly caress.

His hand twitched as he shifted into fourth. He winced at the slight grind to the finely tuned machine. "We had a chance to shoot the breeze this afternoon with Troy."

"Malcolm seems so different when he's away from the spotlight." She stretched her legs out in front of her, kicking off her silvery heels and wriggling her painted toes under the light blast of the heater. "It's difficult to reconcile the guy in holey blue jeans jamming on the guitar in your living room to the slick performer in suits and ties, crooning from the piano."

"Whatever gets the job done." He forced his eyes back on the road before he drove them over a cliff. "You and Hillary seem to have hit it off."

"I enjoyed the day with her, and it was nice to have another woman's opinion when I picked out which dress to wear tonight." She trailed her thumb along her bared collarbone, her black wrap having long ago slipped down around her waist.

The silver gown glistened in the glow of the dash, all but begging him to pull over and devote his undivided attention to peeling off the fitted bodice....

*Eyes on the road.*

He guided the Jag around another curve, yacht lights glinting on the water far below.

She angled her head to the side. "What are you thinking about?"

Nuh-uh. Not answering that one. "What are *you* thinking about?"

"Um, hello?" She laughed dryly. "Exactly what you intended for me to think about. The night we went to see *La Bohème.*"

How neatly she'd turned the tables on him.

He liked that about her, the way she took control, too, which reminded him of how she'd seduced him in his favorite chair once they'd gotten home from *La Bohème.* "That was a, uh, memorable evening."

"Not everything about our marriage was bad," she conceded.

"Italian opera will always hold a special place in my heart."

Except he'd thrown out that damn chair when she left, then found he had to pitch most of the rest of his furniture as well, including the dining-room table, which also held too many sensual memories of her making her way panther-style toward him with a strawberry in her mouth. The only place they'd never made love was in that tomato-red room since she'd said it was meant for guests, which somehow made it off-limits for sex.

She inched her wrap back up and around her shoulders, the night having dipped to fifty degrees. "I thought *Don Giovanni* was your favorite opera."

"The story of a hero landing in hell for his sins?" Appropriate. "A longtime favorite. Although I'm surprised you remember that I liked it."

"You remembered that I prefer cream cheese pastries and chocolate mint tea for breakfast."

He'd made a mental note of many things she liked back then, working his ass off to keep her happy as he felt their marriage giving way like a sandy cliff. "We were together for four years. I intended to be with you for the rest of my life."

"And you think I didn't?" Pain coated her words, as dark as the clouds shifting over the stars. "I wanted to build a family with you."

Another of her dreams he'd crushed. The ways he'd failed this woman just kept piling on, compacting his frustration until he was ready to explode.

Not trusting himself to drive, he pulled off the road and into a deserted rest area. He set the emergency brake and wished the anger inside him was as easy to halt. Anger at himself. "I gave you a puppy, damn it."

"I wanted a baby."

"Okay…" He angled toward her, half hoping she would slap his face, anything but stare at him with tears in her eyes. "Let's make a baby."

She flattened her hands to his chest, hard, stopping just shy of that slap he'd hoped for. Although a telltale flex of her jaw relayed her rising temper. "Don't you dare mock me or my dreams. That's not fair."

"I'm very serious about being with you."

"So you stay away from me all day?" she shouted, her fingers twisting in the lapels of his tuxedo. "You stay away for three whole years?"

Her question stopped him cold. "That bothered you?"

"For three years you ignored my attempts to contact you." She shoved free and leaned against the door, arms crossed under her breasts, which offered too beautiful a view. "Did you or did you not manipulate me on purpose today?"

He chose his words carefully, determined to get through the tough stuff so they could make love without the past hovering over them. "I figured we both needed space after last night if there was any chance of us enjoying our evening together."

"That makes sense," she conceded.

"I'm a logical man." He rested a hand on the back of her seat, his fingers dangling a whisper away from her hair. He was so damn close to having her, he could already taste her.

"You may think you're logical, but I don't understand half of what you do, Conrad. I do know that if you'd really loved me, truly wanted to stay married, you would have been honest. Whatever game you're playing now, it has nothing to do with love." Words tumbled from her faster and faster as if overflowing from a bottle. "You just don't want to lose. I'm another prize, a contest, a challenge. The way you've played me today and for three years? It's a game to you."

"I can assure you," he said softly, his fingers finally—thank God—finally skimming along her silky hair. "I consider the stakes to be very high. I am not in the mood to play."

"Then what are you doing? Because this back and forth, this torment, has nothing to do with peace."

"I have to agree." He traced her ear, down to the curve of her neck.

Her eyes slid closed and the air all but crackled. "Are you doing this to make me stay?"

"I told you what I want. A chance for us to say good-bye." He thumbed the throbbing pulse along her neck, his body going hard at the thought of her heart beating faster for him. "Leaving was your choice, not mine, but after three years I get that you mean business."

Her lashes fluttered open, her blue eyes pinning him. "And you really accept my decision."

"You *were* yelling at me about thirty seconds ago." He outlined her lips, her breath hot against his palm.

"Are you accusing me of being a shrew?" She nipped his finger.

He forgot to breathe. "I would never say that."

"Why not? I've called you a bastard and worse."

"I am a bastard, and I am far worse." He took her face in both hands, willing her to hear him, damn it, to finally understand how much she'd meant to him. "But I'm also a man who would have been there for you every day of your life."

She searched his eyes, her mouth so close to his their breaths tangled together. Something in her expression stopped him.

"Every day, Conrad? Unless it's one of the times you can't be reached or when you call but your number is blocked."

Damn it. He pulled away, slumping back in his seat. "I have work and holdings around the world."

"You're a broken record," she said, her voice weary and mad all at once. "But who am I to judge? You're not the only one who can keep secrets."

A chill iced the heat right out of the air. "What the hell does that mean?"

"Do you know what finally pushed me over the edge?" Her eyes filled with tears that should have been impossible to hold back. "What made me walk out?"

"It took me a couple of days to return your calls, and you'd had enough." He'd fired the secretary that hadn't put her calls through. He'd honestly been working at being more accessible to Jayne.

"Seven days, Conrad. Seven." She jabbed a finger at him, her voice going tight and the first tear sliding down her cheek. "I called you because I needed you. I'd gotten a suspicious report back on a mammogram, and the doctor wanted to do a biopsy right away."

Her words sucker punched *everything* out of him, leaving him numb. Then scared as hell.

He shot upright and started to grab her shoulders, only to hold back at the last second, afraid to touch her and upset her even more. "God, Jayne, are you all right? If I had known…"

"But you didn't." She pushed his hands away slowly, deliberately. "And don't worry, I'm fine. The lump was benign, but it sure would have been nice to have you hold my hand that week. So don't tell me you would have been there for me every day of my life. It's simply not true."

The sense of how badly he'd let Jayne down slammed over him. He closed his eyes, head back on his seat as he fought down the urge to leap out of the car and shout, punch a wall, anything to ease the crushing weight of how he'd let her down.

One deep breath at a time, he regained his composure enough to turn his head and look at her again. "What happened to the puppy?"

"Huh?" She scrubbed the backs of her hands across her wet cheeks.

"What did you do with Mimi after you left?" Mimi, named for the heroine in *La Bohème*.

"Oh, I kept Mimi, of course. She's with…a dog sitter."

Of course she'd kept the dog. Jayne wasn't the kind of person to throw away the good things in her life. He was.

He pinched the bridge of his nose, stared out the window at the churning night sea below and wished those murky waters held some answers. Jayne's ocean-fresh scent gave him only a second's warning before she took his face in her hands and kissed him.

Desperate to forget the past, Jayne sealed her lips to Conrad's. Right or wrong, she just needed to lose herself in the feel of his body against hers. The roar of the waves crashing against the shore echoed the elemental restlessness inside her.

With a low growl, he wrapped his strong, muscled arms around her. He took her mouth as thoroughly as she took his. The taste of coffee from dinner mingled with the flavor of him. And what a mix of the familiar and a first kiss wrapped up in one delicious moment. Goose bumps sprinkled along her arms, shimmering through her, as well.

Her hands slid from the warm bristle of his face to his shoulders and she held on. Because, God, this was what she'd wanted since the second she'd sensed him walk up behind her in the casino, drawn by the intoxicating warmth and bay rum scent of him. The way his hands smoothed back her hair, stroked along her arms, stoked a familiar heat inside her. She'd been right to instigate this. Here, in his arms, she didn't have to think about the pain of the past. To hell with peace and resolving their problems. Rehashing old issues just brought more pain. She wanted this bliss.

And then goodbye.

His mouth trekked to her jaw as he dipped lower, his late-day beard a sweet abrasion against her neck. Her head lolled to the side, a moan rolling up her throat. She stroked along the fine texture of his tux over bold muscles, up and into his hair. Combing through his impossibly soft strands, she urged him to give more, take more. She tugged gently, bringing his mouth back to hers.

Bittersweet pleasure rippled through her, reminding her how good they'd been together. Her breasts ached for his touch and she wriggled to get nearer, pressing against the hard wall of his chest. She struggled to get closer, swinging a knee over and bumping the gearshift.

"Damn it," Conrad's muffled curse whispered against her mouth but the thought that he might stop was more than she could bear.

She shoved her hands under his tuxedo coat, sinking her fingernails into the fine fibers of his shirt. Three years of being without sex—without *him*—crested inside her, demanding she follow through. His hand skimmed up her leg, tunneling under her dress as he'd done years ago. The rasp of his calluses along her skin ignited a special kind of pleasure and the promise of more.

Except that private theater box had been a lot roomier than his Jaguar. And she wanted more than just his *hands* on her.

"Take me…" she gasped.

"I intend to do just that." His voice rumbled in his chest, vibrating against her.

"Not here. Home. Take me home."

He angled back to look at her as if gauging the risk

of pausing. He grazed his knuckles along her cheek. "Are you sure?"

"Absolutely." As sure as anyone could be about making love with the person who'd broken her heart. She scored her nails down his back. "I know what I want. I won't change my mind about being with you tonight."

It wasn't a matter of winning or losing anymore. It was just a matter of stopping the ache and praying for some of that peace. Because wanting him was tearing her apart.

Angling into him, she nipped his bottom lip. "Conrad, I think it's time we break in your new furniture."

Conrad hauled Jayne into the private elevator and willed the doors to close faster. He may have hoped to clear the air of past issues during their drive before jumping right to sex, but now that Jayne had taken that decision out of his hands, he was all in.

He'd made record time driving back to the casino, determined to get to the penthouse before she changed her mind. God help him—both of them—if she backed out now. After tasting her again, touching her again, he was on fire from wanting to be with her. Wanting to bury himself heart deep inside her until they both forgot about everything but how damn good they were together.

Until in some way he made up for how deeply he'd let Jayne down.

He jammed his key card into the slot and the elevator doors slid closed. The mirrored walls reflected multiple images of his wife, tousled and so damn beautiful she took his breath away.

"Come here, now," she demanded, taking control in that way that turned him inside out. She grabbed his

jacket and tugged him to her. "You've been tormenting
me all night with the way you look at me."

He pressed her against the cool wall as the elevator lifted. "You've been tormenting me since the day
I met you."

"What are we going to do about that?" She arched
against him, her hips a perfect fit against his.

"I suggest we keep right on doing this until we can
figure out how we're ever going to quit." He angled
his mouth over hers, teasing her with light brushes and
gentle tugs on her bottom lip.

"That makes absolutely no sense," she whispered
between kisses.

Nothing about the way he felt for her made a damn
bit of sense. But then he'd wanted her since the first
time he saw her. That had never changed, never light-
ened up. He gathered her hair in his hand and—

"Conrad," she gasped, "stop the elevator."

"You want me to *stop*?" Denial spiked through him.

"No, I want you to stop the elevator—" she kissed
him "—between floors—" stroked him "—so we don't
have to wait a second longer."

He slapped the elevator button.

Jayne opened her arms, and he didn't even have to
think. He thrust his hands into her hair, the familiar
glide of those silky strands against his skin as arousing as always. Images scrolled through his mind of her
slithering the blond mass over his chest as she nibbled
her way down, down, down farther still until her mouth
closed around him... Desire pounded in his ears in time
with the bass beat of the elevator music.

As if she heard his thoughts, understood his need
to have her touch him again, her fingers grazed down
the front of his pants, rubbing along the length of him

until he thought he would come right then and there. He gripped her wrist and eased her hand away. Soon, he promised himself, soon they could have it all.

Her hips rocked against him, and he pressed his thigh between her legs, rewarded by her breathy moan of pleasure. The gauzy length of her gown offered little barrier between him and the hot core of her.

Memories of that night at *La Bohème* seared his brain and fueled his imagination. He bunched up her dress in his fist, easing the fabric up her creamy-white legs until he reached the top of her thighs. Only a thin scrap of satin stayed between him and his goal. Between him and her.

They were completely alone in the privacy of his domain. And even if someone dared step into his realm, he shielded her with his body. Never would he leave her vulnerable to anyone or anything. She was his to protect, to cherish.

To please.

He tucked a finger into the thin string along the side and twisted until…the fabric gave way. She purred into his mouth and angled toward his touch. He wadded the panties in his fist and stuffed the torn scrap into his pocket before returning to her.

Stroking from her knee to her thigh again, he nudged her dress up until his fingers found her sweet, moist cleft. He stroked along her lips, swollen with the passion he'd given her. Without rushing, he stroked and explored, giving her time to grow accustomed to his touch, to let her desire build while he kissed her, murmuring against her mouth how damn much she drove him crazy. His other hand cupped the perfect curve of her bottom and lifted her toward the glide of his caress.

Her gasps grew faster, heavier, the rise and fall of

her breasts against his chest making him throb to be inside her. He slipped two fingers into the hot dampness of her, the velvety walls already pulsing around him with the first beginnings of her orgasm. He knew her body, every telltale sign. His fingers still buried deep within her, he pressed his palm against the tight nub of nerves and circled. She writhed against him in response, gasping for him not to stop, she was so close…

He burned to drop to his knees to finish her with his mouth, to fill his senses with the essence of her, but he didn't dare risk leaving her that exposed unless they were behind locked doors. But soon, before the night was over he would make love to her with more than his hand. He would bring her to shattering completion again and again, watching the bliss play across her face.

Her head fell back against the glassed wall, her hands clamped to his shoulders, her nails digging deep. He grazed his mouth along the throbbing pulse in her neck just as she arched in his arms. Her cries of completion echoed in the confines of the elevator, blending with the music drifting from the speakers. And he watched—God, how he watched—every nuance on her beautiful face, her eyes closed, her mouth parted with panting gasps. The tip of her tongue peeked out to run along her top lip and he throbbed impossibly harder. For her. Always for her.

Her body began to slide as she relaxed in the aftermath, her arms slipping around his neck. He palmed her back, bringing her against him, although his feet weren't as steady as he would like right now. The music grew louder, sweeping into a crescendo until…

An alarm pierced his ears, jolting through him. No wait, that was the floor lifting again, the elevator rising.

"Conrad?" Her eyes blinked open, passion-fogged.

He understood the feeling well.

His head fell to rest against the mirrored wall. "That's the backup system in case the elevator breaks."

"Oh…" She froze against him then wriggled, smoothing her gown back in place. "That would have been really embarrassing if we hadn't noticed and the doors had just opened."

"This is only a temporary delay." He cupped her head and kissed her soundly before stepping into the penthouse.

She kicked her shoes off, her eyes still steamy blue, her pupils wide with desire. He flung her wrap over the wine rack and backed her down the hall. Except he didn't intend to stop at the chair or in front of the fireplace. He wanted his wife in his bed again. Where they both belonged.

Later, he would figure out why the notion of one weekend suddenly didn't seem like near enough time with her.

He reached for the light switch only to realize…

Crap. The chandelier was already glowing overhead and he always turned the lights off when he left. Cleaning staff never came at night.

How had he let his instincts become so dulled that he'd missed the warning signs?

Someone was in his penthouse, and he should have noticed right away. His lapse could put Jayne in danger, and all because he'd let himself get carried away making out with her in an elevator. His guilt fired so hot her panties damn near burned a hole in his pocket. He moved fast, tucking her behind him as he scoped the living area and found his intruder.

Wearing his signature gray suit and red tie, Colonel

Salvatore lounged in a chair in front of the fireplace, a cell phone in hand.

Conrad's old headmaster and current Interpol handler set aside his phone and stood, his scowl deeper than usual. "Conrad, we have a problem."

# Five

Her head still fogged from her explosive reaction to Conrad in the elevator, Jayne stared in confusion at their unexpected guest sitting in the living room like family. She recognized Conrad's old headmaster and knew they'd kept in touch over the years, but not to the extent that the man could just waltz into their home while they were out.

*Conrad's* home, she reminded herself. Not hers. Not anymore.

Had her almost-ex-husband grown closer to Colonel Salvatore over the past three years? So much time had passed, even though their attraction hadn't changed one bit, it wasn't surprising there might be things she didn't know about his life anymore.

Although that wouldn't stop her from asking.

Praying she didn't look as mussed as she felt, she walked deeper into the living room, all too aware of her bare feet and hastily tossed aside heels. Not to mention the fact that she wasn't wearing panties. "Colonel Salvatore? There's something wrong?"

Conrad stepped between them, his broad back between her and their "guest." He stuffed his hands into his tuxedo pockets only to pull them back out hastily. "Jayne, I'm sorry to leave, but Colonel Salvatore and I need to talk privately. Colonel? If you'll join me downstairs in my office…"

Except Salvatore didn't move toward the door. "This concerns your wife and her safety."

Safety? Unease skittered up her spine, icing away the remnants of passion from the elevator. If this problem involved her, she wasn't going anywhere. "Whoa, hold on. I am completely confused. What does your being here for some kind of problem have to do with me?"

The colonel looked at Conrad pointedly. "You need to tell her. Everything."

Conrad's shoulders braced. His jaw went hard with a familiar stubborn set. The tender lover of moments prior was nowhere to be seen now. "Sir, with all due respect, you and I should speak alone first."

"I wouldn't advise leaving her here by herself, even for us to talk." Salvatore's serious tone couldn't be missed or ignored. "The time for discretion has passed. She needs to know. Now."

Jayne looked from man to man like watching a tennis match. Something big was going on here, something she was fast beginning to realize would fundamentally change her life. The chill of apprehension spread as her legs folded. She didn't know what scared her more—the fact that this man thought she was in serious danger, or that she could be on the verge of finally learning something significant about her ultrasecretive husband. She sat on the edge of Conrad's massive leather chair, her bare toes curling into the Moroccan carpet.

Muscles twitching and flexing with restraint under his tux jacket, Conrad parked himself by the fireplace. He didn't sit, but he didn't protest or leave, either. Whatever John Salvatore wanted of Conrad, apparently he intended to follow through. The way the colonel issued orders spoke of something more official, almost like a boss and employee relationship, which made no sense at all.

"Jayne," Conrad started, scratching along the same bristled jaw she'd stroked only minutes earlier, "my lifestyle with the casinos gives me accessibility to high-profile people. It provides me with the ability to travel around the world, without raising any questions. Sometimes, authorities use that ability to get information."

"Accessibility to what? Which authorities? What kind of information?" Her mind swirled, trying to grasp where he was going with this and what it had to do with some kind of threat. "What are you talking about?"

Salvatore clasped his hands behind his back and rocked on his heels. "I work for Interpol headquarters in Lyon, France, recruiting and managing agents around the world."

"You work for Interpol," she said slowly, realization detonating inside her as she looked at her husband, all those unexplained absences making sense for the first time. "*You* work for Interpol."

All those years, he hadn't been cheating on her. And he hadn't been following in his criminal father's footsteps. But she didn't feel relieved. Even now, he was ready to make love to her with such a huge secret between them.

Anger and betrayal scoured through her as she thought of all the times he'd looked her in the face while hiding such intense secrets. For that matter, he wouldn't have confided in her even now if his boss hadn't demanded it. She'd had a right to know at least something about a part of Conrad's life that affected her profoundly. But he'd rather ditch their marriage than give her the least inkling about his secret agent double life.

To think, she'd been a kiss away from tearing her clothes the rest of the way off and jumping back in bed with him, even though he hadn't changed one bit. Even now the moist pleasure lingered between her legs, reminding her of how easily she'd opened for him all over again. Part of her hoped he would deny what she'd said, come up with some very, very believable explanation.

Except, damn him, he simply nodded before he turned back to John Salvatore. "Colonel, can we get back to Jayne's safety?"

"We have reason to believe the subject of your most recent investigation may have stumbled on your identity, perhaps through a mole in our organization. He's angry, and he wants revenge."

Salvatore's veiled explanation floated around her brain as she tried to piece together everything and figure out what it had to do with her husband. "Who exactly is after Conrad?"

They exchanged glances and before they could toss out some "need to know" phrase, she pressed on. "If I'm uninformed that puts us both in more danger. How can I be careful if I don't even know what to be careful about?"

Salvatore cleared his throat. "Have you heard of a man named Vladik Zhutov?"

Her heart stopped for three very stunned seconds. "Of course I've heard about him. He was all over the news. He's responsible for a major counterfeiting ring. He single-handedly tried to manipulate some small country's currency to affect the outcome of an election. But he's in jail now. Isn't he?"

The colonel dabbed his forehead with a handkerchief. "Even in prison, he has influence and connections, and we have reason to fear he might be trying to use those against Conrad."

She flattened her hand to the nearest chair to keep her legs from giving way underneath her. Her husband had always been so intent on separating himself from anything to do with his father's world. Even though his parents were both dead, Conrad wouldn't even visit their graves.

Was he on a vendetta of his own? Had he placed his life at risk to see that through?

Anger at Conrad took a backseat to fear for his safety. Her stomach knotted in horror, terror and a total denial of the possibility of a world without Conrad's indomitable presence. "Are you saying this individual has taken out some kind of hit on Conrad?"

She looked back and forth from the two men, both so stoic, giving away little in their stony expressions. How could someone stay this cool when her whole world was crumbling around her? Then she saw the pulse throbbing in Conrad's temple, a flash of something in his eyes that looked remarkably like…raw rage.

Salvatore sat on the chair beside her, angling toward her in his first sign of any kind of human softening. "Mrs. Hughes—Jayne—I'm afraid it's more complicated than that. Intelligence indicates Zhutov has been in contact with assassins, ones who are very good at

what they do. They understand the best way to get revenge is to go after what means the most to that person.
You, my dear, are Conrad's Achilles' heel."

Conrad was certain his head would explode before
the night was through. What more could life catapult
at him in one weekend?

The thought that someone—*anyone*—would dare
use Jayne to get back at him damn near sent him into
a blind rage. Only the need to protect her kept him in
check.

Later, he would deal with the inevitable fallout from
Salvatore ignoring Conrad's request to shield Jayne
from the messiness of his Interpol work. He could think
of a half-dozen different ways this could have been
handled, all of which involved *not* telling Jayne secrets
that could only put her in more danger.

Since Salvatore had dropped his "Achilles' heel"
bombshell, the colonel had taken charge as he did so
well. He'd shown Jayne his Interpol identification and
offered to fly her to headquarters in Lyon, France. He
would do whatever she needed to feel reassured, but it
needed to happen quickly for her personal protection.

One thing was clear. They had to leave Monte Carlo.
Tonight.

Salvatore continued to explain to Jayne in even, reasonable tones designed to calm. "When you make ar-
rangements for work and for your dog, you need to give
a plausible story that also will lead Zhutov's people in
the wrong direction."

She twitched, but kept an admirable cool given everything she'd been told. "My phone is tapped?"

"Probably not." Salvatore shook his head. "And even
if it is, the penthouse is equipped with devices that

scramble your signal. However, that doesn't stop listening devices on the other end. We can use that to our advantage, though, by scripting what you say."

"This is insane." She pressed a trembling hand to her forehead.

"I agree." Salvatore played the conciliatory role well, one he sure as hell hadn't shown a bunch of screwed-up teenagers seventeen years ago. "I sincerely hope we're wrong and all of this will be resolved quickly. But we can't afford to count on that. You need to tell them that you're ironing out details of the divorce with Conrad and it's taking longer than you expected."

Nodding, she stood, hitching her evening bag over her shoulder. "I'll step into the kitchen, if that's not a problem."

"Take your time, catch your breath, but keep in mind we need to leave by sunup."

Jayne shot a quick glance at her husband, full of confusion, anger—betrayal—and then disappeared into the kitchen.

Conrad reined in his temper, lining up his thoughts and plans while his wife's soft voice drifted out.

Salvatore cleared his throat. "Do you have something to say, Hughes?"

Oh, he had plenty to say, but he needed to narrow his attention to the task at hand. "With all due respect, Colonel, it's best that I keep my opinions to myself and focus on how the hell we're going to keep Jayne off of that megalomaniac's radar."

"I have faith you'll handle that just fine."

The colonel's blasé answer lit the fuse to Conrad's anger. He closed the gap between them and hissed low between his teeth so Jayne wouldn't overhear. "If you have such faith in me, why the big show in front of my wife?"

"Big show?" He lifted an eyebrow.

What the hell? Conrad was not sixteen and a high school screwup. This was not the time for games. "Scaring the hell out of her. Springing the whole Interpol connection on her."

"I still can't believe you never told her. I thought you were smarter than that, my boy."

"It doesn't matter what you think. That was my call to make. I told you when I married her I didn't want her involved in that side of my life, for her own safety."

"Seems to me you've put her in more danger by not clueing her in. Even she picked up on that."

There was no way to know for sure now. But the possibility chapped at the worst time possible. "Thanks for the insights. Now, moving on to how we take care of Zhutov? If my cover's been compromised…"

The ramifications of that rolled over him, the realization that even once he had Jayne tucked away safe, this line of work and the redemption it brought could be closed to him forever. Later, he would sift through that and the possibility that without Interpol in his life, he could have his wife back.

Right now, he could only concentrate on making sure nobody touched so much as one hair on her head.

Sagging back against the polished pewter countertop, Jayne hugged her cell phone to her chest. The lies she'd just told left a bad taste in her mouth. Not to mention the fact she'd just been put on an unpaid leave of absence from her job.

This was supposed to have been such a simple trip to tie up the loose ends in her marriage…

Hell. Who was she kidding? Nothing with Conrad had ever been simple.

As if conjured from her thoughts, he filled the archway leading into the kitchen. He'd ditched his tuxedo jacket and tie, the top button of his shirt open. A light scratch marked his neck and she realized she must have put it there sometime during their grope fest in the elevator, along with spiking his hair in her desperate hunger to touch him again. Thank God she hadn't followed through. How much worse this moment would have been had that elevator stayed shut down and she'd made love with him standing up in that cubicle of mirrors.

She set her phone down. "Can I have my panties back?"

He quirked an arrogant eyebrow before dipping into his pocket and passing over the torn scrap of satin. It was ridiculous really, asking for the useless piece of underwear back, but it felt like a statement of independence to her, reclaiming ground and putting space between them.

She snatched the dangling white scrap from his hand. "Thank you."

She jammed the underwear into the trash, a minor victory, before turning back to confront him. "You work for Interpol."

Hands in his pockets, he lounged one shoulder against the door frame. "Apparently I do."

Apparently?

His dodgy answer echoed too many in their past. The time he'd missed their first anniversary weekend retreat that they'd planned for weeks. Or when he'd bailed on going with her to her half brother's incredibly awkward wedding. And no explanations. Ever.

She couldn't keep quiet. Not now with her emotions

still so raw from their explosive discussion in the car and their passionate encounter in the elevator. Even now, a need throbbed between her legs to finish what they'd started, to take him deeply inside her.

"You still won't admit it? Even when your boss confirmed it to me? What kind of twisted bastard are you? Do you get some sick pleasure out of yanking me around this way?"

His eyebrows shot up. "I kept you in the dark for your protection."

"I'm not buying it. I know you too well." Anger, hurt—and yes, more than a little sexual frustration— seethed inside her. "You didn't tell me because then you would have to commit, one hundred percent, to our marriage. You never wanted it to last, or you would have found a way to put my mind at ease all these years."

He could have told her something. Anything. But he hadn't even tried to come up with a rationale for his disappearances. He'd just *left*.

"I thought you would worry more," he said simply.

Although she wondered if there was a flash of guilt in his mocha-brown eyes. That would go a long way toward keeping her from pummeling him with fruit from the bowl on the counter.

"And you think I didn't worry when I had no clue where you were or what you were doing?" Those sleepless nights came back to haunt her. "In the beginning, I was scared to death something had happened to you those times I couldn't locate you. It took me a long time to reach the conclusion you must be cheating on me, like my father fooled around on my mom."

He straightened, his eyes flinty hard. "I never slept with another woman."

"I get that." She raised a hand. "Hell, I figured that out even then. But you still lied to me. You cheated on me with that damn job."

He scrubbed a hand over his scowl. "Do you think operatives have the luxury of printing out an itinerary for their spouses?"

"Of course not. I'm not that naive." More like she'd let herself stay oblivious, clinging to the hope she might be wrong about him hiding things from her. "But Colonel Salvatore made it clear tonight you could have told me something and you chose not to."

"I chose what I thought was best for you." His mouth went tight.

Well, too damn bad. She had every right to be upset.

"You thought it was best to sacrifice our marriage? Because that's the decision you made for both of us, without even giving me the option of deciding for myself."

"I won't apologize for keeping you safe."

His intractable words made her realize how far apart they were from seeing eye to eye on this.

"Fine. But consider how you'd feel if the tables were turned and it was me disappearing for days on end without a word of explanation. Or what you would have thought if I'd left you to celebrate your anniversary by yourself." He'd flown her to a couples retreat in the Seychelles. The island country off the coast of Africa had been so romantic and exotic. Except he'd left her sitting in a dining room full of hormones all alone.

He'd said nothing, as per usual.

Knowing she'd let herself be turned into some kind of doll adorning his arm and decorating his world perhaps stung most of all. "And to think I was that close to falling in your arms again. Well, no worries about that now. I am so over you, Conrad Hughes."

She angled sideways past him, through the door.

He gripped her arm. "You can't leave now. No matter how angry you are with me, it's not safe for you out there."

"I got that from your boss, thanks. I'm just going to pack. In my room. *Alone*."

His hand slid down her arm, sending a traitorous jolt of awareness straight to her belly until she pressed her legs together against the moist ache still simmering.

"You were able to arrange things with work and for Mimi?"

Standing this close to Conrad with her emotions on overload was not a smart idea. She needed to wrap this up and retreat to her room to regroup. "She's settled, but Anthony can't watch her indefinitely. He travels with his job. But I'll figure that out later."

She brushed past.

"Anthony."

Conrad's flat, emotionless voice sent prickles up her spine. She turned slowly, her evening gown brushing the tops of her bare feet. "He's the nephew of a former patient."

Not that she owed him any explanation after the way he'd walled her out for years.

"And he watches our dog while you're out of town." Conrad still leaned in the doorway, completely motionless other than the slow blink of his too-sharp eyes.

"It's not like he and I are dating…"

"Yet. But that's why you came to Monte Carlo, isn't it? So you would be free to move on with Anthony or some other guy." Conrad scratched his eyebrow. "I think I pretty much have the picture in place."

And clearly he wasn't one bit happy with that image. Well, too damn bad after all the tears she'd shed seeing his casino pictured in tabloids, him with a different woman on his arm each time. "You don't get to be mad at me. I'm the one who's been lied to."

"Then I guess that makes it easier for us to spend time alone together." He shoved away from the door frame, his shoulder brushing hers as he passed. "Pack your bag, sweetheart. We're taking a family vacation."

# Six

The bulletproof, tinted windows on his balcony offered Conrad the protection he needed while escaping the claustrophobic air of the penthouse.

Jayne had already picked out his replacement. He realized now that she'd come to Monte Carlo to end their marriage so she could move on with another man. If she hadn't already.

Scratch that.

He didn't think she was sleeping with the guy, not yet. Jayne was an innately honorable woman. And while he didn't assume she would stay celibate for three years, she wouldn't have almost had sex with him if she'd already committed to another man.

Her integrity was one of the things about her that had drawn him right from the start. She had a goodness inside her that was rare and should be protected. For the first time, it hit him how much she must have missed her career when she lived with him, and even though Monte Carlo was his primary residence, he'd traveled from holding to holding too often for her to secure a new job. He'd never thought about how long and lonely her days must have been.

Looking back, he probably should have left her the hell alone. He deserved Jayne's anger and more. He'd been wrong to marry her in the first place knowing he would never choose to tell her about his contract work with Interpol. He'd deluded himself that he held back out of a need to protect her, but deep down he knew he'd always feared he needed the job more than he needed her. That he needed that outlet to rebel, a way to channel the part of his father that lived inside him, the part that had almost landed him in jail as a teenager.

He'd been so damn crazy for Jayne he'd convinced himself he could make it work.

He'd only delayed the inevitable.

Now she was paying the price for his mistake. He resisted the urge to put his fist through a wall. Her life could be at risk because of him. He wouldn't be able to live with himself if anything happened to her.

He scoured the cove below, every yacht and cruise ship lighting up the shoreline suddenly became suspect.

A sound from the doorway sent him pivoting fast, his hand on the 9mm he'd strapped into a shoulder harness.

Troy Donavan lounged in the entrance, his fedora in hand. "Whoa, hold up. Don't shoot your body double."

"My what?"

Donavan stepped out onto the balcony. "Your double. I'll travel as you and you travel as me. If anyone manages to track either of our movements, they'll still be led in the wrong direction." He dropped his hat on the lounger. "Salvatore said we're not heading out for another couple of hours. I can keep watch over Jayne while you catch a nap."

"I'm cool. But thanks. Insomnia has its perks." He glanced sideways at his best friend of over seventeen years. "Did Salvatore send you here to check on me after the showdown with Jayne?"

"He alerted me to the crap with Zhutov and the concerns for your wife. I know how I would feel in your shoes, and it's not pretty."

Damn straight. He didn't know how Donavan handled having Hillary keyed into the Interpol world. She'd even started training to actively participate in future freelance missions.

"I have to get Jayne as far away and under the radar as possible." How long would this nightmare last? Would she end up spending the rest of her life on the run? He wouldn't leave her side until he knew she was safe. He'd wanted to grow old with her, but sure as hell not that way.

"I promise you, brother, if Zhutov has so much as breathed Jayne's name, he will be stopped. You have to believe that."

"After this is over, I have to let her go." Those words were tough to say, especially now with the image of her building a life with another man. "I was wrong to think I could have her and the job."

"People do dangerous jobs and still have lives. You can't expect every cop, firefighter, military person and agent not to have families. Even if we don't get married, there are still people in our lives who are important to us. The best thing you can do for Jayne is stick to her, tight."

"You're right."

"Then why aren't you smiling?" Donavan clapped him on the shoulder. "Want to talk about what else is chewing you up?"

"Not really."

"Fair enough."

And still he couldn't stop from talking. "She just... gets to me."

He remembered the way she'd called him on the carpet for teasing her on the ride home tonight, giving him hell for talking about that evening they saw *La Bohème* together. As if he knew that would turn her inside out the same way it did him. Damn, he'd missed that spark she possessed.

"That's what women do. They burrow under your skin." Donavan grinned. "Didn't you get the memo?"

Conrad didn't feel one damn bit like smiling. He stared down at his clenched fist, at his own bare ring finger. "She's seeing someone else."

"Damn," Donavan growled. "That's got to really bite. But it's been three years since the two of you split. Did you really expect you would both stay celibate?"

Conrad looked out over the harbor, the sea stretching as far and dark as each day he'd spent apart from Jayne.

Troy straightened quickly. "Whoa, wait. Are you telling me you haven't seen anyone else while you've been separated?"

Still, Conrad held his silence.

"But the tabloids..."

"They lie." Conrad smiled wryly at his friend. "Didn't you get the memo?"

Donavan stared back, not even bothering to disguise his total shock. "You haven't been with anybody in *three years?*"

"I'm married." He thumbed his empty ring finger. "A married man does not cheat. It's dishonorable."

Donavan scrubbed both hands over his face then shook his head as if to clear the shock away. "So let me get this straight... You haven't seen your wife since she left you. Which means you haven't had sex with anyone in *three years?*"

"You're a damn genius."

Donavan whistled softly. "You must be having some serious quality 'alone time' in the shower."

Understatement of the year. Or rather, that would be *three* years. "Your sympathy for my pain is overwhelming."

"Doesn't sound like you need sympathy. Sounds like you need to get—"

"Thanks," he interrupted, not even wanting to risk Donavan's words putting images in his head. "I can handle my own life."

"Because you're doing such a bang-up job at it lately. But wait." He thumped himself on the forehead. "Poor choice of words."

Against his will, a smile tugged at Conrad's face. "Really, Donovan. Don't you have some geeky computer tech support work that needs your attention before we all leave?"

"You can call me a geek all night long, brother, but I'll be sleeping next to a woman." Donavan punched him in the arm.

Conrad lifted an eyebrow, but preferred the joking to sympathy any day of the week. Something his best friend undoubtedly understood. "Hit me again, and I'm going to beat the crap out of you."

Donavan snagged his fedora from the lounger. "Everybody wants to beat the crap out of me today. What's up with that?"

"Get out of here before I break you in half."

"Because I feel very sorry for you, I'm just going to walk away." He spun his hat on one finger. "But I'm taking a bottle of your Chivas with me so you won't feel bad for scaring me off."

"Jackass."

"I feel the love, brother. I feel the love." He opened the French doors and paused, half in, half out. "See you inside later?"

"Absolutely." He nodded once. "And thank you."

Donavan nodded back. No more words were needed.

His friend had helped him decompress enough to see clearly again. He needed to keep his eye on the goal now, to keep Jayne safe at all cost.

He might not be the man she deserved, but he was damn well the man she needed.

Jayne rolled her small bag out into the living room, having used the past couple of hours to change out of her evening gown and generally get her head together. If that was even possible after her world had been so deeply shaken in such a short time.

The sun hadn't even risen yet.

If they hadn't been interrupted, she would have been in Conrad's bed now, completely unsuspecting of *this*.

She realized his secret had noble roots, a profession that brought justice, so different than her father's secret life, his hidden second family with a mistress and two children. But the fact that she'd been duped so totally still hurt on a deep level. Trusting her heart and her life to Conrad had been very difficult.

How could she reconcile the fact that she hadn't

even begun to know the man she'd married? Walking away with any kind of peace when she'd thought she understood him was tough enough. But now with so much mystery surrounding Conrad and their life together, she felt like every bit of progress she'd made since leaving had been upended.

And with this possible threat lurking, she didn't even have the luxury of distance to regain her footing.

The Donavans sat in the leather chairs, talking over glasses of seltzer water. She felt uncomfortable having Troy and Hillary pose as decoys for them. The thought of anybody in harm's way because of her made her ill. But she hadn't been given any say on the matter.

She also couldn't help but note how seamlessly Hillary had been brought into the plan. Apparently not all Interpol operatives kept secrets from their spouses.

The stab of envy for that kind of compatibility wasn't something she was proud of. But, damn it, why couldn't she have found her way to that sort of comfort with her husband? What was wrong with her that Conrad had never even considered confiding in her?

Just as she rolled her bag the rest of the way in, Conrad stepped out of his suite. His normal dark and brooding style of clothes had been swapped out for something more in keeping with Troy's metro style. She couldn't take her eyes from the relaxed look of her husband in jeans and a jacket, collar open, face unshaved, his thick black hair spiked.

Troy looked back over the chair, water glass in hand. "Good timing. Salvatore should be done any minute now. He's arranging the travel plans, complete with diversionary stories going out to the press." He glanced over at his wife. "Did I forget anything?"

"Just this." Carrying one of her husband's hats, Hillary walked to Conrad. "You should wear this. And maybe slick back your hair a bit. Here…" She reached for her water glass. "Use some of this since you didn't have time to shower."

Troy choked on his drink.

Conrad glared at him.

Jayne wondered what in the world was wrong with both of them.

Her husband took the fedora from Hillary. "I'm good. Thanks. I'll take good care of his hat."

"Take good care of yourself while you're at it," Hillary said just as her husband looped an arm around her waist and hauled her to his side. "Yes?"

Troy held up his phone. "Text from Salvatore. Time to roll."

With a hurried goodbye, Troy and Hillary stepped into the elevator, his head bent toward hers to listen to something. The two of them looked so right together, so in sync even in the middle of chaos.

Jealousy gripped Jayne in an unrelenting fist.

The doors slid closed and she wished her feelings could be as easily sealed away. She turned back to her husband. "Where are we going?"

Conrad thumbed through his text message, Troy's fedora under his arm. "To the jet."

"And the jet would be going to…"

He looked up, his eyes piercing and closed off all at once. "Somewhere far away from here."

His evasive answer set her teeth on edge. "Now that I know about your double life, you can drop the tall, dark and mysterious act."

She yanked the fedora from under his arm, his jacket parting.

A shoulder holster held a silver handgun.

"Oh," she gasped, knowing she shouldn't be surprised, but still just… "Oh."

He pulled his jacket back over the weapon. "The people I help nail don't play nice. They are seriously dangerous. You can be as angry at me as you want, but you'll have to trust me, just this once, and save your questions for the airplane. I promise I'll tell you anything you want to know once we're airborne. Agreed?"

Anything she wanted to know? That was one promise she couldn't resist. Probably the very reason he'd said it, tossing irresistible temptation her way. But it was an offer she intended to press to the fullest.

She pulled out a silk scarf to wrap over her blond hair. "Lead the way."

Once the chartered jet reached cruising altitude, Conrad took his first easy breath since he'd found Salvatore waiting for him in the penthouse. He was that much closer to having Jayne tucked away in the last place anyone would think to find either of them.

Jayne hadn't moved her eyes off him since they'd left the penthouse. Even now she sat on the other side of the small table, tugging her silk scarf from hand to hand. He watched the glide of the deep purple fabric as it slid from side to side. Until now, he hadn't realized she dressed in bolder colors these days. A simple thing and inconsequential, but yet another sign that she'd moved on since leaving him. She'd changed and he couldn't go back to the way things were.

But back to the moment. Without a doubt, the boom was going to fall soon and he would have to answer her questions. He owed her that much and more. He reached for his coffee on the small table between them, a light breakfast set in front of them.

He wasn't interested in food. Only Jayne. He could read her well and the second she set aside the scarf in her hands he knew. She was ready to talk.

"We're airborne, and you owe me answers." She drizzled honey into her tea. "Tell me where we're going."

"Africa."

Freezing midsip, she stared at him over the top of her cup. "Just when I think you can't surprise me. Are we staying somewhere like the island resort where we planned to spend our first anniversary?"

"No." He couldn't miss the subtle reminder of when he'd bailed on their first anniversary retreat in Seychelles. Without a doubt, he owed her for all the times he'd shortchanged her in the past. He raised the window shade, the first morning rays streaking through the clouds. "We're going to West Africa. I have a house there."

"Another thing I didn't know about you." Her voice dripped with frustration as thick as the extra honey she spooned into her tea. "Do you mean something like a safari resort?"

"Something like that, nothing to do with business, though." She would see for herself soon enough, and he had to admit, he wanted to see her reaction without prior warning. "I purchased the property just before we split. A case led me to… It doesn't matter. You're right. I should have told you about an acquisition that large."

"If it's your home, can't we be found there?"

"The property was purchased under a corporate name, nothing anyone would connect with me. There's not much point in a retreat if the paparazzi can find you."

"Well, if the press hasn't found out about it, then the

place must be secure." She half smiled. "So do we plan to hide in Africa indefinitely?"

"What did you tell Anthony?" He set down his coffee cup carefully.

"It's my turn to ask the questions, remember?" she reminded him gently. Her eyes fell away, and she stared into her cup as if searching for answers of her own. "But in the interest of peace…I told him what we planned for me to say, that divorcing my husband wasn't as simple as I'd expected. That you and I needed time to sort things out. He was understanding."

"Then he isn't as big a threat as I thought." He couldn't wrap his brain around the notion of ever being okay with the prospect of Jayne and some other guy hooking up. His hand twitched around the cup.

"Conrad, not everyone is all alpha, all the time."

He looked up fast, surprised at her word choice then chuckled.

"What did I say? And remember, you promised to answer my questions."

At least he could tell her this and wondered now why he never had before. "Back in high school, my friends, we called ourselves the Alpha Brotherhood."

"You're all still so close." She frowned. "Do they *all* work for…"

"Please don't ask."

"You said I could ask anything," she pressed stubbornly.

He searched for what he could say and still stay honest. "If something were to happen to me and you needed anything at all, you could call them. They can get in touch with Salvatore. Is that answer enough for you?"

She stared at him for so long he thought she might push for more, and truly there was more he could say but old instincts died hard after playing his life close to the vest.

Nodding, she leaned back in her leather seat, crossing her arms. "Thank you. Get back to the Alpha Brotherhood story."

"There were two kinds of guys at the academy, the military sort who wanted to be there to jump-start a career in uniform and a bunch of screwed-up rule breakers who needed to learn discipline."

Did she know that when she'd leaned back her legs stretched out in a sexy length that made him ache? He wanted to reach down and stroke her calf, so close to touching him. The sight of her in those jeans and leather boots sent another shot of adrenaline to his already overrevved body.

He knocked back another swallow of hot coffee to moisten his suddenly dry mouth. "Some of us in that second half realized the wisdom of channeling those rebellious tendencies if we wanted to stay out of jail. After we graduated from college, Salvatore offered us a legal outlet, a way to make amends and still color outside the lines—legally. Honorably."

"That's important to you, honor." She crossed her legs at the ankles, bringing her booted foot even closer to brushing him. "You've been so emphatic about never lying even when you hold back the truth."

He looked up sharply, realizing how much he'd revealed while ogling her legs like some horny teenager. And he realized she was playing him. Just like he'd played her in the past, using sexual attraction to steer their conversations.

It didn't feel good being maneuvered that way.

Remorse took his temperature down a notch. He sat up straighter, elbows on the table as he cradled his coffee. "My father was a crooked bastard, Jayne. It makes me sick the way the rest of the world all thought he was this great philanthropist. He made a crap-ton of money and gave it away to charities. But he made it cheating the same kinds of people he was pretending to help."

Her hand fell to rest on his. "I understand what it's like to lose faith in your father. It hurts, so much."

How strange that he was holding hands with his wife and he couldn't remember the last time he'd done that. He'd touched her, stroked her, made love to her countless times, but he couldn't recall holding her hand.

"I guess we do have that in common. For a long time, I bought into my old man's hype. I thought he was some kind of god."

"You've never told me how your mother felt about your father's crimes?"

"She's his accountant." He shrugged, thinking of all the times he got an attaboy from his parents for making the grade. It never mattered how, as long as he won. "Colonel Salvatore was the first person to ever hold my feet to the fire about anything. Yes, I have my own code of honor now, Jayne. I have to be able to look myself in the mirror, and this job is the only way I know how to make that happen."

"How weird is it that we've been married for seven years and there are still so many things about you I don't know." Her blue eyes held him as tangibly as her hand held his beside the plate of croissants and éclairs.

"That's my fault." He squeezed.

"Damn straight it is." She squeezed back.

The jet engine droned in the silence between them, recycled air whooshing down.

He flipped her hand in his and stroked her lifeline with his thumb. "What happens now?"

"What do you mean?" Her voice came out breathy, her chest rising and falling faster.

Although he could see that even in her anger she still wanted him, he was now beginning to understand that desire alone wouldn't cut it any longer.

"In the elevator we were a zipper away from making love again."

Her hand went still in his, her eyes filled with a mix of desire and frustration. "And you want to pick up where we left off?"

"How will your dog sitter feel about that?"

She sighed. "Are you still jealous even after I told you I'm not dating him?"

"Are you planning on seeing him after you leave?" He had to know, even if the answer skewered him.

What had the other guy given her that he couldn't? He'd lavished her with every single thing a woman could want, and it hadn't been enough for Jayne.

"Honestly," she said, "I thought I might when I flew to Monte Carlo, but now, I'm not sure anymore."

He started to reach for her but she stopped him cold with a tight shake of her head.

"Damn it, Jayne—"

"I'm not done." She squeezed his hand hard. "Don't take what I said as some sign to start tearing our clothes off. I *am* certain that I want a normal life with a husband who will be there for me. I want the happily ever after with kids and a real family sitting down to dinner together, even if it's hamburgers on a rickety picnic table at a simple hometown park. Maybe that sounds boring to you, but I just can't pretend to fit into this jet-set lifestyle of yours where we share a bed and nothing else. Does that make sense?"

He closed his eyes, only to be blindsided by the image of her sitting on a porch swing with some other lucky bastard while their kids played in the yard. "The thought of you with someone else is chewing me up inside."

"You don't have the right to ask anymore," she said gently. "You know that, don't you? We've been separated for three years."

"Tell that to my chewed-up gut."

She tugged her hand free. "You've already moved on. Why shouldn't I?"

He looked up sharply. "Says who?"

"Every tabloid in the stands."

"Tabloids. Really?" He laughed. Hard. Not that it made him feel any better. "That's where you're getting your news from? I thought you graduated from college magna cum laude."

Finally he'd shocked her quiet, silencing those damn probing questions.

But not for long.

Jayne's hand clenched around her discarded scarf. "You're saying it's not true? That you haven't been with other women since we split up?"

He leaned across the table until his mouth was barely an inch away from hers. He could feel her breath on his skin and he knew she felt his. Her pupils widened in awareness, sensual anticipation. And still, he held back. He wouldn't kiss her now, not this way, when he was still so angry his vision clouded.

Not to mention his judgment.

He looked her in the eyes and simply said, "I am a married man. I take that commitment very seriously."

She was his wife. The only woman he'd ever loved.

He should have the answers locked and loaded on how to keep her happy. He was a damn Wall Street genius, entrepreneur billionaire and Interpol agent, for God's sake.

Yet right now, he didn't have a clue how to make things right with Jayne, and he didn't know if he ever would.

# Seven

The gates swung wide to Conrad's home in Africa, and Jayne had to admit, he'd shocked the hell out of her twice in less than twenty-four hours.

She'd expected a grand mansion, behind massive walls with sleek security systems that made Batman's cave look like something from last generation's game system. This place was…

Understated.

And the quiet beauty of it took her breath away.

She leaned forward in the seat, as the Land Cruiser took the uphill dirt road. A ranch-style house perched on a natural plateau overlooking a river. She'd spent four years poring over renovations and perfect pieces of furniture for their different residences, perhaps hoping she could somehow create an ideal marriage if she could only put together an ideal home. She would guess the place was built from authentic African walnut. Everything about the house looked real, nothing prefab or touristy about it.

Porches—and more porches—wrapped around the lengthy wooden home, with rockers, tables and roll down screens to overlook the nearby river. Palm trees had a more tropical than landscaped feel. Mangrove trees reached for the sky with their gnarled roots twisting up from the ground like wads of fat cables.

She glanced at her husband, wondering what led him to purchase this place just before they'd split. But his stoic face wasn't giving away any clues. Although, Lord, have mercy, he was as magnificent as the stark and unforgiving landscape.

With the day heating up fast, he'd ditched the sports coat and just wore jeans with his shirtsleeves rolled up. Like his home, he didn't need extravagant trappings to take her breath away. As if she wasn't already tempted enough around him.

Although the gun still tucked in the shoulder harness gave her more than a little pause.

Their game of twenty questions during the plane ride hadn't helped her understand him one bit better. If anything, she had more questions, more reservations. Being here alone together was complicated now. They'd moved past the idea of sex for the hell of it as some farewell tribute to their marriage. That didn't mean the attraction wasn't still there, fierce as ever, just beneath the surface of their tentative relationship.

Tearing her gaze away, she pressed her hands to the dash. "This isn't at all what I expected."

"How so?" He slowed the SUV then stopped at the half-dozen wooden steps leading to the front door.

"No bells and whistles chiming. No gambling rich and famous everywhere you look."

"The quiet appeals to me." He opened the door and circled the hood to her side.

She stepped out just as he reached her and avoided his outstretched hand, not ready to touch him again, not yet. "If you'd wanted somewhere to be quiet, there were places a lot closer to home than Africa."

The dusty wind tore at her hair. She tugged her scarf from around her neck and tied back the tangled mess.

"True. But this is the one I wanted and since I'm sinfully rich," he said, pulling out her roll bag and a duffel for himself, "I can have the things I want, if not the people."

Was this quieter persona one he donned for his missions or was this a part of her husband she'd never seen? She shivered in spite of the temps already sending a trickle of sweat down her spine. "What about security? I don't see any fences or cameras."

"Of course you didn't see them as we drove up. They're the best, thanks to our good friend Troy. If anyone crosses the perimeter, we'll know." He jogged up the stairs and flipped back a shutter to reveal an electronics panel. "You'll be briefed on how everything works so you're not dependent on me if an emergency arises."

Now wasn't that an eye opener?

She trailed her fingers along a rocker, setting it in motion and thought of his casino with the glassed-in balcony overlooking the sea. And she realized he loved the outdoors. Even now, his ear tipped toward the monkey chattering from some hidden tree branch.

"Jayne?" he called from the open door. "Are you ready?"

"Of course," she lied and followed him inside anyway.

This was definitely not a safari lodge after all.

There weren't any animal heads mounted on the walls, just paintings, an amalgamation of watercolors, oils and charcoals, without a defining theme other than the fact each one portrayed a unique view of Africa.

And in such a surprisingly open space.

Conrad had a style of his own—and a damn good one. But she'd fallen into a stereotypical assumption that he would put a foosball table in her living room if she turned over the reins to him. She thought back to his penthouse remodeling. She'd been so focused on the shock of all her things swept away she'd failed to notice the sense of style even in his man cave.

How much of his "hiding" of himself had she let happen?

She stepped deeper into the room with a massive stone fireplace in the middle. A wood frame sectional sofa dominated the space, piled with natural fiber cushions and pillows. There were no distractions here, just the echo of her footsteps and the sound of the breeze rustling branches outdoors.

The place was larger on the inside than it looked from outdoors, likely another means of security. Her entire condo back in Miami could have fit in the living area with room to spare. A glance down the hall showed at least five other doors, but she was drawn to the window overlooking the river. A small herd of antelope waded in for a drink, while a hippo lazed on the far side of the shore.

Conrad's hand fell on her shoulder. "Jayne?"

She jolted and spun to face him, finding him so close her heart leaped into her throat. Her hands started to press to his chest, but she stopped shy of the silver gun.

"Uh, I was just enjoying the view." She gestured over her shoulder at the window.

"You've been standing there awhile. I thought you'd dozed off." He tugged the end of her scarf, her hair sliding loose again. "You must be almost dead on your feet since we didn't sleep last night, so I'll save the grand tour for later. There's just one place you need to see now."

The kitchen for a snack? His bed to make love before they both fell into an exhausted slumber?

He stopped in front of a Picasso-style watercolor of people in bright colors dancing. He slid the painting to the side to reveal another panel like the one she'd seen on the front door. After a quick tap along the keypad, he stepped back. Boards along the wall slid automatically and stacked, revealing a passage.

"This is the panic room." Conrad pressed a card into her hand with a series of numbers. "This is the code. Do not hesitate to use it in case of an emergency. Don't wait for me. I can take care of myself a helluva lot better if I'm not worrying about you."

Salvatore's words from earlier came back to haunt her, about how she was Conrad's Achilles' heel. Her presence placed him in greater danger. Somehow in the rush to leave Monte Carlo, she'd lost sight of that revelation.

Tears burned her eyes, and she ached to reach for him.

"Jayne, it's going to be okay." He brushed her hair over her shoulder. "You need to sleep, and I need to check the place over. We'll talk more later."

She tried not to feel rebuffed. He was doing his job. *She* had pushed *him* away after Salvatore's revelation.

Her hands fell to her sides. Of course he was right. She couldn't possibly make rational decisions with her head cottony from lack of sleep. And if she couldn't think clearly she became even more of a liability to Conrad.

Yet as he showed her to the guest room, she still couldn't help wishing she could sleep in his arms.

Conrad punched in the code to the safe room where he stored all his communication gear and security equipment. The entire place ran off solar power and a satellite feed, so he couldn't be cut off from the outside world. He kept enough water and nonperishable food in storage to outlast a siege.

Call him paranoid, but even in his infrequent freelance role with Interpol, he'd seen some intense crap go down in the world.

The windowless vault room in the middle of the house had everything he needed—a bed, an efficiency kitchen, a bathroom and a sitting area, small, but useful down to the last detail. A flat screen was mounted on the wall for watching the exterior. And an entire office's worth of computers were stored away, ready to fold out onto the dinette table like an ironing board lowered out of a wall.

He parked himself in front of the secured laptop and reached for the satellite phone. He needed to check in with Salvatore. Halfway through the first ring, his boss answered.

"Yes," the colonel barked.

"We've arrived, and we're settled. No red flags here that I can see. What do you have on your end?"

"The money in Zhutov's wife's account has been withdrawn and we have images—which I'm forwarding to you now—of his known associates in discussion with a hit man. We've got trackers on both individuals."

"I'll review his wife's bank accounts again. Why her assets haven't been frozen is beyond me."

"We do what we can, and you know that."

"Well, let's damn well do more." Scrolling through computer logs of account transfers, Conrad tucked the phone between his shoulder and ear, not wanting to risk speakerphone where Jayne might wake up and overhear.

"Hughes, my people are on it. You should sleep. You'll be more alert."

"Like you sleep?"

The colonel was a well-known workaholic. When they'd all been in school they'd theorized that their headmaster was a robot who didn't need mere mortal things like sleep. Seemed as if he was always walking the halls, day and night.

Salvatore sighed. "Go spend some time with your wife. Repair you marriage. Put your life back together again."

"Sir, with all due respect, you saw her back in Monte Carlo. She was pissed."

"I saw a woman who looked like she'd just been kissed senseless in an elevator."

"You're not helping the problem at hand by playing matchmaker." He'd need more of a miracle worker to untangle the mess he'd made of his life.

"I sincerely hope you and she had a long talk on the airplane about your work with me."

Just what he needed right now, a damn lecture on all the ways he'd screwed up his marriage. "Thank you for your input, sir. I'll take that under advisement."

The colonel laughed darkly. "Still as stubborn as ever, Hughes. Leave the sleuthing to my end this time.

Your job is to fly under the radar, keep you and your wife safe. Let me know if you need anything."

The call disconnected, and Conrad set the phone aside.

Three fruitless hours of database searching later, he slammed the computer shut in frustration. He couldn't figure out if the clues just weren't there. Salvatore's words echoed through his head, about his job being to protect Jayne. The old colonel was right. Conrad wouldn't be any good to her dead on his feet.

Resigned to surrendering, at least for now, he left the panic room and sealed it up tight again. The sectional sofa looked about as inviting as a bed of nails, but it was the best place to keep an ear out for Jayne—other than sleeping next to her, which didn't appear to be an option tonight.

And speaking of Jayne, he needed to check on her, to leave her door open a crack so he could hear her even in his sleep. He padded barefoot down the hall to her room and eased her door open.

Bad idea.

Looking at Jayne sleeping was torture. And apparently he was a masochist tonight because he stepped deeper into her room. Her legs were tangled in the sheets, long legs bared since her nightgown had hitched up. Her silky hair splashed over the pillow in a feathery blond curtain.

She slept curled on her side, with a pillow hugged to her chest just the way he remembered. If they'd still been together, he would have curled up behind her, their bodies a perfect fit. He still didn't understand how something so incredibly good could fall apart like their marriage had.

Tired of torturing himself tonight, he pivoted away and walked back out to the living room. He yanked a blanket off the ladder rack against the wall and grabbed two throw pillows. Even if his mind resisted shutting down, his body demanded that he stretch out and rest. But still his brain churned with thoughts of Jayne and how damn close they'd been to making love again.

If Salvatore hadn't been waiting for them in the penthouse, they would have ended up in bed. He could still hear her cries of pleasure from the elevator. He could feel the silken texture of her clamping around his fingers.

They may have had their problems communicating, but when it came to sex, they'd always been beyond compatible. And they'd had other things in common, too, damn it. They shared similar taste in books and politics. She enjoyed travel and appreciated the beauty of a sunset anywhere in the world.

And they both enjoyed the opera.

In fact, he'd planned to take her to the opera during their forty-eight hours of romance, back when he'd been enough of an idiot to think he could let her go again. He'd chartered a jet to fly them to Venice for a performance. He'd reserved a plush, private opera box where he could replay their *La Bohème* date.

He could still remember what she wore that night, a pale blue gown, feathery light. He'd been riding the rush of a recent mission, adrenaline making him ache all the more for his wife. The moment he'd seen her walk out of their bedroom wearing the dress, he'd known he wouldn't rest until he found out what she had on underneath.

Before Act One was complete, he'd known....

Dreams of Conrad during that hazy realm of twilight sleep always tormented her the most. Fantasy and reality blended until she didn't know whether to force herself awake or cling to sleep longer.

*La Bohème* echoed through her mind, the opening act, except that didn't make sense because she was in Africa with Conrad. So why was the opera playing out on a barge on the river? Confusion threatened to pull her awake. Until the glide of Conrad's hands over her breasts made her cling to the dream realm where she could sit with her husband on the porch and listen.

Savor.

His hands slid down her stomach to her leg. With skillful fingers he bunched her gauzy blue evening gown up, up, up her leg until his hand tunneled underneath. She felt his frown and realized she had jeans on underneath her formal dress?

Confusion churned in her brain as she stared down at her bare feet and well-worn denim. She kicked at the hem of her gown, frustrated, needing to free herself of the voluminous folds so she could wear her jeans.

And so she could feel Conrad's touch.

The roar of frustration grew louder, and louder still until the porch disintegrated from the vibrations. She stood in the rubble, a herd of elephants kicking up dust on the horizon.

Her bare feet pedaled against the covers. She fought harder, frantic to wake herself up and outrun the beasts chasing through her head. Elephants thundered behind her, rumbling the ground along with an orchestra segueing into the closing act. Her chest hurt, and she gasped for air.

She tripped over the gnarled roots of a mango tree. Her hands slapped the ground, but it gave way, plunging her into the Mediterranean Sea outside Conrad's casino. The farther she sank, the darker the waters became until she hit bottom.

Sealed in a panic room.

A window cleared along the top and she looked up, searching for a way out. Desperation squeezed the air from her lungs. Conrad stood on the balcony far, far above, watching her, drinking his Chivas. She couldn't reach him, and he couldn't hear her choked cries of warning to watch out for the thundering herd.

Wasn't a guy always supposed to hear his mermaid call him?

Except she wasn't the one in danger.

His balcony filled with thick, noxious smoke until Conrad disappeared...

Jayne sat up sharply.

Wide-awake, she blinked in the dark, unfamiliar room. Gauzy mosquito netting trailed from all four corners of the canopy. Just a dream, she reminded herself. Not real.

Well, the charging elephants weren't real, but the panic room was very real, along with a looming threat.

Fear for Conrad still covered her like a thick blanket on a muggy day. She'd put him in danger just by being with him. A crummy way to pay him back for all the years he'd tried to keep her safe from a dangerous job. Now that she was past some of the worst feelings of betrayal, she could feel the inevitable admiration beneath it. He was a good man, and she—unknowingly—had been his Achilles' heel.

That hurt her to think about. She had so many regrets about her marriage, and their future had never been more complicated. Her body burned for his touch.

With the pain of losing him still so fresh in her mind, she knew without question, she *had* to be with him tonight.

Conrad stared at the ceiling fan swirling around and around, the click so quiet he knew that couldn't have woken him.

So what had?

The alarms were set. He'd cracked the door to Jayne's room. No one would get in without him knowing, and Jayne wouldn't so much as sneeze without him hearing.

Muffled cries? He'd absolutely heard those.

Hand on his 9mm, he raced down the hall, careful to keep his steps quiet so as not to alert an intruder. He pushed through the guest bedroom door.

And found Jayne standing a hand's reach away in an otherwise empty room. She jumped back to avoid the swinging door. The sight of her hit him clean in the libido.

His hand fell away from his gun.

An icy-blue nightgown stopped just shy of her knees, lace trim teasing creamy flesh. The pale blue was so close to the color of the gown she'd worn to *La Bohème* that memorable night it almost knocked his feet out from under him. The silk clung to her curves the way his hands ached to do, the way he'd dreamed of doing every night since she'd walked out on him.

"Is something wrong? I heard you cry out in your sleep and I just needed to be sure you're all right." Good enough cover story for why he'd burst into the room.

"Just a nightmare. How cliché, huh?" She thrust her hands in her hair, pushing it back—and stretching the fabric of her nightgown across her breasts. "I cry out.

You run to me in my bedroom, afraid something happened to me. I'm still rattled by my bad dream."

He tore his eyes off the pebbly tightness of her nipples against silk. "God forbid we should ever be cliché."

She stepped closer, padding slowly on bare feet, her eyes narrowed with a sensual intent he'd seen—and enjoyed—many times in the past.

"Although, Conrad, clichés become clichés because they worked well for a lot of other people. And if we follow the dream cliché to its conclusion, the next step would be for me to throw myself in your arms so we can make love."

Jayne stopped toe-to-toe with him, still not touching him, and if she did, his control would be shot all to hell. For whatever reason, she was taking charge and seducing him. Except she would be doing so for all the wrong reasons, vulnerable from whatever had frightened her in the dream.

He couldn't take advantage of her while she was riding the memories of a nightmare. But he also couldn't leave her in here upset and alone.

Grabbing the door to keep from reaching for her, he stepped back into the hall. "I think we need to get out of this bedroom."

"Why?" She nibbled her bottom lip.

He swallowed hard. "We need to go. Trust me."

She laughed softly. "Trust you? That's rich, coming from you."

"Fair enough, I deserve that." He always had liked the way she never pulled punches and found it every bit as arousing now as he had when they lived together. "Or you could just trust me because you're a nicer person than I am."

"All right, then." She placed her hand in his, her soft fingers curling around his.

And holy crap, she leaned in closer to him as they walked down the hall. The light scent of her shampoo teased his nose. The need to haul her into his arms throbbed harder, hotter. Damn it, he was supposed to be protecting her, comforting her. He reined in thoughts fueled by three years of abstinence.

*Three. Damn. Years.*

Out in the main living area, he guided her to the sectional sofa, wide palm ceiling fans clicking overhead. "Have a seat, and I'll get us a snack from the kitchen."

She settled onto the sofa, nestling in a pile of pillows. "Just some water, please."

That would give him all of sixty seconds to will back the raging erection. Hell, he could spend an hour creating a five course meal and it wouldn't be enough time to ease the painful arousal.

He snagged two bottles of water from the stainless-steel refrigerator in a kitchen he'd actually learned to use and returned to the living room. He twisted off a cap and passed her the Evian. "Let's watch a movie."

"A movie?"

"I can pipe anything you want in through the satellite." He opened his bottle. "I'm even open to a chick flick."

"You want to watch a *movie?*" She shifted in the mass of throw pillows, looking so much like a harem girl he almost dropped to his knees.

"Or we can talk." And he realized now that Salvatore was right. He should talk to Jayne and tell her more about the man she'd married, the man she thought she wanted to crawl back in bed with. He needed to be sure her eyes were wide-open about him before he could even consider taking her up on what she offered.

She was stuck here because of him. They were both forced to watch over their shoulders—also because of him and the choices he'd made. While he couldn't see much he would do differently, at least he owed her a better perspective on why he'd broken the law.

Why he'd ruined so many lives, including theirs.

He sat by her, on the side that didn't have his gun in the way. On second thought, he unstrapped the shoulder harness and set the whole damn thing on the teak coffee table.

Too bad his past couldn't be tucked away as easily.

He wrestled with where to start and figured what the hell. Might as well go back to the beginning.

Elbows on his knees, he rolled the water bottle between his palms. "You know what I did as a teenager, but I don't think I've ever really explained why."

She sat up straighter, her forehead furrowing, but she didn't speak.

"A teenage boy is probably the dumbest creation on the planet. Pair that with a big ego and no moral compass, and you've got a recipe for trouble."

Seventeen years later and he still couldn't get past the guilt of what he'd done.

"You were so young," she said softly.

"That's no excuse. I was out of control and hating life. This girl I liked had dumped me because her parents didn't want her around my family." He glanced at her. "Her dad was a cop. My ego stung. And I decided to show him and the justice system what screw-ups they were, because I—a teenager—was going to do what they couldn't. I would make the corrupt pay." Starting with two leches he'd caught hitting on his sister, damn near assaulting her, and his dad hadn't done more than shrug off his friends' behavior by insisting no harm, no foul.

"You had good intentions. All of the news reports I read said as much. And yes, I searched every one of them since you're usually closemouthed about your past." She set aside her drink and clutched his forearm, squeezing. "While it's admirable you feel bad, you can also cut yourself some slack. You were exposing corrupt corporations."

"Not so much. See, I could have infiltrated my dad's records and those of his crooked friends, then turned them over to the authorities. And I could have had a better motivation than getting back at some girl or showing up my old man. But I wanted to make a statement. I wanted to make him see that even if I didn't do things his way, damn it, I was still every bit as smart. Because I would get away with it."

She didn't rush to reassure him this time, but she hadn't pulled away in disgust. Yet.

"Twisted, isn't it?" He set aside his water bottle to keep from shattering it in his fist. "I wanted to bring him—as well as a couple of his friends—down *and* make him proud of me."

"That had to make getting caught all the worse." She gathered a pillow to her, her voice steadier than her hands.

"That's the real kick in the ass irony." His hand fell to the lacy edge on the short sleeve of her nightgown and he rubbed it between two fingers. "I didn't get caught. I would have gotten away with it."

"Then how did you end up in reform school?"

"I found out that one of the CEOs of a business I'd helped tank with my short sales… He took his life."

Acid fired at the lining of his stomach, burning up to his throat with a guilt that would never leave, no matter how many missions he completed or how much money he donated to charity. "I turned myself in to the police, with all the information on what I had done, everything I could dig up on my father."

"And the police gave you a more lenient sentence because you came forward." Her hand settled on his back, soothing. "What happened was horrible, but you did come forward with all that evidence, even when it incriminated you. That counts for something."

Laughter rumbled around in his chest, stirring the acid and mixing in some shards of glass for good measure to flay his insides. "Turning myself in didn't count for jack. I only got sent to that school instead of juvie because my dad hired the best lawyers. He got off of every major charge, and I could not beg my way into prison."

His dad's lawyers had made sure the press learned—through an "anonymous" leak—that every targeted company had been guilty of using child laborers in sweatshops overseas.

Once the media got wind of that part of his case, he'd been lauded the white knight of orphans. The pressure had nudged the judge the rest of the way in cutting him a deal. Through the colonel's mentorship, he and his friends had learned to channel their codes of right and wrong. Now they had the chance to right wrongs within the parameters of the law.

"I'm just damn lucky I landed in Salvatore's program. I owe him more than my life, Jayne." His voice strangled off with the emotion clogging his throat and squeezing his chest. "I owe him my self-respect."

Wordlessly she slipped her arms around him and

pulled him to her. He pressed his forehead into her shoulder and drew in the pure, clean scent of her. She was too good for him, always had been. There just hadn't been anyone in her life to warn her away from him the way his teenage girlfriend's dad had.

"Conrad, Colonel Salvatore couldn't have built something within you if the foundation and all the essential parts weren't already there. You're a good man."

He didn't know how long they sat there, and a part of him knew he should let her go back to bed before he took anything more from her. But having her this close again felt better than he'd remembered, different, too. The glide of her fingers along the back of his neck soothed as much as they aroused. She was such a mix of contradictions, everything he wanted and all he didn't deserve.

She turned her face to graze a kiss across his temple before taking his face between her hands and looking him in the eyes. "I think we've both been hurting long enough."

Oh, God, this was it. The moment she would send him packing for good. She wouldn't wait around for him to sign the papers. She would pursue the divorce without his consent, an option that had always been open to her due to their lengthy separation. He hadn't realized until now how much hope he'd been holding on to. Like a sap, with every day that passed and no divorce, he'd allowed himself to believe there was a chance they would reconcile.

Now he had to face up to the fact that it was over between them, and she would move on to live the life she deserved. The one he'd never come close to offering her. She would find the man she deserved who would give her a real home and cute babies.

Forcing out words to set her free damn near split him in half. "Jayne, I never wanted to hurt you." He clasped her wrists, holding on to her for what would be the last time. "I only want you to be happy."

She angled back to stare deep in his eyes. "Then make love to me."

# Eight

Leaning forward, her hip digging into the sofa cushions, Jayne skimmed her mouth over Conrad's, praying he wouldn't push her away again.

Desperate to see this through.

His admissions, his outpouring from deep in his soul only confirmed her conviction that he was a much better man than he realized. And regardless of whatever else had happened between them, she wasn't turning back from right now, right here with Conrad.

She sensed his restraint, his lingering concerns about protecting her from her dream or from herself. Whatever. To hell with holding back. She poured all her frustration and bottled emotions into the way her body ignited around him. Arching upward, she swung her leg around and over until she straddled him, bringing her flush against the hard length of his erection. She rocked once, twice, her hips to his until she felt the growl rumble in his chest. His arms shot up and around her, locking her to him.

A purr of relief spiraled up her throat.

"Jayne, are you sure this is what you want?" he asked between possessive kisses.

"Absolutely. We've both waited long enough. Stop talking and take me, damn it."

And thank heaven he listened and agreed. Angling her back onto the sofa, his solid body pressed her into the welcoming pile of pillows. He hooked a finger along the lacy edge of one sleeve, sliding along her shoulder and around until he skimmed her breast, launching delicious shivers of anticipation.

Desire surged liquid heat through her veins in a near-painful, all-over rush. She'd laid awake so many nights, aching for him, tempted to reach for the phone and just hear the sound of his voice. The rumbling timbre of him speaking her name then and now sent her spine bowing up toward him, as she wriggled to get closer.

She thumbed the buttons on his shirt free and yanked the fabric off his shoulders, sending it sailing to rest on a water bottle. Sighing, she splayed her fingers over his chest, up along his shoulders to pull him to her again. The heat of his bare flesh seared through her nightgown, her breasts tingling with awareness. How had she made it through the past three years without him, without this?

Her hand slid between them, down the front of his jeans, stroking his erection straining against his fly until he throbbed impossibly harder against her touch. She fumbled with the top button then eased the zipper down. Her fingers tucked inside his boxers, and he groaned low in his throat.

The steely length of him fit to her hand, familiar even after years apart. Although in some ways it seemed like no time at all, given all the hungry dreams she'd had of him coming to her bed again. Or in some of her more uninhibited fantasies he'd come to her in other places. Whisking her away from work to make love in the car. Joining her on a beach walk where they slipped behind a sand dune together. Or appearing next to her in a dark theater...

But she always woke up alone, unfulfilled and knowing he would never come for her. She had to move on with her life.

God, her thoughts were running away from her, threatening to steal this moment from them again.

Conrad shifted on top of her, and she gripped his shoulders to hold him in place. "Where are you going?"

"Jayne, I'm not leaving." His hands never stopped moving and arousing her even while he talked. "I packed a box of condoms in my suitcase, because even though I didn't just assume we would sleep together, I sure as hell wasn't going to lose the chance due to poor planning."

"Guess what?" She slid her hands around, digging her nails into his buttocks. "I'm a good planner, too."

"Then lucky for us, we have plenty to get through the night." He slid off her and stood, wearing nothing but his jeans, open and low slung on his hips in a tempting V. "So do I go get mine and come back, or do we move to the bedroom?"

Her brain was so fogged just staring at him that she struggled to form an answer. She didn't want to think. She just wanted to feel him over her, moving into her. But if they stayed here, there would be the awkward moment afterward when they pulled themselves together afterward and walked to separate bedrooms—which was insane, since she was his wife. For now at least.

And she realized exactly what she wanted. To be in his bed, to make love there and sleep in his arms.

"Let's go to your room."

Before she could say another word, he swept her against his chest in such a macho show of strength she smiled just before she flicked his earlobe with her tongue then drew it between her teeth, enjoying the slightly salty taste of him.

The lingering scent of his aftershave mixed with the musk of perspiration on his skin. She drew in the smell of him, the feel of him, until even the silk of her nightgown felt itchy against her oversensitized skin. The hard wall of his muscled chest wasn't the one of a paper pusher or a man who'd become soft from years of high living. He could take charge in every realm, intellectually and physically, and that duality turned her on all the more.

He shouldered open his door, revealing a massive teak bed sprawling in front of a window overlooking the river. Then she didn't see anything other than the linen drapes on the ceiling over the bed as he settled her in the middle of a simple cotton comforter. He angled to his suitcase on the stand, pulled out a box of condoms and tossed it on the bed before leaning over her again.

With competent and quick hands he bunched her gown in his fists and swept it away. The breeze over her skin made her want the press of his body but he sprinkled kisses along her stomach, took the edge of her bikini panties between his teeth and tugged. She thought of the panties he'd torn from her body in the elevator, of how he'd given her such an intense release.

At the first nuzzle between her legs, her knees fell

apart and her bones turned to liquid. The flick of his tongue and gentle suckling brought her to the edge too fast, too soon. She clawed at his shoulders, drawing him up, but he stopped, teasing the tight nipple the way he'd licked and laved the tight bud of nerves.

He had her writhing on the comforter, aching to take this further, faster. His hand slid down to replace his tongue with a knowing touch. He inched his way back up her body until his mouth settled on her breast and his fingers between her legs teased in synchronicity, playing her perfectly. He knew her, just like the night at *La Bohème*. Except now she was naked and they were alone so he had free rein for more. He stroked the tight bundle of nerves with his thumb while sliding two fingers deep, crooking at just the right spot.

She gasped and pressed harder against his hand even as she wanted all of him. "No more playing. I just want you inside me."

"And you can be damn sure that's exactly where I want to be." He rolled her nipple lightly between his teeth. "But I want that—want you—so much and it's been so long, I'm not going to last. I need to take care of you first."

She circled him, stroking…her thumb rolling over the damp tip. And yes, she was every bit as close to coming apart.

"That works both ways you know, the part about having gone without sex for too damn long." She reached for the condom box and tugged free a packet. "No more waiting. If we come fast, then we get to linger later, but I can't wait anymore."

Determined to delay not a second longer, she sheathed him with a familiarity and newness that she still didn't quite comprehend. The fan rustled the curtains around their haven.

He held her face, looked into her eyes and said, "There hasn't been anyone since you. No one comes close to turning me inside out the way you do. And even when I resent it like hell, there's no denying it. I only want you."

His words stilled her hands. *No one* since her? For three years?

She wanted to believe him, ached to believe him. Because she felt the same. She even understood the part about resenting the way this feeling for each other took over her body and her life.

And then he kissed her. He thrust his tongue as he pushed inside her. Filling her, stretching her with more of that newness after so damn long away from each other. The sweet abrasion of his chest rasped along her nipples. The hard roped muscles of his legs flexed with each pump of his body. She dug her heels into the mattress and angled up against him until the gathering tension in her pulled even tighter, bringing her closer.

Her hand flung out to grab the headboard, the intense sweetness was almost too much. She wanted to hang on to the sensations as tightly as she held the headboard, but he'd taken her too close to the edge with his mouth and his skillful touch.

One more deep stroke finished her. Pleasure rippled from her core, pulling through her, outward until the roots of her hair tingled. She bowed upward into him, even as her head thrashed on the pillow.

He chanted encouragement as her release pulsed and clamped around him, his voice growing hoarse until he hissed between gritted teeth. And while she'd doubted so much about their relationship, she knew he'd told her the truth about the past three years. He belonged to her.

She hugged him in the aftermath as he collapsed on top of her. The ceiling fan overhead click, click, clicked, gusts shifting the drapes around the towering teak bed. She trailed her fingers along his broad back, her foot up his thigh, and didn't take for granted the feel of him.

Not anymore.

It was one thing to be angry at him for the past thirty-six months. And another altogether to accept he'd been every bit as torn apart by their breakup as she had. With what he'd shared about his father tonight, she started to realize she'd never fully grasped what made him tick. Maybe if she dug for more clues about his relationship with his father in particular, she might understand how he'd arrived at his place of such emotional isolation.

Because she realized more than ever that she couldn't just walk away again.

Conrad held his wife spooned against him while she slept. She was back in his bed. He'd won.

And he didn't feel one bit peaceful about letting Jayne go.

Moonbeams reflected on the river water, the dock light glowing. If she was awake, he would have liked to sit out there with her and just listen to the night sounds, then walk with her up to the house, shower with her in the outdoor stall with the stars above them.

He'd made love to her twice more and still it wasn't enough. He rested his chin on her head, the sweat of their lovemaking lightly sealing their bodies, her spine against his chest. Each breath pressed her closer again, stirring his hard-on to a painful intensity. His hand slid around to cup her breast, filling his palm with her creamy roundness. She moaned in her sleep, her nipple drawing up into a tight bead.

She was in his blood. Rather than clearing away the past, making love with her had churned up all the frustration of the past three years. The thought of letting her go—unbearable. But he couldn't envision taking her back to Monte Carlo.

Although, how to blend her into his old life could be a moot point. If his cover had been blown, his Interpol work would be over. He angled to kiss her shoulder over the light red mark of his beard bristle from last night. He could have Jayne back and no more unexplained absences.

But the thought of ending his Interpol work… hell. He wouldn't have considered it before. Although since Zhutov might have taken that choice from him, he might as well make the best of the situation. And he couldn't just let Jayne wander off with God knows what kind of threat looming. These sorts of crooks did not forget.

His path became clear.

Protect Jayne.

His life came into focus. He realized his past mistake. He'd tried too hard to blend her into his world in Monte Carlo. He'd let her too close to the darker side of himself. Somehow, he must have known that, since he'd chosen to bring her here, to a place that represented the man he'd once wanted to be.

Jayne shifted in her sleep, arching her breast into his hand, her bottom wriggling against him. He throbbed against the sweet dip in her spine and the beginning of his need for her pearled along the tip of his erection. He clamped a hand on her stomach to hold her still.

Sighing, she looked back over her shoulder at him with sleepy half-awake eyes.

"Is it morning?" she asked in a groggy voice.

"Not yet. Keep sleeping." He had a packed day planned, showing her the full extent of the compound he'd built here. "We have plenty of time."

"Hmm... Except I'm not sleepy." She reached behind her to stroke his hair. "What's on the agenda for today?"

He nuzzled her hair. "I have some ideas. But what do you want?"

"At some point, breakfast. A very big breakfast, actually. After last night, I'll need more than pastries and tea."

"I'm certain I can figure something out."

"You cook?"

He was a little insulted by the assumption that he didn't, until he remembered all the times he'd burned toast when they were still together. His cooking was a more recently acquired skill. "I make some pretty fierce eggs Benedict these days."

"Sounds heavenly." Her head rested back against his chest. "I also noticed you've taken up redecorating."

Did he detect a note of pique in her voice? He opted for honesty. "Having your things around brought back too many memories. It was easier to move forward if I got rid of them."

Her feet tucked between his. "But you didn't replace everything. The red room stayed the same."

"That was the only room in the penthouse where we never had sex."

"So let me get this straight. You tossed out every piece of furniture that reminded you of the two of us having sex there."

"Pretty much."

She stayed silent, and he wished he could see her face to gauge her mood. So much of her was familiar and then other times not so much. She'd changed. So had he. They were both warier.

Finally she smiled back at him over her shoulder. "Good thing we never made love in the Bentley. It would have been a damn shame for you to have to get rid of such a cool collector's item."

"You have a point." He kissed her, wondering if he would have to burn this bed if she walked out on him again. "I guess we've both made some changes. What prompted you to swap from being an E.R. nurse to Hospice care?"

"You've obviously kept tabs on me. Why do you think?"

Was that a dig? "You know you don't have to work, right? No matter what happens between us, I will take care of you."

She flipped back the covers and started to sit up. "I don't need to be 'taken care of.'"

"Whoa... Hold on now." He looped an arm around her waist. "I didn't mean to offend you. I was just commenting on the fact that we're married. What's mine is yours. Fifty-fifty."

"Don't let your lawyer hear you give up your portfolio that easily."

"Not. Funny."

Still, she sat on the edge of the bed, the vulnerable curve of her back stirring his protective urges. She could shout her independence all day long. That wouldn't stop him from wanting to give her nice things. And more importantly, it wouldn't stop him from standing between her and anything that threatened her.

Shifting up onto an elbow, he rubbed her back and tried to backtrack, to fix what he'd screwed up. "Tell me about your new job."

Was it his imagination or did the defensive tensing of her shoulders ease?

"When I came back to Miami, my old job had obviously been filled. I took the Hospice opening as a temporary stopgap until a position more in my line of expertise became available. Except I found I didn't want to leave the job. It's not that I was unhappy with my work before, but something changed inside me."

"Like what?" He smoothed his hand down to the small of her back, the lolling of her head cluing him in to keep right on with the massage.

"I think I was drawn to E.R. work initially because there wasn't as much of a chance of my heart being engaged." She glanced back. "I don't mean to say that I didn't care for the patients. But there wasn't time to form a relationship with someone who's out of your care in under an hour. I had a set amount of time to help that person, and then we moved on."

He massaged along the tendons in her neck. "Your dad's stunt hiding a second family really must have done a number on you."

"I had trouble connecting with others." She sagged back onto the bed and into his arms. "Now I find there's a deep satisfaction in bringing comfort to people when life is at its most difficult. It may sound strange…"

"Not at all," he said as he tucked her tight against him, this amazing woman he damn well didn't deserve but couldn't bring himself to give up.

"Enough depressing talk about the past. I don't know about you, but I can think of a far more enjoyable way to spend our time now that I am completely awake."

She stretched out an arm to slide a condom from the bedside table and pressed it into his palm.

Smiling seductively over her shoulder, she skimmed her foot along his calf, her legs parting ever so slightly for him, inviting him. And call him a selfish bastard, but he wasn't one to turn down an invitation from Jayne. He'd been without her for so long he couldn't get enough of her. Time and time again he'd been tempted to fly to Miami and demand she come home.

Like that would have gone over well.

Instead he'd sent back those damn divorce papers repeatedly, knowing eventually she would have to come to him. She'd been well worth the wait. He skimmed his fingers around her again, slipped them down between the damp cleft, stroking as she opened farther.

With two fingers, he circled, faster, pressing and plucking with the amount of pressure he knew she enjoyed, bringing a fresh sigh from her. And just when he'd brought her to the edge, he hooked his arm under her knee and angled his sheathed erection just right, so close to everything he'd dreamed of and fantasized about when he'd taken those long and unsatisfying showers without her.

As he slid inside Jayne, *his wife,* he vowed he would not lose her. And he would never, never let anything from his past touch her again.

Jayne stood at the river's edge and watched the gazelle glide through the tall grasses on the other side of the mangrove swamp. The midmorning sun climbed up the horizon in a shimmering orange haze, echoing the warm glow inside her after a night of making love with Conrad.

Again and again. He'd given her explosive orgasms

and foreplay to die for. He'd brought her a late-night snack in bed of flatbreads and meats, fed to each other. He'd fed her perfectly prepared eggs Benedict this morning. They'd talked and laughed, everything she'd dreamed could happen for them again.

How different might things have been if they'd come here for their first anniversary? If they'd talked through all the things they were only beginning to touch on now?

And she couldn't completely blame him anymore. As she looked back, she accepted the times she'd let things slide rather than push him, because deep in her heart she was scared she wouldn't be able to walk away.

Her mother hadn't deserved what happened to her. God knows Jayne hadn't deserved it, either.

But she refused to be passive any longer. If—and that was a *big* if—she and Conrad stood a chance at patching things up, he needed to be completely open with her. They needed a true partnership of equals.

Glancing over her shoulder up to his home on the plateau, she saw her husband pacing, talking on his cell phone. He'd said he needed to check in with Salvatore before he took her on a tour of the property. Apparently there were other buildings and even a small town beyond the rolling hills and she had to admit to curiosity about what drew him here. The home—the whole locale—was so different from the glitz of his other holdings.

It gave her hope.

So much hope that she'd called Anthony. She'd arranged for a friend from work to pick up Mimi. If she was going to even consider making things work with Conrad, she had to cut off any ties to Anthony, a man she'd considered dating.

Watching Conrad walk down the incline toward her now, she wasn't ready to pack her things and bring Mimi across the ocean yet, but for the first time in three years, she was open to the possibility. She just needed the sign from Conrad that he would compromise this go-round.

He closed the distance between them, stopping at the shoreline with tall grasses swaying around his calves. He draped an arm around her shoulder. "Salvatore's staff is still wading through backlogs of visitors, letters, emails, any contact with the outside world. A suspicious amount of money was moved from Zhutov's wife's account. Salvatore hopes to have concrete answers by the end of the day."

The threat sounded so surreal, but then Conrad's whole hidden career still felt strange to her. "What about Troy and Hillary?"

"They're safely in the Bahamas at a casino and no signs of anyone tracking them, either. By all accounts, they're enjoying the vacation of a lifetime."

"So this could all be a scare for nothing?"

He kissed her forehead. "Not nothing. We're here, together."

For how long? Long enough to find a path back together? She wished they could stand here by the river watching the hippo bathe himself in mud.

She tucked closer to Conrad's side, the sun beaming down on them. "Did you get any sleep last night?"

"Three or four hours. I'm good."

"Yes, you are." Turning in his arms, she kissed him good-morning and wondered just how private this spot might be. She looked at the dock, then up the incline at the deck and the outdoor shower stall. Her mind swirled with possibilities....

With a final kiss to her forehead, he angled back. "Ready to go for the tour?"

"Absolutely." Walking alongside him to the Land Cruiser, she tucked away her fantasy for another time, intensely curious about this tour and the opportunity to dig deeper into what made her husband tick.

The wilds of Africa were definitely a world away from Monte Carlo. Instead of flashy royalty in diamonds and furs, a spotted cheetah parted the grasslands not far from a mama giraffe with her baby. They walked with a long-legged grace much more elegant than any princess.

She rolled down her window, letting the muggy air clear away the images of the glitzier lifestyle, immersing herself in the present. "We know each other well in some ways and in others not at all—no dig meant by that. I feel like it's my fault, too."

"None of this is your fault. I'm the one responsible for my own choices and actions, no excuses from the past." Wind tunneled in his white polo shirt, his faded jeans fitting to his muscled thighs.

It wasn't about the clothes with him. She couldn't help but think—not for the first time—how he had a powerful presence just by existing, whether he was in a tuxedo in Monte Carlo or dressed for the desert realms of Africa.

She studied the hard line of his jaw, peppered with stubble. "Why can't you let me feel sorry for what you went through as a teenager?"

"I don't want sympathy. I want you naked." He shot a seductive grin her way. "We can pull over and…"

"You're trying to distract me." And she was determined to talk. "You promised to answer my questions."

Only the wind answered, whispering through the

window as they drove toward a small cluster of buildings in the distance, with cars and lines of people,
adults and kids. Perhaps this was a school?

Regardless, her time to talk would be cut short soon.

"Conrad? You promised," she pressed as birds
ducked and dove toward their windshield only to break
away at the last instant.

He winced, looking back at the narrow rural road.
"You're right. I promised."

"Where did you stay on school breaks? Or did you
stay at the school, like juvenile hall or something?"

The smile left his eyes. "I went home for holidays
with an ankle monitor."

Thoughts of him as a teenager walking around with
that monitoring device chilled her. "That had to have
been awkward after you tried to turn in your father."

"My dad told me I could make it all up to him by
connecting him with the families of my new friends."
He steered around a pack of dwarf goats in the road.
"Why don't we talk about your dad instead, Jayne?"

He guided the car back on the road again, leading
them closer to the long stucco building, surrounded
by smaller outbuildings. The slight detour off the road
jounced her in the seat, hard, almost as if he'd deliberately bounced her around.

She held up her hands in surrender. "Okay, message received."

Her husband wasn't as open to talking this morning, but she wouldn't give up. She would simply wait
for a better opening while they spent their day at...
Not a school at all.

He'd driven her to a medical clinic.

# Nine

Conrad watched his wife, curious as to what she would think of the clinic he'd built. Because yes, he'd built it as a tribute to her and the light she'd brought to his world. Regardless of how their marriage had broken up in the end, his four years with her were the best in his life.

She asked him all those questions about his father and the arrest, looking for ways to exonerate him because she had such a generous and forgiving heart. But she didn't seem to grasp he'd done the crime. He was guilty of a serious wrong, no justification.

His life now had to be devoted to a very narrow path of making things right. The small hospital was a part of that thanks to a mission to the region nearly four years ago that had left a mark on him. He'd been aiding in an investigation tracing heroin traffic through a casino in South Africa, the trail leading him up the coast. He wasn't an agent so much as a facilitator to

lend effective covers and information about people in
his wealthy world. They'd taken down the kingpin in
that case, but Conrad hadn't felt the rush of victory.

Not that time.

His nights had been haunted by visions of the *Agberos,* street children and teens also known as "area
boys." They were loosely organized gangs forced into
crime. And no matter how many kingpins Conrad took
out, another would slide into place. There was no Salvatore to look after those boys, to change their lives
with a do-over.

Conrad opened Jayne's car door, her reaction so
damn important to him right now that his chest went
tight with each drag of air. Lines of patients filed into
the door, locals wearing anything from jeans and
T-shirts to colorful local cloths wrapped in a timeless
way. They were here for anything from vaccinations
to prenatal care to HIV/AIDS treatment.

The most gut-wrenching of all? The ones here for
both prenatal care and HIV treatment. There was a
desperate need here and he couldn't help everyone, but
one at a time, he was doing his damnedest.

He wasn't a Salvatore sort, but he could at least give
these kids some relief in their lives. He could make sure
they grew up healthy, and those that couldn't would
have a fighting chance against the HIV devastating so
many lives in Africa.

Jayne placed her hand in his and stepped out of the
SUV. "Interesting choice for an outing."

"I thought since you're a nurse, you would like to
see the facility."

"It's so much more than I would have expected in
such a rural community."

"It feeds into the population of three villages, and there are patients who drive in from even farther."

She shaded her eyes against the sun, turning for the full three-hundred-and-sixty-degree view of everything from the one-story building to storage buildings. The place even had a playground, currently packed with young kids playing a loosely organized game of soccer, kicking up a cloud of dust around them. A brindle dog bounded along with them, jumping and racing for the ball, reminding him of little Mimi.

Patients arrived in cars and on foot, some wearing westernized clothes and others in brightly colored native wear. A delivery truck and ambulance were parked off to the side. Not brand-spanking-new, but well maintained.

They'd accomplished a lot here in a few short years.

He pointed to the doctor pushing through the front double doors. Conrad had given the doc a call to be on the lookout for them. "And here's our guide. Dr. Rowan Boothe."

Another former Salvatore protégé.

Jayne halted Conrad with a hand on his arm. "Is it okay if we just wander around? I don't want to get in anyone's way or disrupt anyone's routine."

The doctor stopped at the end of the walkway, stethoscope around his neck, hands in the pockets of his lab coat.

"Ma'am, don't worry about the tour. He owns the place." Boothe said it in a way that didn't sound like a compliment.

Not a surprise.

He and Boothe hadn't been friends—far from it. From day one, the sanctimonious do-gooder had kept to himself. Getting a read off him had been tough. On the one hand, he'd picked fights and then on the other, Boothe damn near martyred himself working community service hours.

The doc didn't much like Conrad, and Conrad didn't blame him. Conrad had given Boothe hell over his do-gooder attitude. But Conrad couldn't deny the guy's skill and his dedication. Boothe was the perfect fit for this place, and probably even a better fit for Jayne.

Damn.

Where the hell had that come from?

Suddenly it mattered too much to him that Jayne approve of the clinic. He was starting to want her to see him as the good guy and that was dangerous ground.

Damn it all to hell. He needed distance, or before he knew it, she would start asking more questions, probing around in his past for an honorability that just wasn't there.

"Jayne, you're in good hands here. I'm going to tend to some business."

Jayne's head was spinning as fast as the test tubes in the centrifuge. Her slip-on loafers squeaked along the pristine tile floors as she turned to follow Dr. Boothe into the corridor, her tour almost complete.

One wing held a thirty-bed hospital and the other wing housed a clinic. Not overly large, but all top-of-the-line and designed for efficiency. The antibacterial scent saturated each breath she took, the familiarity of the environment wrapping her in comfort.

She'd expected Conrad to romance her today. That's what Conrad did, big gifts and trips. He remembered her preferences from cream-filled pastries to Italian opera.

But this? He'd always seemed to think her nursing

was just a job and she'd followed his lead, figuring someone else needed the job she would have taken up. She'd had plenty of money as his wife… But God, after six months, she'd become restless and by the end of the first year, she'd missed her job so much her teeth ached.

Walking down the center hall of the clinic, she couldn't stop thinking maybe he had seen her need there at the end, that he'd been planning this for her. Had she given up on them too soon?

Dr. Rowan Boothe continued his running monologue about the facilities and their focus on childhood immunizations as well as HIV/AIDS treatment and education.

She was impressed and curious. "You and Conrad seem to know each other well. How did you meet?"

The doctor looked more like a retired model than a physician. But from what she'd heard so far, his expertise was undeniable. "We went to high school together."

North Carolina Military Prep? Was he the kind who'd gone in hopes of joining the military or because of a near brush with the law? Asking felt…rude. And then there was the whole Salvatore issue…an off-limits question altogether. "Hmm, it's nice when alumni can network."

He quirked a thick blond eyebrow as they passed the pharmacy. "Yes, I was one of the 'in trouble' crowd who now use their powers for good instead of evil."

"You have a sense of humor about it."

"That surprises you?" he asked as he held open the door for her, a burst of sunshine sending sparks in front of her eyes.

"What you face here, the tragic cases, the poverty, the limited resources and crime…" She stepped onto the front walkway, shading her eyes. Where was Conrad? "How can you keep that upbeat attitude under such crushing odds?"

"People are living longer here because of this clinic. Those children playing over there would have been dead by now without it." He gestured to a dozen or so boys kicking a soccer ball on a playground beside the clinic. "You said you're a Hospice nurse now, an E.R. nurse before that. You of all people should understand."

He had a point.

"You're right, of course." Her eyes adjusted to the stark sunshine and out there in the middle of the pack of boys, her husband joined in, kicking the soccer ball.

Laughing?

When was the last time she'd heard him laugh with something other than sarcasm? She couldn't remember. The sound of him, the *sight* of him, so relaxed took her breath away. He looked...young. Or rather he looked his age, a man in his early thirties, in the prime of life. Not that he'd looked old before but he'd been so distant and unapproachable.

She glanced at Dr. Boothe. "What was he like back in high school?"

"Moody. Arrogant. He was gangly and wore glasses back then, but he was a brilliant guy and he knew it. Folks called him Mr. Wall Street, because of his dad and what he did with the stock market." He glanced at her. "But you probably could have guessed all of that."

She just smiled, hoping he would keep talking if she didn't interrupt.

"I didn't come from money like most of the guys there, and I wasn't inordinately talented like Douglas. I had a monster chip on my shoulder. I thought I was better than those overprivileged brats. I caught a lucky break when I was sent there. I didn't fit in so I kept my distance." He half smiled. "The sense of humor's a skill I acquired later."

"Yet, Conrad brought you here. He must respect you."

"Yeah, I guess. I have the grades, but so do a lot of doctors who want to save the world. If we're going to be honest, I'm here because of a cookie."

"Pardon me? I'm not sure I understand."

"My mom used to send me these care packages full of peanut butter cookies with M&M's baked into them. Damn, they were good." The fond light in his eyes said more about the mother who sent the baked goods. "One day, I was in my bunk, knocking back a couple of those cookies while doing my macro-biology homework. And I looked up to find Conrad staring at those cookies like they were caviar. I knew better than to offer him one. He'd have just thrown it back in my face."

He leaned against a porch pillar. "We were all pretty angry at life in those days. But I had my cookies and letters from Mom to get me through the days when I didn't think I could live with the guilt of what I'd done."

He shook his head. "But back to Conrad. About a week later, I was on my way to the cafeteria when I saw him in the visitation area with his dad. I was jealous as hell since my folks couldn't afford to fly out to visit me—and then I realized he and his dad were fighting."

"About what?" She couldn't help but ask, desperate for this unfiltered look into the teenager Conrad had been during a time in his life that had so tremendously shaped the man he'd become.

"From what Conrad shouted, it was clear his father wanted him to run a scam on Troy's parents and convince them to invest in some bogus company or another. Conrad decked his dad. It took two security guards to pull him off."

The image of that betrayal, of the pain and humiliation he must have felt, brought tears to her eyes she knew her overly stoic husband would never have shed for himself. "And the cookie?"

"I'm getting there. Conrad spent a couple of days in the infirmary—his dad hit him back and dislocated Conrad's shoulder. The cops didn't press charges on the old man because the son threw the first punch. Anyhow, Conrad's first day out of the infirmary, I felt bad for him so I wrapped a cookie in a napkin and put it on his bunk. He didn't say anything, but he didn't toss it back in my face, either." He threw his hands wide. "And here I am today."

Her heart hurt so badly she could barely push words out. "You're killing me, you know that don't you?"

"Hey, don't get me wrong. He's still an arrogant ass, but he's a good guy if you dig deep." He grinned. "Really deep."

She looked back out at her husband playing ball with the kids. His voice rode the breeze as he shouted encouragement and tips, and she couldn't help but think of the father that had never been there for him. No wonder he was wary of being a parent himself.

But if he could only see himself now. He was such a natural.

She'd dreamed of them having children one day, and she'd hoped he could be a good father. But she'd never dared imagine him like this. She should be happy, hopeful.

Instead she was scared to death. It was one thing to fail at her second chance with Conrad if she would have had to walk away from the same failed marriage she'd left before. But everything was different this time. What if she lost the chance to make Conrad genuinely happy? This chance to touch lives together in Africa?

That would level her.

An older boy booted the soccer ball across the field, a couple of smaller boys chasing it down. The ball rolled farther away, toward a moving truck stacked with water jugs. The vehicle barreled along the dirt road without the least sign of slowing even as the child sprinted closer on skinny little legs.

Her heart leaped into her throat. Dr. Boothe sprang into motion but there was no way he would make it to the child in time.

"Conrad!" Jayne screamed, again and again.

But he was already sprinting toward the kid, who was maybe six or seven years old. Conrad moved like a sleek panther across the ball field, faster than should have been possible. And in a flash, he'd scooped the child up with one arm and stopped a full ten yards away from the truck. He spun the kid around, sunshine streaming down from the sky around them. The little boy's giggles carried on the breeze as if all was right in the world. And it was. Conrad had the situation firmly in hand.

Her heart hammered in her ears.

A low laugh pulled her attention away from her husband and back to Dr. Boothe. A blush burned up her face over being caught staring at her husband like a lovesick teenager.

God, her feelings for Conrad were so transparent a total stranger could read her.

What did her husband think when he looked at her? Did he think he'd won her over today? If so, she needed to be damn clear on that point. Yes, she was hopeful, but that didn't mean she was willing to compromise on her dreams.

But what about his dreams?

This close brush with danger revealed her husband's competence in a snapshot. She'd spent so many nights worried about why he hadn't called home, but seeing him in action gave her a new appreciation for how well equipped he was for quick action in risky work. He was smart, strong and he had resources. Furthermore, he had lightning reflexes and a will to help others.

Was she being as selfish as she'd once accused him of being by denying him a job that obviously meant a lot to him? A job that was, she now understood, a conduit to forgiving himself for his past? Clearly Conrad needed his work as badly as she needed hers.

That realization hurt, making her feel small and petty for all the accusations she'd hurled at him. He'd deserved better from her then, more understanding. She couldn't change the past and she didn't know if they had a future together or not.

But she could control what she did today.

Conrad started the Land Cruiser, sweat sticking his shirt to his back from the impromptu ball game and the surprise sprint to keep the little Kofi from dashing in front of a moving truck. His head still buzzed with the kick of fear when he'd seen the kid sprint toward the vehicle, unaware of anything but reaching that soccer ball.

Thank God the worst hadn't happened.

Playing with the kids was the high point of these visits for him, something he always did when he had time here. But today, he'd also needed the outlet after watching Jayne with Boothe, their heads tucked together as they discussed the ins and outs of the clinic.

The day had been a success in every way that mattered, and he was a petty bastard for his foul mood. He wanted to blame the stress on Zhutov, and God knows that added to his tension. There wasn't a damn thing he could do but wait until the enemy made a move. And once that wait was over?

Hell. The need to take his wife home and imprint himself in her memory, deep in her body, took hold of him. And he couldn't think of a reason why he shouldn't follow through on the urge to make love to her until they both fell into an exhausted sleep.

He put the car in Drive and accelerated out of the parking lot. His wife sat beside him with that expression on her face again, like she'd put him under a microscope. He prepped for what he knew would come next.

"That was amazing how fast you reacted when the child ran toward that truck."

"I just did what anyone would have." And he'd also had a word with the truck driver about the dangers of speeding past a playground. "Kofi—the kid—spends a lot of time here with his older brother, Ade. Their mother comes regularly for her HIV treatments."

"Do you know all the kids' names?"

"Some," he answered noncommittally.

She sighed in exasperation. "You said before we got on the plane you would tell me anything. Did you mean that?"

"I should have put a limit on how many questions you could ask." A flock of geese scattered in front of him.

"I'll go easy on you then. What's your favorite kind of cookie? I realize I should already know that, and I feel awful for having to ask when you have my favorite pastry memorized, but I realized I really don't know."

Cookie? What the hell? "Um, anything with M&M's. I'm, uh, partial to M&M's in my cookies."

She smiled and touched his knee. Apparently he'd answered that one correctly.

"Next question?"

"Why don't you wear glasses anymore? And why didn't you ever mention that you used to? You'd think there would be pictures."

"Boothe," he said simply. Now he understood why they'd been standing under the awning so long. Boothe had been spouting out crap about the past. "I had Lasik surgery on my eyes so I don't need glasses anymore. As for photos of me wearing them? They perished in a horrible accident, a trash can fire in Salvatore's office. A fire extinguisher was sacrificed in the line of duty."

Her hand stayed on his knee. "You have a sense of humor when you want to—sarcastic, sure but funny."

She stroked higher up his thigh and he damn near drove into a ditch. He clasped her wrist and moved her back to her side of the car.

"You'll need to put that thought on hold."

Laughing softly, she hooked an elbow out the window, her blond hair streaking across her face. "I want to know more about your job with Interpol."

Apparently the easy questions had just been to soften him up.

"What do you want to know?"

"I keep trying to wrap my brain around the whole notion of you and your friends living a James Bond life, and it's blowing my mind. How did I miss guessing for four years?"

Because he was a damn good liar?

That didn't seem like a wise answer. He measured out a smarter answer, balancing it with what was safe to tell her.

"We're more freelancers, and we don't take jobs often. It actually keeps the risk of exposure down." But the longer he went between assignments, the more restless he grew. If this Zhutov case blew up in his face, would Salvatore cut him out or relegate him to some paper-pushing research? "I only worked six 'projects' in the entire time we were together. An assignment could take anywhere from a week to a month."

She nodded, going silent while she stared out the window at an ostrich running on pace with them at forty-two miles per hour. Her deep breath gave him only a flash of a notice that she wasn't giving up.

"Sounds to me like your Alpha Brotherhood has morphed into a Bond Brotherhood." She tipped her face into the wind, her eyes closed, her neck arched and vulnerable. "Troy is definitely the Pierce Brosnan Bond type, with his charm and his metro-sexual style. Malcolm is the Roger Moore type, old school Bond with his jazz flair. I only recall meeting Elliot Starc once, but he fits well enough for the Timothy Dalton slot, rarely seen but very international. The doctor, Boothe, he's the Daniel Craig Bond, the tortured soul."

"Who said Boothe was part of the Alpha Brotherhood?" And yes, he noticed she'd aptly insinuated they were all working for Salvatore as well, something he didn't intend to confirm.

"Just a guess." She glanced at him, her perceptive blue eyes making it clear she hadn't missed the nuance. "By the way, *you* are absolutely the Sean Connery Bond."

"I think you're paying me a compliment." He

glanced over and found her staring at him with a familiar sensual glint.

He went hard at just a look from her—and the promise in her eyes.

"You're sexy, brooding, arrogant and too damn mesmerizing for your own good. It's not fair, you know."

"I'm not sure where you're going with this."

"Just that I can't resist you. Even now, I'm sitting here fighting the urge to jump you right here in the middle of nowhere. I'm trying to play it cool and logical because I don't want either of us to get hurt again."

"Can we go back to the Sean Connery discussion?" He hooked an arm around her and tugged her to his side.

She adjusted her seat belt and leaned against him. "I wonder sometimes if we were drawn to each other because of feeling like orphans."

He forced himself not to tense as she neatly shifted the conversation again. "We had parents."

"Don't be so literal."

"Don't be such a girl."

"Um, hello? I have breasts."

"Believe me." His hand slid along the generous curve. "I noticed."

"You're not paying attention." She linked fingers with him, stopping his caress.

He squeezed her hand, driving with the other hand down the deserted private road leading back to his house. "You have my complete and undivided attention."

"Good, because there will be a quiz afterward," she said smartly.

He nuzzled her hair, and wondered when just sitting beside her, holding her hand had become such an incredible turn on. "I've missed you."

"I've missed you, too." Her head fell to rest on his shoulder. "That's what I was getting at. You have your brotherhood, but you lead these separate lives with just periodic high octane reunions. Day by day, neither of us has a family."

He laughed darkly. "Dysfunctional is drawn to dysfunctional, I guess."

"Not exactly how I would have phrased it, but that works well enough." Her hand fell to rest on his knee, stroking lightly.

To arouse or soothe?

"Jayne, your dad's a loser just like mine was." Anger simmered in his gut over how her father had hurt her. "End of story. We overcame it."

"Did we?" She drew circles on his jeans, her touch heating him through the denim. "Or are we still letting them control our lives?"

His hand clenched around the steering wheel. He wanted to be with her, but damn it, she needed to leave discussions of his father in the past. He'd said all he cared to say about the old man who didn't warrant his time. This whole twenty questions game was officially over.

"If I wanted therapy I would pay a shrink." He turned off the road, hitting the remote for the gate, which also triggered a timed release for the other layers of security along with a facial recognition program.

"Wow, Conrad," she said, sliding back to her side of the vehicle, "that was rude."

He reined his temper in even as sweat beaded his brow. "You're right." He stopped the car beside the house. "Of course."

"If you don't agree," she snapped, throwing her door open wide, "then just say so."

"I disagree, and I'm rude." He threw his arms wide as he circled to the front of the car. "I agree, and you tell me not to?"

"I just meant disagree politely." She crossed her arms over her chest, plumping her breasts in the simple white T-shirt.

His hard-on throbbed in his jeans, aching as much as the pain behind his eyes.

"I just want to get a shower and some lunch." He yanked his sticky polo shirt off and pitched it on the porch. To hell with this. He stalked toward the outside shower stall along the side of the house. "Not pick a fight."

"Who's picking a fight?" Her voice rose and she all but stomped a foot. "Not me. I'm just trying to have an honest discussion with you."

"Honest?" He barely kept his voice under control. That shower was sounding better and better by the second. Maybe it would cool down his temper. "You want to talk honest then let's talk about why you want to rewrite history so I'm some pathetic sap who blames the world for all his problems."

She stalked closer to him one step at a time until she stopped an inch shy of her breasts skimming his bare chest. "Conrad? Shut up and take me to the shower."

# Ten

As much as Jayne ached to find answers that would give them a path to reconciliation, clearly Conrad didn't want to talk anymore. And to be honest with herself, the trip to the clinic had left her more than a little vulnerable. She'd seen a side to her husband she hadn't known existed. Beyond just funding a building, he was obviously hands-on at the place, well-known and liked. The way he'd played with the kids still tugged at her heart until she could barely breathe.

She definitely needed to give them both time and space. She was a patient woman, and right now she could think of the perfect way to pass that time.

Making love to her husband.

And if she was using sex to delay the inevitable? Then so be it. She couldn't leave the protection of this place so she might as well make the most of this time.

She linked fingers with Conrad and tugged him toward the side of the house.

"Jayne, the front door's that way."

"And the exterior shower is this way." She walked backward, pulling him with her. "Unless there's some reason we should stay inside? I figured since we walked around the grounds earlier, the security system outside is as good as inside."

"You are correct. I wouldn't have built an outdoor shower if it wasn't safe to use it. No one can get within a mile of this place without my knowing about it." He reassured her with a fierce protectiveness in his voice and eyes.

The magnitude of that comforted her and unsettled her at the same time. She was a dentist's kid from Miami. Prior to meeting Conrad, the extent of her security knowledge included memorizing the pin code for the security box on the garage leading into her condo.

She shoved aside distracting thoughts and focused on the now. Seducing Conrad. She pulled a condom from her purse and tucked it into his hand. "And that takes care of our last concern."

He flipped the packet between his fingers. "You were planning this all day?"

"Actually—" she tossed aside her purse "—I intended to get you to pull over on a deserted side road—since this whole place is essentially deserted that wouldn't have been tough—and I would seduce you in the car. Since the Land Cruiser is conveniently roomy, we would finish off the fantasy we started in the Jaguar in Monte Carlo."

He jerked a thumb over his shoulder. "Do you want to go back to the car?"

"I want you. In the shower. Now."

He hooked his thumbs in her jeans. "Happy to accommodate."

She grabbed the hem of her T-shirt and peeled it over her head, baring her white lacy bra. Late afternoon rays heated her skin almost as much as his eyes as she toed off her canvas loafers. The gritty earth was warm beneath her feet, pebbles digging into her toes.

Her hands fell to her belt buckle, and she unfastened her jeans, never taking her eyes from his sunburnished face. She wriggled denim down her hips, enjoying the way his gaze stroked along each patch of revealed flesh. One last shimmy and she kicked aside her jeans, grateful she'd invested in new satin and lace lingerie before this trip.

That panty set forced her to admit she'd been hoping for just this when she'd come to Monte Carlo to deliver her five-carat ring and divorce papers. Deep in her heart, she'd hoped he would tear up the papers and slide the ring back on her hand.

Life was never that clear-cut. Today's answers had shown her more than ever how far more complex the situation—and her husband were.

But one thing was crystal clear. She had amazing lingerie and her husband's interest. And she intended to enjoy the hell out of their afternoon together.

She teased the front clasp open and tossed her bra aside. The extravagant scrap of satin and lace landed on top of her jeans. After they'd met in Miami, he'd rented a yacht to live on while he concocted business reasons to stay in town. Even though she'd been tempted to sleep with him from the first date, she'd held back, overwhelmed by his wealth, concerned about his past. But two months into the relationship, she couldn't ignore her heart any longer. She'd fallen irrevocably in love with him.

They'd made love on his yacht that night. They'd eloped four weeks later.

Memories of the optimism of that day and the heartbreak that followed threatened to chill her passion. She refused to let that happen, damn it.

Turning toward the shower, she called over her shoulder, "Someone's way overdressed for this party."

His eyes took on a predatory gleam, and he walked toward her, taking off his jeans and boxers with a speed and efficiency that sent a thrill of anticipation through her.

He stalked toward her, his erection straining hard and thick up his stomach. She reached behind her, her fingers grazing along the teak cubicle until she found the latch. She pulled the door open.

The slate tile floor cooled her feet after the scorched earth outside. She turned on the shower just as Conrad filled the entrance with his big, bold presence. The spray hit her in a cold blast, and she squealed, jumping back.

Laughing, Conrad stepped deeper inside, hooking an arm around her waist and hauling her against the delicious heat of his body until the spray warmed. She arched up on her toes to meet his kiss, water slicking over her skin in thousands of liquid caresses. She knew they couldn't continue like this forever. They were merely delaying the inevitable decision on where to take their relationship next.

That only made her all the more determined to indulge in every moment now. She scored her nails lightly down his back, down to his hips, her fingers digging into his flanks to urge him closer. The rigid press of his arousal against her stomach brought an ache and moisture between her thighs that had nothing to do with the sheeting water.

He caressed her back, her breasts, even her arms, the rasp of his callused fingertips turning every patch of her skin into an erogenous zone. One of his hands fell away, and she moaned against his mouth.

"Patience," he answered, his hand coming back into sight cupping a bottle of shampoo.

He raised his arm and poured a stream onto her head before setting aside the bottle. Suds bubbled, dripping, and she squeezed her eyes shut a second before he gathered her hair and worked up a lather. Pure bliss.

The firm pressure of his fingers along her scalp was bone melting. She slumped against the sleekly varnished walls. With her eyes closed, her world narrowed to the sound of the shower, the wind, the distant cackle of monkeys, a natural symphony as magnificent as any opera.

Certainly Conrad played her body well, with nuances from his massage along her temples to the outlining of her ears. Bubbles rolled down her body, slithering over her breasts and between her legs. She rubbed her foot along the back of his calf, opening her legs wider for the press of his erection against the tight bud of nerves already flaming to life. Each roll of her hips, each thrust of his fingers into her hair took her higher, faster.

The pleasures of the whole incredible day gathered, fueling the tingling inside her. He'd always been a generous lover and their chemistry had been explosive from their first time together. She opened her eyes and found him watching her every reaction.

Time for *her* to take *him*.

She scooped the bar of soap from the dish and

worked up a lather. He lifted an eyebrow a second before she used her hands as the washcloth over his chest, down his sculpted arms and down to stroke his erection, cupping the weight of him in her hands. He twitched in her clasp, bracing a hand against the shower wall.

He clamped her hand to stop her.

"Jayne—" his voice came out choked and hoarse "—you're killing me."

"As I recall…" She sipped water from his chest, her tongue flicking around the flat circle of his nipple. "You never complained in the past when I took the initiative."

"True enough." He skimmed his hand over her hair, palming the back of her head.

"Then why won't you let me…"

He stepped back, the shower spraying between them. "Because you've called the shots for the past three years."

That was debatable, given how many times he'd sent her papers back unsigned. "Then this is a punishment? I'm not sure I like the context of that mixed with what's happening between us."

"Do you want to stop?" His question was simple enough, but the somber tone of his voice added weight and layers.

They were talking about the future. She wasn't ready to have this discussion with him.

"You know I don't want to stop. I never have. How about my turn now, yours later?" Clamping hands on his shoulders, she nudged him down to the shower seat. "Any objections to that?"

"None that come to mind." He spread his arms wide. "I'm all yours."

"Glad to hear it."

Anticipation curled through her. Kneeling in front of him, she took him in her mouth, the shower sheeting along her back. She gripped his thighs. The flex of muscles thrilled her as she took in every sign of his arousal increasing. His head thudded back against the cubicle wall, and yes, she delighted in tormenting him as much as he'd teased her last night, drawing out the pleasure.

She knew his body as well as he knew hers, thanks to years of great sex and exploring what drove the other crazy. And she drew on every bit of that stored knowledge now until his fist clenched in her hair, gently guiding her off him. She smiled, reveling in the powerful attraction, the connection that couldn't be denied even after three years apart.

His hands slid under her arms, and he lifted her onto his lap. She straddled him, the tip of him nudging between her legs, and she almost said to hell with birth control. Never had she been more tempted, her womb aching to be filled with his child. Aching to have a whole damn soccer team with this man. But after what her parents had put her through, she wouldn't risk bringing a child into an unstable relationship.

And, damn it, even thinking about those lost dreams threatened to wreck the mood. She grabbed the condom from the soap dish and passed it to him. Her hands were shaking too much to be of any help.

Her hands braced on his shoulders, and she raised up on her knees, taking him deep, deeper still inside her, lifting again. She slid her breasts up and down his chest. Every brush of flesh against flesh launched a fresh wash of goose bumps over her. Faster and faster they moved, his hands on her hips, guiding her as he thrust in synch with her.

Moans rolled up her throat, wrung from her, each breathy groan answered by him. And yes, she took added pleasure in controlling this much of her life, bringing him to the edge, knowing that his feelings for her were as all-consuming as her own were for him.

His hands slid under her bottom and he stood, never losing contact, their bodies still linked. He pressed her back to the wall, driving into her, sending her the rest of the way into a shattering orgasm. Her arms locked around him, her head on his shoulder as her cries of completion rippled through her.

Thank goodness he held her because she couldn't have stood. Even now, her legs melted down him, her toes touching the slate floor. His hot breath drifted through her hair as he held her in the aftermath of their release.

They'd made love in a shower numerous times and the tub, too, but never in an outdoor shower. His adventurous nature had always appealed to her. She'd always been such a cautious, practical soul—her mother had always been so stressed, Jayne had worked overtime to be the perfect daughter and that regimen eventually became habit. Rigid attention to detail was a great trait for a nurse, but not in her personal life. Then Conrad had burst into her world.

Or rather he'd hobbled into the E.R. on that broken foot, stubbornly refusing to acknowledge just how badly he'd been hurt. Even in a cast, he'd been more active than any human she'd met. He'd swept her off her feet, and for the first time in longer than she could remember, she'd done something impulsive.

She'd married Conrad after only knowing him for three months.

If they'd dated longer might they have worked through more of these issues ahead of time? Had a stronger start to their marriage, a better foundation?

Or would she have talked herself out of marrying him?

The thought of having never been his wife cut through her. She wanted a future with him. She couldn't deny that, but she also couldn't ignore what a tenuous peace they'd found here.

And the least bump in the road could shatter everything.

Conrad lounged on the shower bench with the door open, watching his wife tug her clothes back onto her damp body. Damn shame they couldn't just stay naked, making love until the world righted itself again. "I read once that 'The finest clothing made is a person's skin, but, of course, society demands something more than this.'"

She tugged her T-shirt over her head, white cotton sticking to her wet skin and turning translucent in spotty places. "Where did you read that?"

"Believe it or not, Mark Twain."

"I always think of you as a numbers man." She pulled her hair free of the neckline, stirring memories of washing her, feeling her, breathing in the scent of her.

Her legs glowed with a golden haze, backlit by the sunset. There was still time left in this day.

He gave her a lazy smile. "You've been thinking of me, have you?"

"I do. Often." Her smile was tinged with so much sadness it socked him right in the conscience.

He stood and left the shower stall, sealing the door after him. He reached for his jeans. "And where do you think of me? Somewhere like in bed? Or in the shower? Because I thought of you often in the shower and now..."

She rolled her eyes. "Where doesn't matter."

"It's been a long three years without you. I'm making up for lost time here." He tried to lighten the mood again, to bring them back around to level ground. "That's a lot of fantasies to work through."

"If only we could just have sex for the rest of our lives. That would probably cure your insomnia." She gave her jeans an extra tug up her damp legs, her breasts moving enticingly under the T-shirt.

She'd been his wife for seven years and still his mouth watered when he looked at her. Her blond hair was slicked back wet, her face free of makeup, and she was the most beautiful woman he'd ever seen.

"The last thing I think about when I'm with you is sleep." What a hell of a time to remember how their marriage had cured his insomnia in the beginning.

"Eventually we would wear out." She sauntered up to him and buttoned his jeans with slow deliberation, her knuckles grazing his stomach.

"Is that a challenge?" His abs contracted in response to the simple brush of her fingers against him.

And he could see she knew that.

She patted his chest before stepping back. "You enjoy a challenge. Admit it."

He grabbed her hips, hauled her against him and took her mouth. He would eat supper off her naked body tonight, he vowed to himself. He would win her over and bring her into his life again, come hell or high water. The past three years without her had been hell. The thought of even three days away from her was more than he could wrap his brain around.

The possibility that he might not be able to persuade her started a ringing in his ears that damn near deafened him. A ringing that persisted until he realized...

Jayne pulled back, her mouth kissed plump and damp. "That's my cell phone. I should at least check who it is."

Disappointment bit him in his conscience as well as his overrevved libido. "Of course you should."

She snatched her purse from the ground and fished out her cell phone. She checked the screen and frowned before pushing the button. "Yes, Anthony? What can I do for you?"

Anthony Collins? Conrad froze halfway down to pick up his polo shirt off the ground. What the hell was the man doing still calling Jayne? She said she'd ended any possible thoughts of romance between the two of them.

The way her eyes shifted away, looking anywhere but at Conrad wasn't reassuring, either. He didn't want to be a jealous bastard. He'd always considered himself more logical than that. But the thought of Jayne with some other guy was chewing him up inside.

She turned her back and walked away, her voice only a soft mumble.

Crap. He snatched his shirt off the ground and shook out the sand. He stood alone, barefoot, in the dirt and thought of all the times he'd isolated Jayne, cut her off from his world without a word of reassurance. He was a bastard. Plain and simple. She'd deserved better from him then and now.

Jayne turned around, and he willed back questions he'd given up the right to ask. He braced himself for whatever she had to say.

"Conrad." Her voice trembled. "Anthony said he's been getting calls from strangers claiming to be conducting a background check on me for a job I applied for. It could be nothing, but he said something about the questions set off alarms. He wondered if it might be someone trying to steal my identity. But you and I know, it could be so much worse than that…."

Her voice trailed off. She didn't need to state the obvious. His mind was already shutting down emotion and revving into high gear, churning through options for their next move.

And most of all how to make sure Jayne's safety hadn't been compromised.

Up to now his gut had told him Zhutov didn't have a thing on him. He didn't make mistakes on the job. But he couldn't ignore the possibility of Zhutov's reach when it came to Jayne so he'd been aggressively cautious.

Had he been cautious enough? Or had something slipped through the cracks while he was lusting after his wife? He shut down his emotions and started toward the house.

"We need to get inside now. I have to call Colonel Salvatore."

Jayne hated feeling useless, but what could she do? She wasn't some secret agent. Hell, she didn't even have her car or access to anything. She felt like she'd been turned into an ornamental houseplant—again.

Conrad had locked the house down tight before going to the panic room to talk to Salvatore and access his computers. She padded around the kitchen putting together something for supper while listening to one side of the phone conversation, which told her absolutely nothing.

Only a couple of hours ago, he'd shown her the clinic and it was clear he'd been trying to reach out to her by sharing that side of his life. Although the spontaneous soccer game had touched her just as much.

She tugged open the refrigerator and pulled out a container of Waldorf salad to go with the flaky croissants on the counter. And she vowed, if she found one more of her favorite anything already waiting here for her she would scream.

How could the man have ignored her for three years and still remember every detail about her food preferences? For three long years her heart had broken over him. She would have given anything for a phone call, an email, or God, a surprise appearance on her doorstep. Did he really think they could just pick up where they left off now?

She spooned the salad onto plates, her hands shaking and the chicken plopping on the china with more than a little extra force. Would he have continued this standoff indefinitely if she hadn't come to him? She couldn't deny she loved him and wanted to be with him, but she didn't know if she could live the rest of her life being shut out this way.

Slumping back against the counter, she squeezed her eyes shut and forced herself to breathe evenly. She thought about that teenage Conrad whose trust had been so horribly abused by his father. Conrad, who'd grown into a man who built a health clinic and devoted his life to a job he could never claim recognition for doing.

Boothe was right. Conrad was a good man.

She just needed to be patient. And instead of peppering him with questions nonstop, she could start offering him parts of her past, things that were important but that she'd been hesitant to dredge up. But, good God, if she couldn't tell her husband, who could she talk to?

Yes, she still loved Conrad, but she wasn't the same woman she'd been three years ago. She was self-reliant with a clear vision for her future and a sense of her own self-worth.

She also knew that her husband needed her, whether he realized it or not. Pushing her own fears aside, she opened a bakery box full of cookies.

No matter how hard he worked to shut down emotions, still he couldn't ignore the weight of Jayne's eyes on him, counting on him. At least they had one less thing to worry about.

He leaned against the kitchen doorway. "Salvatore's looking into the calls, but so far he said everything looks on the up-and-up. He's confident it was just a hiring company for a hospital running a background check."

"Thank God. What a relief." Her eyes closed for an instant, before she scooped up two plates off the counter. "I made us something to eat. We missed lunch. Could you pour us something to drink?"

She walked past him, both plates of food in her hands. He opened a bottle of springwater, poured it into two glasses with ice then followed her into the dining room. Already, she sat at her place, fidgeting with her napkin.

No wonder she was on edge. All the pleasure of their day out, even making love in the shower, had been wrecked with a cold splash of reality. He sat across from her and shoveled in the food more out of habit than any appetite.

Jayne jabbed at the bits of apple in her salad. "Did I ever tell you why I'm such an opera buff?"

He glanced up from his food, wondering where in the world that question had come from. But then he had given up trying to understand this woman. "I don't believe you did."

"I always knew my parents didn't have a great marriage. That doesn't excuse what my father did to us—or to the family he kept on the side. But my parents' divorce wasn't a huge surprise. They argued. A lot."

He set his fork aside, his full attention on her. "That had to have been tough for you to hear."

"It was. So I started turning on the radio to drown them out." She shrugged, pulling her hair back in her fist. "Opera worked the best. By the time they officially split, I knew all the lyrics to everything from *Madame Butterfly* to *Carmen*."

The image of her as a little girl sitting in the middle of her bed singing *Madame Butterfly* made him want to time travel to take her bike riding the hell away from there. But was he doing any better at protecting her in the present?

She leaned forward on her elbows. "Just so we're clear, you have absolutely no reason to be jealous of Anthony. Nothing happened with him, and I made sure he understood that when I spoke to him yesterday. I even had a friend from work pick up Mimi. I would never, never betray your trust that way."

"I believe you." And he did. He knew how she felt about what her family had been through with her father's longtime affair.

"What's wrong then?" She clasped his arms, holding on tight, her eyes confused, hurt and even a little angry. "Why are you so…distant? You know those walls destroyed us last time."

He shoved away from the table, holding himself in check. Barely. But he wouldn't be like her father, shouting and scaring the hell out of her. "This whole mess with Zhutov and you having to second-guess every call that comes into your life. Do you expect me to be happy that there are people asking around about you? That I had to take you to a remote corner of the world to make sure no one is after you—because of me?"

"Of course you have a right to be worried, but if Colonel Salvatore says there's nothing to worry about, I believe him."

"Nothing to worry about—this time."

"We don't always have to assume the worst here."

A siren split the air like a knife, cutting her off mid-sentence.

He recognized the sound all too well. Someone had tripped the alarm on the outer edges of his property.

Holy crap. His body went into action, his first and only priority? Securing Jayne.

"Conrad?" Her face paled with panic. "What's that?"

"The security system has been tripped. Someone's trying to break into the compound." He grabbed her by the shoulders and hustled her toward the front steps. "You need to lock yourself in the panic room. Now."

# Eleven

Jayne hugged her knees, sitting on a sofa in the panic room. Her teeth chattered with fear for her husband. She'd barely had time to process Anthony's confusing call before the alarm had blared. Conrad had hooked an arm around her waist, rushed her indoors and opened the panic room. He ushered her in and passed over a card with instructions for how to leave…

If he didn't return…

Horror squeezed her heart in an icy fist with each minute that ticked by. She'd already been in here for what felt like hours, but the clock on her cell phone indicated it had only been sixteen minutes.

Someone was trying to break in and there was nothing she could do except sit in this windowless prison while the man she loved faced heaven only knew what kind of danger. Desperately, she wanted to be out there with him, beside him. But Colonel Salvatore had been right. She was Conrad's Achilles' heel. If he had to worry about her, he would be distracted.

She understood that problem well.

There wasn't anything she could do now other than get her bearings and be on guard. Surveying the inside of her "cell," she took it in, for all the good that did her.

As far as prisons went it wasn't that bad, much like an efficiency apartment, minus windows and with only two doors—one leading out and the other open to a small bathroom. A bed filled a corner, a kitchenette with a table in another. A table and television rounded out the decor.

A television? She couldn't envision anyone in a panic room hanging out watching their DVD collection. Angling sideways, she grabbed the remote control off the end table. She turned on the TV. A view of the front yard filled the flat screen.

Oh, my God, she was holding the remote to a surveillance system. She wasn't isolated after all. Relief melted through her. She could help by monitoring the outside. She yanked her cell phone from her pocket and saw…she still had a signal so the safe room hadn't blocked her out.

She thumbed through the remote until she figured out how to adjust the views—front yard, sides, the river—all empty. Her eyes glued to this thin connection to Conrad, she clicked again to a view of the outward perimeter including the clinic.

Not empty.

In fact, a small crowd gathered outside, even this late in the day with the sun setting fast. In the middle of the crowd, four lanky figures sat with their hands cuffed behind their backs.

Teenagers.

Probably not more than fifteen.

And if she guessed correctly, they were some of the same kids who'd played soccer with Conrad just that afternoon.

She clicked the remote, the camera scanning the view until she found Conrad standing with Dr. Boothe. Her husband had his phone out, talking to the doctor while thumbing the keypad. She sagged back on the sofa. If there was any danger to her here, Conrad wouldn't be so far away.

Still, she stayed immobile, waiting for his call. She wouldn't be the fool in the horror films who walked right into a killer's path in spite of all the warnings. But how many times in her life had she sat waiting and worrying, unable to connect or help? She couldn't be a helpless damsel in distress or a passive bystander in her own life.

Her cell phone buzzed beside her, and she saw an incoming text from Conrad.

All clear. Just a break-in at the clinic for drugs. I'll be home soon.

A moment of sheer fright was over in an instant. Was this how Conrad lived on the job? Not fun by any stretch of the meaning. But then, not any more stressful than the time she'd been working in the E.R. when a patient pulled a knife and demanded she empty the medicine cabinet. He'd been too coked up to hold the knife steady, and the security guard had disarmed him.

There weren't any guarantees in life, regardless of where she lived.

She picked up the clearance code and punched in

the numbers to open the door back into the house.
She texted Conrad an update.

Made it out of the panic room. No problems with the
code.

She hesitated at the urge to type "love you" and instead opted for...

Be safe.

Seconds later the phone buzzed in her hand with an
incoming text.

This will take a while. Don't wait up.

Not so much as a hint of affection coated that stark
message, but then what did she expect? He was in the
middle of a crisis. She shook off the creeping sense of
premonition.

For a second, she considered returning to the panic
room and just watching him on the screen, but that
seemed like an invasion of his privacy. If she wanted
this relationship to work between them, she needed to
learn to trust him while he was gone. And he needed to
learn to trust that she could handle the lifestyle.

So what did a woman do while her man was out saving the world? Maybe she didn't need all the answers
yet. She just needed to know that she was committed
to figuring them out.

She knew one fact for certain. Living without Conrad was out of the question.

The moon rose over the clinic, lights blazing in a
day that had run far too long. Bile burned his throat as

he watched the last of the *Agberos* loaded into a police car. Ade, a teen from the soccer game, stared over the door at him with defiant eyes that Conrad recognized well. He'd seen the same look staring back at him in the mirror as teenager.

Jayne and the house were safe, but four teens he'd played with just this afternoon had tried to steal drugs from the clinic. While one of them tried to escape, he'd strayed too close to the house. Boothe had said the attempts were commonplace. *Agberos* weren't rehabilitated in a day—and many of the Area Boys could never be trusted.

Now wasn't that a kick in the ass?

Intellectually he understood what Boothe had told him a million times. In a country riddled with poverty and lawlessness, saving even a handful of these boys was a major victory.

Still, defeat piled on his shoulders like sandbags.

The ringleader of this raid really got to him. Conrad had played soccer with Ade and his younger brother Kofi earlier. He thought he'd connected with them both. And yeah, he'd identified with Ade, seen the seething frustration inside the teen, and wanted to help him build a stable life for himself. Would the little Kofi follow in his big brother's footsteps?

There wasn't a damn thing more Conrad could do about it tonight. He jerked open the door to the Land Cruiser, hoping Jayne had turned in for the night, because he wasn't in the mood for any soul searching.

The drive home passed in a blur with none of his regular pleasure in the starkly majestic landscape that had drawn him to this country in the first place.

Ahead, his house glowed with lights.

The house where Jayne waited for him, obviously

wide-awake if the bright windows were anything to judge by.

Conrad steered the Land Cruiser along the dirt road leading up the plateau, his teeth on edge and his temper rotten as hell. He floored the Land Cruiser, the shock absorbers working overtime. He couldn't put enough space between him and the mess at the clinic, now that the cops had everything locked down tight again.

He parked the Land Cruiser in front of the house, but left the car in idle. He couldn't just sit here thoughtlessly losing himself in his wife's softness in order to avoid the obvious. He needed to take action, to do something to resolve the questions surrounding Zhutov. And he needed to tuck Jayne somewhere safe—most likely somewhere far the hell away from anything in his world since his judgment was crap these days.

Bringing her here had been a selfish choice. He'd wanted to be alone with her. Like some kid showing off an A-plus art project, he'd wanted her to see his clinic, to prove to her there was something good inside him. There were plenty of other places she could stay that were safer. He would talk to Salvatore once Jayne was settled for the night.

He turned off the car, leaped out and slammed the door. Already, he could see her inside on the sofa, lamps shining. He should have tinted these windows rather than depending on the security system.

Just as he hit the bottom step, Jayne opened the front door. Her smile cut right through him with a fresh swipe of guilt.

"Welcome back." She leaned in the open door, a mug of tea cradled in her hands. "What a crazy evening. But at least you know your security system works as advertised."

"You figured out how to work the surveillance television?" If so, that should cut down on the questions for tonight, a good thing given his raw-as-hell gut.

"I did, although I'm still a bit fuzzy on the details." She followed him inside, the weight of her gaze heavy on his shoulders.

"Some of the local *Agberos* tried to steal some drugs from the clinic. When the alarms went off at the clinic, one of the kids—Ade—ran away and tripped the security system here."

"Thank goodness they didn't get away with it. And I'm glad everything was resolved without anyone getting hurt."

"A guard was injured during the break-in." He pinched the bridge of his nose, pacing restlessly past a ladder against the wall covered with locally woven blankets. He needed to get to his computer, to plug into the network and start running leads.

"Oh, no, Conrad. I'm so sorry." Her hand fell to rest on his shoulder. "Will he be all right? Do they need my help at the clinic? I'm sorry now that I didn't go with you."

Her touch made him restless, vulnerable.

He walked to the window, looking out over the river. "You were here, safe. That's the best thing you could do for me."

"What's wrong?" She stopped beside him. "Why are you avoiding me?"

Because if he lost himself in her arms right now, he would shatter, damn it. His hands clenched. "This isn't the right time to talk."

She sighed, a tic tugging at the corner of her eye. "It's never the right time for my questions. That's a big part of what broke us up before." She squeezed his forearm. "I need for you to communicate with me."

Her cool fingers on his skin were a temptation, no question. She'd always been his weakness from the day he'd met her.

"I would rather wait for any discussion until we get the report in from Salvatore."

"What changes if we hear from him?" She frowned, staring into his eyes as if reaching down into his soul. "You think if that man Zhutov has blown your cover, then you don't have to make tough choices. You won't have to do the work figuring out how to let me into your life if you keep the job."

"Or maybe I'm not sure if I'll be a man worthy of you without the job." The admission hissed out between clenched teeth, something he'd known deep in his belly even if he hadn't been willing to admit it until now.

Her eyes went wide. "How in the world could you think that?"

"I'm looking reality in the face, and it sucks. You saw it all on the surveillance camera. You saw those kids in the handcuffs." The memory of it roared around inside him, echoing with flashes from his arrest, the weight of an ankle monitor, the sense of confinement that never went away no matter how freely he traveled the world. "They were stealing drugs to sell. And we could dig into why they needed the money, but bottom line is that they stole medication that's hard as hell to replace out here and they injured a guard in the process."

She gripped his arm harder, with both hands. "It had to be painful seeing the boys you'd played with betray you that way."

The sympathy in her eyes flowed over him like acid

on open wounds. "Damn it, Jayne, I was one of those kids. Why can't you get that?"

"I do get it. But you changed, and there's a chance they'll change, too. Is that such a horrible thing? To believe in second chances?"

The roar inside him grew until it was all he could do to keep from shouting. She didn't deserve his rage. She didn't deserve any of this.

"I'm not the good guy you make me out to be. Yes, I took the job with Interpol to make amends, but I do the work because it gives me a high. Just like when I was in high school, like when I broke the law. I've only figured out how to channel it into something that keeps me out of jail." He looked her dead in the eyes and willed her to hear him. "I'm not the family guy you want, and I never will be."

"What if I say I'm willing to work with that? I think we can find a balance."

He would have given anything to hear those words three years ago, to have that second chance with her. But he knew better now. "And I don't. We tried, and we failed."

"Are you saying this because you're afraid I'll get hurt from something related to your job?"

Holding back a sigh, he dodged her question. He'd had plenty of practice after all. "If that was the case, I would just say it."

"Like hell. You would stage a fight to get me to walk. It's cliché, just like when I woke up with nightmares, and we're not cliché kinds of people. We lead our lives doing difficult jobs that rational people would shy away from. I love that about you, Conrad. I love you."

Damn it, why was she pushing this tonight? Did she want to end things?

And ultimately, wouldn't that be the best thing for her?

"Jayne, don't make this harder on both of us. We've been separated for three years. It's time to finalize the divorce."

Too stunned to cry, Jayne closed the bedroom door and sagged back on the thick wood panel. At least she'd made it out of that room with her head high and her eyes dry.

How in the hell was she supposed to sleep in here tonight with the memories of a few hours ago still so fresh in her mind, the scent of their lovemaking still clinging to the sheets?

Damn him for doing this to her again. And damn her for being such an idiot.

She ran to her suitcase and dug through it, tossing things onto the floor until she found the little black shoulder bag she'd worn to the casino that first night. She dug inside and pulled out her wedding ring set, the five-carat yellow diamond and matching diamond-studded band.

Her fist clenched around the pair until the stones cut into her palm. She grounded herself in the pain. It was all she could do not to run outside and throw the damn things into the river.

She squeezed her eyes closed and thought back over their fight.

Conrad meant every word he'd said. She'd seen the resolution in his eyes, heard it in his voice. And while she still believed he'd made the choice out of misconceptions about himself, she also accepted she couldn't change his mind. She couldn't force him to let go of his past.

She'd waited for him for three years. She'd come here to try one last time to get through to him, only to have him tear her heart to shreds all over again. She didn't regret trying. But she knew it would be a long time before she got over loving Conrad Hughes, if she ever did.

Now there was nothing left for her but to leave with her head high.

Putting the pieces of her life back together would be beyond difficult and, God, she needed a shoulder to cry on, someone to share a bucket of ice cream and put life into perspective. Her mother was gone. She didn't have any sisters. Seeing Anthony again was out of the question, and her friends from work would never understand this.

The answer came to her, a place to go where Conrad couldn't argue about her safety, a person who could offer the advice, support and the sympathetic shoulder she needed. She placed her wedding rings on the bedside table, letting go of them and of Conrad for the final time. She wasn't chasing after him anymore.

She picked up her cell phone and called Hillary Donavan.

She was gone. He'd lost her for good this time.

Watching the lazy hippo roll around in the mud, Conrad sat on the dock with a bottle of Chivas, hoping to get rip-roaring drunk before the sun set. The night had been long, sitting on the couch and thinking about her in the next room. He'd prepared himself for the torment of watching over her until Salvatore cleared him to leave.

But she'd walked out first thing in the morning with her own plan in place, already cleared by Salvatore. A solid plan. As good as any he could come up with himself. Boothe would take her to the airport where Hillary would meet her.

Jayne was a smart and competent woman.

He tipped back his glass, not even tasting the fine whiskey, just welcoming the burn in his gut.

The rumble of an approaching car launched him to his feet. Then he recognized Boothe's vehicle and dropped back down to sit on the dock. He must be returning from taking Jayne to the airport.

Just what he needed. His old "friend" gloating. He topped off his drink.

Boothe's footsteps thudded down the embankment, rustling the tall grass. "You're still sitting around here feeling sorry for yourself. Damn, and I thought you were a smart guy."

Conrad glanced over his shoulder. "I don't need this crap today. Want a drink?"

"No, thanks." Boothe sat beside him, a handful of pebbles in his fist.

"Always the saint."

He pitched a pebble in the water, ripples circling outward. "People see what they want to see."

"Is there a reason you came by?"

"I've been thinking about offering your wife a job. Since you live here and own the clinic, I thought I should run the idea past you first."

Boothe surprised him again, although hadn't he had the same thought about moving Jayne to Africa and settling down? Would she actually take the position even though their paths would cross? "And you're asking my permission?"

"She's a Hospice nurse. She's already on unpaid leave from her other job because of what we do. Only seems fair to help her out." He flicked a couple more pebbles into the water. "Or did you just plan to assuage your conscience by writing her a big fat check?"

Damn, Boothe went for the jugular. "You're offering her a job to get back at me, aren't you?"

"Contrary to what you think, I don't dislike you… anymore."

"So you concede you hated my guts back then, even if you had the occasional weak moment and shared your cookies with a soulless bastard like me."

Boothe's laugh echoed out over the river, startling a couple of parrots and a flock of herons. "Hell, yes, I resented you. You were an arrogant bastard back then and you haven't learned much since."

"Remember that I write your paycheck." Conrad knocked back another swallow. "I fund your clinic."

"That's the only reason I'm here, because I'm grateful." He flung the rest of the pebbles into the water and faced him. "That woman is the best thing that's ever going to happen to you. So, because I owe you a debt, I'm going to give you a piece of advice."

"Thanks. Can I have another drink first?"

Boothe ignored him and pressed on. "In the work world, you're aggressive. You go after what you want. Why the hell haven't you gone after your wife?"

The question stunned him silent through two more rolls of his pet hippo out there.

Disgusted with himself, Conrad set aside his glass.

"She wants a divorce. She's waited three years. I think that's a good sign she's serious."

"Maybe." Boothe nodded slowly. "But is that what you want? You made her come to you again and again. And if you do get back together again, she's stuck waiting for you, repeating the old pattern that wrecked her the first time."

"You're more depressing than the alcohol."

Boothe clapped him on the back, Salvatore style. "It's time for you to quit being a stupid ass. I'll even spell it out for you. Go after your wife."

"That's it?" Just show up? And he hadn't realized until now how much he'd been hoping Boothe might actually have a concrete solution, a magic fix that would bring Jayne home for good this time. Even though he'd told her to leave, the quiet afterward had been a damn hefty reminder of how empty his life was without her. He'd made a monumental mistake this time and Boothe thought that could fixed with a *hey, honey, I'm home?* "After how badly I've screwed up, that doesn't seem like nearly enough."

"For her, that's everything. Think about it." He gave him a final clap on the back before he started walking up the plateau again.

Conrad shoved to his feet, his head reeling from a hell of a lot more than booze.

"Boothe," he called out.

Rowan stopped halfway up the hill. "Yeah, brother?"

Conrad scratched along his collarbone, right over the spot that had once been broken. "Thanks for the cookie."

"No problem." The doctor waved over his shoulder.

As Boothe's car rumbled away, Conrad let his old

classmate's advice roll around in his brain, lining up with memories of the past. Damn it, he'd fought for his wife. Hadn't he?

But as he looked back, he had to accept that he'd expected the marriage to fail from the start. He'd expected her to walk every bit as much as she'd expected him to follow the pattern of her old man. And when she didn't walk this time, he'd pushed her away.

Except Jayne wasn't like his parents. She couldn't be any further from his criminal of a dad or his passively crooked mother and he should have realized that. Countless times he'd accused Jayne of letting the past rule her, and he'd done the same thing. Convinced she would let him down, because, hey, he didn't deserve her anyway. So he'd pushed her away. He might not have been the one to walk out the door, but he hadn't left her any choice by rejecting her so callously. He hadn't left physically, but no question, he'd emotionally checked out on her.

She deserved better than that from him. She'd laid her heart out, something that must have been tough as hell for her after all they'd been through. He should have reassured her that she was his whole world. He worshipped the ground she walked on and his life was crap without her.

And his life would continue to be crap if he didn't get himself together and figure out how to make her believe he loved her. He'd panicked in telling her to leave. He realized now that even though he wasn't good enough for her, he would work his ass off every single day for the rest of his life to be a man worthy of her. No matter what Salvatore uncovered, regardless of whether Conrad had a career or not, he wanted to spend his life with Jayne. He trusted her with anything. Everything.

He would even answer her million questions, whatever it took to make her trust him again.

To make her believe he loved her.

# Twelve

The Bahamas shoreline was wasted on Jayne.

She lounged in a swimsuit and sarong on the well-protected balcony with Hillary. Most people would give anything for a vacation like this at a Nassau casino with a friend to look out for her. Her new gal pal sure knew how to nurse a broken heart in style. But for all Jayne's resolve to stand her ground, this split with Conrad hurt so much worse than the one before and she was only one day into the new breakup.

The familiar sounds drifted from the casino below and wrapped around her, echoing bells and whistles, cheers of victory and ahhhs of disappointment. Glasses clinked as the drinks flowed in the resort, while boaters and swimmers splashed in the ocean. This place had its differences from Monte Carlo, a more casual air to the high-end vacationers in sarongs and flowing sundresses, but there were still plenty of jewels around necks, in ears…and in navels.

She wasn't in much of a gambling mood. Besides, she'd left her rings behind.

What had Conrad thought as he looked at them? Did he have any regrets about pushing to finalize the divorce? How could she have been so wrong to hope he would come around this time and fight for their marriage the way he tackled every other challenge in his life?

God, she wanted to scream out her pain and frustration and she would have had she been alone. She turned to Hillary, who was stretched out on a lounger with a big floppy hat and an umbrella to protect her freckled complexion.

"Thanks for taking me in until Salvatore can clear everything up. Once he gives the go-ahead, I'll be out of your hair and back to work."

Hillary looked over the top of her sunglasses, zinc oxide on her freckled nose. "You know you never have to work again if you don't want. I don't mean to sound crass, but your divorce settlement will be quite generous."

Jayne hadn't wanted Conrad's money. She wanted the man. "I don't see myself as the dilettante type."

"Understandable, of course." Hillary twirled her straw in the fruity beverage, not looking the least like an undercover agent herself. "During my years planning events, I met many different types of people—everything from conspicuous consumers to truly devoted philanthropists. It's amazing to have the financial freedom to make a difference in such a sweeping fashion. Just something to think about."

Like opening a clinic in Africa? Conrad had definitely used his money and influence to change the world for the better. Why the hell couldn't he accept the happiness he'd earned?

The sound of the French doors opening pulled her attention back to the present.

Hillary sat up quickly, her fingers landing on the folded towel that covered a handgun. "Troy?"

A tiny canine ball of energy burst through in a frenzy of barking. Jayne gaped, stunned. Surely it couldn't be her little…

"Mimi?"

Her French bulldog raced on short legs in a black and white blur straight into her arms. Oh, my God, it *was* her dog. Mimi covered her chin in lapping kisses.

Jayne's heart tumbled over itself in her chest because there was just one way Mimi could have gotten here. Only one person who would have known how important it was to have her dog with her right now.

The final question that remained? Had Conrad delivered the dog in person as a peace offering or just arranged the travel in a final heartbreaking gesture of thoughtfulness? She squeezed her eyes shut and buried her face in Mimi's neck to hold off looking for a moment longer, to hold on to the possibility that her husband might be standing behind her even now.

Bracing herself, she looked back and found, thank God, Conrad stood in the open doorway. Her heart leaped into her throat and her eyes feasted on the sight of him after a nightmarish day of thinking she would never see him again. He wore jeans, a button-down shirt with rolled-up sleeves—and dark circles under his haunted eyes.

She didn't rejoice in the fact that he'd been miserable, too—okay, maybe she did a little—but above all she wanted him to be happy. He deserved to be happy. They both did.

A rustling sounded from the lounger beside her as Hillary stood. "Is there word on Zhutov?"

Jayne sat upright, swinging her legs to the side of her own lounger. Why hadn't she considered he might be here for that reason? If Zhutov had broken Conrad's cover, ending his career with Interpol, then she would never know if he would have returned to her on his own. Trust would be all the tougher when they already had so much between them.

Bottom line, she wanted what was best for him, his cover safe, even if that meant he walked away from her.

Conrad shook his head. "No word on Zhutov yet. I'm here for Jayne. Just Jayne."

He stared straight into her eyes as he spoke, his voice deep and sure. She almost forgot to breathe. And while she was disappointed not to have Salvatore give them the all clear, she couldn't help but be grateful that whatever Conrad had to say wasn't motivated by losing his work with Interpol.

Hillary grabbed her bag and her hat. "I'll, uh, just step into the kitchen and make, um… Hell. I'll just leave." Her hand fell on Jayne's shoulder lightly. "Call if you need me."

Angling sideways past Conrad, Hillary slipped away into the suite, closing the door behind her.

Jayne hugged her dog closer as Mimi settled into her lap. "This was thoughtful of you. How did you get her here?"

He stuffed his hands in his pockets and eyed her warily. "I phoned your friend Anthony and asked for help retrieving the dog."

"You spoke to him?"

Conrad nodded, pushing away from the door and stepping closer. "I did. He's a nice guy actually, and he was glad to pick up Mimi and take her to the airport because he knew seeing her would make you smile." He crouched beside her, one knee on the ground. "Which I have to tell you, makes me feel like a mighty small bastard, because I should have thought to do this sooner. I should have thought to do and say a lot of things. But I'm here to make that right."

The hope she'd restrained in her heart swelled as she heard him out, her thoughtful husband who knew she would appreciate her precious dog far more than a lifeless diamond bracelet. "I'm listening."

"I'm sorry for telling you we should make the divorce final. I was certain I would let you down again, so I acted like an idiot." He drew in a shaky breath as if…nervous. The great Conrad Hughes, Wall Street Wizard and casino magnate was actually anxious. "I'm a numbers man, always have been, ever since I was a kid counting out my French fries into equal piles. I'm not good at seeing the middle ground in a situation. But I'm getting there."

"What do you propose?" she asked and saw no hesitation in his eyes as he opened up and answered her.

"Compromise." He met her gaze full-on, such sincerity in his espresso dark eyes they steamed with conviction. "On *my* part this time. When we were together before I asked you to do all the changing and insulted you by giving nothing in return."

And clearly that was tearing him apart now.

"Not nothing. You're being too tough on yourself. You always are." She sketched her fingers along his unshaven jaw. Apparently he hadn't wasted a second getting to her, between arranging to pick up Mimi and flying to the Bahamas. He hadn't even stolen a second to shave.

"Then you'll help me work through that." He pressed a kiss into her palm. "Jayne, I've faced down criminals. Made and given away fortunes. But the thought of losing you nearly drives me to my knees. I see you with all that unconditional love in your eyes, a total openness I never gave back. You knew the truth about me and my crooked family, and you loved me anyway. I'd put us in an all-or-nothing life. Well, the past three years of 'nothing' has been hell."

"I completely agree with you there." Her eyes burned, but with happy tears and hope.

"But back to my compromise. And if it's not good enough, tell me and I promise you, I will listen to you this time. After you left, I realized I can't go through this again. I let you go once, and it almost killed me."

"Conrad? I don't know what to say." How funny that *she* was the one speechless now. She'd hoped for a moment like this, prayed that Conrad could find the peace to embrace a life together, but the reality of it sent joy sparkling through her.

"If you want me to quit the Interpol work, I will."

"Shh!" She touched her fingertips to his mouth, moved that he would offer, hopeful that he truly was willing this time to make the compromises needed to build a life together. "You don't have to do that. I just need reassurances that you're all right."

He nipped her fingers lightly, smiling his appreciation. "I can do that. I will tell you everything I'm cleared to share about my work with Salvatore. I can promise you I'll check in every twenty-four hours so you won't worry."

"And that's safe for you?"

"We have the best of the best technology. And I intend to make use of it to keep you reassured—and to keep you well protected. I kept pushing you away to keep you safe, but all it did was tear us both apart. I will do better. And if you change your mind about the job with Interpol, say the word, I'm out. I would give up anything to keep you. I honest to God love you that much, Jayne."

Unable to hold back any longer, she leaned forward into his arms and kissed him, pouring all the love, hope and dreams out and feeling them flow right back to her, from him. There was something different in him now; the restlessness was gone. And while it had shredded her heart to walk away from him again, maybe that's what it had taken to make him see what she'd already realized—they needed each other. Two pieces of the same whole. Conrad seemed to understand that now. He'd found a new peace and maybe even some forgiveness for himself.

Mimi squirmed to get free, squished between them. Laughing, they eased apart and her dog—their dog— jumped from Jayne's lap to sniff the balcony furniture and potted plants.

Jayne looked back at Conrad, still kneeling in front of her. "Is it all right to have a dog here?"

"I bought the place two years ago. I can have a whole damn pack of dogs inside if I want."

"And is that what you want? A pack?" She toyed with the open V of his collar, the fire rekindling inside her.

"Actually I was thinking more like a soccer team of kids. Our kids, babies first, of course."

Shock froze her. She stared into his eyes and found one hundred percent sincerity.

"I'd like that, too," she whispered.

She'd learned to leave the past behind and step outside her safety zone without losing the essence of herself. Life wasn't an all-or-nothing game. It was a blending of the best of both sides. A marriage.

Her marriage.

Just as she started to reach for her husband, the French doors opened and Hillary stuck her head out, cell phone in hand. "Folks, you're going to want to hear this update from Salvatore."

Jayne's stomach knotted. Was it bad news? Could their newfound peace be so short-lived? She felt Conrad take her hand and squeeze reassuringly. She looked into his eyes and realized she wasn't alone—and neither was he. They truly were a team now and whatever happened, they would face it together.

She turned back to Hillary, and realized the woman was smiling so brightly the news couldn't be that bad.

Conrad said, "We're ready. What's the update?"

Hillary tapped speakerphone and Salvatore's voice rumbled over the airwaves, "Authorities apprehended Zhutov's hired assassin and given his confession and the photos he had on his cell phone, we're certain you two were not the targets. You're in the clear. Your cover is secure."

Grinning, Conrad grabbed Jayne around the waist, lifted her from the chair and spun her around. Mimi barked, dancing around their feet. Laughing, Hillary put the phone to her ear and stepped back into the hotel suite.

Jayne grasped Conrad's shoulders as he lowered her back to the ground again. "Oh, my God, that is amazing news."

"Damn straight it is." He hauled her to his chest, a

sigh of relief rattling through him. "And Lord willing, the day's about to get even better."

Stepping back again, he pulled his hand out of his pocket, their wedding rings rested in his palm. "Jayne, I've loved you from the first time I saw you and will love you until I draw my last breath. Will you please do me the honor of wearing this ring?"

She placed her hand over his, their rings together in their clasped hands. "I'm all in. I want to be a part of your big, bold plans for the future, to help others in the clinic in Africa and build more clinics in other parts of the world. I accept you, as you are... I *love* you as you are."

His hand slid into her hair, and he guided her mouth to his with a fierce tenderness that reached all the way to her soul.

The stakes had been high, but she knew a winning hand when she saw one.

Smoothly, Conrad slid on his wedding band and then he slipped hers back on her finger. Where it would stay put this time.

Because one pair, the two of them, had won it all.

# Epilogue

*Two months later*

Coming home to his wife was one of life's greatest pleasures.

Conrad parked the Land Cruiser beside the clinic where his wife worked. Their clinic, in Africa. He'd offered Jayne diamonds and a splashy jet-set lifestyle, but his wife had chosen a starkly majestic home in Africa, caring for the ill and orphaned in the area villages.

God, he loved her and her big, caring heart.

His eyes were drawn to her like a magnet to the purest, strongest steel. He found her on the playground with the kids, kicking the soccer ball, her hair flying around her.

She'd stepped in to help run the foundation that oversaw the clinic. In the two months since she'd relocated here, she'd already come up with plans and funding to add an official childcare center so when adults came for treatment they didn't have to bring their kids inside where they could catch anything from pneumonia to a simple cold.

He'd tried to tell her she didn't have to work this hard, but she'd only rolled her eyes and told him they could sneak away for an opera once a month—if he promised to be incredibly naughty before intermission. In spite of his efforts to pamper her, he'd discovered his wife had grown fiercely independent. The way she took charge, her visionary perspective, reminded him of Colonel Salvatore.

Zhutov was no longer even a remote threat. One morning a month ago, guards had found him dead in his bunk, smothered. Most likely by someone as payback for any one of his criminal acts over the years.

Life was balancing out.

Conrad started toward the soccer field. Now that the loose ends had been tied up this past week he'd spent at Interpol Headquarters in Lyon, France, he was free until the next assignment rolled around.

He liked coming home to her, here. He could manage his holdings from a distance with good managers in place, and he could jet over with his wife whenever she was ready to take in an opera.

Right now, though, he just wanted to have dinner with his wife. The soccer ball came flying in his direction, and he booted it back into play. Jayne waved, smiling as she jogged toward him.

"Welcome home," she called, throwing her arms around his neck.

He caught her, spinning her around under the warm African sun. Already, she whispered about her plans for making love in the shower before supper and how good it would be to sleep next to him again.

And he had to agree, his insomnia was now a thing of the past. Everything was better with her in his life. He knew, in his wife's arms, he'd finally come home.

\* \* \* \* \*

# "I can't date you, Max."

"I can't stop wanting you, Cara."

She lifted her long lashes, her crystal-blue eyes looking directly into his. "Try, Max. Summon up some of your famous fortitude, and try."

He couldn't help but smile at that. "I'm not here for inside information. I was genuinely concerned about you."

"As I said—"

"You're fine. I get it."

That was her story, and she was sticking to it.

Dear Reader,

Welcome to the Mills & Boon® Desire™ series DAUGH-TERS OF POWER: THE CAPITAL. I was delighted to be invited to write the opening book. In *A Conflict of Interest*, Cara Cranshaw's loyalties are tested. She is thrilled by the election of President Ted Morrow, but it means an end to her romantic relationship with network journalist Max Gray.

While Max searches for the scandal behind the president's illegitimate daughter, Cara struggles to hide her unexpected pregnancy, since Max has made his opinion on fatherhood crystal clear.

It's always great fun to watch a strong hero discover his softer side. I hope you enjoy *A Conflict of Interest* and all the books to follow in the DAUGHTERS OF POWER: THE CAPITAL series.

Happy reading!

*Barbara*

# A CONFLICT OF INTEREST

BY
BARBARA DUNLOP

MILLS&BOON

Published in Great Britain 2013
by Mills & Boon, an imprint of Harlequin (UK) Limited,
Eton House, 18-24 Paradise Road, Richmond, Surrey TW9 1SR

© Harlequin Books S.A. 2013

Special thanks and acknowledgment to Barbara Dunlop for her contribution to the DAUGHTERS OF POWER: THE CAPITAL miniseries.

ISBN: 978 0 263 90466 6
ebook ISBN: 978 1 472 00585 4

51-0313

Harlequin (UK) policy is to use papers that are natural, renewable and recyclable products and made from wood grown in sustainable forests. The logging and manufacturing processes conform to the legal environmental regulations of the country of origin.

Printed and bound in Spain
by Blackprint CPI, Barcelona

**Barbara Dunlop** writes romantic stories while curled up in a log cabin in Canada's far north, where bears outnumber people and it snows six months of the year. Fortunately she has a brawny husband and two teenage children to haul fire-wood and clear the driveway while she sips cocoa and muses about her upcoming chapters. Barbara loves to hear from readers. You can contact her through her website, www.barbaradunlop.com.

For my husband

CHOICE OF **TWO** GIFTS!

A **treat** from us to **thank you** for reading our books!

Turn over **now** to find out more

# Thanks for reading!

We're treating you to **TWO** fabulous offers...

# One

It was inauguration night in Washington, D.C., and Cara Cranshaw had to choose between her president and her lover. One strode triumphantly though the arches of the Worthington Hotel ballroom to the uplifting strains of "Hail to the Chief" and the cheers of eight hundred well-wishers. The other stared boldly at her from across the ballroom, a shock of unruly, dark hair curling across his forehead, his bow tie slightly askew and his eyes telegraphing the message that he wanted her naked.

For the moment, it was investigative reporter Max Gray who held her attention. Despite her resolve to turn the page on their relationship, she couldn't tear her gaze from his, nor could she stop her hand from reflexively moving to her abdomen. But Max was off-limits now that Ted Morrow had been sworn in as president.

"Ladies and gentlemen," cried the master of ceremonies above the music and enthusiastic clapping that was spreading like a wave across the hall. "The President of the United

States." His voice rang out from the microphone onstage at the opposite end of the massive, high-ceilinged room.

The cheers grew to a roar. The band's volume increased. And the crowd shifted, separating to form a pathway in front of President Morrow. Cara automatically moved with them, but she still couldn't tear her gaze from Max as he took a few steps backward on the other side of the divide.

She schooled her features, struggling to transmit her resolve. She couldn't let him see the confusion and alarm she'd been feeling since her doctor's visit that afternoon. *Resolve,* she ruthlessly reminded herself, *not hesitation and definitely not fear.*

"He's running late." Sandy Haniford's shout sounded shrill in Cara's ear.

Sandy was a junior staffer in the White House press office, where Cara worked as a public relations specialist. While Cara was moving from ball to ball tonight with the president's entourage, Sandy was stationed here as liaison to the American News Service event.

"Only by a few minutes," Cara shouted back, her eyes still on Max.

*Resolve,* she repeated to herself. The unexpected pregnancy might have tipped her world on its axis, but it didn't change her job tonight. And it didn't alter her responsibility to the president.

"I was hoping the president would get here a little early," Sandy continued, her voice still raised. "We have a last-minute addition to the speaker lineup."

Cara twisted her head; Sandy's words had instantly broken Max's psychological hold on her. "Come again?"

"Another speaker."

"You can't do that."

"It's done," said Sandy.

"Well, *un*do it."

The speakers, especially those at the events hosted by organizations less than friendly to the president, had been vetted weeks in advance. American News Service was no friend of President Morrow, but the cable network's ball was a tradition, so he'd had no choice but to show up.

It was a tightly scripted appearance, with only thirty minutes in the Worthington ballroom. He would arrive at ten forty-five—well, ten fifty-two as it turned out—then he was to leave at eleven-fifteen. The Military Inaugural Ball was next on the schedule, and the president had made it clear he wanted to be on time to greet the troops.

"What do you want me to do?" asked Sandy. "Should I tackle the guy when he steps up to the microphone?" Sarcasm came through her raised voice.

"You should have solved the problem before it came to that." Cara lifted her phone to contact her boss, White House Press Secretary Lynn Larson.

"Don't you think I tried?"

"Obviously not hard enough. How could you give them permission to add a new speaker?"

"They didn't *ask*," Sandy pointed out with a frown. "Graham Boyle himself put Mitch Davis on the agenda for a toast. Two minutes, they say, tops."

Mitch Davis was a star reporter for ANS. Graham Boyle might be the billionaire owner of the network, and the sponsor of this ball, but even he didn't get to dictate to the president.

Cara couldn't help an errant glance at Max. As the most popular investigative reporter at ANS's rival, National Cable News, he was a mover and shaker himself. He might have some insight into what was up. But Cara couldn't ask him about this or anything else to do with her job, not now and not ever again.

Cara pressed a speed-dial button for her boss.

It rang but then went to voice mail.

She hung up and tried again.

She could see that the president had arrived at the head table, in front of and below the stage. He was accepting the congratulations of the smartly dressed guests. The men wore Savile

Row tuxedos, while the woman were draped in designer fabrics that shimmered under the refracted light of several dozen crystal chandeliers.

The MC, popular ANS talk show host David Batten, returned to the microphone. He offered a brief but hearty welcome and congratulations to the president before handing the microphone over to Graham Boyle. According to the schedule, Graham had three minutes to speak. Then the president would have one dance with the female chair of a local hospital charity and a second with Shelley Michaels, another popular ANS celebrity. That was to be followed by seven minutes at his table with ANS board members before taking his leave.

Cara gave up on her cell phone and started making her way toward the stage. There was a staircase at either end, nothing up the middle. So she knew she had a fifty-fifty chance of stopping Mitch Davis before he made it to the microphone. Too bad she wasn't a little larger, a little brawnier, maybe a little more male.

Once again, her thoughts turned to Max. The man dodged bullets in war-torn cities, scaled mountains to reach rebel camps and fought his way through crocodiles and hippos for stories on the struggles of indigenous people. If Max Gray didn't want a person up onstage, that person was not getting up onstage. Too bad she couldn't enlist his help and would have to rely on her own wits.

She chose the stairs at stage right, wending her way through the packed crowd.

Graham Boyle was waxing poetic about ANS's role in the presidential election. He'd taken a couple of jabs at President Morrow's alma mater and its unfortunate choice of mascot given current relations with Brazil. But that was all fair game.

Cara wished she was taller. At five foot five, she couldn't see the stairs to know if Mitch was waiting to go up on the right-hand side. She regretted having gone for the comfortable two-inch heels instead of the flashy four-inch spikes that her sister, Gillian, had given her for Christmas. She could have used the height.

"Where are you going?" It was Max's voice in her ear.

"None of your business," she retorted, attempting to speed up and put some distance between them.

"You have that determined look in your eyes."

"Go away."

He tucked in close beside her. "Maybe I can help."

"Not *now,* Max." She was working. Why did he have to do this to her?

"Your destination can't possibly be a state secret."

She relented. "I'm trying to get to the stage. Okay? Are you happy?"

"Follow me." He stepped in front of her.

His six-foot-two-inch height and broad shoulders made him an imposing figure. She supposed it didn't hurt any that he was famous, either. Last month, he'd been voted one of the ten hottest men in D.C. The upshot was he could move through a crowd far faster than she could. Resigned, she stuck to his coattails.

Even with Max clearing the way, they eventually got stuck behind a crowd of people.

"Why do you want to get to the stage?" He turned to ask her.

"For the record," she responded, "I don't know any state secrets. I don't have that kind of job."

"And since I'm not a foreign spy, we should be able to carry on a conversation without compromising national security."

An unmistakable voice came over the sound system. "Good evening, Mr. President," drawled Mitch Davis.

A murmur of surprise moved across the room, since Mitch was a known detractor of President Morrow. Cara rocked back on her heels. She'd failed to stop him.

"First, let me say, on behalf of American News Service, congratulations, sir, on your election as President of the United States."

The applause came up on cue, though perhaps not as strong as usual.

"Your friends," Mitch continued with a hearty game-show-host smile, "your supporters and your mother and father must all be very proud."

Cara strained to catch the president's expression, wondering if he would be angry or merely annoyed by the deviation from the program. But there was no way to see through the dense crowd.

"The president is smiling," Max offered, obviously guessing her concern. "It looks a little strained though."

"Davis is not on the program," Cara ground out.

"No kidding," Max returned, as if only an idiot would think otherwise.

She glared at him, then elbowed her way past, maneuvering through the crowd toward the president's table below the stage. Lynn Larson was going to be furious. It wasn't exactly Cara's responsibility to ensure that this specific ball went smoothly, but she had been working closely with the staffers coordinating each one. She was partly to blame for this.

Thankfully, Max didn't follow her.

"I expect nobody is prouder than your daughter," said Mitch, just as Cara reached a place where she could see Mitch on stage.

There was a confused silence in the room, because the president was single and didn't have any children. Confused herself, Cara rocked to a halt a few feet from Lynn at the president's table. Lynn glanced toward the stairs at the end of the stage, as if she was gauging how long it would take her to get there.

Mitch waited a beat, microphone in one hand, glass of champagne in the other. "Your long-lost daughter, Ariella Winthrop, who is with us here tonight to celebrate."

It took half a second for the crowd to react. Maybe they were trying to figure out if it was a sick joke. Cara certainly was.

But she quickly realized it was something far more sinister than a joke, and her gaze flew to the corner of the stage, where she'd glimpsed her friend Ariella, whose event-planning company had been hired to throw the ANS ball. When Cara focused on Ariella, her stomach sank like a stone. As soon as it was pointed out, the resemblance between Ariella and the president was quite striking. And Cara had known for years that Ariella was adopted. Ariella didn't know her birth parents.

The crowd's murmurs rose in volume, everyone asking each other what they knew, had heard, had thought or had speculated. Cara could only imagine at least a thousand text messages had gone out already.

She took a half step toward Ariella, but the woman turned on her heel, disappearing behind the stage. There were at least a dozen doorways back there, most cordoned off from the guests by security. Hopefully, Ariella would make a quick getaway.

Mitch raised his glass. "To the president."

Everyone ignored him.

Cara moved toward Lynn as the crowd's questions turned to shouts and the press descended on the table.

"If you would direct your questions to me," Lynn called, standing up from her chair and drawing, at least for a moment, the attention of the reporters away from President Morrow.

The man looked shell-shocked.

"We obviously take any accusation of this nature very seriously," Lynn began. She looked to Cara, subtly jerking her head toward the stage.

Cara reacted immediately, skirting around the impromptu press conference to get to the microphone onstage. Damage Control 101—get ahead of the story.

She quickly noted that the security detail had surrounded the president, moving him toward the nearest exit. She knew the drill. The limos would be waiting at the curb before the president even got out the door.

She had no idea if the accusation was true or if Mitch Davis had simply exploited the resemblance between Ariella and the president. But it didn't matter. The texts, tweets and blogs had likely made it to California and Seattle, probably all the way across the Atlantic by now.

Cara scooted up the stairs and crossed the stage, staring Mitch Davis down as she went for the microphone.

He relinquished it. His work was obviously completed.

Mitch's gaze darted to the crowd. His confident expression faltered, and she saw Max, his eyes thunderous as he moved along below the stage, keeping pace with Mitch as the man made his way to the stairs.

"Ladies and gentlemen," Cara began, composing a speech inside her head on the fly. "The White House would like to thank you all for joining the president tonight to celebrate. The president appreciates your support and invites you all to enjoy yourselves for the rest of the party. For members of the press, we'll provide a statement and follow-up on your questions at tomorrow's regular briefing."

Cara turned to applaud the band. "For now, the Sea Shoals have a lot of great songs left to play tonight." She gave a signal to the bandleader, which he thankfully picked up on, and the energetic strains of a jazz tune filled the room.

Covered by the music, Cara quickly slipped from the stage.

Max was standing at the bottom of the stairs to meet her, but her warning glare kept him back—which was probably the first time that had ever happened. But then he mouthed the word "later," and she knew they weren't done.

There were times when being a recognizable television personality was frustrating and inconvenient. But for Max Gray, tonight wasn't one of them. He'd only been to Cara's Logan Circle apartment a handful of times, but the doorman remembered him from his national news show, *After Dark,* and let him straight into the elevator without calling upstairs for Cara's permission.

That was very convenient for Max, because there was a better than even chance Cara would have refused to let him come up. And he needed to see her.

The ANS inaugural ball debacle had been a huge blow to the White House, particularly to the press office. Cara and Lynn had handled it professionally, but even Cara had to be rattled. And she had to be worried about what happened next. The scandal whipping its way through D.C. tonight had the potential to derail the White House agenda for months to come. Max needed to see for himself that Cara was all right.

He exited the aging elevator into a small, short hallway. Her apartment building had once been an urban school, but it now housed a dozen loft apartments, characterized by high ceilings, large windows and wide-open spaces. Cara's had a small foyer hall off the public hallway. From there, a winding staircase led to a light-filled, loft-style grand room with bright walls and gleaming hardwood floors. The single room had a marble-countered kitchen area in one corner, with a sleeping area separated by freestanding latticework wood screens.

Max had loved it at first sight. It reminded him of Cara herself, unpretentious, breezy and fun. She was practical, yet unselfconsciously beautiful, from her short, wispy, sandy-brown hair to her intense blue eyes, from her full, kissable lips to her compact, healthy body. She never seemed to run out of energy, and life didn't faze her in the least.

The short public hallway had four suite doors. The last time Max had been here was mid-December. Cara had kept him at arm's length after Ted Morrow won the election in November. But he'd bought her a present while he was in Australia, pink diamond earrings from the Argyle Mine. He'd selected the raw stones himself, them had them cut and set in eighteen-karat gold, especially for her.

She'd let him in that night, and they'd made love for what was likely the last time—at least the last time during this administration. Cara had been adamant that they keep their distance, since he was a television news host, and she was on the president's staff. Max shuddered at the thought. He really didn't want to wait four years to hold her in his arms again.

He knocked on Cara's door, then waited as her footsteps sounded on the spiral wrought-iron staircase.

He heard her stop in front of the door and knew she was looking through the peephole. There were a limited number of people who could get through the lobby without the doorman announcing them. So she probably expected it was Max. That she'd come down the stairs at all was a good sign.

"Go away," she called through the door.

"That seems unlikely," he responded, touching his fist to the door panel.

"I have nothing to say to you."

He moved closer to the door to keep from having to raise his voice and alert her neighbors. "Are you okay, Cara?"

"Just peachy."

"I need to talk to you."

She didn't respond.

"Do you really want me to talk from out here?" he challenged.

"I really want you to leave."

"Not until I make sure you're okay."

"I'm over twenty-one, Max. I can take care of myself."

"I know that."

"So, why are you here?"

"Open up, and I'll tell you."

"Nice try."

"Five minutes," he pledged.

She didn't answer.

"Ten if I have to do it from the hallway."

A few seconds later he heard the locks slide open. The door yawned to reveal Cara wearing a baggy, gray T-shirt and a pair of black yoga pants. Her feet were bare, her hair was slightly mussed and her face was free of makeup, showing the few light freckles that made her that much cuter.

"Hey," he said softly, resisting an urge to reach out and touch her.

"I'm really doing fine," she told him, lips compressed, jaw tight, her knuckles straining where she held the door.

He nodded as he moved inside, easing the door from her hands to close it behind himself. He looked meaningfully at the spiral staircase.

"Five minutes," she repeated.

"I can finish a soft drink in less than five minutes."

She shook her head in disgust but headed up the stairs anyway. Max followed, resisting once again the urge to reach out and touch. There was a time, a very short time in the scheme of things, when he'd felt free to do that.

"Cola or beer?" she asked, coming to the top of the stairs and padding across the smooth floor to the kitchen area.

"Beer," Max decided, shrugging out of his tux jacket and releasing his bow tie.

He moved to the furniture grouping of two low, hunter-green leather couches, a pair of matching armchairs and low tables with lamps, all tastefully accented by a rust, gold and brown patterned rug. Her view of the city was expansive. The night had turned clear, with a new blanket of snow freshening up the buildings and the trees, reflecting the lights in the park across the street.

Cara returned with a can of beer for him and a cola for her. She handed the can to Max and then curled into one of the armchairs, popping the top on her own drink.

"Four minutes," she warned him.

He opened his beer and eased onto the corner of a couch. He pulled off his wristwatch and set it on the coffee table, faceup where he could see it.

He caught her slight, involuntary smile at the gesture.

"You okay?" he asked in a soft voice.

"I'm fine," she assured him one more time.

"Did you know?" he couldn't stop himself from asking.

"You know I can't answer that."

"Yeah," he agreed. "I was counting on being able to read your expression when you told me to back off."

She lifted her brows. "And did you?"

"You're as inscrutable as ever."

"Thank you. It helps in my business." She took a sip.

He followed suit. Then he set the can down on a coaster. "You know I'll have to go after the story."

"I know you will."

"I don't want to hurt you. And I respect the hell out of this president. But a secret daughter?"

"We don't know for sure she's his daughter."

Max stilled. He was surprised Cara had offered even that much insight. "We will soon enough."

She nodded.

"Have you talked to Ariella?" He knew the two women were friends. Cara had casually introduced Max to Ariella at a fundraising event right before the election.

Cara set her cola down on a table beside her. "Do you honestly think that would be in anyone's best interest?"

"That's neither a yes nor a no."

Cara's expression remained completely neutral.

"You're very good," he allowed.

She sat forward. "I know you have to go after this, Max. But can you at least be fair about it? Can you please take into account all the facts before you help ramp up the public hysteria?"

Max leaned forward, bringing them close enough that he could feel her faint breath, inhale the coconut scent of her shampoo, close enough that it was hard to keep from kissing her.

"I always take all the facts into account."

"You know what I mean."

He reached for her hand.

But at his faintest touch, she snapped it away. "This is going to get ugly."

He knew that was an understatement. The press, not to mention the opposition, smelled blood in the water, and they were already circling. "Are you going back to work tonight?"

"Lynn's taking the night shift. I'll go in early tomorrow morning."

"It's going to be a long haul," Max noted, wishing there was something he could do to help her. But he had a very different job from Cara, a job that was certain to be at odds with hers.

"Yes, it is." She sounded tired already.

"I'll be fair, Cara."

"Thank you." There was a wistful note to her voice. For a moment, her blue eyes went soft and her expression became less guarded.

He reached for her hand again, this time squeezing before she had a chance to pull away.

She glanced at their joined hands. Her voice turned to a strained whisper. "You know all the reasons."

"I disagree with them."

"I can't date you, Max."

"I can't stop wanting you, Cara."

She lifted her long lashes, and her crystal-blue eyes looked directly into his. "Try, Max. Summon up some of your famous fortitude and try."

He couldn't help but smile at that. "I'm not here for inside information. I was genuinely concerned about you."

"As I said—"

"You're fine. I get it."

That was her story, and she was sticking to it.

Her skin was creamy and smooth, her lips dark, soft and slightly parted. He imagined their feel, her taste, her scent, and instinct took over. He tipped his head, leaning in.

But she pulled abruptly away, turning and dipping her head before he could kiss her. "Your five minutes are up."

He heaved a sigh, giving up, letting her small hand slip from between his fingers. "Yeah. I guess they are."

*　*　*

Max had left his watch behind in Cara's apartment. She had no way to know if he'd done it on purpose. It was a Rolex—platinum, with baguette-cut emeralds on the face. She couldn't even imagine the price. Being a popular television personality definitely had its perks.

When she'd gone to bed, Cara had set the watch on the table beside her. She'd used its alarm as a backup, since she'd had to get up at three-thirty.

Then she'd put it in her purse before heading for her West Wing office at the White House. If Max called about it, she'd drop it off for him on her way home. She had no intention of letting him use it as an excuse to come back to her apartment again.

She flashed her ID tag through the scanner in the White House lobby, and passed through security in the predawn hours. A cleaner was vacuuming, while deliverymen made their way along the main hall. It was quiet out front, but closer to the press office, the activity level increased. Movers were lugging furniture and boxes into the newly appointed offices. She passed several people on her way to her small office.

"Morning, Cara." Her boss, Lynn, fell into step with her.

Cara unbuttoned her coat and unwrapped her plaid scarf from around her neck as they walked. "Did you get a chance to talk to the president?"

Lynn shook her head, shifting a file folder to her opposite hand. "The Secret Service was with him for an hour. Then Barry went in for a while. And after that, he went back to the residence."

"Is it true?"

One of the communications assistants appeared to take Cara's scarf and purse. Cara shrugged out of her coat and added it to the pile in the woman's arms.

"We don't know," said Lynn, pushing open her office door.

Cara followed her inside. "Barry didn't ask him?"

Chief of Staff Barry Westmore knew the president better than anyone.

As press secretary, Lynn's office was the largest in the communications section. It housed a wide oak desk, a long credenza, a cream-colored couch and three television screens mounted along one wall playing news shows from three different continents. In English, German and Russian, reporters were speculating on the president's personal life.

Lynn plopped down in her high-backed leather chair, twisting her large, topaz ring around and around the finger of her right hand. Lights from the garden broke the darkness outside the window before her. "Even if it's true, the president wasn't aware that he had a daughter."

"That's good." From a communications perspective, deniability was key in this situation.

Lynn didn't look as relieved as Cara felt. "There's more than one possible woman."

Cara's eyebrows shot up.

"Barry and I did the math," said Lynn. "Accounting for possible variations in gestation period. Since the baby might have been premature, there are three possible mothers."

"Three?" Despite the gravity of the situation, Cara found herself fighting a smile. "Go, Mr. President."

Lynn frowned at her impertinence. "It was senior year in high school. The man was a football star."

"Sorry," Cara quickly put in, lowering herself into one of the guest chairs opposite the desk.

Her boss waved away the apology. "He's refusing to give us the names."

"He has to give us the names."

"First, he wants to know if Ariella is his daughter. If and only if she is his daughter, then we can look at the ex-girlfriends."

"The press will find them first," Cara warned, her mind flitting to Max. The networks and newspapers would pull out all the stops to find Ariella's mother. They wouldn't wait on a DNA test. This was the story of the century.

"Yes, they will," Lynn agreed. "But the president is unwilling to ruin innocent lives."

In Cara's opinion, the women's lives were already ruined. Anyone who'd had the misfortune to sleep with President Morrow in high school would be fair game. It wouldn't even matter whether the lovemaking squared up with Ariella's birth date; they'd still be hunted down and hounded with questions.

Lynn twisted her ring again. "It's always that thing that you don't see coming. And it's always sex. Next time, remind me to back a nerdy candidate. Maybe president of the chess club or something."

"These days, nerds are hot," Cara pointed out.

"That's because we expect them to grow up rich."

"That's why I hang out at the local internet café looking for dates."

Lynn grinned, putting a little life into her exhausted expression. "I should have married a nerd in high school."

"Instead of a smoking-hot navy captain?"

Lynn gave a self-conscious shrug, but her eyes took on a secretive glow. "It was spring break. And he rocked those dress whites."

"You didn't even look twice at the nerds," Cara accused.

"The hormones want what the hormones want."

Cara's brain conjured up a picture of Max, but she quickly shook it away. "Have you spoken to Ariella?"

"Nobody can find her."

"Can't blame her for that." If it had been Cara, she'd have crossed the Canadian border by now.

"Think you can find her?" Lynn asked.

Cara would love nothing better than to find Ariella and make sure she was okay. But she wasn't going to abandon Lynn to go on a wild-goose chase. "You need me here."

"We can live without you."

"Just what every woman wants to hear. You're going to have to give a statement to the press today. And you need me to write it. *You* need to get some sleep."

Cara wished she'd had more than three hours' sleep herself. She knew she had to pay more attention to things like eating and sleeping now that she was pregnant. But time for sleep and time to prepare nutritious meals were pretty hard to come by while working for the president. Especially during this crisis.

"I will get some sleep," Lynn agreed. "Barry's working on a statement, and we'll put the press off until the afternoon. Do you think you'd be able to find Ariella?"

Cara got to her feet. She had to believe her womb was a safe place for the first few weeks of gestation no matter what chaos was going on outside it. She reassured herself that many women wouldn't even know they were pregnant this early.

"I can try," she told her boss.

"Then go. Get out of here."

Cara headed for her own office, quickly retrieving her coat and purse. If she could find Ariella, at the very least they could offer her Secret Service protection. She wrapped the scarf around her neck before heading out into the snow.

If the story was true, Ariella would need protection for the rest of her life, and that would only be the start of the chaos. Merely being a member of the White House staff had sent Cara's personal life into a tailspin. She couldn't imagine what Ariella was going through.

# TWO

After combing the city for countless hours, looking everywhere she could think to find Ariella, Cara gave up. It was nearly nine in the evening, and she'd left dozens of messages and asked everyone who might know anything. She was exhausted when she finally took the elevator back to her loft. Maybe Ariella really had fled to Canada.

Cara twisted her key in the dead bolt, then unlocked the knob below, pushing open the solid oak door.

As soon as she stepped inside, she knew something was wrong. A light was on upstairs and someone was playing music.

Her hand reflexively went to her purse, where she'd stashed Max's watch. If he'd used it as an excuse to come back, if the superintendent had actually let him into her apartment, well, there was going to be hell to pay for both of them. Max might be a famous television personality, trusted and admired by most of D.C., but that didn't give him the right to con the super, break into her apartment and make himself at home.

She tossed her coat and scarf on the corner bench in the

entry hall and pulled off her boots, not even bothering to put them in the closet. She paced her way up the spiral staircase, working up her outrage, planning to hit him with both barrels before he had a chance to start the smooth talk.

Then she realized Beyoncé was playing. And it smelled like someone was baking. She made it to the top of the stairs and stopped dead.

Ariella stood in the middle of her kitchen, surrounded by flour-sprinkled chaos. She had one of Cara's T-shirts pulled over her short dress and a pair of red calico oven mitts on her hands. Midstep between the oven and the island counter, she held a pan of chocolate cupcakes.

"I hope you don't mind." She blinked her big, blue eyes. "I didn't know where else to go."

"Of *course* I don't mind." Cara quickly made her way across the room. "I've been out looking for you."

Ariella set down the cupcake pan. "They've staked out my house, the club, even Bombay Main's. I didn't dare go to a hotel, and I was afraid of the airport. The doorman always remembered me, and I pretended I misplaced your spare key."

"You were right to come here." Cara gave her a half hug, avoiding the worst of the flour.

Then she glanced at the trays of beautifully decorated cupcakes. Vanilla, chocolate and red velvet, they were covered in mounds of buttercream icing, and Ariella had turned marzipan into everything from flowers and berries to rainbows and butterflies.

"Hungry?" she jokingly asked Ariella.

"Nervous energy."

"Maybe we can take them to the office or sell them for charity." There had to be five dozen already. They couldn't let them go to waste.

Ariella pulled off the oven mitts and turned off the music. "You got any wine?"

"Absolutely." Cara's wine rack was small, but she kept it well stocked.

She moved to the bay window alcove to check out the selection. "Merlot? Shiraz? Cab Sauv? I've got a nice Mondavi Private Selection."

"We might not want to waste a good bottle tonight."

Cara laughed and pulled it out anyway.

"I'm going for volume," said Ariella.

"Understandable." Cara returned to the kitchen, finding a small space among the mess to pull the cork. "Glasses are above the stove," she told Ariella.

Ariella retrieved them, and the two women moved to the living room.

Ariella peeled off the T-shirt, revealing a simple, steel-gray cocktail dress. She plunked into an armchair and curled her feet beneath her. "Do we have to let it breathe?"

"In an emergency—" Cara began to pour "—not necessary."

Ariella rocked forward and snagged the first glass.

Cara filled her own and sat back on the couch. Then she suddenly remembered the pregnancy and guiltily set the glass down beside her. What was she *thinking?*

"Mine can breathe for a few minutes," she explained. Then focused on Ariella. "How are you holding up?"

"How would you guess I'm holding up?"

"I'd be flipping out."

"I am flipping out."

"Could it be true?" Cara asked. "Do you know anything at all about your biological parents?"

Ariella shook her head. "Not a single thing." Then she laughed a little self-consciously. "They were Caucasian. I think they were American. One of them might have grown up to be president."

"I always knew you had terrific genes."

Ariella came to her feet, moving to a mirror that hung at

the top of the stairs, gazing at her reflection. "Do you think I look anything like him?"

Cara did. "Little bit," she said, rising to follow Ariella and stand behind her. "Okay, quite a bit."

"Enough that…"

"Yes," Cara whispered, squeezing Ariella's shoulders.

Ariella closed her eyes for a long second. "I need to get away, somewhere where this isn't such a big deal."

"You should stay in D.C. We can protect you. The Secret Service—"

"No." Ariella's eyes popped wide.

"They'll take good care of you. They know what they're doing."

"I'm sure they do. But I need to get out of D.C. for a while."

"I understand." Cara wanted to be both sympathetic and supportive. Ariella was first and foremost her friend. "This is a lot for you to take in."

"You are the master of understatement."

Their eyes met in the mirror.

"You need to take a DNA test," said Cara.

But Ariella shook her brunette head.

"Not knowing is not an option," Cara gently pointed out.

"Not yet," said Ariella. "It's one thing to suspect, but it's another to know for sure. You know?"

Cara thought she understood. "Let us help you. Come to the office with me and talk to Lynn."

"I need time, Cara."

"You need help, Ari."

Ariella turned. "I need a few days. A few days on my own before I face the media circus, okay?"

Cara hesitated. She didn't know how she was going to go back to her boss and say she'd found Ariella and then lost her again. But her loyalty was also to her friend. "Okay," she finally agreed.

"I'll take the DNA test, but not yet. I don't think I could wrap my mind around it if it was positive."

"Where will you go?"

"I can't tell you that. You have to keep a straight face when you tell them you don't know."

"I can lie."

"No, you can't. Not to the American press, you can't. And not to your boss, and definitely not to your president."

Cara knew she had a point. "How can I contact you?"

"I'll contact you."

"Ariella."

"It has to be this way."

"No, it doesn't. We can help you, protect you, find out the truth for you."

"It has to be this way for me, Cara. Just for now. Only for a while. I know it's better for the president if I stay, better for you if I stay and face the music." Her voice broke ever so softly. "But I just can't."

"None of this is your fault," Cara felt compelled to point out, putting an arm around Ariella's shoulders.

Ariella nodded her understanding.

"He's a very good man."

"I'm sure he is. But he's the president. And that means…" Ariella's voice trailed off.

"Yeah," Cara agreed into the silence. That meant the circus would never end.

Her cell phone chimed a distinctive tone, telling Cara it was a text from Lynn. She moved away and pulled it from her pocket. The message told her to turn on ANS.

"What?" asked Ariella, watching Cara's expression.

"It's from Lynn. There's something going on. It's on the news." Cara moved to the living area and pressed a button on the remote, changing the channel to ANS.

Ariella moved up beside her. "Oh, I have a bad feeling about this."

Field reporter Angelica Pierce was speaking. She was speculating about Ariella and her relationship to the president, and
was saying something about a woman named Eleanor Albert
from the president's hometown of Fields, Montana. Then old
yearbook photos of the president and Eleanor Albert came up
side by side on the screen. With a dramatic musical flourish,
a picture of Ariella settled in between them.

Cara's eyes went wide.

Ariella sucked in a breath, gripping the sofa for support.
"No," she rasped.

Cara wrapped her arm around her friend and held on tight.
There was no mistaking the resemblance. Cara wasn't even
sure they needed a DNA test.


Max knew the excuse of having forgotten his watch in
Cara's apartment was lame. But it was the best he'd been able
to come up with on short notice. She was home now. He could
see the lights on in her apartment.

He'd just seen the pictures of the president, Ariella and Eleanor on a news site on his tablet. All hell was about to break
loose at the White House, and it was doubtful he'd be able to
see Cara again for weeks to come.

He exited from his Mustang GT, turning up his coat collar
against the blowing snow. He was on his way home from dinner with the NCN network brass and wearing dress shoes, so
he was forced to dodge puddles, taking a circuitous route on
his way across the street.

He made it to the awning, brushed the flakes from his
sleeves, then looked up, straight into the eyes of Ariella Winthrop. They both froze.

"Ariella?" He swiftly glanced both ways to see if anyone
else was out on the dark street.

"Hi, Max."

He moved close, taking her arm to guide her away from
the streetlight. "What are you doing? You can't be out on the

street." There didn't appear to be any other reporters around, but it wasn't safe for her. He'd met her only a few times, but he liked her a lot. She was Cara's close friend, and Max seemed to have a protective streak when it came to Cara.

"The doorman called me a cab."

"A cab? Have you seen the news? You're plastered all over it."

"I saw."

"Let me take you home." He immediately realized that was a ridiculous suggestion. "Let me take you to a hotel. I'll take you anywhere you need to go. But you can't stand out here alone waiting for a cab."

He made a move toward his own car, but she stood her ground, tugging her arm from his.

"Max," she commanded.

He reluctantly stopped and turned to her.

"You're one of the guys I'm avoiding, remember?"

"I'm not a reporter right now."

"You're always a reporter."

"You don't have to talk. Don't say a word." He paused. "But can I ask you one question?"

She shot him an impatient look.

He asked anyway. "Was it you? Did you leak tonight's information to ANS?"

"I'd never even heard of Eleanor Albert before tonight. And the pictures don't prove a thing. I still don't know for sure."

He recognized that she was in denial. "The rest of the world knows for sure," he told her gently. "Let me take you to the White House."

"No!"

"You'll be safe there." And maybe it would earn him some goodwill with the administration, maybe even with Cara.

*Wait a minute. Cara.* Why was Cara letting Ariella leave her apartment all alone? Why hadn't she called in reinforcements?

"Did you talk to Cara up there?" It occurred to him that maybe Cara wasn't home.

"That's two questions," said Ariella.

"Is she upstairs? She let you leave?"

"I'm a grown woman, Max."

"And you're the president's daughter."

"Not until they prove it, I'm not."

A new thought occurred to Max. And, if he was right, it wasn't a half bad idea. "Are you going into hiding?"

Her silence confirmed his suspicions.

"I can help. I can take you somewhere safe."

This time she rolled her eyes. "It won't be hiding if an NCN reporter knows where I am. You're already going to report this entire conversation."

Max was used to walking fine ethical lines. He couldn't lie to his network, but he could choose the facts he shared and the order in which he disclosed them. "It's up to me to decide how to frame my story."

Her expression was blatantly suspicious. "What does that mean?"

"What do you want me to report?"

She hesitated, then seemed to decide she had little to lose. "That I have no knowledge of my biological parents, and I've left the D.C. area."

"Done."

"You'd do that for me?"

"Yes," he told her with sincerity.

But her guard was obviously still up. "Are you serious?"

"I am serious."

After a moment, her expression softened. "Thank you, Max."

"At least let me take you to Potomac Airfield. You'll be able to grab a private charter and take it anywhere you want to go. If you need money—"

"I don't need money."

"If you need anything, Ariella."

"How can you take me to Potomac and not report on it?"

He put on his best broadcaster voice. "Sources close to Ariella Winthrop disclose that she has left the D.C. area, likely on a private plane out of Potomac. Nothing is known about the destination, the aircraft or the pilot."

He gave another glance around the dark street to make sure they were still alone. "You can put up your hair, Ariella. We'll stop somewhere and buy you a pair of blue jeans, a baseball cap and dark glasses. Take a Learjet or something even better. Those guys don't talk about their passengers."

He could feel her hesitation. Her teeth came down on her lower lip.

"You got a better idea?" he asked.

"What's in it for you?"

"Goodwill. Yours, eventually the White House's and the president's. Plus, I'm a nice guy."

"You're with the press."

"I'm still a nice guy. And I'm a sucker for a maiden in distress."

That brought a reluctant smile to her lips.

"My car's across the street." He nodded to the Mustang. "Every minute we stand out here, we risk someone recognizing you."

Just then, a taxi pulled up and stopped at the curb, its light on.

Ariella glanced at it. But then she nodded to Max. "Take me to Potomac Airfield."

"Two things," Lynn said to Cara from behind her office desk.

It was ten the next morning, and Lynn had just finished addressing reporters in the press room for a second day in a row. So far, President Morrow had remained out of sight, his schedule restricted to small, private functions where the White

House could control the guest list. But Cara knew that was about to change. He was scheduled to attend a performance tonight at the Kennedy Center.

"Eleanor Albert is an obvious priority." Lynn counted her points off on her fingers. "Who is she? *Where* is she? Is she really Ariella's mother? And what will she say publicly about the president? Two, there's a whole town full of people out in Fields, Montana. We need to know what they know, what they remember and what *they're* going to say publicly."

Then she glanced up, her attention going to someone in the doorway behind Cara.

"There you are," she said, waving her hand for the person to enter. "You might as well come on in."

Cara turned, starting in astonishment as she came face-to-face with Max. He was dressed in blue jeans and square-toed boots, with an open-collar white shirt beneath his dark blazer. He was freshly shaved. His perpetually tousled hair, wide shoulders and rugged looks gave him a mantle of raw power, even though he was just a visitor to the West Wing.

He met her gaze, his expression neutral.

Even with Lynn in the room, Cara had a hard time controlling her annoyance. Max had gone on national television last night, disclosing what he knew about Ariella's whereabouts. She didn't know who his source had been, but he'd milked it for all it was worth, tossing both Ariella and the White House to the wolves in his quest for ratings.

"Have a seat." Lynn pointed to the chair next to Cara's. The two chairs were matching brown leather, low backed but rounded and comfortable, with carved mahogany arms.

Max moved guardedly, but he did as Lynn asked.

"Who's your source?" Lynn shot out without preamble.

"Seriously?" asked Max with an arch of one brow, a carefully placed thread of amazement in his tone.

"How did you learn about Ariella?"

Cara was curious as well. Even she hadn't known Ariella

was headed for Potomac Airfield. She couldn't imagine who had found out, or why they would tell Max of all people.

"You know perfectly well that I can't disclose my sources," Max said to Lynn, but he cast a glance Cara's way, as well.

"You can when it's a matter of security," Lynn countered. "This might even be national security."

Max sat back in his chair, "Really? Go on."

"If she's kidnapped," said Lynn, twisting her ring. "If a foreign entity, or heaven help us all, a terrorist, gets their hands on the president's daughter, it will absolutely be a situation of national security."

"You don't know that she's his daughter."

"Do you think the terrorists care? I was convinced by those pictures. And I'm pretty sure the rest of the nation was convinced by them, too. Do you think the president will take the chance that's she's not?"

Max's body became alert. "So, you're saying the president slept with Eleanor Albert."

Lynn's face paled a shade. "I'm saying nothing of the kind."

But Max pounced on her small misstep. "If he hadn't slept with her, this couldn't possibly be a matter of national security."

For a moment, Lynn was speechless.

Cara stepped in. "Who told you Ariella was going to Potomac Airfield?"

Max twisted his head to look at her. His eyes were cool, his expression a perfect, professional mask.

Cara pressed him. "Come on, Max. You don't want Ariella hurt any more than we do. She's innocent in all this. She needs Secret Service protection."

"No kidding," said Max. "And did you tell her that last night?"

Cara blinked, her insides clenching up.

He continued, "Did you tell her she needed the Secret Service?"

There was only one way for him to have known Ariella had

come to Cara. "Of course I did. I begged her to let me help. I just finished explaining that to Lynn."

Max turned back to Lynn. "You want to know my source? Ariella is my source. I know she went to Potomac Airfield because I drove her there. She's gone, Lynn."

Lynn sat up in her chair. "Why on earth didn't you stop her?"

"Because the power of the press doesn't extend to kidnapping and forcible confinement. She's a grown woman. She's an American citizen. And she's free to come and go as she pleases."

"Is she still in the country?" Cara asked.

"She told me she had her passport."

"You didn't report on any of that last night."

He slowly turned back to Cara, his expression reproachful. "I didn't, did I?"

"You want points for that?" Cara demanded.

"It would be nice. A little credit. A little consideration. Maybe a scoop or two. I ran into Ariella. I offered her assistance. And I put her safety and the good of my country ahead of my own interests. She was determined to leave D.C. without notice. I thought it was best to give her a fighting chance at successfully doing that."

Cara found herself nodding in agreement with his words. She knew from personal experience that there'd been no talking Ariella out of her plans. She only hoped she came back soon. A DNA test was in everyone's best interest.

Lynn's demeanor changed. "The White House appreciates your efforts," she told Max.

"I would imagine you do." He came to his feet. "I'm not the bad guy here. But I do have a job to do."

As he left the office, Lynn's phone rang. Cara quickly took the opportunity to jump up and go after him.

"Max?" She hurried down the hall.

He stopped and turned back, and she canted her head toward her own office.

He followed her inside, and she closed the door. Sure, he'd done the right thing. But he wasn't completely off the hook.

"Where did you run into Ariella?" she fired off.

"Logan Circle."

"My apartment."

"Yes."

"You stalked her."

He moved toward Cara, making her heart reflexively race and her breath go shallow. It didn't seem to matter how hard she fought or how much logic she sent through her brain, over and over again. She was compulsively attracted to Max Gray. It seemed to be embedded in her DNA.

"Really?" he demanded. The distance between them was far too small. "That's what you think? That I was staking out your apartment on the off chance that Ariella would come by?"

Cara admitted the mathematical odds had been low on that happening. She took a step back, bumping against the edge of her desk.

His eyes glittered meaningfully as he moved again, keeping the distance static. "You can't think of any other reason? None at all?"

"I told you no, Max."

"I was there for my watch."

"We both know that was a ruse."

"Yeah. We do. But you won't let me play it straight, Cara. I have no other choice."

"Your choice is to stay away."

"That's not working for me."

There was a shout in the hallway and the sound of two sets of footsteps going swiftly past.

"We can't do this here," she told him.

"When and where?"

"Never and nowhere."

"Wrong answer."

"It's the only answer you're going to get. I have to go to work, Max. In case you missed it in the papers, we're having a crisis."

His tone went suddenly soft. "I'm sorry for that. I truly am."

"But you have a job to do, too," she finished for him.

"And I better get to it."

He brushed the backs of his knuckles against hers, sending a spike of awareness ricocheting through her system, squeezing her heart and tightening her abdomen.

Before she could protest, he'd turned and was gone.

Cara made her way around her desk, dropping into her chair. She gave a reflexive glance at her computer screen, knowing that a million things needed her attention, but the email subject lines didn't compute inside her brain.

Her hand dropped to her stomach and rested there. She was barely pregnant. If not for her ultraregular cycle and modern, supersensitive home pregnancy tests, she wouldn't even know it yet.

But she did. And she was. And Max's baby was complicating an already dicey situation. Max was one of the ten hottest men in D.C. She didn't need a magazine to tell her that. He was also smart, funny, innovative and daring.

He wanted her. That much was clear. But what he didn't want, what he'd never wanted and never would want, was home, hearth and family. He'd told her about his single mother, how his father walked out on them, how he was no genetic prize and had no plans to carry on his questionable family legacy.

He'd found his niche in broadcasting. He had an incredible instinct for a story, and he was absolutely fearless about going after it. It didn't matter if it was in Africa or Afghanistan, flying high in the air or on the bottom of the ocean. He'd chase a story down, and once he caught it, he'd bring it home and broadcast it to the awe and attention of millions of Americans. Max had everything he'd ever wanted in life.

She'd tried to stay away from him from the very start. Given their careers, a relationship was risky during the campaign, foolish after the vote count and impossible now that the president had taken office.

On more than one occasion, it had occurred to Cara that Max might want her for the sole reason that he couldn't have her. And sometimes, in the dead of night, Cara fantasized about giving in to him, spending as much time as she wanted in his company, in his bed. She wondered how many days or weeks it would take for him to tire of her. She also wondered how fast and far he'd run if he knew the extent of her feelings for him.

For Max, this was just another lark, another fling, another woman in the long line that formed a part of his adventurer, bachelor lifestyle. But for her, it was different. She'd all but given him her heart. And now she was having his baby.

If he'd run fast and hard from the knowledge of her true feelings, he'd rocket away from the possibility of fatherhood. He'd be on the next plane to Borneo or Outer Mongolia.

Cara gave a sad smile and coughed out a short laugh at her musings. In the dead of night, when she fantasized about Max, it was those initial few days and weeks that occupied her thoughts. She glossed over the part where he left and broke her heart. Some days, she actually thought it might be worth it.

# Three

The things Max put up with for his job. He'd hacked his way through jungles, gone over waterfalls, battled snakes and scorpions, even wrestled a crocodile one time. But nothing had prepared him for this. He was slope side in the president's hometown of Fields, Montana, among five hundred darting, shrieking schoolchildren let loose on skis and snowboards.

While the president was growing up, Fields had been a small town, mostly supported by the surrounding cattle ranches. But over the years, its scenic mountain location and pristine slopes had been discovered by skiers and snowboarders. Lifts had been built and high-end resort chains had moved in, fundamentally changing the face of the entire town.

Ranch access roads still lined the highway, but the old-guard cowboys now rubbed shoulders with the colorfully attired recreation crowd. It seemed to Max a cordial if cautious relationship. While the newer parts of town were pure tourism, the outskirts were a patchwork of the old and new. A funky techno bar had been built next to the feed store, while a tavern with sawdust and peanut shells covering the floor shared a parking lot with a high-end snowboard shop.

Max's cameraman, Jake Dobson, sent up a rooster tail of snow as he angled his snowboard to a halt next to Max. The two men had first worked together at a small, local station in Maryland. When Max had been asked to join the team at NCN, he'd made it clear that Jake coming with him was a condition of the contract. Jake was the unsung hero in every single one of Max's news stories.

"Another run?" asked Jake.

"I don't think so," Max scoffed, glancing at the multitude of children on the slope. "I was scared to death out there."

Jake laughed at him. "They're quite harmless."

"I'm not worried about them hurting me. But it's like dodging moving pylons. Pylons that bruise easily. I'm not about to have running over an eight-year-old girl on my conscience."

"We could do a black diamond run."

They had a couple of hours left before dark.

"Sure. Up there, I can take out a twelve-year-old. That'll help me sleep better." Max bent down to pop the clips on his own snowboard.

"It's a statewide outdoors club jamboree," Jake put in helpfully as he released his own bindings. "They'll be here for a week."

"We've got work to do anyway." Max stood his board up in the snow, removing his helmet and goggles.

The two men had spent the morning in the older part of Fields, talking to the ranching crowd. So far, they'd met a number of people who'd known the president when he was a teenager. Unfortunately, none of them were willing to go on camera. And none would admit to knowing anything about Eleanor.

"I think the ranchers have all headed home by now," Jake observed. "Early to bed and early to rise."

"Maybe. But their kids and grandkids will be at clubs dancing with the tourists. Who knows what kind of stories have been passed down about the Morrows?"

"You're going to play the tourist and mix and mingle?"

"Why not?" Max had been pleasantly surprised by how respectful the people of Fields seemed to be. It was obvious many of them recognized him from his television show, but they mostly smiled and nodded and kept their distance. Few even asked for autographs.

Back in D.C.—and in New York and L.A.—people were much more aggressive. It was impossible for him to walk into any restaurant, lounge or club in D.C. without being approached by a dozen people. Being in Fields was quite refreshing.

"Can we get a burger first?" Jake asked, brushing the snow off his board with the back of his glove. "I'm starving."

"Works for me." Max started to walk back to the lodge. "Are those pip-squeaks really going to be here all week?"

His and Jake's rooms were uncomfortably close to the indoor pool complex. There'd been a steady stream of shrieking and stomping children up and down their hall both last night and this morning.

"Yes, they are," Jake responded. "I talked to one of their leaders up top."

"Lovely," Max drawled.

He wasn't a kid person. Some people seemed to see right past the noise, the mess, the smell and the irrationality to the cute, lovable little tykes beneath.

Max was in awe of those people. He preferred rationality. Or, at least, predicable irrationality. If there was one thing he'd learned about adults, it was they could always be counted on to act in their own best interests.

"I called down and asked the hotel manager to move us," said Jake.

Max brightened. "You did?"

"I've got your back, buddy." Jake smacked him on the shoulder. "We're each in a one-bedroom villa up on the hillside. It's adults only."

"I love you, man."

Jake chuckled. "It was the hot spring pools that made up my mind. Well, that and the fact that Jessica walked out on me last week. I don't want to spend my first assignment as a bachelor surrounded by grade-schoolers."

"Jessica walked out on you?"

Jake pulled off a glove with his teeth. "She'll be back. But until then, I am under no obligation to be faithful to her."

"She's clear on that?"

They took the staircase leading to the equipment lockers.

"I'm single and she's single. She can bang half of D.C. while I'm gone for all I care."

"I take it she's not 'the one.'"

"It's way too soon to tell."

Max couldn't help but grin at that as they entered the cavernous, warehouselike building. "Trust me, Jake. If she was the one, you'd kill any guy who looked sideways at her, never mind slept with her."

"You're an expert?" Jake scoffed.

"I know that much."

Max wasn't even Cara's boyfriend and he had a hard time thinking about her with any other guy. Technically, the two of them were single. But that was only a technicality, based on current circumstances. It didn't mean he'd look twice at another woman.

They stowed their boards and gear, changed out of the snowboard boots and headed for the Alpine Grill on the street out front. Max was still pondering his and Cara's single status when the waitress brought them each a mug of red ale from a local microbrewery.

He and Jake had taken seats on the lounge side of the rustic, hewn-beam restaurant, which was adults only. But the shrieks and cries of children came through the doorway from the restaurant. Then a group of people burst into a rollicking rendition of "Happy Birthday." Evidently, someone named Amy had reached a milestone.

"Shall I mention that it's your birthday?" asked Jake.

"Now that would be a treat," Max returned dryly.

He took a drink of the foamy beer. He'd turned thirty today. Some people thought of it as a milestone. Max didn't see it that way. He'd been twenty-nine and three hundred and sixty-four days yesterday. Thirty was only twenty-four hours older. He really didn't get the big deal.

Jake craned his neck. "Good grief, they gave those little kids sparklers."

Max turned to look.

When he did, it wasn't the potential fire hazard that caught his eye. It was Cara. She was standing in the restaurant foyer, looking adorable in a waist-length, puffy, turquoise jacket, a pair of snug blue jeans and set of ankle-high black books. Her cheeks were bright red, her lips were shiny and her blue eyes were as striking as ever.

Max's chest went tight. He scraped back his chair and rose from the table.

"Nobody's on fire," Jake pointed out. "Yet."

Max didn't respond. His attention was locked on Cara as he instinctively wound his way through the other tables. The shrieks of the children, the smell of grilling beef, the rainbow of ski clothing disappeared from his perception.

"Hello, Cara." He offered her a friendly smile.

In response, her eyes went round with obvious shock and her jaw dropped open a notch. "Max," she managed. "You're in Fields."

"I'm in Fields," he returned.

She gave her head a little shake, as if she was trying to wake herself from a dream. But Max wasn't going anywhere.

The hostess appeared in front of them. "For two?" the young woman asked, glancing from Cara to Max.

"Just one," said Cara.

"Join us," said Max. "Jake is here," he quickly finished, so she wouldn't think it would look like a date.

Cara had met Jake a couple of times over the past few months. As far as Jake was concerned, Cara was an acquaintance of Max's, no different than hundreds of other people on the periphery of his life as a news reporter.

Cara hesitated while the woman waited, her bright, welcoming smile flickering with confusion.

Cara glanced to Jake, then obviously concluded refusing his offer would garner more curiosity than accepting it would.

"Sure," she said to Max. "Why not?"

Max thanked the hostess, then guided Cara to their table.

When they got there, Max introduced her. "You remember Cara Cranshaw."

Jake got to his feet. His smile was warm and his eyes alight as he shook Cara's hand. "It's *very* nice to see you again."

Max instantly realized his mistake. Jake and Cara were both single. Sure, Jake was in the news business like Max. But a cameraman was quite a few steps removed from the people who actually researched and crafted the stories. He'd be a much safer choice for Cara.

And Jake certainly seemed to appeal to women. He was tall, physically fit, square-chinned and gray-eyed, with a devil-may-care attitude that got him a steady string of offers from women all around the world.

"Cara doesn't date newsmen," Max announced.

Cara shot him an appalled expression.

But Jake laughed easily. "I'm sure she can make an exception in this case."

This time she blanched, gripping the back of her chair. And Max realized she'd drawn the conclusion Jake knew about their relationship.

"Jake means for him," Max pointed out.

"What do you say?" Jake asked her easily. "My girlfriend just dumped me. I'm wounded and terribly lonely."

Cara seemed to recover from her shock very quickly. She smoothly took her seat and unfolded the burgundy cloth napkin in front of her.

Then she looked to Jake. "I'm afraid I don't go on pity dates."

Jake clutched at his chest as if he'd been stabbed.

"Better for you to stay away from the ones with brains, anyway," Max said to Jake.

"Aren't you cynical," Cara chided Max.

"Because I don't think Jake can get a date with a woman whose IQ is over one hundred?"

"Because you seem to think there's a critical mass of low-intelligence women for him to choose from."

"Ouch," said Jake.

"I didn't mean to offend your gender," said Max.

"Which makes it that much worse," she said tartly.

"Keep digging, buddy," said Jake, making shoveling motions with his hands. To Cara, he said. "Can I get you a drink?"

Max cursed himself for being slow on the uptake.

"Thank you," Cara responded with a sweet smile for Jake. "Ginger ale, please."

Jake glanced around the crowded pub, obviously checking for their waitress. After a moment, he rose to walk over to the bar himself.

"He's a gentleman," said Cara, her tone a rebuke to Max as she smoothed the napkin out in her lap.

"He's flirting with you."

She rolled her eyes. "Really, Max. Thank you for clearing that up, since, like many women, I'm of low intelligence and wouldn't have figured it out for myself."

Max clamped his jaw, fighting the urge to defend himself. Instead, their gazes locked, and an instant rush of desire washed through him as the noise of the crowd ebbed and flowed.

Cara cracked first. "So, what are you doing in Fields?"

"Same thing as you."

"I doubt that."

"We're both here after the story."

She straightened in her chair. "No. You're here after the story. I'm here looking for the truth."

"Don't get all self-righteous on me. It's not an attractive quality."

She leaned in and hissed, "You think I want to be attractive? To you?"

He lowered his voice, matching her posture. "There's no way for you to help it, sweetheart."

Jake's arrival broke the moment. "Your ginger ale, ma'am."

Cara turned to him and smiled. "Thank you, sir."

"Pleasure to be of assistance."

Max snagged his beer mug by the handle, struggling not to gag on the syrupy sweetness. "Give me a break."

"Did you know it was Max's birthday?" Jake asked Cara in a hearty, if slightly malicious, voice.

"I did not." She gave Max an overly sweet smile. "Happy birthday."

"I think we should get the staff to sing."

Max glared his annoyance at Jake. "I think the fistfight that would break out between us afterward would reflect badly on NCN."

Jake laughed easily, leaning back in his chair.

Just then, the "Happy Birthday" chorus came up again in the restaurant. This time it was Billy being celebrated.

Before the voices died down, a little girl shrieked and cried. Probably Billy's little sister, jealous because he was getting all the attention. She sounded very young, and Max could only hope they didn't appease her by handing her a lit sparkler.

"Kid heaven," he muttered under his breath. "Adult hell."

Cara shot him an odd look. But then her cell phone rang and she dug into her purse to retrieve it.

"Sorry," she apologized to them both before raising the phone to her ear. "Hi, Lynn."

Cara ran her finger up and down against the condensation of her ginger ale glass, distracting Max while she listened.

"Uh-huh," she finally answered. "Will do. Tomorrow?" She went silent. "Got it. Thanks." She hung up and slipped the phone back into her purse.

"Care to share?" Max asked.

She gave him a secretive smile that tightened his stomach. "You wish," she teased.

"I think she's one up on us," Jake joked.

That wasn't news to Max. Cara had been one up on him from the first moment they'd met.

Later that day, Cara had started her search with the school yearbook. It was easy enough to find the president's and Eleanor Albert's classmates. The ones she'd tracked down so far didn't remember enough to help the press with the story. That was encouraging. As long as they continued to say they didn't know anything, and as long as Eleanor didn't surface, there wasn't much more to report.

Despite the encouraging news, by the end of the first day, Cara returned to her hotel room exhausted. She was worried about running into Max again, and she knew there would be other reporters in town, so she decided on room service.

She found herself adding a glass of milk to the order, making sure she had both green and yellow vegetables and a good balance of protein and complex carbs. She'd have loved to go for the chocolate cake for dessert, but settled instead for frozen yogurt with strawberries.

She'd also added a multivitamin to her diet, and booked an appointment with an obstetrician for later in the month. She wasn't ready to pick up any baby books yet, but she did browse a few sites on the internet. She found she could think about diet and exercise and body changes without panicking, but if she let her mind go to an actual baby, she'd find herself dizzy and short of breath.

Like now. When an ad came up for infant formula and a cherubic little baby smiled out from her phone, she quickly shut down the browser, closing her eyes until the feeling passed. She knew she had to wrap her head around this. To do that, she needed someone to confide in, and there was only one person in the world who fit the bill.

She pressed a speed dial button on her cell phone.

After a few rings, her sister Gillian's voice came on. "Hey, Cara."

Cara forced a cheerful tone. "Hey, yourself."

"How are things in D.C.?"

"Hectic. Seattle?"

"Right back at you. We're opening up a sales office in Beijing next month. You would not believe the red tape." Gillian's voice went muffled for a moment. Then she came back to the call. "Sorry about that."

"Are you still at work?"

"It's only seven on this side of the country. You home?"

"Are you…" Cara hesitated. "I mean, I know you're always busy, but…is it worse now than normal?"

"Not particularly. Hey, Sam, tell them I'll sign it off, but only if it's under a million… Sorry again."

Cara couldn't help but smile at Gillian's familiar pace of life. Her sister was CEO of her own technology company. They'd broken into the health-care market with GPS organizational devices that tracked everything from room cleaning to medication dispensing three years ago and never looked back.

"No problem," said Cara. "I'm the one who's sorry to bother you."

"It's no bother. So, what's going on?"

Cara didn't know how to answer that.

Gillian jumped back in. "I mean, I read about the secret daughter and all. I assume that's taking up most of your time."

"It is."

"Did he know? I mean… Okay, this isn't a secure line, and even if it was…" Gillian took a breath, speaking by rote. "I know you wouldn't give away confidential information about the president to your sister. So, all you FBI guys listening in can stand down."

Cara laughed. She appreciated her sister's caution, but it wasn't necessary. The FBI wasn't listening in on her phone calls.

Gillian's voice went warm again. "So, what do you need, baby sister?"

Though they were only fourteen months apart, Gillian had teased Cara with the term most of their lives.

"Any chance you could take a trip to Montana?"

"Montana? Why in the heck would I go to Montana?"

"Fields, Montana."

"Ooohhh," Gillian drawled. "*That* Montana. Back where the whole thing started. Why? You need me to sleuth something out? Bribe someone?"

"You know, if the FBI really was listening, you would end my career in a single phone call."

"Did I say bribe?" Gillian came back. "I meant *find*. You want me to *find* someone?"

"I want you to come and see me."

There was a split-second pause. "You're in Montana."

"Yes."

"Right now?"

"Right now."

"That's less than an hour away. I can have the jet ready by eight."

Cara allowed herself to hope. "Can you come?"

"Is something wrong?"

"No." Cara scratched at a flaw in the hotel desktop. "No, no. Nothing much."

Again Gillian hesitated almost imperceptibly. "But it's something. Is it work?"

"Nothing to do with work. What you see on the news is pretty much it right now. There's the Asia Pacific Summit coming up in L.A., but beyond that it's all Ariella all the time. Is she or isn't she, and when did the president know."

"So, it's personal?"

"Can you come?"

"Are you sick?"

"No."

"Did you break the law?"

"Gillian."

"Do you need money? Do you have a secret gambling addiction? Is the mob after you?"

*"No."*

"Because, I've got a lot of capital tied up in Beijing right now, but I'm sure I could free up—"

"I don't need your money."

"Okay. So, what's going on? Are you pregnant?"

Cara froze. She knew she should toss out something flippant to throw Gillian off the truth, but she couldn't for the life of her think of what that might be.

"Cara?"

"Please. Just come."

"I'm on my way."

Cara was the last person Max expected to see walking into the small Fields airport this late at night. Despite its small size, it was an attractive airport, themed around the frontier spirit of the region, with lots of polished pine logs, leather and fieldstone. But it had also been designed and built with the high-end ski clientele in mind, so it was tasteful and welcoming.

Right now, it was all but deserted. The concourse shops

and cafés were closed. The waiting areas were empty. Most of the staff still on site were cleaners, with the exception of a lone clerk behind the check-in counter. Max moved from the alcove where he'd sat down, crossing the floor toward Cara.

Hearing his footsteps, she turned.

As she had in the Alpine Grill, she looked startled and none too pleased.

"You *are* stalking me," she charged, glancing around, probably checking for Jake and his camera.

"I was about to accuse you of the same thing." He came to a halt beside her.

"I'm here to meet someone," she told him.

"There are no flights this time of night."

"It's a private jet."

"Uh-huh." He watched her expression, trying to guess her intentions. If she'd simply been following him on spec, then she didn't know who he was meeting. On the other hand, if she somehow found out who he was meeting, she might have followed him here because of it.

She remained inscrutable. "And you?"

"Meeting someone myself." He'd give her that much.

"Who?" she fired back.

He shook his head. "Uh-uh."

She crossed her arms over her chest. "I don't believe you."

He widened his stance. "Believe whatever you want."

"You promised you wouldn't take advantage of our relationship."

"What relationship?" If they were having a relationship, Max would dearly love to know.

"You know what I mean. You can't..." She glanced around. "It's not fair...." She seemed to force herself to gather her thoughts. "Can't you just leave? This is nothing. I promise you, this is nothing."

"Do I have to remind you this is a public airport and a free country?"

She had him curious now. If she hadn't followed him here, there was a chance she was hiding something herself. Maybe he'd stumbled across something important.

"Cara!" a woman called from across the concourse.

Cara immediately left Max's side, rushing to meet the woman who had emerged from an airside doorway.

The two met in the middle of the room. The woman dropped her overnight bag, and they hugged. It was then Max realized how much they looked alike. Their hairstyles were similar, same wispy, short look. The light brown hair color was nearly identical, and their eyes, noses and mouths were almost copies. The other woman was slightly taller, and Cara was a little leaner.

Max automatically started toward them.

"Max Gray." He stuck out his hand to the other woman.

"Really?" the woman singsonged, glancing at Cara as she disentangled from the embrace. "Then you must be—"

"He's a reporter," Cara blurted out. "And we have to be *very* careful what we say around him." Her warning to the woman was surprisingly blunt.

"I host an investigative news show," Max corrected her. "It's called *After Dark* on NCN." He wasn't particularly snobbish about the difference, but he didn't want the woman to think he was some lowlife tabloid stringer, either.

"I'm Gillian Cranshaw. Cara's sister."

"There's certainly a family resemblance."

"We have to go now." Cara hooked her arm through Gillian's, scooped up the overnight bag and all but dragged her sister in the direction of the exit.

"Let me." Max stepped forward, reaching for the bag.

"I've got it," said Cara, quickening her pace. Something obviously had her rattled.

"Catch you later," Gillian called back over her shoulder.

Before Max could give much thought to Cara's bizarre behavior, a man appeared through the same airside doorway as

Gillian. Cara glanced fleetingly at him but otherwise paid no attention.

Clearly, there was some kind of family drama on top of the political drama. Otherwise, Cara might have taken a moment to wonder who exactly Max was meeting at almost ten o'clock at the Fields airport. And it was worth wondering about. But Max certainly wasn't going to do her job for her.

"Liam Fisher?" Max asked as the man approached.

"Hello, Max. I recognize you from your program."

"Thank you for coming."

"Thanks to NCN for thinking of me."

The two men shook hands.

Since arriving in Fields, Max had learned two things. One, the town was intensely loyal to the president. And two, Eleanor Albert hadn't ever made much of an impression. Few people remembered her, and even fewer people associated her with Ted Morrow.

Combined, those two details told Max one very important thing. The story of Eleanor's daughter Ariella had been hard to get. And conventional means likely hadn't been enough to dig it out in the first place. That meant unconventional, possibly illegal, means had been used to obtain the scoop.

Liam Fisher was a former staffer at ANS. He'd left under a cloud of secrecy and at odds with the current owner, Graham Boyle. Max's instincts were telling him that the real story wasn't Eleanor Albert. The real story was ANS and how they'd found out about Eleanor Albert in the first place.

# Four

Cara hustled her sister around a small airport café, past a candy store and behind the security kiosk toward the side door that led to the parking lot.

"For a minute there, I thought he was the daddy," said Gillian as they briskly walked toward the exit. She twisted her head for a final look at Max, then did a quick check of her cell phone.

"He's a reporter," Cara responded, not about to get into an explanation right now. "And I think he's following me."

"I think he's meeting the guy who came in on the Cessna," said Gillian. "They were landing behind us."

"Reinforcements," Cara guessed. "The place is crawling with press."

"I read about it. You know that Ariella person, don't you? Isn't she the caterer who did that Thanksgiving thing? The one where the singer fell into the cake."

"That's her," Cara acknowledged.

They made their way down a concrete ramp to the mostly deserted parking lot where Cara had left her rented SUV.

"She seems like she has a good sense of humor," Gillian observed.

"So does the president."

"So, you think it's true then?"

"What do you mean?"

"You just compared Ariella's sense of humor to the president's. You must think she's his daughter. Or do you *know* she's his daughter?"

"I don't know anything for sure." Cara hit the unlock button on the remote and got a double beep in response. "But you must have seen the pictures on TV."

"Nope."

"Well, Ariella looks an awful lot like them. I mean, not only does she look like Eleanor Albert. She looks like the president, too. A perfect combination of genes." Cara opened the hatchback door and tossed her sister's bag inside.

"Then that's that. It must be true."

"If I had to bet," said Cara. "My money would definitely be on yes."

"But they'll do DNA."

"They will."

"Surely the president can put a rush on it."

Cara headed for the driver's door. "You really don't watch much TV, do you?"

Gillian's cell phone rang. "I've been mostly paying attention to tech sector news coming out of China and India." She raised the phone to her ear. "Hello?" Using her free hand, she opened the passenger door and climbed into the vehicle.

Cara followed suit, buckling up and starting the engine. Then while Gillian talked business on her phone, Cara backed out of the parking spot and headed for the parking lot exit.

Judging from Gillian's side of the conversation, it sounded as though there was trouble with a supplier in India. Then Gillian took another call and had an argument with her accountant about staff pension plans. By the time she hung up, they were nearly back to town.

"It would have been a genetic jackpot," she announced, tucking the phone back into her slacks pocket.

"For Ariella?" Cara glanced from the snowy road to her sister, then quickly back again.

"No. That Max guy, the reporter. Tall, good-looking, seemed athletic. And you have to be a quick thinker to host a news show. So he must have a brain up there."

Cara wasn't so sure about Max's reasoning skills. "He does a lot of dangerous fieldwork. Jungles, war zones, mountaintops."

"So brave, too?"

"I meant that his testosterone seems to be crowding out his intellect. You want to stop for a drink?" On impulse, Cara wheeled into the Pine Tree Lounge parking lot. It was a newer log building on the outskirts of Fields, with inviting yellow lights on a pine-pillared porch.

"Sure," Gillian agreed. "I'm up for liquor."

They locked the vehicle and made their way along the shoveled walkway, up a wide, stone staircase and into a wood-paneled entry. A country tune played softly through the speakers, and the polished wood tables were lit with tiny oil lamps. The chairs were red leather, and vintage horse tack adorned the walls.

Cara moved to a quiet table near the back, checking to be sure they were out of earshot of the other patrons.

The waitress arrived immediately, setting down glasses of ice water. Gillian gave a cursory look at the extensive wine list, then simply asked for something "really good" in an old-world cabernet sauvignon.

Finally, they were alone. Cara wasn't driving, and Gillian's cell phone wasn't ringing.

"So," said Gillian with a deep breath as she reached for the bowl of mixed nuts in the middle of the table.

"So," Cara returned, bracing herself. "It's him. He's the guy."

Gillian glanced both ways, looking over her shoulder.

"What guy?"

"Max. He's the father."

Gillian's hand dropped to the tabletop. "Then why—"

"He doesn't know. He can't know. We're not supposed… He's a reporter, and I work in the White House press office."

"But you slept with him anyway?"

"That was before the election." Cara defended herself. "And, okay, once after the vote count, but it was all before the inauguration. And that was a mistake. It never should have happened."

"Whoops," Gillian deadpanned.

"That's pretty much what I said. And he… And I… And then…" Cara waved her hand in the air. "You know what I mean."

Gillian fought a smile. "I'd know what you meant if you finished your sentences, or at least finished your clauses."

Cara dropped her chin to her chest and shook her head. "I mean, I'm screwed."

Gillian waited until Cara looked up. Her eyes were glowing with what looked like joy. "You are not screwed. You're going to have a baby. *We* are going to have a baby." She reached for Cara's hand. "You don't have to worry about a thing. It doesn't matter how this happened. It's great that it did. Babies are never bad news. Especially yours."

"He doesn't want children," said Cara. "He's never wanted children. He wants to chase stories to dangerous places around the world and not have to worry about anyone back home."

"Bully for him."

"And even if he did," Cara continued, "we can't even think about a normal relationship. He's a conflict of interest. We're less than a week into the president's term, and I have this albatross hanging around my neck."

"You're saying it's not in your best interest to tell him?" Gillian asked.

"Absolutely not."

"Never?"

"I can't picture it."

Gillian cocked her head, clearly pondering the facts of the situation as she reached for another handful of nuts. "Then what you need to do is sleep with someone else."

Cara thought she must have misheard. *What?*

"I don't mean literally. I mean, make it clear to Max that you haven't been exclusive. When he finds out you're pregnant, he might insist on a DNA test, but if he's not daddy material, he might be content to let the matter drop. What he doesn't know won't cost him anything."

Cara digested her sister's words. "You're very cynical."

Then she tried to picture the conversation where she casually informed Max that she'd been sleeping with other men while they'd dated. No, not while they'd dated. That was dressing it up too much. She meant while they'd tried and failed to keep their hands off each other.

"I've been around a lot longer than you have," Gillian retorted.

"Fourteen months?"

"I've always been more worldly than you."

The waitress arrived, opening the bottle and pouring a glass for Gillian. Cara refused and asked for a hot chocolate instead.

"So, you think it's okay for me to keep it from him? I mean ethically?" Cara asked.

Gillian shrugged. "Why not?"

Cara leaned back, slouching more comfortably in the chair. "That wasn't what I expected you to say."

"You thought I'd tell you to run to him, 'fess up and see if he wanted a white picket fence and all the trimmings?"

Cara hated to admit it, but that was kind of where her thoughts had been going. Not that she'd have agreed. Still, it would have been nice to have some moral support for her out-rageous fantasy.

"Oh, Cara." Gillian's face screwed up in pity. "That's not good."

"No, that's not what I thought," Cara lied. "And that's not what I want. The last thing I need is some miserable martyr of a man, hanging around my house, trimming my hedges, clean-ing my barbecue and blaming me for having ruined his daz-zling career. Thank you, but no. I don't need that kind of grief."

Gillian was silent for a moment. "Well, you almost con-vinced me. But you might want to work on your delivery."

"Excuse me?"

"You protested a little too much there."

Cara hated to admit that Gillian was right. She knew Max would never want them to be a family, but sometimes she just couldn't help but wish for it herself.

Max and Jake listened with rapt attention while Liam Fisher outlined some of the underhanded tactics ANS had used in the past to track down big stories. The three men were at the Apex Lounge at the topmost stop of the ski gondola. It was lunchtime, and the facility was quickly filling up with fami-lies and children.

"It became exponentially worse when that producer Mar-nie Salloway arrived," Liam was saying. "The woman has no conscience. I'd be surprised if she has a soul."

"Do you have an example?" Max asked. Marnie was his former boss, and he could well believe she was up to no good. He and Jake had been working in Fields for three days now. They'd undertaken countless interviews, all of which were next to useless. They had hour upon hour of footage where the townspeople praised the president and looked puzzled when asked about Eleanor Albert.

"It went beyond manipulation," said Liam. "There was downright coercion. I never passed on an envelope full of cash, but I definitely wined and dined a few people, a five-star resort for a weekend, a three-hundred-dollar bottle of wine and then the carefully framed question to get just the right sound bite."

"That's not illegal," Max pointed out.

A young boy shrieked and rushed past the table with three of his friends, each of them bumping Max's elbow. Max glanced around for parents, or maybe an adult supervisor for the jamboree kids, but didn't see anyone paying the slightest attention to the hooligans.

Max cussed under his breath.

"That was a straw that broke my back," said Liam.

For a split second, Max thought he was talking about the unruly children.

"She, I mean Marnie, wanted me to hide a microphone in a victim's house. A teenage boy who was bullied by a sports team. She was convinced he'd exaggerated the problem and wanted to expose what she considered a conspiracy against a popular coach."

Jake scoffed in disgust, while Max drew back in absolute shock.

"You have got to be kidding me," Max spat.

"That's when I quit. Or when I was fired for insubordination, depending on whose story you want to believe."

Squeals of high-pitched laughter sounded from outside on the gondola deck. Max reflexively glanced up to see a mob of kids had gathered there. They were jostling for their snowboards, pushing and teasing, tossing each other's hats and gloves in the air.

"How can a person even think around that?" Max complained.

Jake laughed at him. "Chill out, Max. They're just having fun." Then he turned his attention back to Liam, getting serious once more. "You have any proof of this stuff?"

Max also focused on Liam.

"Just my word against theirs," said Liam. "But I haven't

delved too deeply before. Once I was out of there, I got on with my life. So, you never know what we might find out if we go looking."

"How do we start?" asked Max as the waitress cleared their plates. He handed her his credit card.

"I've got a few favors I can call in," said Liam.

"We're not quite done in Fields," said Max. "But we can meet you back in D.C."

Liam nodded his agreement. "Are you two boarding down now or taking the gondola?" asked Liam.

"I'm boarding," said Max, feeling the need to get some exercise and clear his head. Liam sounded like he was going to lead them in exactly the right direction, and Max knew things were going to get intense very soon.

Max raised his brow in a question to Jake, even though he already knew the answer. Jake would never take the easy way down.

"We'll meet you in the lobby," Jake told Liam with a grin.

Max signed the credit card slip and shrugged into his jacket as he headed for the exit.

Happily, most of the kids had vacated the deck. He assumed they were boarding their way down the hill. He could only hope they'd had enough of a head start to stay well ahead of him.

While Liam waited for the next gondola car, Max and Jake made their way to the rack that held their snowboards. Max's path to his board was blocked by a boy of about eleven who was struggling with his bindings.

Inwardly sighing at the delay, Max crouched down on one knee. "Need some help?" he asked, masking his frustration with a friendly tone.

He couldn't help but wonder where the kid's parents were or why a member of the jamboree staff or even the ski hill staff hadn't already assisted the boy. Max had seen numerous officials wandering the slopes in bright yellow jackets with the name of the hill plastered across the back.

"It's stuck," the boy whined, jamming at the buckle with his fingers.

Max looked at the kid's face and realized the boy was fighting back tears.

"Don't worry." He did his best to sound reassuring. "We can fix it up."

Stripping off his gloves, Max straightened a bent buckle on one of the mechanisms. Then he pulled the strap through, tightening it until it was secure.

"How does that feel?" he asked the boy.

The boy flexed his foot. "Okay." He sniffed.

Max straightened as Jake came up behind them, one foot secured to his board, the other pushing himself along the even ground.

As Max reached for his own board, he noticed the boy glancing worriedly around.

"Are you here with you parents?"

"My friends."

"Oh." Max glanced around for a likely looking group. "Can you see them?"

"They left." The boy pointed to the start of a medium-difficulty run. "That way."

"They left you behind?" *Nice friends.*

The boy nodded, looking both embarrassed and upset.

Moving a few feet to the top of the slope, Max strapped his boots to his board while Jake secured his free foot. This was really none of their concern. But it wasn't like they could leave the poor kid to his own devices.

"What's your name?" Max asked the kid.

"Ethan."

"Well, Ethan." Max snapped his goggles into place and did a quick check to make sure Ethan was all set to go. "I guess you'd better ride down with us."

The boy brightened.

"I'm Max, and this is Jake. I'm sure we can find your friends at the bottom."

As they headed down the run, it quickly became obvious that Ethan's enthusiasm outstripped his skills.

Max slowed his pace, pulling behind the kid, cringing at his sloppy technique and his wobbling balance. Ethan gamely tried to take a few, small jumps, but he took fall after fall on the landings.

Finally, Max couldn't stand it any longer. He pulled up beside him and helped him to his feet.

"Bend your knees," Max instructed. "Go back on your heels," he demonstrated. "But don't overbalance the landing. Here, hold out your arms, like this."

To his credit, Ethan watched carefully. He bit his lower lip and nodded in obvious determination.

"You want to watch me do it once?" asked Max.

"Yeah. That would be good."

"Okay." Max pointed to a small mound downhill from them. "That one."

He took it slow and easy, jumping just enough to get some air, exaggerating his balancing movements on the other side.

Ethan took a turn. Surprisingly, he kept his feet on the landing. He grinned at the accomplishment, punching a celebratory fist in the air.

Max chose another small one, and Ethan followed.

It was the longest run of his life, but when they came to a rest point midway, Ethan took the most impressive jump so far, getting a fair degree of air, then landing it and keeping upright.

Max found himself shouting in celebration, while Ethan sprayed up a small rooster tail of snow and grinned ear to ear.

The sound of cheering erupted beside them, and Max turned to see a group of six boys calling congratulations to Ethan.

"Nice ollie!" shouted one.

"Bangin'," called another.

"How'd you get so rad in the last hour?" asked a third, coming closer.

Head up, shoulders square, Ethan jerked his thumb in Max's direction. "This guy knows how to rip."

One of the boys peered up at him. "Aren't you that Max something? The crocodile-wrestling guy on TV?"

The group's interest swung to Max.

"That's me," Max admitted. He pulled off his glove to shake the boys' hands. "Max Gray."

"Awesome," someone whispered.

One of the boys elbowed Ethan. "Ethan, how d'you know Max Gray?"

Ethan suddenly seemed a little starstruck.

"We met up top," Max offered into the silence. "Took a ride down together."

Ethan seemed to find his voice. "Can you show us something else?"

Max glanced at Jake, who was clearly struggling not to laugh at his predicament.

"Sure," Max agreed fatalistically. Part of his job was being nice to the viewers. Though the viewers were generally quite a bit older than these.

He made his way down the rest of the mountain, stopping and starting, seven young boys in tow, each struggling to execute his instructions. He had to admit, it wasn't all bad. The kids were friendly and polite, and most of them made some improvement in the course of the run.

At the end, they met up with the broader jamboree group. Someone produced a marking pen, and he signed all the boy's helmets. Jake, of course, got footage of the whole thing. Max knew he was never going to hear the end of this.

"I heard some of the kids talking about him this morning in the lobby," Gillian said as she and Cara made their way along the shoveled sidewalk. It was shortly after noon, and they were checking out the restaurants along the street. "Said he taught them to snowboard yesterday. It was total hero worship."

"Are you sure it was kids?"

"Yes. I can tell the difference between ten-year-olds and twenty-year-olds. He signed their helmets. I don't see how he can hate kids that much."

"That doesn't sound like Max," Cara ventured.

"Maybe you're wrong about him," said Gillian.

"He told me himself that he didn't like children," Cara pointed out. There wasn't any ambiguity in Max's opinion about having a family. If he was teaching them to snowboard, it must have been under duress.

Gillian stopped in her tracks and pointed to the door of the Big Sky Restaurant. "Here?"

The upscale family restaurant advertised gourmet burgers, and Cara was starving. "Looks fine to me."

They entered to find it warm inside, with a big stone fireplace at one end and cushioned leather seats at generous-size tables. Gillian chose a half-round booth and slid inside. Each of them snagged a menu.

"It must be the mountain air," said Cara.

Gillian grinned at her.

"Hey, you're hungry, too," Cara pointed out.

"Not as hungry as you."

Cara didn't argue the point. Instead her interest was snagged by pictures of burgers and fries.

"You'll have a whole new fan base after tonight," said a familiar voice next to their table.

Cara glanced up to meet Jake's surprised eyes.

"Cara," he greeted her with a smile. Then he looked at Gillian and his smile widened further. "And...*friend*. Do you ladies mind if we join you?"

"Please do," Gillian answered before Cara could find her voice.

"Hello, Cara." Max gave her a slight nod.

"New fan base?" asked Gillian as Jake took up the seat beside her.

"Young snowboard enthusiasts," Jake answered, holding his hand out to Gillian. "Jake Dobson, Max's cameraman."

"Gillian Cranshaw. Cara's sister."

"Not hard to guess you're related," said Jake, glancing from one woman to the other.

Max seemed to take his seat next to Cara rather reluctantly. "You sure you don't mind?" he asked.

"No problem." She could do this. She'd force herself to do this, coolly, casually, unemotionally.

They were both in Fields. It was a small town. For the next few days, she'd have to cope with running into Max. It was probably good practice.

She turned her attention back to the menu. "I think I'll have a milk shake," she mused, her sweet craving still out in full force. "Chocolate."

"Cara always did go wild at lunchtime." Gillian laughed.

"What about you?" Jake asked Gillian. "You ever get wild?" His intimate tone drew Cara's attention. Appreciation of Gillian's beauty was clear in his eyes.

Cara had seen that look from men a hundred times. Although she and Gillian looked very much alike, Gillian had always had a glamorous streak, a little more makeup, a little heavier on the jewelry, professional highlights in her hair, designer clothes and an eye for accessorizing that Cara admired.

Gillian rolled her eyes at Jake's interest, then she deftly shifted her attention to Max. "Nice to see you again, Max. The kids were all talking about you in the lobby this morning."

"No good deed goes unpunished," Max drawled.

"Did something happen?" asked Cara, glancing from man to man.

"Montana isn't the strongest market for *After Dark*," Jake explained. "Max was hoping to stay a little bit under the radar."

"Not that you're helping me any," Max pointed out to Jake.

"I got some good footage yesterday. There's a chance editing can turn it into a sweet human interest story." Jake closed his menu. "It's not like we're getting anything on the president."

Cara looked at Max, curiosity piqued. "You don't say?"

"Don't give away our information," Max admonished Jake.

"Not blowing the case wide open?" Cara pressed Max.

"Too busy teaching small children to snowboard," he replied laconically as he perused the sandwich section of the menu. "And you?"

"Haven't been teaching anything to small children." She felt her arm drop reflexively to her lap.

Then Gillian smiled innocently over her menu at Max. "Do you have any children of your own?" she asked.

Cara nearly choked. Had her sister lost her mind?

Jake coughed out a hearty laugh. "Not Max. At least, none that he knows about."

Cara felt light-headed for a moment.

"No children," Max told Gillian in a firm voice. "You?"

"No children," Gillian responded. "No husband. No boyfriend."

*"Really?"* Jake angled his body toward her.

"Down, boy," Gillian put in, dropping her gaze to the open menu. "I think I'll go with a strawberry shake."

"I'm recently single myself," Jake told her smoothly.

"Quit hitting on Cara's sister," said Max.

"It's fine," Gillian assured Max with an impish smile that said she dealt with it all the time. Cara knew she did.

"You think this is hitting on her?" Jake asked in a mock-wounded tone. "Clearly, you've never seen me in action."

"I've seen you in action on six continents," Max replied. "I like Cara, and I don't want you messing with her family."

Gillian's gaze met Cara's. *He likes you,* was her silent message. *Makes no difference,* was Cara's message back. She and

Max were headed in completely different directions in life. They were already in opposing worlds, and no amount of liking each other was going to change that.

# Five

They'd had to cut their lunch short. News that Max was in town had spread around Fields, and the level of attention on him continued to grow. Cara could tell that it frustrated him. And after the tenth polite but intrusive autograph request, they took their meals to go.

"We should head up to one of the hotel rooms," Jake suggested as they converged on the sidewalk.

"I'm in a closet," Cara responded. "The press office can't be extravagant with the taxpayers' money."

"I've got this suite thing on the top floor," said Gillian. "I take it we're hiding out?"

"I don't think I'm going to get any peace." Max frowned. "But the rest of you can do whatever you want." He looked a cross between brave and pathetic.

Cara shook her head. "Are you trying to be a martyr?"

"How'm I doing?"

"Poorly," said Cara.

"We're not going to abandon you," Gillian put in staunchly.

Cara wished her sister hadn't said that. Hanging out with Max seemed to send her on an emotional roller-coaster.

"Let's go to Max's villa," Jake suggested. "It's bigger than mine, and it's the highest one on the hillside. The place has a killer view, and if you want to wear off the milk shake, there's a path that leads to the hot springs."

"More like a goat track," Max put in. "Going down's not bad, but on the way up I kept wishing we had ropes and crampons."

"Works for me," Gillian said brightly.

Cara shot a sidelong glance at her sister. She sure hoped Gillian wasn't trying to throw Cara and Max together in the hopes that something sparked between them. If she was, the plan would definitely fail.

The men's SUV was closest, parked over in the hospital parking lot. Since it was starting to snow, and the road to the villas was slippery and steep, they all piled into the four-wheel-drive with Max at the wheel. The snow grew heavier as they approached the first of the villas. The local radio station was predicting six inches of new powder up in the peaks.

"I'm definitely taking a few runs tomorrow," said Jake from the backseat.

"As long as we can do it alone," Max put in. Then he glanced at Cara, who was sitting in the front passenger seat watching the big snowflakes splatter against the windshield. "I don't think I'm giving away any deep secrets if I tell you we're getting squat from our interviews."

"The most interesting footage I've taken this week was Max's snowboard lessons," said Jake. "Everything else was a waste of time and effort."

"What's not working for you?" Cara asked Max. From her perspective, things were terrific. She hadn't unearthed any time bombs that would hurt the president.

"Nice people saying nice things about what a nice boy the

president was as a teenager doesn't exactly make for riveting television."

"Just as I suspected." Cara couldn't keep the smug satisfaction from her voice. "You're going after the salacious story. You'd love it if you unearthed a scandal. No matter how detrimental to the country's governance or who you hurt."

The tires slid out beneath them, and Max wrestled the steering wheel to bring the vehicle back under control. "That's hardly fair."

"You want ratings, Max." It was no secret how the news media worked.

"My producer wants ratings," Max responded. "I want to know about Eleanor Albert."

"For the pure pursuit of knowledge, I'm sure."

"Well, I'm sure not going to cover anything up."

Oh, those were fighting words to Cara. "Are you implying that I will?"

The SUV automatically shifted to a lower gear, jerking everyone back in their seats.

"I'm implying that your loyalty is to the president." His gaze locked with hers.

"You're right about that." Her jaw tensed. Spending time with Max was an even worse idea than she'd imagined. "You should take us back to the hotel."

"No."

"Excuse me?"

"The burgers are already cold, and the milk shakes are already warm. And we're here." He skidded into a driveway and ratcheted the SUV into park.

"Maybe we could call a truce?" Gillian suggested from the backseat.

"The man's impossible," Cara ground out.

"He's just doing his job," Gillian responded.

Cara flashed her sister an annoyed glare. How dare she

be on Max's side? She opened her mouth to argue, but she stopped herself.

She didn't need to get petty to make her point. Max was doing his job. And Cara was doing hers. The conflict between them wasn't going to be resolved, and Gillian was going to figure that out very quickly.

"Fine," she agreed. "Truce."

Max didn't answer. But he did exit the vehicle, grabbing the bag of burgers.

Gillian came up beside her as they took the fieldstone staircase to the front door of the villa. "Are you trying to create a self-fulfilling prophecy?" she hissed in Cara's ear.

"What are you talking about?"

"You know how you get. He's a perfectly decent guy."

"He's a reporter who hates children."

"Right. I'm surprised he didn't throw those boys down the mountain, instead of, you know—"

"Yeah, yeah. I get it. He was nice to them, even though he didn't like them."

"I'm just saying, pay it forward for those young boys, be nice to their hero while he eats his burger. Can you do that?"

Cara could do that. She would do that. She was a professional. Then Gillian's other words echoed in her mind. "What do you mean 'how I get'?"

But Gillian skipped the last couple of steps to enter the villa. Max held the door, standing to one side, as Cara followed her sister inside.

The place was magnificent. Perched on the steep hillside, it had floor-to-ceiling windows across a two-story living and dining area. An archway at one end of the massive room led to a kitchen. On the opposite side of the foyer, was a large ski storage room, where they all hung their coats. A staircase led to an open second-floor hallway, which Cara presumed gave access to the bedroom. And beneath the bedroom, behind the living area, was a media room and a library.

"You can't see it through the falling snow," said Jake, "but the town is down there." He pointed. "And the lake is off to the south. You can see the highway winding away into the mountains. And if you go out on the balcony—"

"Pass," Gillian put in.

Jake smiled at her. "From the balcony, if you look north, you can see the lights from the ski runs at night."

"Clearly not the taxpayers' money," Cara muttered under her breath.

"I heard that," said Max, as Jake and Gillian moved off on an impromptu tour.

"Sorry," Cara responded, realizing Gillian was right. She was definitely being pricklier than usual.

"Let's eat," he suggested dryly, making his way to a dining table for eight.

"How many bedrooms?" Cara asked, forcing herself to be pleasant. She followed him and took up a chair facing the window.

She could easily imagine the view Jake had described. Though right now, it was turning into a wall of white. She'd been told about the sudden storms in the mountains and how they disappeared just as quickly as they came up, leaving miles and miles of champagne powder on the slopes.

"Just the one," said Max. "The villas are adults only. I think they cater to honeymoon couples and romantic weekends. Jake moved us up here when we discovered the jamboree down at the hotel."

"It must be nice and quiet."

"Very quiet." Max smiled. "And very nice."

Cara wanted to protest that kids weren't all bad. But instead she peeled the foil from her cheeseburger.

Max took a large bite of his and chewed. Then he wiped his mouth with a paper napkin. "Man, that's good."

Cara tasted her own burger and nodded in agreement. Lukewarm or not, the burger was delicious. She followed it up with a sip of her melting chocolate shake, and her stomach rumbled softly in appreciation.

If Max heard, he didn't comment. "Are you heading back to D.C. soon?" he asked.

"Likely tomorrow," she answered between bites.

"Same here. I don't think the story's in Fields, and we need to start prep work for South America."

"South America?" Cara prompted, popping a couple of cool fries in her mouth.

"We're going up into the Andes, looking at the impact of global mineral prices on exploration and on indigenous people." Max's jade-green eyes grew more intense as he spoke. "I'm particularly interested in the influence of China on local governments, labor standards and immigration."

She was struck, as she often was, by the depth of his understanding of his stories. He truly was a committed and ethical journalist. She felt guilty all over again for some of the accusations she'd tossed his way. "You're a very smart man, aren't you?"

"What I lack in intellect, I make up for in curiosity. I love a puzzle."

Cara didn't think Max was lacking anything in intelligence. She was beginning to agree with her sister. Her baby might have hit the genetic jackpot by having Max for a father.

"What about the president's paternity mystery?" she asked. "Does it make you curious?"

To her surprise, Max gave a careless shrug. He took a drink of his milk shake before answering. "Not really. Ariella's either his daughter or she's not. He either knew about it or he didn't. Neither case is going to fundamentally shift national policy in any way. And, honestly, I don't think Ariella's the story."

That statement surprised Cara. It worried her as well. "What is the story?" she couldn't help asking.

"You know I can't tell you that."

She knew that. Of course she knew that. Their entire relationship had centered around avoiding conflicts of interest. As a journalist, Max wasn't permitted to share his story angles with the White House press office.

She set down her burger, wiping her fingertips on the paper napkin. "I'm sorry I asked."

"It never hurts to ask."

"Yes, it does. It hurts to ask a question that puts someone else in an awkward position." She'd insisted he not do that with her, and now she was breaking her own rule.

"I'm a big boy, Cara." His expression went soft. "You don't scare me."

"You scare me plenty," she offered honestly.

"Okay, I can tell you this much."

"No, don't." She dramatically put her hands over her ears.

Jake's voice drawled as he and Gillian entered the room. "What is the man saying to you now?"

"Nothing," Cara quickly put in, removing her hands from her ears. "We were just joking around."

"You two?" Jake raised a brow. "I find that hard to believe." Then he glanced at the burgers and shakes. "Okay, this is sad."

"They're not bad," said Max, finishing his last bite.

"This from a man who once ate chocolate-covered ants." Jake looked to Gillian. "Believe me, you do not want to trust his opinion on cuisine."

"It was pretty good," said Cara, backing up her claim by polishing off the last bite of her own burger.

But Gillian frowned at the paper bag and cardboard cups. "Think I'll pass."

"Let's go grab something fresh," Jake suggested to her.

Cara started to protest, but her sister was nodding at Jake in agreement.

"We'll just be a few minutes," Jake promised, moving swiftly to the storage room, retrieving Gillian's coat and holding it out for her.

"What about the storm?" Cara tried, pointing out the window. Her next move was going to be to offer to go with them.

"It's letting up," said Gillian, allowing Jake to help her with her puffy white coat.

"We've got four-wheel drive," said Jake.

Gillian spoke directly to Cara. "You can stay here and play nice with Max."

Cara returned her sister's mischief with a glare. Gillian's not-so-secret plan was never going to work. No matter how nice Cara was to Max, he wasn't going to have an epiphany and realize he'd wanted to be a family man all along.

She started to rise. "I don't mind coming along for—"

"Not necessary," Jake put in. "Put up your feet. Finish your milk shake. The view's going to be spectacular in about fifteen minutes. We'll be back before you know it."

With that, they were out the door, leaving silence behind them.

"Do you think they wanted to be alone?" Max drawled.

Cara turned to him. "Huh?"

"It was pretty obvious."

That hadn't been Cara's read of the situation at all. She watched the black SUV back out of the driveway and head downhill. "You think?"

"Short of a neon sign, I don't think they could have made it any plainer."

No. Cara was pretty sure this was Gillian's not-so-subtle way of giving her some time alone with Max in the ridiculous and romantic hope that something would come of it.

"Sorry you got stuck with me," Max offered, watching her expression closely.

"I'm not stuck with—"

Okay, so she was stuck with Max. He definitely wasn't her first choice for a companion this afternoon. And it occurred to her that Jake and Gillian had left with the only vehicle. There was no escaping the villa until they returned. Good thing they were coming right back.

"Tell me more about South America." She forced herself to sit back in her chair and take the situation in stride.

Max's phone beeped, signaling that he had a text. He glanced at the screen.

"It's Jake."

"Already?"

"He wants us to turn on the local NCN news affiliate. It's five o'clock in D.C., and he wants to see if they run the snowboarding story."

"You don't look too happy about that," Cara observed.

"I don't like fluff."

"I thought it was the kids you didn't like." The words jumped out before she thought them through.

"Those, too," Max agreed.

Cara knew she needed to stop probing like that. Every time she asked a question about kids, he answered it honestly, and she felt even more depressed about her future.

While he located the TV remote control, Cara polished off the last of her fries and finished the milk shake. Normally, a burger and fries would have left her feeling stuffed. But she was still a little hungry. If this was the pregnancy affecting her, she'd have to be careful for the next nine months. It was embarrassing, but Gillian's abandoned burger was starting to look good.

Max located the NCN affiliate and turned up the volume. He sat down on one of two matching sofas. Cara moved to join him in the living room area, choosing an armchair that faced the television.

Sure enough, they ran with the story. Jake had even managed to get some sound of Max explaining the fundamentals of snowboarding and the kids cheering each other on.

The segment was brief, but Cara was astonished by Max's patience with the boys. It was clear they were in awe of him and just as clear that they were learning. Their techniques improved as they made their way down the slope. And, at the end, they were all obviously proud of their performance and overwhelmed by getting that kind of attention from a celebrity.

When Max signed everybody's helmets, she had to blink back a tear.

"Wow," said Max, shutting off the television. "That was quite the fluff piece."

Cara's emotion evaporated. "I thought it was nice."

"They'll milk it for suburban mom viewers, I guess," said Max.

"You looked like you were having fun." She couldn't bring herself to believe he'd hated it. She found her hand resting on her stomach again, and her mind started down the dangerous path of Max's suitability as a father.

"The whole time I was with them, I was wishing I could snowboard alone," he told her. "But they were viewers, so I had to behave. It'll never make the story. But given a choice, I'd have ditched the kids."

Well, that certainly put a stop to Cara's fanciful musings. "Are you saying it was all PR?"

"I'm saying that I'm not the saint the network would like me to be."

"So, you still don't like kids."

"There's a lot of real estate between liking kids and being friendly to the viewers. Just because I did my job, doesn't mean I'm going to become a grade-school teacher."

His phoned chimed, and he moved to the dining room table to retrieve it.

"Hey," he said simply.

Then he paused. "Right now?" Another pause. "Yeah, we'll be here. I'll tell her. Okay. Bye." He hung up.

"What is it?"

"Jake and Gillian won't be coming back right away, because Gillian had to get on a conference call."

Cara stomach fluttered. "Are you kidding me?"

"Apparently, it's morning in China, and the Chinese office needed to talk to her before the start of business. Her laptop is in her hotel suite, so they've gone back there."

"But…they…"

"Does that sound plausible to you?" Max asked, his face taking on a knowing expression. "Because I know Jake pretty well, and there's every chance they might be—"

"That's my *sister* you're talking about."

"Your sister doesn't have a sex life?"

"She's not sleeping with Jake." The two had only just met. "She has business interests in China, important business interests in China. I'm sure it's exactly what they say it is."

"Okay." Max held up his hands in surrender.

"I'm not blindly defending my sister's honor."

"You are, but that's admirable."

"I'm saying she does business with China."

"And I'm saying Jake is attracted to her."

"That doesn't mean the feeling is mutual."

Max returned to the living area. "We'll likely never know."

"I already know."

"You're cute, you know that?"

His smile sent an insidious warmth spreading through her body. It suddenly struck her exactly how foolish she'd been to let them end up alone.

"Max—" she began to protest, but then a rumbling sound distracted her. It was deep and low, a vibration as much as a sound.

Max's face blanched. He stiffened for a second then let out a guttural cussword. Before she knew what was happening, his arm was around her waist and he was dragging her.

"What?" she managed to sputter, even as the sound grew louder and the floor began to shake.

Max pulled her through the door to the bathroom, lifting her into the giant tub. "Lie down!" he commanded, disappearing.

They were having an earthquake. She'd never heard of a bathtub as a refuge place, but it seemed as good a place as any. She lay down.

In a few seconds, Max was back with her. He'd dragged the big square coffee table into the bathroom. He quickly lay down above her and put the table facedown over the tub.

The roaring grew to a piercing screech. The entire world was shaking around them. Cara reflexively clung to him, burying her face in his shoulder.

"Earthquake?" she managed in a hoarse voice.

"Avalanche." His arms tightened around her.

The lights flicked out, and the world turned murky gray.

"Are we still alive?" Cara's voice was barely a whisper in Max's ear.

The air had been silent around them for a full minute.

"We are," he answered, straining to hear any sounds around them.

"Is it over?"

"Maybe."

"*Maybe?*"

"One avalanche can trigger another." He kept his voice low, shifting onto his side to put her in a more comfortable position. In his rush to get her protected, he'd come down directly on top of her. "Am I hurting you?"

"No. I don't think so." She flexed. "Do we need to whisper?"

"No."

They both fell silent.

"How long do we wait?" she asked.

He slipped his fingers into the crack between the upside-down table and the tub, pushing the table aside. "I think we're okay."

He levered himself out of the tub, then turned to offer Cara his hand. She took it, and he hoisted her out, making sure she was steady on her feet.

His cell phone chimed from the living room.

Her voice held a slight tremor. "Do you think anybody was hurt?"

"I don't know." Max feared the worst.

His villa was still standing, but he'd experienced avalanches close-up before, and this had been a big one. The phone trilled again.

"You should get that," said Cara.

"You okay?"

She disentangled her hand from his. "I'm fine."

She looked pale but seemed all right.

He went after his phone, noting Jake's number.

"You guys okay?" Max said in greeting.

"Man, am I glad to hear your voice," said Jake. "How's Cara?"

"We're fine." Max watched as Cara came through the bathroom door. She paused to steady herself with a hand on the sofa back.

"They're fine," Jake informed someone at his end of the conversation. Max assumed it was Gillian.

"It must have just missed you," Jake said to Max.

"I haven't had a chance to look out. But I thought the villa was going to come off its foundation. What can you see from down there?"

"Half a mountainside covered in snow. The street is full of frightened people."

"Did it reach the town?"

"No. And the main slide didn't hit the ski hill."

"Thank goodness for that. Anyone hurt?" Max was itching to get into the fray. But there was no way off the mountain.

"Search and rescue is scrambling. But I don't think we're going to know anything for a while. You two okay where you are?"

"Sure," said Max. "The power's out, but we've got the fireplace."

"Judging from what I'm seeing here, you'll be there overnight."

"I guessed as much," said Max with a glance at Cara. Some of the color was coming back to her face. "Can you keep the two of us out of the news?"

"Sure," said Jake.

Max knew Cara wouldn't want anyone to know they were together. "I'm a little tired of being the story."

"Understood. I got some footage of it coming down. Had to use my tablet instead of a camera, but it looks like it came out okay."

Max couldn't help a half smile at that. Jake saw the world in video clips. While most people's reaction to danger was to wisely turn and run, Jake's reaction was to grab the nearest video recording device.

Jake wasn't finished. "If your phone battery's holding up, can you take a few minutes of footage from your vantage point?"

"I'll see what I can get."

"Can you put Cara on? Gillian wants to talk to her."

"Sure." Max moved to where Cara was sitting and held out the phone. "Gillian."

Cara seemed to brace herself. "Hello?"

She listened for a moment. "Yes. I am." Another pause. "Not a scratch. Well, maybe a little shell-shocked." Then she gave a nervous laugh. "Really?"

Curious to see what had happened outside, Max headed onto the snowy balcony, pulling the door closed behind him.

The scene around him was surreal. The bulk of the slide had fallen to the north of the villa complex. It had created a jagged slope of solid packed snow. The edge of it had stacked up against the side of the villa. Max knew from experience it would be hard as concrete.

Max and Cara weren't the only ones who'd been incredibly lucky in avoiding the disaster. The rest of the villas were south of Max's, farther down the hill. To that side, the slide paths were smaller, narrow, crashing their way through ravines and gullies, sticking to the low ground and, from what Max could see, missing the buildings.

He heard the door slide open behind him.

"Oh, my—"

He turned to where Cara had stopped dead in the doorway, staring at the moonscape beside the villa.

"The road's gone," she stated in astonishment, remembering to come outside and close the door behind her.

"It'll take a while to dig that out."

She moved up beside him at the rail. "Are we stranded?"

"For now. They could send a helicopter for us. But they probably don't have all that many resources, and the injured have to be their priority."

"Of course," Cara agreed. "Gillian said she offered them the use of her jet. They may need to evacuate some of the injured people to bigger hospitals and bring in more rescuers."

"It'll be dark soon," Max couldn't help observing. He sure hoped nobody was stranded on the ski hill in all this.

Cara shivered as she focused on the setting sun.

"We should go inside." His instinct was to put an arm around her shoulders. But he quickly stopped himself.

She'd been firm on the boundaries of their relationship, and he couldn't discount the possibility of telescope lenses trained on the avalanche damage picking them up.

"We really should go inside," he repeated.

If there was any chance of prying eyes, he wanted Cara out of sight. The fewer people who knew she was with him, the better off she'd be.

This time, she turned. He swiftly moved to pull open the sliding glass door, letting her through first.

With the power out, it was going to get cold and dark inside the villa very soon. He was guessing other people were trapped at other villas, but they were spaced too far apart for him to know for sure. At least he hadn't seen any villas with obvious structural damage. That was a good sign.

There was newspaper, matches and firewood next to the big stone fireplace. He'd also noticed two oil lamps on the mantel, and candles were placed at various spots around the room.

He lit the oil lamps, then handed the matches to Cara, keeping one for himself. "You want to look around and light a few candles?"

"Sure." She took the matches from his hand.

He knew it was better to keep her busy. If she stood around thinking about their close call, there was still a chance she could go into shock.

While she moved around the room, he crouched down on one knee and began laying a fire.

Luckily, the villas seemed well-prepared for a rustic lifestyle. Either they'd done it for the ambiance or power outages were common up here. But he knew there was a larger wood box at the back of the storage room. They'd be fine overnight, for a few days if it came to that.

He lit the newspaper, watching as flames curled up around the smaller pieces of kindling. "Your sister has a jet?" he opened.

"Her company has a jet."

"But she owns the company."

"That she does." Cara had lit half a dozen candles, and the room was filled with a soft glow of yellow light.

"Is it a big company?" Max added a couple of larger pieces to the fire. Satisfied with the crackling sound and the height of the flames, he closed the glass doors, adjusting the damper to the open position.

"It gets bigger all the time." Cara handed back the matches, and he put them on the stone mantel.

"Define *bigger*." He gestured to the sofa directly across from the fireplace. They might as well make themselves comfortable. Then he gave a laugh at his own question. "I guess it's big enough to buy a jet."

"One of their software applications has been widely adopted by the international health-care industry. Since that started, I think the sky's the limit." Cara settled into one corner of the sofa.

Max gave a low whistle as he took up the other end of the couch. "Successful family you've got going."

"I think that depends on who you ask."

"A member of the White House staff and an IT entrepreneur? Under what benchmark is that not successful?"

"Rural Wisconsin."

"Wisconsin has something against high tech?"

"If my parents had their way, Gillian and I would have found ourselves a couple of nice dairy farmers, settled down in the Rim Creek area and started producing grandchildren."

"Ahh." Now he understood.

"Fortunately for everybody, my brother found a wonderful local girl and fell in love. She's pregnant with their third at the moment, and they seem perfectly happy living on the farm."

"Farm life's not for you?"

Cara gave an exaggerated shudder. "Gillian and I couldn't wait to leave."

Then, unexpectedly, she smiled. "When I was in fifth grade, Gillian studied with me every night. We had a secret plan for me to skip grade six so we'd graduate the same year, and we could go off to college together."

"Did it work?"

"Not that year. But I got far enough ahead that I was able to take extra classes in high school and finish early."

Max couldn't help but be impressed. "So it did work."

"Eventually. We left together for Milwaukee. After a couple of years, I switched to Harvard, and she went to MIT."

He couldn't help taking in Cara's fresh-faced beauty in the firelight. The young men of Rim Creek must have been very disappointed when she left. "You'd have made a cute dairy-maid."

"I'd have failed miserably."

"Funny how you grew up in the country and ended up in the big city. I grew up in the middle of the city and ended up craving the wilderness."

She glanced around. "You must love this."

He did. But not for the reasons she meant. They were all alone for the entire night, and his imagination was working overtime on the implications.

# Six

Candlelight bounced off the polished cherrywood table. The leather dining chairs were deep and luxurious, the fire crackled and popped in a soothing backdrop and the expensive crystal and china shone in the flickering light.

The only thing out of place was the instant oatmeal where a five-star dinner should have been. Cara's was apple cinnamon, while Max had gone with maple sugar.

Cara wasn't about to complain. Though they had no power and no heat, Max had dug out the propane barbecue on the balcony. He'd cleaned it up, got it running and boiled some water in the kettle. The hot water, along with the few provisions in the villa's kitchen, had yielded both oatmeal and tea. Left to her own devices, she wouldn't have had even that much.

Jake had sent another message from town, with the encouraging news that a group of children with only minor injuries had been rescued from one of the slopes. Work would go on all night, bringing stranded people down from the Apex Lounge at the top of the gondola. Cara had texted her boss, letting them all know she was safe, but with the warning that she was conserving the battery in her phone.

She and Max had then shut down their communication devices, and now, except for the distant glow of the town below, they were cut off from the world.

"You really were a Boy Scout," said Cara, as she blew gently on a first spoon of oatmeal.

"What makes you say that?" Max was seated directly across from her at one end of the long table. She had a view out the glass wall at the far end, and heat from the living room fire warmed her back.

"You lit the fire. You thought to use the barbecue to boil the water. I bet you know first aid and how to whittle."

"Yes to the first aid, but there weren't a lot of Boy Scouts in my neighborhood."

Cara knew Max had grown up in south Chicago, and she knew his single mother had worked as a waitress. "So how did you learn all that?"

"Trial and error. Mostly error. While I was in college, I took some adventure vacations, embarrassed myself, nearly got people killed. When you grow up in a basement apartment without so much as a hammer or a screwdriver, never mind camping equipment or a father to show you how they're used, you hit your eighteenth birthday with a bit of a handicap."

Cara was sorry she'd asked. "I didn't mean—"

"I'm not upset with you. I'm not upset with anybody. Life is what it is sometimes. I can't control how I grew up. I can only control what I do from here on in."

She knew she shouldn't ask, but she couldn't help herself. "Is that why you don't want a family? Because of your bad memories?"

"There are a lot of reasons why I don't want a family. Experience, yeah. I wouldn't wish my childhood on anyone. And I wouldn't wish my mother's life on anyone. Every single day of her life was a grind."

"Poverty was a big part of that," Cara pointed out.

Max didn't respond to her comment. "Don't even get me started on genetics," he said. "I'm the product of a father who was willing to walk out on the mother of his child, walk out on his own son, walk out on his responsibility. You think the world needs more people from that particular gene pool?"

"You're not like him."

"Oh, yes, I am. I'm here today, but I'll be gone tomorrow. I may use a jet plane instead of a bus, but I'm living in my own, selfish world, following my own, selfish dreams."

"But you're not leaving anyone behind." Cara knew it was a completely different situation.

"Exactly," Max agreed. "That's the beauty of the system. I'm not hurting anyone. I could get shot and killed in a conflict zone or swept down a waterfall and drown and it wouldn't matter one little bit."

"It would matter."

"Yeah, well, NCN's ratings might drop. But that would be a temporary—"

"Your *friends* would miss you." She couldn't stand to hear him talk that way. He was loved and respected by his friends, his peers, even his viewers.

"Hey, I don't mean that as a bad thing. I mean it as a source of freedom. Of course my friends would miss me. If they died, I'd miss them, too. But losing a friend is nothing compared to losing parents or a spouse. I'm not going to be the guy who leaves loved ones behind to fend for themselves."

"Let me get this straight. You're protecting your potential wife and your potential children by never allowing them to exist?"

Max gave a thoughtful nod. "Yeah, that's pretty much it."

"There's something wrong with that logic." More than she would tell him. More than she could ever tell him.

"Not from where I'm sitting."

"You can't live in a bubble, Max."

She tried to tell herself that none of this was a surprise. She'd known all along Max wasn't father material. He wasn't even relationship material. She had no right to get all maudlin now just because he'd laid it out in no uncertain terms.

Nothing had changed in the last five minutes. She still had a couple of months before she'd even have to hide her pregnancy. She'd decided to ask Lynn about an international posting. There was an ongoing need for communications support in the embassies. She'd like London, or maybe Sydney, or even Montreal. Her child could learn French while he or she was growing up.

"I'm not living in a bubble," Max countered. "I jump out of airplanes, climb mountains, ford rivers. I even wrestled a crocodile once."

"Ah, the infamous crocodile story." She forced herself to lighten things up, taking another bite of her oatmeal.

"Okay," he said. "In the interest of full disclosure—but I warn you, what happens while trapped by an avalanche, stays in the avalanche."

She managed a smile at that. "Good grief, what are you about to confess?"

"My guide on that trip? He was nearby in the boat. And I think, well, I know, he conked the gator on the head with his paddle before the wrestling match started."

Cara worked up a censorious frown, her tone clearly disapproving. "Are you saying the crocodile was incapacitated?"

"I'm guessing. But Jake got the footage, and we all kind of agreed to pretend it was a bigger deal than it was."

"You fought a punch-drunk crocodile?"

"And won."

"And parlayed it into the he-man, adventurer reputation you now enjoy amongst your innocent and apparently duped fans."

There was a twinkle in his eye. "I never claimed to be a Boy Scout."

"Okay. I guess I'm in no position to be snooty. I've never wrestled any kind of crocodile."

"Just the vultures in the press."

"Some days, I wish somebody would clonk them on the head with a paddle."

Max turned thoughtful. "There's nothing in Fields for either of us. I mean about Eleanor."

Her guard went up. "You know I can't discuss that with you."

"I'm not asking for information. I'm just making an observation. Nobody's talking. Nobody admits to remembering anything of significance. Which means either there's a conspiracy going on here worthy of the CIA or people truly don't remember."

"I think they don't remember," Cara put in before she could stop herself.

"I agree," Max returned. "And doesn't that beg the question of how Angelica Pierce and ANS found the story?"

Cara had to agree that it did. "Do you have a theory?"

Max leaned slightly forward. "Are you offering quid pro quo on an information exchange?"

"You know I can't do that."

"Then I don't have a theory." He paused. "Except that I do. And it's a good one."

It was her turn to lean forward. "You're bluffing."

"Only one way for you to find out."

There were, in fact, two ways for her to find out. But the second one was worse than the first.

"I can tell what you're thinking," he taunted.

"No, you can't."

"You're thinking that if you got naked, I'd tell you anything."

"I am *not* going to bribe you with sex."

He seemed to consider that. "Too bad. Because it'd work."

* * *

Max knew he had to keep himself busy for the rest of the evening. Because if he let his attention get stalled on Cara, he'd go stark, raving mad.

He'd cleaned up the dishes, refilled the wood box and checked the walls for damage where the avalanche snow had piled up. Now he was methodically working his way through the drawers and cupboards in the living area, looking for anything that might be useful to them if they were stuck here for a couple more days.

Cara had hung her blazer in the closet, commandeered a fuzzy robe from the powder room to help her keep warm and borrowed a pair of Max's socks to use as slippers. She should have looked comical, curled up in a corner of the sofa with a magazine in her hand, but she was sexy.

"What did you find?" she called across the room, having noted he was staring vacantly into the bottom of a cabinet.

He stopped himself from turning to look at her again. "Board games." He pulled one out at random. "Monopoly?"

"I haven't played that in years."

"What do you play? *Angry Birds?*" he asked her.

She laughed. "Angry voters."

He couldn't help but smile at that. "Are you winning?"

"Hardly ever."

He came to his feet, Monopoly game in hand. "Care to take me on?" He was about to run out of busywork, and concentrating on Monopoly was better than concentrating on Cara.

"I thought I was already taking you on," she returned. But she closed the magazine and set it on the table.

He decided to take that as a yes.

He made his way to the dining room table, moving a couple of candles to one side, then opened the old box to see if enough of the pieces were there to play a game.

Surprisingly, the contents seemed mostly intact, if a bit dog-eared and faded.

Cara pulled up a chair. "Is the dog there?"

"We have the dog." Max unfolded the board between them and handed her the game piece.

"What are you taking?" she asked, reaching for the piles of colored money and starting to sort.

"Top hat," he decided.

"Not the race car?"

He frowned. "It looks like an import."

"You're an American muscle car guy?"

"That's right. Nothing quite like touring a Mustang GT convertible out on Route 1." He got comfortable in the chair across from her, then located the dice and stacked the game cards in their respective piles.

Cara paused, her blue eyes going dreamy. "That sounds nice."

"I'll take you anytime you want to go. Well, we might want to wait for April or May. Unless we start in Georgia." In the winter, he always used a hardtop.

"You have a convertible?"

"I have three."

"You don't think that's a little excessive?"

"They're part of my collection."

She gave him a knowing smile. "In my book, 'collection' is merely a justification for excess."

"No argument from me."

She looked him straight in the eye. "Now there's a first."

"Ouch," he told her softly.

"How many cars do you own?"

Max did a quick calculation in his head. "Seventeen. But three of them are in the middle of restoration work. Most of them are vintage."

"You restore old cars?"

"I do."

"How come I didn't know this?"

"There are many things you don't know about me."

"But where? How? You live in a penthouse on Connecticut Avenue."

"I also have a house in Maine."

"Seriously?"

"Why would I make that up?"

She went back to sorting the money. "I'm just surprised. You've never mentioned it before."

"Cara, we haven't had that many dates." And most of their time alone together had been spent debating the political issues and events of the day. Or in bed. They'd spent an awful lot of their time alone together in bed. Which might explain his rather Pavlovian urge to kiss her right now.

Her hand slowed in the money sorting, then came to a stop on the stack of fifties. She looked up at him, and he could see the same thoughts making their way through her brain.

"What else don't I know about you?" she asked.

"Many, many things. Most of them good."

Her mouth twitched in a smile. "Tell me the bad ones."

"You first."

She drew back in what was obviously mock affront. "There's nothing bad about me."

"You've got the hots for a maverick, daredevil news reporter."

"Ha. Me and about a million other women."

"Thanks for the compliment." He gave her a nod. "But you're different, and you know it."

"I'm not different. I'm exactly like all those other women who run panting after the famous, sexy crocodile wrestler."

"You're different to me," he told her honestly.

"Only because I'm the one in front of you at this moment."

"Beautiful women are in front of me all the time. I don't feel this way about them."

"Then it's because you can't have me."

Max had considered that. In fact, he'd considered it quite a lot. Could the fact that Cara was off-limits make her even more appealing? Was it possible his mind was playing tricks on him? Was it possible he was that shallow?

"It's true," she crowed triumphantly at his silence.

"I sometimes wish it was," he returned. "It would make things a whole lot easier."

She tapped her index finger on the table. "If I was available. If I was, I don't know, let's say a bank manager. If I was nobody in public or political life. If I'd confessed my passionate, undying love for you and told you I wanted to spend the rest of my life with you, marry you, have your babies—"

*"What?"* Everything inside him recoiled. "Where did that come from?"

She shook her head. "You don't want me, Max."

"I don't see going from zero to a hundred in two seconds flat. I don't see pretending you're a completely different person than you are. If you were you, but had stayed on the dairy farm and were looking for a hick, hayseed husband to read *Farming Today* and escort you to the barn dance on Saturday night, I wouldn't have fallen for you."

"Well, aren't you shallow."

"But you're not that. You'd never be that. I like you just the way you are, Cara. In your current life. In your current circumstances. With your current hopes and dreams and value system."

"Where I'm the forbidden fruit."

"It's more complicated than that."

"You have no idea."

He reached across the table and covered her hand with his. "I have a very, very good idea. You and I are trapped in separate worlds. Those worlds are incompatible."

Her gaze locked on to their hands. "I'm glad to know you've been listening."

He squeezed her hand, and she didn't fight him.

"Come here," he told her softly.

"No."

"Then I'll come there." He rose and rounded the end of the dining table.

"Max." She sighed in obvious frustration.

But he took her hand again, drawing her to her feet.

She looked confused and vulnerable. "I have to protect myself from you."

"You're doing a terrific job."

"No, I'm not."

"But not tonight. You don't need to stay away from me tonight."

"Max—"

"It's just you and me, Cara. For the first time, maybe the one and only time, our lives beyond these walls are irrelevant."

"I can't—"

He put a finger across her lips. "I'm not asking for state secrets or any other kind of information. You can stop talking right now and not say another word until morning if you want."

She rolled her eyes at that.

He grinned. "That's not how I meant it, and you know it." Then he sobered, moving closer, inhaling deeply, letting her scent waft over all his senses. "For now, and only for right now, I'm simply Max and you're simply Cara. That's not going to happen again for another four years."

"Eight years," she corrected around his finger.

"That's even worse."

"Not for President Morrow."

"Do you want to be serious?"

"No. Absolutely not. I can't stand here and reasonably, logically rationalize sleeping with you tonight."

"You're overthinking, Cara."

"It's better than underthinking."

He tipped his head toward her. "Forget thinking. I'm kissing you now."

"Max," she protested softly.

It wasn't a no, he told himself. Maybe he was the one rationalizing now, but she definitely hadn't said no.

When Max's lips touched hers, Cara all but melted in the firelight. His strong arms enveloped her, pulling her tight, bringing her home. His scent was familiar, as was the pressure of his full lips, the tease of his tongue and the way his hands roamed her back, as if he needed to press every individual inch of her body against his own.

She told herself one minute, then two, then three. But Max's embrace was the best place in the world to be. He was her biggest weakness and her hopeless addiction.

He whispered against her mouth, "I've missed you so much."

He tugged the sash of her robe, his gaze penetrating hers as he pushed it off her shoulder, spreading it on the thick carpet in front of the fire. He flicked the buttons of her white blouse, one by one, until he revealed her lacy bra.

She reached for his tie.

The breath whooshed out of his body as she worked the knot. Then he stood still as she pushed his shirt buttons through their buttonholes.

The fire flickered on his tanned body, highlighting the half-dozen scars that marred his chest. She traced the longest one with her finger, and he sucked in a breath.

"Hurt?" she asked softly.

"Not at all."

She traced another. "Gator?"

"Tree branch. Parachute landing." His thumbs stroked across her midriff, teasing the skin beneath her breasts. "You are so soft, so perfect."

"That's because I don't jump out of airplanes." She stretched up for another kiss.

"Don't ever get hurt."

She had no idea how to respond, so she kissed him instead.

"I couldn't stand it if you got hurt." He deepened the kiss, pushing her blouse from her shoulders, letting it drop to the floor. The fire crackled in the quiet room, warming the air, scenting it with the light fragrance of cedar smoke.

She discarded his shirt, and he deftly removed her bra. Then he wrapped her in his arms once again, skin to skin. She let her fingertips trail down his strong back. Giving in to impulse, she feathered kisses along his chest, tasting his skin, drawing his essence into her mouth.

His hand cupped her breast, and pulsing desire skipped its way to every corner of her body. Her hands convulsed against his back.

He eased her down to the floor, laying her gently on her back against the thick robe. The villa was cooling with the night, but the fire was warm on one side and Max's body radiated heat on the other. He leaned up on one elbow. His index finger traversed a line from her neck to the tip of her shoulder. He moved over one breast, then down to her navel.

"How can you be so beautiful?" he asked as his explorations moved back higher.

He grazed the tip of her nipple, sending waves of pleasure through her body, tightening her muscles, making her spine reflexively arch.

He did it again, and her eyes fluttered closed. Then he moved to the other breast, and she felt a wash of heat and desire suffuse her skin. Goose bumps rose, and a pulse began to throb low in her belly.

He released the button of her slacks, easing down the zipper and quickly stripping them off.

Her body rife with growing arousal, she reached blindly for him.

"Lie still," he whispered in her ear.

She complied, only because her bones had gone limp and it seemed like the easiest thing to do.

"I could watch you all night long." His words made her open her eyes.

His expression was intent as his hands moved along her thighs, over the white lace of her panties, skimming the jut of her hip bone, up to the indentation of her waist.

He had beautiful green eyes, a strong chin, a chiseled nose and dark lips that she knew were near magic. Every woman in D.C. was attracted to him. Yet he was staring at her with reverence.

He teased the edge of her panties, fingers dipping beneath, finding her smooth, sensitive skin. Her back arched again, eyes closing, hands curling into involuntary fists.

"Kiss me," she rasped.

She felt him bend toward her.

She parted her lips.

But instead of tasting him, she felt his hot mouth cover her nipple. He drew it inside his mouth, tongue curling around the bud. She groaned with pleasure, one hand moving to his head, grasping tight to his dark hair.

He switched to the other breast, and the fire seemed to grow hotter. She was awash with pleasure mixed with an urgent desire. Her thighs twitched apart, primed and ready for his touch.

"Max, please," she choked out, struggling to speak around the roar in her brain.

He kissed her swollen lips, and nothing had ever felt so satisfying. His mouth opened hers, and his tongue plunged deep, over and over again.

Without breaking the erotic kiss, he stripped off her panties. He kicked off his own pants. And then he was on top of her, his satisfying weight pressing her into the carpet. She was surrounded by heat from all sides.

She kneaded his back, his buttocks, widening her thighs, urging him in.

He eased up on his elbows, brushing her mussed hair from her face, trapping her gaze with his. "There's nobody else in the world," he told her. "Nobody."

He was quick with a condom. Then he kissed her lips and

flexed his hips. Her body welcomed him in. Her legs wrapped around him, her hips tilting up. There was nobody else in the world for her, either. She couldn't imagine these feelings, this connection, coming around more than once in a lifetime.

Tonight was precious. Tonight Max was hers. She curled her body around him and hung on tight. Time and space disappeared as his rhythm pounded reality from her brain.

His broad hand found the small of her back, pulling her up, holding her to him, rocketing shock waves of pleasure to every corner of her being.

She cried out his name, and he kissed her hard and deep. Her body bucked, and her world exploded over and over again.

She sucked in gulps of air, as the world slowly righted itself again. Max's breathing was ragged in her ear. He firmed his hold on her, carefully rolling them both so that she was on top. The fire crackled beside them, sending curls of warmth across her damp, bare back.

"That was…" she began. But she didn't have the first clue what to say after that.

"It was," Max agreed. "It truly was."

Streaks of dawn stretched pink across the overcast sky, the light revealing the snowy mountain peaks behind the villa. In the king-size bed on the second floor, Max kept his breathing even, his arms still and easy where they wrapped around Cara. She was asleep, her naked body spooned in front against his, and he didn't want to disturb her.

They were toasty warm beneath the covers. But the fire had gone out hours ago, and the villa was rapidly cooling off. The cold was like reality. They could stave it off for a little while, but eventually, they'd have to face it.

Cara stirred in his arms; the movement sent a fresh wave of desire through his body.

"Is it morning?" she asked, tone husky with sleep.

"Close." He gave in to impulse and pressed his lips against the back of her neck.

"Thanks," she murmured.

"Anytime." He kissed her again, lingering.

A laugh burbled up from her chest. "I meant for last night."

"Even better."

"For being here. The fire, the tea, the oatmeal. For knowing what to do and how to do it."

"I get that a lot." He slid his palm up her smooth stomach. "What to do…" He cupped the curve of her breast. "How to do it."

She trapped his hand. "I was about to say you were a knight in shining armor."

"And you're the maiden in distress? I can work with that."

"You're blowing it, Sir Max."

He shifted so that she rolled onto her back and he could look into her face. "Where you couldn't be doing better, fair Cara."

She shook her head but was obviously fighting a smile.

"Call me Sir Max again," he cajoled.

That got him a feeble smack on the shoulder.

He laughed and wrapped her in his arms, rolling once more so that she lay full on top, the length of her naked body pressing against his.

"You need to be serious," she told him.

He sobered. "No problem." He cradled her face, urging her forward, kissing her once, then again, then deeper.

She resisted at first, but within seconds she was returning his kiss. Her body turned pliant on his, molding around him.

He inhaled her scent, reveled in the softness of her skin, tasted her sweet mouth and let his fingertips absorb the texture of her silky hair. Passion arced the length of his body, bringing it to life. His hands were itchy to explore, and they slipped to her neck, over her smooth shoulders, to the small of her back, over her buttocks to the seam of her sculpted thighs, to—

She groaned against his mouth.

He stilled. "Too soon? Sore?"

"No." She shook her head. "Well, yes. But no. Not enough to…"

He struggled to keep himself still while she made up her mind, his muscles twitching with anticipation, a pulse beginning to throb inside his ears. She was wet and hot and sweet, and he could only hover on the brink for so long.

She drew slowly back a few inches. "Max?" Her voice was breathless.

"Yeah?" he managed, his free hand curling into a fist.

"You have to promise me something."

Anything, anything, *anything*. "Now?"

"It's—"

He moved his hand, and she sucked in a breath.

"Good or bad?" he asked.

Her eyes fluttered closed, and her mouth dropped open, her back arching into his hand.

He was taking that as good. He leaned up to kiss her, drew her down to meet him and pushed everything else to the back of his mind. His body took over, mouth roaming, hands ranging. He turned her onto her back, settling between her legs.

She was all motion beneath him, her fingertips digging into his back, her kisses deep and passionate. She suckled his neck, dampening his skin, her breath then cooling the spot. Her hand moved between them, her thighs parting, her fingertips closing around him, guiding him.

"Condom," he managed as some scrap of sanity dredged up from the base of his brain.

But she kept going. "It's fine. It's good." She sucked in a couple of deep breaths. "So good," she groaned.

In reaction, his hips flexed. Her heat engulfed him, and there was no going back. He fought to measure his pace, his mind telling him to go slow, while his body strained to gallop forward.

They were a perfect fit, a perfect rhythm, and she breathed

his name over and over in his ear. He buried his face in her neck, planting wide-open kisses, reveling in the salty tang of her skin, likely leaving marks.

Her spine arched, her neck stretched and her hips bucked up against him. Passion boiled in his body, obliterating everything but Cara.

He groaned her name and felt her hot, damp body convulse around his. He fell over the edge to oblivion.

Max took long, deep breaths, his limbs like jelly, his weight pressing Cara into the soft mattress. He decided he must be getting old, because it sure shouldn't take him this long to recover from lovemaking.

"Max?" Her tone was hollow against his ear.

"Am I squishing you?"

She shook her head. "Don't move."

"Okay."

"You feel good."

"I feel amazing." He felt like he'd been drugged, in a good way, in a way that could make him an instant addict.

"You have to promise me something," she told him, voice still quiet and husky.

Right. He remembered now. He'd interrupted her. Or she'd interrupted him. Clearly, it was something important.

"For the president?" he asked.

"For me."

Regaining just enough strength to operate his arms, Max lifted up on his elbows. "For you? Anything." He meant it. Procedure be damned. Protocol be damned. Laws be damned. If Cara needed something from him, he'd move heaven and earth to make it happen.

She moved her gaze away from his. "When they get here… When we're rescued and we go back to D.C.…"

"I'm not telling anybody anything," he pledged. What had happened between them was personal and private. It had no bearing on their professional lives, and it was nobody's business but their own.

"I need you to stay away from me."

He didn't like it. But he understood. They disagreed on how their relationship could work while the president was in office. He got that. And he wouldn't presume that last night changed anything.

"I know how you feel," he began.

But she put a finger across his lips to silence him. "I mean it, Max. You have to stay away from me, completely away. I'm not strong enough to fight you. You'll win. And you winning will be very, very bad for me."

"There's nothing that says we can't be friends."

She glanced down at their naked, entwined, joined bodies. "We can't be friends, Max."

He felt as if he'd been sucker punched. He wasn't ready to say he'd wait four years for her. But he wasn't ready to say he wouldn't. He didn't know where this was going. But she didn't, either, and they couldn't just walk away.

"Promise me," she pressed, capturing his gaze. "No more dropping by my apartment. No more seeking me out at events. No more leaving your watch behind."

"No." No way, no how. She was entitled to her perspective, but he had a right to make his case.

A sheen formed in her eyes, and he felt like the worst jerk in the world.

"You have to let me try." There was a pleading tone in his voice.

She blinked. "If you try, I'll get hurt."

"I won't hurt you, Cara." He found himself gathering her close again, voice rumbling with emotion. "I swear I won't hurt you."

There was a catch in her tone. "Stay away, Max. If you care about me at all, then stay away."

Max felt a block of ice settle into his chest. He'd sworn he'd do anything for Cara. And this was the thing she asked of him. For that reason, it was what he'd do. He'd do it for her. Even if it killed him.

# Seven

It had been midmorning when the snowmobiles arrived at the villa to rescue them. Cara used the helmet and a scarf to camouflage her identity as they headed back into town. But it turned out she needn't have bothered. The town was busy, people focused on repairs to the ski runs and on the final rescue activities. A few fingers pointed at Max when he dismounted and removed his helmet. But Cara was far across the parking lot, being shadowed by a different rescuer, and it didn't seem to occur to anyone they might have been together.

Thankfully, she quickly learned that everyone was accounted for. Those with injuries had been taken to the Fields medical center, with a few of the more serious cases shipped to hospitals in larger towns nearby. All were expected to recover.

Cara had met up with Gillian in the lobby of the hotel and learned that Jake was taking Max out to cover the avalanche story. Cara, on the other hand, was needed back in D.C. So they packed and made their way to the airport.

There was no excuse for her to stay in Fields any longer.

But as Cara climbed the narrow staircase to Gillian's jet, she felt like she was leaving something precious behind. She knew her mind was playing tricks. What she was sad to leave was a fantasy where Max was a perfect husband and father. The reality was something altogether different, and she was going to have to get used to that.

She ducked her way through the jet's door, inhaling the soft scent of new leather. The dozen white seats looked more like armchairs than airplane seats, each pair facing one another with a polished rosewood table between. Near the back was a sofa, oriented sideways, across from an entertainment center. Burgundy throw pillows gave a decorator's touch, and large, oval windows illuminated the pale interior.

Cara made her way to one of the luxurious seats in the forward half of the cabin. The copilot had relieved her of her luggage, and she tucked her purse beside the seat as she sat down.

"Did you turn into a billionaire when I wasn't looking?" she asked her sister.

Gillian grinned from the doorway. "Not yet." Then she turned to speak to the pilot, her voice too soft for Cara to hear.

"Yet?" Cara prompted as Gillian moved toward her.

"Maybe someday. Well, really, depending on how things go in India," said Gillian as she plunked down across from Cara. "Fingers crossed. If you're curious, I can check with my accountant and see how close we're getting."

The hydraulics whirred as the jet plane door folded into the closed position.

"Do you ever stop and let it boggle your mind?" Cara had always considered her sister a genius. And she'd known for a few years now that Gillian's business was growing in leaps and bounds.

"You let it boggle your mind when you're in a room with the president?"

"Yes," Cara answered honestly.

"But not enough to stop you from doing your job."

"I suppose."

Gillian opened a recessed compartment next to her seat, extracting a bottle of water from a bed of ice cubes. "Why are we talking about this?"

"Because we're sitting in a ridiculously expensive jet, being pampered beyond what is reasonable."

Gillian buckled up, then gestured to the small trapdoor next to Cara's seat. "Thirsty?"

"Not really."

Cara tightened the seat belt across her hips. The jet began to taxi, turning on a dime to head for the runway.

Gillian unscrewed the cap on her bottle. "We should be talking about Max."

"I don't want to talk about Max." Cara changed her mind about the water, lifting the small, wood-grained lid of her seat compartment and taking a bottle.

Gillian leaned back against the headrest of her seat. "Was that a thump I heard in the middle of the night?"

"You mean the avalanche?"

"You falling off the wagon."

"Wagon?" Cara took a drink of the chilled water.

"The no-Max-Gray wagon."

Cara choked, struggling not to spit out the mouthful of water.

Gillian laughed at her struggle. "I'll take that as a yes."

"You should take it as shock," Cara wheezed. "At the audacity of your question."

Gillian waved a dismissive hand as the engines whined to full power. "But you did it, didn't you?"

"Yes," Cara admitted. "I did. Thanks to you. And I really don't want to talk about it."

"Why not?"

"Because I'm trying not to think about it."

"Is it working?"

"Not particularly."

Gillian's voice lowered, her expression going softer. "Sorry I left you."

"Why *did* you leave me?"

Gillian had been fully aware that Cara was fighting her feelings for Max. Leaving them alone together hadn't been a particularly supportive move.

"I was hungry," Gillian sheepishly admitted. "Jake seemed like a decent guy. I didn't expect the conference call. And I sure didn't expect an avalanche."

"You thought you'd be back before Max could seduce me?"

"I did. I didn't count on the two of you rushing for the bedroom the minute we cleared the driveway."

"That's *not* how it happened."

"No kidding."

"I held out for a while. But he practically saved my life. I mean, well, he would probably have saved my life. If the avalanche had hit the villa and the roof had caved in." Cara's memory went back to those few moments when she'd thought they might die, the feel of Max's body sheltering her, his strength, his ingenuity.

The jet sped its way along the frozen asphalt, lifting smoothly into the air before banking around the mountain peaks.

"How did it happen?" asked Gillian.

Cara frowned at the question. "I think you want us to be closer than sisters ought to be."

"We've always been closer than sisters ought to be."

It was true. "You want to know which position we used and what he whispered in my ear?"

Gillian answered with a broad grin. "I want to know what you were thinking the moment before you said yes and took off your clothes."

"I was thinking no, no, no, no, *no*."

"Clearly, that worked."

"I was making a reasoned and logical argument inside my head for keeping my hands completely to myself."

"And?"

"And he told me I was overthinking."

"Were you?"

"I'm always overthinking. There's nothing wrong with overthinking. You generally come to much better decisions when you're overthinking."

"So what happened?" Gillian prompted.

"He kissed me."

"Just up and kissed you?"

"Just up and kissed me. He didn't have a counterargument. There wasn't a single point for his side."

"So he kissed you instead."

Cara felt a little shiver at the memory. "And that was all she wrote. Next thing I knew, I was naked."

Gillian laughed. "I'm sorry. I know it's not funny. But I love that my coolly logical, self-contained, controlled sister got swept away by inappropriate passion."

Cara sent her a glare. "Well, I didn't love it at all," she lied.

"Was it bad?" asked Gillian, sobering.

"No." Cara couldn't bring herself to lie about that.

"Good?"

"So good," Cara swallowed. Forget the top ten, Max had to be the hottest man alive, and heaven had to be just like those moments in his arms.

"So what now?"

"Nothing now. It's done. It's over."

"You broke up with him?"

"There was nothing to break. We were never together. But I made him promise that he'd stay away from me. He has principles. He'll keep his word."

Gillian was silent for a long moment. "You think that was smart?"

"It was brilliant." Cara trusted Max more than she trusted herself.

"I guess that's one problem solved." As the plane leveled off, Gillian unbuckled her seat belt. "But what will you do when your pregnancy starts showing? D.C.'s a pretty small town. Max is going to hear that you're pregnant."

"I have a plan," said Cara, shifting to get comfortable in her seat, telling herself it was past time to stop talking and thinking about Max. It was her and the baby from here on in.

"Oh, do tell," Gillian encouraged.

"I'm requesting a transfer to one of our foreign embassies. Maybe Australia, maybe Canada or England. There are plenty of places for me to go." She made a show of glancing around the plane's interior. "And it's not like you can't come and visit whenever you want."

"Would they give you a transfer?"

"I hope so. Maybe. I think I have a good chance."

"And, if they don't?"

"They will."

"Cara—"

"I don't need plan C, D and F."

Gillian opened her mouth, but Cara didn't let her get in a word. "I'm not you," said Cara.

"And I'm not pregnant," Gillian retorted.

"Really? You're going to go there?"

"I'm just sayin', you were probably hoping the birth control would work, too."

"What made you so mean?"

"If your big sister won't tell you the truth, who will?"

"That's not the truth. That's your paranoid view of the world."

"If we don't break into the India market," Gillian said reasonably, "we'll try for Brazil."

"So, you'll still become a billionaire."

"Exactly."

"And that was a metaphor for good contingency planning?"

"It was. You can't do these things on the fly. I already have staff in South America. We've got a dozen in-market consultants working from Chile to Colombia. But, for your circumstances, good contingency planning says you need to let Max know the two of you weren't exclusive. And you need to do it now, before any hint or whisper of pregnancy comes up."

"Just call him up?" Cara challenged, knowing it was ridiculous. She could never pull that off. Not with Max. Maybe not with anyone.

"You could be a little more subtle than that."

"He'd know I was lying."

"How would he know?"

"Because I could never do it with a straight face."

"Really?"

"Yes, really."

"Hmm." Gillian went silent for a moment. "Okay, then I'll do it for you."

Cara scoffed. "I think we're above and beyond sisterhood again."

"I'd do anything for you."

Cara cocked her head and cast her sister a baleful look. "You'll tell Max that I've been sleeping with other men?"

"Please. Give me a little credit. I won't tell Max. I'll tell Jake."

Cara gave a slow blink of astonishment. "Jake?"

"He liked me," said Gillian. "Or at least he was attracted to me. He was definitely flirting with me."

Cara had no doubt it was true. "You don't think it'll look suspicious if you call him up to talk about my sex life?" The idea was so preposterous, she didn't know whether to laugh or shriek.

"He'll call me."

"What? When? Wait a minute. Did you sleep with Jake?"

"No," Gillian huffed. "I did not sleep with Jake. I only just met the man."

"But he stayed in your hotel suite last night."

"Where else was he going to stay? The hotels were completely full, and his villa was hit by an avalanche."

Cara quirked a meaningful eyebrow.

"Listen, missy." Gillian wagged her finger in mock admonishment. "It was a big suite, and I behaved myself."

"Did you like him?" Cara asked, contemplating the possibilities.

"I don't know. I suppose." Gillian's gaze moved to the window. "He's kinda cute and funny. He's got a wicked sense of irony. You know, it's been a long time since any guy completely ignored my money."

"He didn't notice the three-thousand-dollar-a-night hotel suite?"

"If he did, he didn't say much. But back to you. All I have to do is mention to Jake that I'm in D.C. He'll talk me into a drink and voilà."

"Voilà? In between martinis, you bring up your sister's sex life?"

"Easy, peasy."

"No," Cara told her with conviction.

"You don't have to lift a finger."

"*No.*"

Gillian looked carefully into her eyes. "You sure?"

"I'm positive." She was. Sort of. Maybe.

She couldn't deny the utility of Max thinking someone else was the father. But she wasn't ready to let him think she'd betrayed him.

Then again, maybe *betrayal* was too strong a word. They'd dated casually, never had an understanding of any kind. Maybe he already thought she'd been with other men. Maybe he'd been with other woman.

She swallowed. She knew it wasn't her right to care. But she cared very much.

\* \* \*

"Your instincts are second to none." Max's former boss, Marnie Salloway, hit the remote, shutting off the video segment from the Fields avalanche. Max hadn't worked with the woman in years, not since she was an associate producer and he was fresh out of college at in Maryland. But he'd answered her summons for a meeting. He wanted to look her in the eyes and ask a few questions.

"Right place, right time," said Max, turning in his chair at the long, oval table in the office boardroom.

"Juxtaposed with the snowboard lessons, you look like the all-American guy."

"Hardly," Max scoffed.

Marnie gave him a knowing smile. "And you look so darn good doing it."

"Are you flirting with me?"

She was at least ten years older than Max. He'd been the object of her attention in the past, and he had no wish to repeat the experience. He also hoped to throw her off her game. If Liam Fisher was right and ANS was playing fast and loose with the law in getting their info on the Ariella Winthrop scandal, Marnie would be in the thick of it.

"Absolutely not," she trilled. "Please. I'm merely saying what we both know. You're a star, Max. Though now that we're talking about it, I think you've gone just about as far as you can go over at NCN. When are you going to consider joining a real network?"

"NCN feels pretty real to me."

"Not according to the latest ratings. Well, your show is doing fine."

"Which would be my primary concern."

Marnie sat forward, her fire-engine-red nails clashing with her rather orange-hued hair. "I'm not talking about how your show is doing now. I'm talking about what you could be doing from here. Our budget is higher. We have more viewers. And we'd be willing to look at giving you some producer responsibilities. Think about it, Max. You could influence the direction of your stories and your show."

"I'm happy with my show's budget and direction."

She cocked her head, showing a brittle, knowing smile. "You need me to sweeten the pot?"

Max didn't respond, curious where she was going and how much she might divulge.

"I have a drawer full of stories, juicy stories, stories that nobody else even knows are out there."

"Tell me more," he encouraged. "What does ANS have that others don't?"

"Superior investigative skills."

"Did you use them on the Ariella Winthrop story, Marnie? How exactly did you get that?"

Suspicion came into her blue eyes.

"How do I know you can get more?" he persisted, trying to throw her off his main purpose.

She was obviously hesitant. "Are you telling me you're ready to jump ship?"

"I'm willing to think about it. How'd you do it?"

"Right place, right time," she told him softly.

But it was triumph he saw in her eyes, pride and triumph. He'd bet a whole lot of money that ANS had done something underhanded and that Marnie was behind it.

He gazed levelly across the table. "Anybody can get lucky once."

"ANS gets lucky a whole lot more than once."

"And I'd be able to take advantage of that luck?"

"Absolutely."

After a silent moment, Max realized he wasn't going to get anything more here today. "Can I have a few days to think about it?"

The caution was back in her expression. "Don't take too long."

He rose from his chair. "Thanks for inviting me to the meeting, Marnie."

She rose with him. "Thanks for thinking of ANS."

"You're all I've been thinking about."

She smiled at that, and he was positive she didn't understand the irony. Thank goodness. It had been a stupid, self-indulgent thing for him to say.

He left the boardroom, took the elevator to the lobby and exited onto the street. Jake was waiting two blocks down, around the corner at Rene's Café.

As Max took the concrete stairs to sidewalk level, his phone chimed. It was his boss at NCN, producer Nadine Clarke.

"Hey," he greeted. The sounds of the busy production office echoed in the background.

"What's this I hear about you meeting with Marnie Salloway?"

"Are you kidding me?" Max glanced behind him at the office building. "That was barely three minutes ago."

"What can I say? We're a news network. People love to leak to me."

"I'm impressed," said Max, stopping for the light.

It was late afternoon, and the sun was setting behind the downtown office buildings. A few flakes of snow wafted down, making an already cold evening feel colder.

"Do I have something to worry about?" asked Nadine.

"Not a thing."

"Good." Her tone was crisp and no-nonsense. "I need you to pack for L.A. The president's leaving for the Pacific Rim Economic Summit in a couple of days, and I need you to stay on the story. We're going to do a remote episode from L.A., haven't figured out the details yet."

"I wanted to talk to you about that," said Max, navigating around a taxi as he moved with the crowd across the street. "I'm not sure the president is the real story here."

"Really?" Nadine drawled in a tone Max recognized. The

woman had already made up her mind and wasn't interested in hearing anything that conflicted with her own view.

He persevered, "I think we should figure out how ANS discovered the story."

"And I think we should figure out how NCN finishes the story. And since I'm the producer, let's try it my way, shall we?"

"Do you even want to know why?" Max pressed.

"Max, you already talked me into hiring Liam. I assume he's going to eventually tell us why."

"Liam needs some help."

"He's doing fine for the moment. But you can tell me more when you get back from L.A."

"Yes, boss," Max drawled.

"That's what I like to hear." Then there was a slight pause. "Unless, of course, you truly are considering an offer from ANS. In which case, let's do dinner so I can massage your ego for a while and offer you a raise."

"Not necessary."

"Good. Your flight leaves at nine." Nadine rang off.

Phone to her left ear, Lynn waved Cara into her office.

"Without any new facts, it's hard to keep them from speculating," Lynn said into the phone.

Cara's coworker Sandy followed her into the office and set a stack of papers on the corner of Lynn's desk.

*"The Morning News,"* said Sandy. *"The Night Show, D.C. Beat* and *Hello Virginia.* They all want the president."

Lynn covered the mouthpiece. "Nobody's getting the president."

*"Hello Virginia* promised to be nice and let him tell his side of the story."

"No, Barry," Lynn said into the phone to the chief of staff. She clenched her jaw for a moment. "Because I don't have magical powers. I don't. No." She shook the telephone receiver dramatically in front of her before putting it back to her ear. "You do that. Tell me what he says." She slammed down the phone.

"Like hell they'll let him tell his side of the story," she said to Sandy, her hand going to her ring.

Cara agreed with her boss. The second *Hello Virginia* got the president in front of a microphone, they'd hit him with every awkward question possible.

Lynn twisted her topaz ring. "We need you on the trip, Cara."

"Which trip?" Cara asked, taking a seat.

"The Pacific Rim Economic Summit. L.A."

Cara was surprised. It was a plum assignment. "You're not going?"

She caught Sandy's annoyed glance as the woman left the room, but forced herself to dismiss it. If it was professional jealousy, Sandy would just have to deal with it. Barry and Lynn set the agenda, nobody else.

"I'm not going," Lynn confirmed. "Barry wants me here. And he was impressed by the way you handled the fallout at the inaugural ball."

"I was just doing what you taught me." Cara wasn't flattering her boss. She was honestly in awe of Lynn's skill at spin. The woman might be a bit prickly, but she was also brilliant.

"Well, you caught Barry's attention, and the president heard how well you did."

Cara slumped back in her chair. "Really?"

"Yes."

"Really?"

"Don't act so shocked." Lynn turned to her keyboard and typed a few words. "You'll need to head for L.A. a couple of days early. Tomorrow would be best. Security and the advance team are already there."

Cara sat up straight. "You bet."

"I'm emailing you the events list. His speeches are in editing, but we'll want some additional speaking points in anticipation of ad hoc questions. Barry will try to keep him away from the press, but somebody might shove a microphone in front of his face on a red carpet somewhere."

"Will do." Cara jotted down a few notes to herself.

"So you'll be handling most of the informal questions."

Cara jerked her head up. "Huh?"

"We can't give them the president."

"But—"

"You'll be fine," Lynn reassured her.

"I haven't done anything unscripted for the president." Cara was nowhere near ready for that.

"What do you call the inaugural ball?"

"An emergency."

"And you stepped up to the plate."

Cara swallowed. "I'm, uh, flattered, of course."

Lynn's expression turned serious. "This is a golden opportunity, Cara."

"What if I blow it?"

"Would I set you up to fail?"

At Cara's hesitation, Lynn answered her own question. "I would not."

"Not intentionally," Cara allowed.

"Are you questioning my judgment?"

"No, no, of course not."

"Good. The president wants you in L.A. Barry has faith in you. And so do I. Don't psych yourself out."

"I won't," Cara vowed. She rose to her feet.

"Go pack your evening gowns. There'll be some parties."

# Eight

It was unseasonably warm in L.A., especially for January. It was barely 7:00 a.m., but Cara was hot jogging along the beach path at the Santa Monica shore. She stripped off her sweatshirt and tied it around her waist, letting her bare arms drink in the cool breeze coming off the ocean. She'd been sweating against her tank top, and the cooling dampness reenergized her pace.

The waves foamed rhythmically against the sand, while early traffic wound its way along Ocean Avenue. The president's advance contingent was set up at the Jade Bay hotel, where the high-level trade meetings would take place. The president was due to attend three luncheons, two dinners and a final reception following a formal joint statement from the participants on the results of the summit.

Cara's cell phone chimed on her hip, and she extracted it from its case. It wasn't a number she recognized.

"Yeah?" she breathed.

"Cara?"

"Ari—" She stopped herself from saying Ariella's full name.

"It's me," Ariella responded.

"Are you okay? Where are you? No. Wait. Don't answer that."

"I'm in Seattle."

As she approached the pier, Cara slowed to a walk. "I told you not to answer."

Ariella's voice turned wistful. "I'm not staying here much longer. I thought it would be more remote. You know, trees and mountains, maybe a log cabin by a stream."

Having visited her sister in Seattle, Cara couldn't help but smile.

"It's huge," said Ariella. "And there are so many people."

"Over half a million," said Cara. "Is everything okay?"

"I'm getting scared."

"Of what?"

"Of being found out, of being recognized. I'm staying in the hotel as much as possible, but when I go out, people look at me like they know me, but they can't quite place me."

"I guess you've seen the TV reports," said Cara.

"I have. It's bad, isn't it?"

"The opposition is calling for the president's resignation. But they do that at the drop of a hat. What's worse is that he's been steadily dropping in the polls."

"I'm not helping, am I?"

"None of this is your fault."

"But I want to help," said Ariella. "I admire the president. You know how much I respect him."

"I do."

"What can I do?"

"Do you want me to answer that question as the president's public relations specialist or your friend?"

"What can I do to help the president?"

Cara drew a deep sigh, raking back her damp hair and plunking down on a bench beneath a palm tree. "Take the DNA test."

Ariella went silent for a moment. "I guess I knew that was going to be your answer."

"It's what's best for the president. I'll be honest with you, we need to move on from the uncertainty. Whatever the outcome, we can spin it a number of ways. Ironically, either answer would make it less newsworthy."

"I understand."

"I'm sorry," Cara said softly.

Ariella gave a light laugh. "It's not your fault, either. Anything else?"

"What do you mean?"

"Is there anything else I can do? I thought hiding out was the best move. But I realize it was the selfish move. I left all of you behind to face the music."

"It's what I'm paid for," Cara pointed out.

"What about that guy?"

Cara didn't understand. "There's a guy?"

"Max Gray. He helped me get away the night after the ball."

Cara's stomach lurched in response to Max's name. "I heard about that," was all she said.

"All the stations keep running the same footage over and over, the president looking shocked when that horrible Mitch person made the toast. I was thinking that if I went on Max's show and made a new statement, gave them something fresh, it would take some of the heat off the president."

"That's not a good idea, Ariella." Max and NCN, like any news organization, couldn't be trusted to act in the best interest of anything but their story.

"You're talking as my friend, aren't you?" Ariella asked.

It was true. Cara was speaking as a friend.

"You should turn into the president's public relations specialist for a minute."

"Ariella."

"I'm asking the public relations specialist. Would it help if I went on Max's show?"

"It would be dangerous. It could go either way."

"I trust Max."

"I don't." Right now, Cara couldn't afford to trust a single member of the press.

"Talk to Lynn," Ariella encouraged her. "See what she thinks I should do."

Cara knew she had to do exactly that. She wouldn't be doing her job if she didn't bring this opportunity to her boss's attention. But she also feared she knew what Lynn would say to the offer. She'd take it in a heartbeat.

"I will," Cara promised. "And I'm also calling my sister. She's in Seattle, and she can help you while you're there."

"I won't be here much longer."

"Gillian can help. Her house is huge and secluded, and she has security."

"Okay," Ariella agreed, a trace of relief in her voice.

Cara ended the call and came to her feet. The Jade Bay hotel was directly across the street, and she needed a secure line for the conversation with Lynn.

When Max's phone rang, he was deep in Malibu Creek State Park, racing Jake downhill on a mountain bike, coming around a tight switchback, avoiding the rocks and scrub brush while ducking beneath an overhanging tree. He splashed through the creek to a wide, grassy spot and skidded his back tire to a stop, cursing out loud.

Jake slammed on his own brakes, but he passed Max before pivoting his bike and sliding to a stop.

"What?" he demanded.

Max ripped off his helmet, fishing into a pocket of his khakis for the phone. He held it up to show Jake, who rolled his own eyes as he removed his helmet.

"Nadine," Max told Jake.

"Impeccable timing, as always," Jake responded, dismounting to lay his bike on its side.

"Hey, Nadine," Max greeted a little breathlessly, following Jake's lead and leaning his own bike down on the grassy patch.

"Have I got a show for you." There was no mistaking the excitement in Nadine's voice.

"Good to hear," Max responded. Whatever it was, he was glad Nadine was happy. When she was happy, everyone was happy. He bent to retrieve his water bottle from the rack on the bike frame, popping the top.

"I just got off the phone with Lynn Larson."

Max stopped. "You got the president for my show?"

"No, no. Not the president. You think I have superpowers? And what's the matter with you, anyway? Everything's going to be anticlimactic after that guess."

"Sorry," said Max.

Nadine harrumphed at the other end.

"Tell me about it," Max prompted. "I promise to be excited." He squirted a stream of water into his dry mouth. The scenery in the park was fantastic, but the dust was pervasive, and, as usual, Jake set a harsh pace.

"Oh, you will be excited," said Nadine. "I got Ariella."

"Ariella Winthrop?" Max raised his brows in Jake's direction.

Jake crossed his arms over his chest, obviously waiting for the conversation to continue.

"Yes, Ariella Winthrop," Nadine returned sarcastically. "Is there another Ariella in the world at the moment?"

Max ignored the rhetorical question. "I thought she'd left town."

"Well, she's coming back. Or, rather, she's coming there."

"To L.A.? You know this how?"

"Lynn Larson. Didn't I just say that?"

"I don't understand," said Max.

Judging by the expression on Jake's face, he was equally confused.

"I don't know what you did, Max. But Ariella herself requested your show. They have some restrictions, of course. But nothing we can't live with. It'll be a short segment, but what a coup. And Caroline Cranshaw will be there."

Max stomach contracted. "Cara?"

Nadine didn't seem to hear him. "I assume Caroline will be the handler, so we don't get too much out of Ariella, but—"

"Cara Cranshaw, from the White House, has agreed to come on my show?" Max locked gazes with Jake.

Jake now knew all about Max's relationship with Cara. After what had happened in Fields, it seemed much safer to have Jake working with them, rather than getting curious.

"She's already in L.A. with the advance team. Lynn's going to call and let her know, and then we'll nail down the details."

It sounded like Cara didn't know about this yet. Max could only imagine how she was going to react.

"I'm just giving you a heads-up," said Nadine.

"I appreciate that."

"What time is it there?"

"Coming up on seven."

"It's ten here. I probably won't hear any more tonight. So, talk tomorrow."

"Talk tomorrow," Max parroted, then ended the call.

"You want to catch me up?" asked Jake.

"Why would Ariella surface?" Max mused to himself.

"I thought you were going to respect a certain perimeter when it came to Cara."

"I did, too." Max dropped the phone back into his pocket. "Her boss may not have talked to her yet. But we've got her and Ariella for the remote from Grauman's Chinese Theatre. It sounds like Cara's already in L.A."

"What about her sister?" asked Jake.

Max lifted his bike. "Forget about her sister. Gillian's smart, gorgeous and filthy rich. She can have any guy in the world."

"Hey, I'm a guy. I'm in the world. My odds are just as good anyone else's."

"No, they're not. The woman's got a master's degree from MIT. She hangs out with the who's who of international commerce. They have private jets, yachts moored in the South of France, hotel buildings and their own sous chefs."

Jake retrieved his own bike, tipping his chin in the air with mock indignation. "I don't like to throw this around a lot. But I'm a graduate of the Stony Hills Digital Film Academy."

"I've seen your résumé," Max drawled. "I've also seen your apartment, and I know your net worth. Forget Gillian. Go back to Jessica."

Jake remounted. "Jessica's history. I've been told I'm good in bed."

Max balanced one foot on a pedal. "By women you were paying to be there?"

"Well, if you're gonna get all picky about it."

Max grinned. "How many miles to the parking lot?"

"Seven," said Jake, cinching up his helmet. "And then, buddy, is it ever Miller time."

"The Jade Bay hotel lounge?"

Jake chuckled. "You've got it bad."

"I want to see what I'm up against."

"Really?" Jake asked. "You're going to give me that kind of an opening?"

"Get stuffed," said Max, rolling his bike toward an incline.

"You're up against Cara," Jake called out from behind. "At least you were at one time. Not so much anymore."

Max poured on the power on his way up the hill, wishing his pulse would pound the memories out of his mind. Keeping his promise to Cara was enough of a battle while she was on the other side of the country. Working with her on a show was going to make it impossible.

Feeling irritated and determined, Cara spotted Max from across the patio lounge of the hotel. The night was cool, propane heaters humming between tables, steam wafting from the pools that were lit underwater with red, blue and green lights. Tiny white lights twinkled in the trees, while men in suits and women in cocktail dresses enjoyed an evening drink among the dining tables, the deeply padded loungers and the private cabanas.

Max was sitting at the bar, his back to her, and the seats on either side of him were empty. His shirt was white, sleeves rolled up to the middle of his forearms. He wore black slacks and casual shoes. A tall, elegant glass of amber beer sat on the bar in front of him.

Cara was returning from a dinner meeting with her White House colleagues in a private room on the top floor of a neighboring hotel. Lynn's direction had been clear: NCN wanted Ariella, and they wanted Cara. And the White House was going to take advantage of the opportunity.

Careful of her dignity in her little black dress, Cara shimmied up onto the bar stool beside Max, hooking her four-inch heels on the crossbar of the high chair.

"Is this your idea of a loophole?" she asked without preamble. "Getting me assigned to your show?"

Max half turned, showing no surprise at seeing her in Los Angeles. "It wasn't my idea."

"I'm sure," she drawled.

The bartender appeared in front of her.

"Orange juice, please."

"Your boss called my boss and offered up Ariella. What were we supposed to do?"

"And you added me in the bargain," Cara accused, reaching for an almond from the small dish on the bar. Though she'd just eaten a chicken breast, stir-fried garden vegetables and rice pilaf, she was ridiculously hungry.

Max swiveled to face her head on. "When I want you, Cara, I'll come after you. I'm not going to sneak around behind your back."

"I don't believe you." This had to be more than a coincidence.

"Don't you?" he asked softly.

She couldn't bring herself to answer. As far as she knew, he'd never lied to her before. And he looked sincere now.

"We can't do this, Max." There was a husky tremor to her voice. She hadn't realized until this moment how much she missed him. Life had been colorless since they'd parted. Sitting this close, it was a struggle to keep from reaching for him, touching his hair, stroking his cheek, pressing her lips to his.

"We're professionals," he countered, green eyes darkening, as if he was reading her mind.

For a moment, she forgot to breathe.

The waiter set a tall glass of orange juice on the bar.

"Hey, Cara." Jake's voice broke the moment.

She gave herself a mental shake, raising her gaze as Jake eased into the seat on the opposite side of Max.

"Hi, Jake. I didn't know you were here."

Jake scooped up a handful of the almonds. "I don't dare stay far away from this guy. Stories have a way of finding him."

She couldn't disagree with that. Max was three thousand miles from D.C., and Ariella was about to be plunked in his lap.

"I hear NCN is getting a scoop," she said to Jake.

He grinned in return. "How's your sister?"

Max shot Jake a dark look.

"What?" Jake asked with mock innocence.

"Can we keep Gillian out of this?" asked Max.

"She's fine," said Cara, thinking her sister had obviously been right about Jake's interest. No huge surprise there.

Jake dumped the remainder of the almonds into his palm. "Had dinner?" he asked Cara.

It was on the tip of her tongue to admit she had, but her stomach rumbled beneath the black dress. "I could eat," she admitted.

Jake came to his feet. "Let's grab a table."

"You are not going to use dinner as an excuse to grill her for information," Max warned.

"Gillian's on her way here," said Cara, tucking her tiny black evening purse under her arm.

Jake pulled up short. "Hello?"

Even Max looked interested by that.

"She's flying Ariella down from Seattle in her jet."

Gillian had made the decision to come to L.A. the second she'd heard Max was in town and that Cara was going to be forced to do a show with him. Cara tried to tell her she didn't need hand-holding. But Gillian had insisted she did. And maybe Gillian was right. It would be good to have her here.

"Seattle," Max mused under his breath. "Not a bad place to hide."

"When's she getting here?" asked Jake.

Max shook his head at Jake. He motioned to a passing waiter and asked for a table.

"Tomorrow night," Cara answered Jake, falling into step behind Max as they wended their way across the patio.

Jake walked beside her. "Moral support?" he asked.

Cara shot him a curious look. "What do you mean?"

"I know about you and Max."

Cara was struck speechless.

"Trying to keep your hands off each other," Jake finished.

"What?" she managed to choke out.

Max came to a halt beside a round table, turning and pulling out a chair for Cara.

"You *told* him?" she demanded, refusing to sit down.

The waiter glanced from one to the other and smoothly withdrew.

"I can be trusted," Jake put in.

"We're better off with him covering for us than snooping around."

"You swore you wouldn't tell anyone."

"Did you tell Gillian?"

"Yes, but…" That was different. Gillian was her sister. She was intensely loyal, and she'd never do anything to harm Cara.

Max lifted a brow.

"That's different," she finished.

"How?" he asked reasonably.

Wasn't it obvious? "She's my sister."

"I've put my life in Jake's hands more than once," said Max.

"And I've put my life in his," said Jake.

Cara turned to look at Jake. Despite her anger, she regretted that she was put in the position of insulting him. He'd always struck her as a perfectly decent guy, and none of this was his fault. But the only way to keep secrets was to hold them close.

"I've got your back," he told her, sincerity in the depths of his gray eyes. "You should sit down and have something to eat."

Something told Cara to trust him. Max obviously did. She wasn't happy about Max sharing, but she had to believe Jake wouldn't betray Max.

She sat down in the padded rattan chair.

A split second later, the waiter reappeared, placing a white linen napkin in her lap with a flourish.

Max and Jake took the chairs on either side of her.

"Wine?" asked Max, reaching for the dark green, leather-bound list.

Just then, another waiter arrived with the drinks they'd left at the bar, setting them on the table.

"I think I'll stick with the juice," she answered, lifting the glass and taking a sip.

"Afraid of losing control around me?" he teased.

"Yes."

Her answer seemed to throw him, and their gazes locked.

Jake glanced from one to the other, his voice going low as he bent across the table. "Just so I'm clear. Do you want me to cover up what happened in Montana, or do you need me to stop it from happening again while we're here?"

"We're fine," said Max, but just then his knee brushed

Cara's. An electric current ran the length of her thigh, settling at the apex, causing her muscles to contract. She knew she had to draw away, break the connection, but she was powerless to do it.

"You sure?" Jake drawled. "Because I'm available for, you know, standing guard at hotel room doors or hosing you down."

Max turned to frown at his friend.

Jake gave an unrepentant grin. "Unless, of course, I make some headway with Gillian. In that case, you two are on your own."

"Let's talk about the show," said Max. His tone turned crisp, but his eyes were still warm when they returned to Cara, and he kept his knee pressed up against hers.

"Sure," she squeaked, earning a curious glance from Jake.

"We've been told we have two minutes with Ariella. It'll be pretaped, three scripted questions, no deviation."

"Can you tell us about your childhood?" Cara listed the questions Lynn had given to her. "Do you know anything about your birth parents? And did you ever have reason to suspect President Morrow might be your father?"

"I can live with those," said Max.

"I'll be there to make sure you don't deviate." She'd seen enough of Max's work to know he'd try to catch Ariella off guard by chatting casually, then create some B-roll footage to exploit later.

"I'll behave," Max vowed, but something in his tone made her nervous.

Max shifted, and Cara was quickly reminded that he was still touching her. How had she forgotten?

"I'll also need to see the edited version."

"Nadine agreed to that?" Max sounded skeptical.

"I guess Lynn can outnegotiate Nadine."

Jake laughed. "Wow. Then I'd hate to be across the table from Lynn."

"She's a force of nature," said Cara.

"You can't fight nature," Max told her in a soft voice.

She tried to pull away from his touch, but her limbs weren't cooperating. He was pressed more fully against her now, and her body was absorbing little pulses of sensation.

"Am I missing something?" asked Jake, taking in their expressions.

"Nothing," said Max, but he didn't back off. "Nadine also wants a few minutes on the summit and a couple of clips of the president," he told Cara. "What's he going to be talking about here?"

"Energy." She struggled to keep her voice even. "Natural gas. And technology, aerospace and aviation in particular. They're a big deal under the free trade talks."

"Manning Aviation?" Max asked Jake. "We can probably get something on the Stram-4000 prototype."

Just then, the waiter arrived, setting a gold-embossed, leather-bound menu in front of each of them.

"You should be talking to Gillian," Cara put in without thinking.

Jake instantly glanced up.

"She's working on a technology deal with China and another one with India. She has exactly the kind of company that will benefit from these trade negotiations."

Max and Jake exchanged a look.

"Would she do it?" asked Max.

"Is her deal confidential?" asked Jake.

Cara hadn't thought about that. "We'd have to ask her."

"I'll do that," Jake quickly volunteered. "I can pick her up at the airport." Then he smirked. "But you two have to promise to behave while I'm gone."

Cara couldn't help stealing a glance at Max.

He was looking straight back, his eyes smoldering with obvious desire. She felt the impact right down to her toes.

# Nine

"Do you think it's fate?" Gillian called from the bedroom of her suite at the Jade Bay hotel.

"I think it's karma," Cara replied, moving from the dining room to the butler's pantry, then peeking into the powder room. "Clearly I did something terrible in a past life. Why do you get such huge hotel rooms?"

Gillian was on the eighty-first floor, with a panoramic view of the Santa Monica Pier. Cara was down on ten, with a view of the lobby roof and the financial building across the street.

Gillian emerged through the double doors of the bedroom. "I don't book them myself. I think we have a travel person who does that. And you couldn't have done anything bad in a past life. You're an incredibly good person."

"Then why is Max in L.A.? Why did Ariella offer to do his show? And why did I open my big mouth and tell them you had a deal with China?"

"It'll be publicity for me," said Gillian. "That never hurts."

"So, clearly, you were very good in a past life."

Gillian grinned at that.

"They want to film your interview at the Manning Aviation facility. Their jet prototype has a technology angle."

"Being pregnant's not a cosmic punishment, you know," Gillian pointed out.

Cara wandered to the wet bar, checking out the liquor selection and the complimentary hors d'oeuvres and glancing at the dozens of crystal glasses in assorted shapes and sizes. "The situation feels like a punishment."

"You should tell him."

Cara shook her head.

"He might surprise you."

"He's not going to surprise me." Cara prided herself on being honest and practical.

Gillian moved across the room. "He's going to know eventually." She put her hand gently on Cara's stomach. "This little guy or girl is not going to stay hidden forever."

"I have a while yet."

"If you're not going to tell him, then you need to get some distance from Max."

Cara gave a pained laugh. "I came all the way across the country."

"Not that kind of distance. Maybe find yourself a new boyfriend. Make it obvious you're dating someone else."

"And bring them in on a conspiracy?" Cara couldn't see that working.

"Max needs to think it's not his baby."

"Yeah, I know he does," Cara admitted softly.

But for the moment, Cara needed to stop dwelling on her problems. She twisted open a bottle of imported water and helped herself to a savory pastry. "Dear sister, have you actually gotten used to all this luxury?"

It was Gillian's turn to glance around the massive suite. "I usually end up hosting business meetings and impromptu receptions. So having the big table is a plus."

"We could throw one heck of a party here," Cara noted.

The living and dining areas could fit thirty or forty people; add to that the huge deck, and the number probably went up to seventy. The dining table alone sat fourteen. The master suite was twice the size of Cara's hotel room.

"You want to have a party?" Gillian asked.

Cara shook her head. "The president arrives tomorrow, and I've got two formal dinners in a row. And I'm so tired lately. By ten, I'm ready to fall into bed. And hungry. I swear I could eat five meals a day."

"You should be eating well."

"I'm definitely eating very well. But I will be happy to get home to my own bed."

"I got Ariella set up with a lab in D.C.," said Gillian, changing the topic. "She's heading home after the show to take the DNA test."

Cara had seen Ariella briefly when they had arrived at the hotel. But Gillian had arranged for private security, who'd whisked her up to her own room right away.

"How's she doing?" Cara asked softly.

Gillian moved to one of the comfy sofa groupings. "Ariella's fine. Better than I expected. You're the one I'm worried about. The more I think about it, the more I realize it's not good for you to be around Max."

"It would be better if he wasn't here," Cara readily agreed, sinking down into a cream-colored armchair. "It all just feels so complicated. I know what I'm supposed to do. I know how I'm supposed to feel."

Gillian sat down across from her. "But you don't?"

"He's so…I don't know. I mean, I'm not supposed to want him. I shouldn't even like him, because he's so obstinate and sarcastic. But he's smart, Gilly. He's funny. And every time he touches me, my entire body lights up."

Gillian sat forward. "He's been touching you?"

"Not like that. Inadvertently, little brushes, things like that."

"They're on purpose," Gillian told her with authority.

"I know they're on purpose," Cara admitted. "And I don't pull away. It's a little game."

"I know that little game. It's called playing with fire."

Cara couldn't help a reflexive grin. "Do you think that's what makes it so sexy? That it's illicit and clandestine?"

"Illicit and clandestine always makes things sexy."

"So, maybe it's not just Max. Maybe I'd feel this way about any guy who was off-limits."

"Maybe." But Gillian looked doubtful. Then she paused, seeming to choose her words. "Cara, is there any chance you've fallen in love with him?"

Cara's stomach caved in on itself. "No," she insisted with a shake of her head. "No. It's not that."

It couldn't be that. Falling in love with Max would be a colossal mistake. And, anyway, she hadn't known him nearly long enough to have fallen in love.

"I like him," she told Gillian. "But I don't love him. I mean, I admire some things about him. But on some fundamental levels, like how we feel about family and children, we're on two completely different planets."

"That's good," Gillian told her with conviction.

"It's great," Cara readily agreed. Maybe if she said it often enough, it would come true.

Since Cara knew Ariella so well, she could tell she was nervous on the stage of the theater. But to a casual onlooker, Ari would only look poised and beautiful. Max sat in the opposite armchair, and the two were surrounded by a jumble of cameras, cables, lights and bustling crew members.

Cara stood off to one side, her heart going out to Ariella. She was incredibly brave to do this for the president.

Finally, it got quiet. The director gave a signal, and everyone stepped out of the shot. The sound and camera crews confirmed their readiness, and Max sat straight in his chair, putting on his formal interviewer's expression.

"We're here in L.A. with Ariella Winthrop, who has been in hiding since news broke of her possible link to President Morrow."

Cara wasn't crazy about the in-hiding reference, but it wasn't enough to shut it down.

"Ariella, welcome to the show." Max turned on the charm. "We all know you were adopted. Can you tell us about your childhood with Berry and Frank Winthrop?"

"Thank you, Max. I'm pleased to be here. The Winthrops were wonderful parents. They raised me in Chester, Montana. My father was very involved in the community. He coached my softball team." She gave what looked like a fond, wistful smile. "I wasn't a star player, but I loved spending Sundays with my father. My mother worked from home, so she was always there when I came home from school. She loved to bake. I kept her secret recipes, and they were the foundation of my current catering and event planning business."

"I understand your parents were killed in a light plane crash?"

Cara moved into Max's line of sight, giving him a warning glare for going off script.

But Ariella stepped up with aplomb.

"I miss them every day," she said. Then she stopped talking, leaving it to Max to fix the silence.

Cara smiled.

"Do you know anything about your birth parents?" Max asked.

Ariella shook her head. "I always knew I was adopted. My mother used to tell me they picked me because I was the best baby in the world. I understood the records were confidential, and I respected that. Many people have valid reasons for giving a baby up for adoption. And thank goodness they make that unselfish decision. I couldn't have asked for a better child-hood, Max."

"Do you think the president lied about—"

"Stop the filming." Cara marched right into the camera shot, holding her hand in front of it, ensuring they wouldn't be able to use the question.

She glared at Max. "Stop it. Right now."

He held up his hands in surrender. "Sorry. Old habits die hard."

"Like hell," she muttered.

He grinned at her and pointed to his live mike.

"Don't do it again," she warned.

"I'm trying my best."

"Ms. Cranshaw," the director called out in obvious frustration. "Can you please get out of my camera shot?"

"Tell your interviewer to stick to the script."

"Stick to the script, Max," the director parroted without a trace of conviction.

Cara stepped back, staying poised and ready.

"Ariella," Max began again. "Before the inaugural ball, did you ever have reason to suspect President Morrow might be your father?"

"No reason at all, Max. I understand the American people are anxious to find out. But I have to say, I have the utmost respect for the president. I look at his positions on the economy, health care and international diplomacy, and I can't help but admire him. The voters made a great decision when they elected him, and I'm sure he will meet all of our expectations."

Ariella stopped speaking, and Cara all but cheered.

Max opened his mouth, but he caught Cara's warning glare and seemed to decide it wasn't worth it.

The director called a halt, and Ariella got to her feet.

Max stood. "Have you taken a DNA test?" he asked conversationally.

"Don't answer that." Cara quickly scooted in. "You're still wearing a microphone."

Ariella stood silently while the techs removed her mike and Max's.

"Can't blame a guy for trying," said Max.

"I can," Cara put in tartly.

"I'm sorry I couldn't help you more," Ariella said to Max.

"I hope you're doing okay," he responded, looking genuinely concerned.

"I'm—"

"Ariella," Cara warned. "He's not on our side."

"That's not strictly true," Max said to Cara, a rebuke in his tone.

"He seems like a good guy," Ariella told Cara. "You should really give him a chance."

Cara wished she could. But she didn't dare.

Max suspected Cara was keeping her distance from him at the Manning Aviation facility. She was far across the big hangar, chatting with a company vice president. The man was obviously taking advantage of having some face time with a member of the president's staff. The segment including the interview with Gillian had been taped and was finished. Most of the film crew had left, and Max and Jake were now checking out the new, single-engine planes being built at the facility.

They were ten passenger propeller planes, hot off the assembly line. They came with bush wheels, floats and skis. Both Max and Jake had private pilot licenses, and Max had been thinking about moving from his Cessna to something a little larger.

"Thought I'd try for another date with Gillian tonight," Jake was saying to Max while the Manning technician replaced the engine cover. Jake's gaze kept drifting to where Gillian was surrounded by half a dozen Manning employees, all men, all clearly vying for her attention.

"Looks like you've got some competition," Max observed.

"True enough." Jake seemed to hesitate. "Then again, there's competition everywhere," he stated, an odd note to his voice.

Max checked out his expression. "You mean for Gillian?"

"Gillian, Cara, any woman really."

Max's gaze flicked across the room. "I think that guy is more interested in President Morrow than in Cara." Not to mention that the vice president of Manning was at least sixty years old.

"Not him," said Jake.

"Then who?" Max drew back. "Not you."

"No, not me. But, you know, plenty of other guys probably find her attractive."

"Maybe," Max allowed.

He didn't really dwell on it, but he knew there had to be plenty of men interested in Cara. Maybe he didn't like to dwell on it because he didn't like the jolt of jealousy that invaded his gut when he did.

"You guys ever talk about stuff like that?" Jake asked, bending to check out the underside of the plane's tail.

"Talk about what?"

"Other guys." Jake ran his fingertips along the rounded edges.

"Why would we talk about other guys?" Apprehension prickled along Max's neck. "Where are you going with this?"

Jake straightened, expression tight. "Has Cara ever mentioned anyone else?"

"That she's dated?"

Had someone come out of the woodwork? From her past? Were they causing a problem? If that was the case, why didn't Jake just come straight-out and say it?

"What's going on?" Max demanded.

Jake glanced across the cavernous complex, then he seemed to check to be sure the technician was out of earshot. "Something Gillian said last night. It led me to believe you and Cara maybe weren't exclusive."

Everything inside Max went perfectly still and cold. "*What did Gillian say?*"

"I know the two of you are basically broken up, but what I don't understand is—"

"*What did Gillian say?*" Max had to stop himself from grabbing Jake by the collar.

"That you and Cara weren't exclusive."

"In those words."

Jake nodded. "In those words. I thought it was odd. I mean, you said you two have always kept it casual. But I thought that was because of your jobs. Cara never struck me as the kind of woman to have more than one lover." Jake glanced furtively away from Max's expression. "Not that it's any of my business. But I thought you should know."

Anger roiling, Max pivoted to glare across the hangar. He knew Cara was over there, but he couldn't focus on her through the red haze forming in front of his eyes.

His hands clenched into fists by his side. "Did Gillian mention a name?"

"Uh, Max."

"*Did she mention a name?*" Max felt perfectly capable of committing murder.

"No name." Jake touched his arm. "I think maybe you and I should—"

"Back off," Max warned Jake, stepping away.

"Come on, Max. I didn't think you'd—"

"Care?" Max barked, turning to glare at Jake.

"Go off the deep end."

"I'm not off the deep end. I'm going to kill the son of a bitch with my bare hands, but I'm not off the deep end."

"I couldn't care less about what you do to some nameless guy. But I'm a little worried about Cara."

"Don't worry about Cara," said Max. He wasn't angry with

Cara. Okay, so maybe he was angry with her. But he wasn't furious with her. He wanted an explanation. And then he wanted to kill someone. And then he wanted to make her forget every other man on the planet.

"I *am* worried," said Jake.

"I'm not going to hurt Cara."

Jake rolled his eyes. "Of *course* you're not going to hurt her. I don't want you upsetting her. I don't want you yelling at her. Gillian told me this in confidence."

Max let out a cold laugh. "Well, you blew that, buddy. Because there's no way in hell I'm going to pretend I don't know."

"Yeah." Jake sighed. "And there was no way in hell I was going to keep it from you." Then Jake gave his head a sad shake. "I really hate to blow my chances with her. I haven't found one single thing I don't like about her." His gaze moved to Gillian and her ring of admirers. "Not one single thing."

Max spat out a pithy swearword. He hated compromising his best friend, but he had no choice here. "I gotta ask her."

"I know you do." Jake looked resigned. "Just don't make it any worse than it has to be, okay?"

"I'll try," Max promised. His feet were already in motion, carrying him across the vast concrete floor toward Cara. He honestly didn't know what he was going to do.

His brain was swirling, his emotions raw, by the time he got to Cara and the vice president.

"I'm sorry," he told the man, voice carefully controlled. "I'm afraid we're running late."

Without giving Cara a moment to react, Max linked her arm in his and all but dragged her away.

"What?" she sputtered, struggling to get her feet sorted out beneath her. She glanced behind them, then she looked up at Max. "Slow *down*."

"Sorry." He measured his pace but kept them on course for the exit.

"Where are we going? What are you doing? What about everyone else?"

"We have to talk."

"About what?"

"Not here."

"Max," she demanded.

"Gillian can ride back with Jake."

There were three NCN production vehicles still sitting in the parking lot outside. Max was taking one for him and Cara. He didn't much care how the others worked it out.

"They had a date last night," he said to Cara. "Did you know they had a date last night?"

"I know they went to a club after dinner." There was confusion in Cara's tone. "Did something happen? Is something wrong? Gillian said she had a good time."

"Nothing happened." But something was terribly, horribly wrong.

Outside in the hot parking lot, Max swung open the passenger door to one of the SUVs.

Cara shook off his hand, turning to face him. "Why are you doing this? What's wrong?"

"Get in."

"I'm not getting in."

"Get in, Cara. We need to talk."

She glared at him a moment longer, but then something in her expression faltered. She paled a shade, then she gave a shaky nod and got into the vehicle without another argument.

It seemed like she'd figured it out, knew that he knew. He sure hoped she was ready to explain herself. Not that any explanation would be satisfactory. They might not have come out and said it, but given all that had happened between them, it was absolutely unconscionable that she should be with another guy.

A fresh wave of anger rolled over Max as he stomped around the front of the SUV, nearly ripping off the driver's door.

Another guy.

Another guy?

What the hell was the *matter* with her?

He stabbed the key into the ignition and tore out of the parking lot, heading down the deserted, industrial road toward the mountain drive.

"Max," Cara began in a small, shaky voice.

"Don't," he warned her. "I can't talk about this and keep us on the road at the same time."

She fell quiet, her fingertips going to her temples.

Max took the curves as fast as he dared. It wasn't until they'd climbed several thousand feet, leaving the city behind, that he pulled off onto a narrow dirt road. He took them far enough that they wouldn't be disturbed, pulled onto a narrow track and stomped on the brakes, rocking the vehicle to a halt.

He shoved it in Park, killed the engine and set the brake. Silence closed in around them, and he could hear the thump of his own heart.

"Max," she tried again.

He turned in his seat and held up a finger to silence her. "Who is he?" he rasped.

She blinked in apparent confusion.

"Who is he?" Each syllable cut through his throat like broken glass.

Cara was shrinking back against the passenger door. "Who is who?" Her voice had turned to a dry rasp.

"I want to kill him, Cara." Max smacked his palm on the steering wheel. "Heaven help me, I want to wrap my hands around his neck and squeeze."

She swallowed convulsively. "Who?"

"The guy. Whoever he is. Whatever guy you've been with—" Max couldn't bring himself to say any more. He turned to face the windshield, gripping hard on the steering wheel.

Long moments went by in silence.

The wind whistled outside, the odd bird sounding in the distance.

He realized he couldn't do this. He was too angry right now. Whatever Cara had done, whatever her motivation, he needed to calm himself down before they talked about it. This wasn't fair to her.

"I'm sorry," he managed, reaching for the key.

"Max, I don't know what you're talking about."

"Gillian," he admitted. Then he turned to look at her again. He didn't want to make things worse for Jake, but the dishonesty had to stop somewhere. "Gillian told Jake you'd been with another guy. It made me angry. Too angry for us to have this conversation."

"Gillian?" Cara's voice was barely a squeak.

"She told him in confidence. He broke that confidence. He thought I should know." Max looked her square in the eyes. "And he was right. I should know. I don't know why you wouldn't tell me." He felt his anger rising all over again. "Hell, I don't know why you would have done it."

Cara blinked rapidly, her eyes taking on a bright sheen. "Max, I—"

"You don't have to explain." He hadn't meant to make her cry. He fought for calm again. He was heartsick but calmer now. And he knew he had to answer for his outburst.

"Gillian shouldn't have said that." A single tear escaped from Cara's bright blue eyes, streaking down in the sunshine that illuminated her face.

Despite everything, the tear ripped at his heart. He couldn't breathe. He could barely speak. "You don't have to tell me anything."

She drew a shaky breath. "There was no other guy."

"Don't lie. Please, just stop talking. I couldn't stand it if you lied to me."

She swiped the back of her hand across her damp cheek. "There was no other guy, Max."

He didn't know what to say to that. He wanted to believe her. He so very desperately wanted to believe her. And she looked sincere. She looked sincere and fragile and more beautiful than ever.

"There hasn't been any other guy since I've been with you. Since before I was with you. Since about a year before I was with you."

Hope flickered inside Max.

She reached out and touched his arm. "Gillian was wrong. She must have misunderstood something... Maybe something I said."

Anger and despair shuddered their way in waves out of Max's body. "Are you serious?"

"Nobody but you, Max." She gave a watery smile. "Nobody but you."

Max couldn't resist. He couldn't stop himself. He reached for her, pulling her across the seat, setting her in his lap, pushing back her hair, stroking her soft cheeks with his thumbs as he bent to kiss her mouth.

Her sweet taste invaded him as relief poured through him. He parted her lips, delving deep, tasting and possessing her essence. He inhaled her scent, felt the softness of her skin on his fingertips and the slight weight of her bottom against his lap.

He was instantly aroused and kissed her again, deeper this time. She kissed him back, a purring sound forming in her throat as her arms encircled his neck. The coolness of her fingers soothed the heat of his skin. The last vestige of his temper vanished, replaced by a driving need to make love to her.

His hands moved to her rib cage, sliding upward, thumbs beneath her round breasts. He plucked at her buttons, freeing her blouse, cupping his palm over the smooth satin of her bra.

She squirmed in his lap.

"Cara," he groaned, wishing she'd protest or smack him away, something, anything to slow this down.

A primal need had hijacked his brain. She was his, his, *his*. There was no way he was going to stop on his own.

But she wasn't slowing this down. Her hands were on his

shirt, releasing his buttons. Between kisses, she gasped for breath. Then she tipped her head back, her teeth biting down on her lip.

He kissed her exposed neck, drawing the succulent skin into the heat of his mouth. Her breasts were soft under his hand, the nipples beading against his palm. His body was on autopilot, free hand reaching beneath her skirt, tugging at her panties, stripping them off.

He touched her, and she groaned, thighs twitching, parting. She moved to straddle him, and her skirt bunched up around her hips.

He drew back an inch, staring into her eyes. They breathed deeply in unison, neither of them saying a word.

He reached for his slacks, unfastening, loosening, until there was no barrier between them.

"Only you," she whispered, the sheen back in her eyes.

"Oh, Cara." He pressed inside her, all rational thought flying from his brain.

Her hot body closed around him, and his hips flexed. He spread his fingers into her hair, bracing her for his kiss, opening wide, delving deep. Her fingernails dug into his shoulder. He wrapped an arm around her waist, pulling her to him, crushing her breasts against his bare chest.

He measured his rhythm, desperate to make it last. He ran his hand across her stomach, along her thighs, to the tender spot behind her knee.

Then he retraced the route, savoring her smooth, soft heat. She gasped at his touch, then moaned softly, pressing herself against his caress.

"You're beautiful," he whispered, increasing his pace. "So incredibly off-the-charts beautiful."

A haze moved through his brain, the world disappearing. Nothing mattered but Cara. Nothing ever would.

"Max," she cried, her breathing turning to quick pants.

"Yes," he groaned, speeding up, struggling to drag oxygen into his own lungs.

Her body stiffened then contracted around him.

"Oh, yes," he gasped, letting himself launch into endless waves of blissful oblivion.

Sounds came back first, the birds and the rustle of the leaves outside. Then came the sweet scent of Cara. Max opened his eyes and blinked against the bright sunshine, waiting for her gorgeous face to come back into focus. Inside the car, the air was stifling and she was slick against his skin.

"Can you breathe?" he asked her.

"Barely."

He managed to flick the ignition key to the accessory setting and press the buttons for the front windows. A welcome breeze flowed over them.

"Thanks." She smiled, pushing back her damp bangs.

He couldn't help but grin, kissing her playfully on the tip of the nose. "You are more than welcome." He paused, sobering. "Anytime."

Her smile also disappeared. "That's not what I meant."

"I know," he acknowledged.

They both went silent, but neither of them moved.

"I didn't plan this," Max told her. It wasn't an apology. He wasn't sorry. But he didn't want her to think he'd driven her into the woods to make love.

"I don't know what to do," she responded in a small voice.

He wasn't sure what she meant. "Right now?"

Her tone was searching. "Always before, I thought I knew. I might not have liked it, but I knew what it was I was supposed to do."

Her gaze studied his. "But we can't date. We sure can't have an affair." She gave a helpless little laugh. "And every time we try to stay away from each other…"

"Fate intervenes?" he offered.

"I don't think we can call this fate."

"I think we can call it anger," he admitted. Then he touched his forehead to hers. "I was so angry, Cara. We might not be officially dating but, apparently, you can't sleep with any other man without me losing it."

"I'm not."

"I know."

"I'm sorry," she whispered.

"You didn't do anything."

Unexpectedly, her arms wound around his neck.

He wrapped his own around her waist and held her close.

"I don't know what to do," she told him again, a catch to her voice.

He stroked his palms up and down her bare back. "You don't have to decide right now. We shouldn't decide right now. We can't."

"We have to do something."

"I'll finish the show, and you'll do your job." He eased back to look at her. "You are amazing."

"I'm a mess." She gave a nervous laugh, wiping her fingertips under her eyes, ineffectually rubbing at her smeared makeup.

Her hair was mussed, her clothes askew. Her cheeks were bright red, and she was covered in a dewy glow in the soft sunshine. He wanted her again already.

But he forced himself to close her blouse, fastening the buttons before he could change his mind.

"We're professionals," he told her. "We'll finish our work here, and we'll go back to D.C. And we won't decide anything, one way or the other, until we have time to think."

He sounded far more confident than he felt. Because he couldn't see any way forward, but he also couldn't see himself giving her up.

Gillian all but hauled Cara over the threshold into her hotel suite. "What happened? Where did you go? Why didn't you answer your phone?"

"Here's one for you," Cara returned as Gillian shut the door behind them. "*What* did you tell Jake?"

Gillian looked confused. "About what?"

"About me. My sex life. Other men in my sex life."

"Oh, that."

"Oh, *that?*" Cara marched into the center of the enormous room and spun around to face her sister.

Gillian seemed confused. "You said you wanted me to do it."

"When? When did I say anything remotely like that?"

"Last night. Right here in the room. We were talking about how you had to start telling people you were pregnant, if only to keep yourself out of danger."

"I said I wouldn't tell Max I was pregnant." Cara remembered it well.

"And I said, 'Max needs to think it's not his baby.' You responded, and I quote, 'Yeah, I know he does.'"

"And you took that to mean you should lie to him?"

"I took that to mean you finally understood what we had to do. And Jake gave me the perfect opening. You'd have been proud, Cara. I slipped it in there like nothing."

"I thought Max knew I was pregnant," Cara told her sister. "When he hauled me away to talk like that, I thought he'd figured it all out. I was about to confess everything."

"But you didn't?"

"I didn't."

Gillian motioned for Cara to follow her to two big armchairs recessed into a bay window overlooking the sunny city. "What did he say? What happened?"

"He was furious." Cara found herself shuddering at the memory.

Gillian sat down and Cara followed suit, sinking into the deep, plush cushions. "I realized he didn't know I was pregnant. But he took *great* exception to the idea of me sleeping with another man."

"Really?" Gillian mused.

"Don't act so surprised."

"Well, it's hardly the 1950s."

"Fidelity doesn't go out of style," said Cara.

"You said the two of you hadn't agreed to be exclusive."

"I'm not promiscuous, either."

Gillian straightened. "I didn't mean to insult you."

Some of the fight went out of Cara. "I know you were trying to help. But, man alive, I've never seen anything like it."

"He didn't hurt you?"

"No. No. Nothing like that. But he threatened to kill the guy." Cara let her mind slip back to the conversation. "But then he calmed himself down. I don't think he's used to losing his temper. And then…"

Gillian waited.

Cara could feel her cheeks going warm.

"And then?" Gillian prompted, curiosity rising in her blue eyes.

"After I swore there'd been no other guys—"

"You what? Wait. You wasted my perfectly fantastic setup? Why would you tell him there'd been no other guys?"

"I couldn't lie to him, Gilly. For some reason, the one thing in this world I can't do is lie to Max."

"That's ridiculous. He's just a man. You know this puts you right back where you started."

"I'd be thrilled to be back where I started."

Gillian went on alert. "What aren't you telling me?"

Cara tugged a wrinkle out of her skirt. "God, I miss wine." She'd give anything right now for a glass of Merlot, or two or three.

"For the taste or the alcohol?" asked Gillian.

"Do you think they make a baby-safe margarita?"

"Sure. Unfortunately, you have to leave out the tequila." Gillian leaned forward and took Cara's hand. "You slept with him again, didn't you?"

"If by slept, you mean had frantic sex with him in the front seat of his car, yes."

"Makeup sex?"

"Turns out, it really is the very best kind."

Gillian have her a squeeze. "Oh, Cara."

"I know. I'm addicted. I have to do something. I have to take drastic action. Can your jet make it to Australia?" It was the farthest place Cara could think of where they spoke English and she might reasonably get a job in the U.S. embassy.

"With a stopover in Hawaii, sure. You want to go now?"

Cara let herself fantasize for a moment about walking out of this hotel room and getting far, far away. Unfortunately, Max popped up in the middle of the fantasy.

"Can we talk about something else?" she asked Gillian.

A second went by. "Sure."

"My misery needs some company. Please tell me you make mistakes. Have you done anything stupid lately?"

"I did something tacky today."

"Good." Cara settled into the armchair. "Tell me all about it."

"I flirted with the pilots at Manning Aviation."

Cara couldn't help feeling a little disappointed. "How is that tacky? You mean because there were six of them?"

Gillian laughed. "Are you hungry?"

"I'm always hungry."

"Let's get room service." Gillian reached for the cordless phone on the table beside her chair. "What do you want?"

"A milk shake."

"Seriously? Again? Is the pregnancy and ice cream thing true?"

"I don't want pickles." Cara couldn't help but cringe as she imagined the tart taste. "But I'd take a sundae instead of a milk shake. Hot fudge, whipped cream, a cherry on top."

"You're out of control."

"I am."

"What do you really want?"

Cara really wanted a sundae. "Get me a wrap of some kind. And I'll take a salad with it. But I do want the milk shake."

"Is it okay with you if I order wine?"

"No, it's not okay for you to order wine, Auntie Gillian. If I'm staying dry, so are you. Get a milk shake."

Gillian pressed a button on the phone. "If I can't fit into my jeans, it'll be all your fault."

"Do an extra hour at the gym."

Gillian ordered two of everything and then put down the phone.

"Tell me about the tacky flirting," said Cara. She needed something to take her mind off Max, and off the baby, and off her daunting future.

Gillian kicked off her shoes, lifting her feet onto the chair, propping one elbow on her upraised knee. "I was trying to make Jake jealous."

Cara was confused. "I thought he was already interested in you."

"I think he is. A little, anyway. We danced pretty late last night. And it was fun. And he walked me back to the hotel. And then he said good-night at the elevator."

"Did you want him to come up?"

Gillian gave a sheepish shrug. "I wanted him to *want* to come up."

"But you didn't invite him."

"No."

"So he didn't turn you down."

"Please. He's male."

Cara coughed out a laugh. It felt good. "Do you even know what you want?"

"I don't," Gillian admitted. "Okay, I do. He blows hot and cold. One minute, he's all friendly and attentive, and the next minute I might as well be a lawn ornament."

"I think becoming a billionaire has messed with your head," Cara observed.

"I'm not a billionaire."

"You're used to being the center of attention. I bet when you walk into a room, every man snaps to."

"Only because I sign their paychecks."

"But Jake doesn't do it, and it makes you crazy."

Gillian groaned, raking her hands through her hair. "Have I turned into a spoiled princess?"

"Did the pilots flirt back?" asked Cara, struggling not to smile at her sister discomfort.

"Yes. And they weren't there for the interview, so they didn't know who I was. So money or not, I know I've still got it."

"And Jake knows you've got it."

"He does," Gillian agreed.

"Was he jealous?"

"I hope so."

"Are you seeing him again tonight?"

"I don't know. What are you doing?"

"The president is hosting a dinner and welcome reception for the summit heads of state. It's private, about two hundred people. Luckily, no press." Cara glanced at her watch. "I have to get dressed in an hour."

"When are you going back?"

"To D.C.?"

Gillian nodded.

"Tomorrow night, after the closing statements. I'm hitching a ride on Air Force One. I'll be busy every minute between now and then." It was just as well. The less time Cara had to think, the better.

# Ten

Max had been back in D.C. for three days.

Though Ariella's brief interview had momentarily taken attention off the president, it had also renewed interest in Eleanor Albert. Max's boss, Nadine, was more determined than ever to find the elusive woman. At the same time, Liam Fisher had come up with solid evidence that somebody from ANS had hacked into a computer in the president's campaign headquarters.

"We don't have a name yet," said Liam, rolling out a chair to take a seat next to Jake at the oval oak table in the NCN boardroom.

"We'll get there," said Max. "At least we know we're on the right track."

There was no evidence yet to implicate owner Graham Boyle, nor was there anything pointing to Marnie Salloway, but Max was still suspicious of his old boss. She'd been vague and smug the last time they spoke, and he was sure she was hiding something. Not that his suspicions got him any closer to the truth.

Nadine breezed into the room, an assistant in tow. "You went way too easy on Caroline Cranshaw in L.A.," she accused Max without preamble.

"She's a pro," Max returned while Nadine sat down. "She wasn't going to give us anything."

Jake slid a glance Max's way, silently indicating that he agreed with Nadine.

"The real story is ANS," said Max, looking to Liam for support. "We know they broke the law."

"We know somebody they once employed broke the law," Nadine retorted. "But we also know they targeted the president in their efforts to find information. That means somebody at the White House knows more than they're letting on."

"No," Max disagreed. "It means ANS *thinks* somebody at the White House knows more than they're letting on."

"And who knows the most about the scandal?" Nadine challenged, drumming her polished fingers on the table top.

Max didn't respond to the rhetorical question.

"ANS knows most about the scandal," Nadine answered her own question. "And they're targeting the White House for information. Eleanor Albert is the story. Find her."

Liam sat forward in his chair, folding his hands on the table, looking both dignified and wise. Even Nadine stopped to listen.

"If this hacking can be traced to ANS," he stated, "if it goes up to the reporters or up to Marnie Salloway or all the way up to Graham Boyle, then NCN has its own scoop."

"*If* they did it," Nadine retorted. "And *if* we can prove it. And *if* we can prove it before anyone else."

"They did it," said Liam with conviction. "And the campaign office is just the tip of the iceberg."

"I'd put money on Marnie having her fingers in this particular pie," Max added.

"Comforting," Nadine drawled sarcastically. "But the Eleanor story is a sure thing. If we find her, we've got a ready-made scoop." She looked at Liam. "She went somewhere after Fields. Even if she died, she did it somewhere."

"On it," Liam agreed, accepting the decision.

Then Nadine turned her attention to Max. "We just did Lynn Larson a big favor."

"I thought it was Lynn Larson who did us a favor." The press secretary could have called any network and made a deal for Ariella's statement.

"You're going down to the White House to collect."

Max immediately thought of Cara at the White House. He suspected she'd been avoiding him since their return from L.A. He knew the entire White House was scrambling to stop the slide in the president's popularity, and the press office was right in the thick of things. Still, he'd left half a dozen messages and she wasn't calling him back.

He missed her more than he could have imagined. The upside of approaching Lynn was that he had a decent chance of seeing Cara. His chest tightened in anticipation.

"Fine," he agreed. "What do you want me to ask her?"

Nadine came to her feet. "You're the investigative journalist. You figure it out."

Her assistant immediately hopped up, following Nadine out the door.

The three men waited a full minute.

"How far can we go investigating ANS on our own?" asked Jake.

Max responded, "Before it turns into flat-out insubordination?"

Liam grinned. "We're fairly safe if we do it after business hours."

"I'm on board," Max agreed.

He knew the best way to help his situation with Cara was to deal with the scandal that was taking all of her time. If they did prove something against ANS, then the public's attention would shift from the president. Cara's time would free up in a heartbeat. As he worked the coming long hours, Max would cling to that.

Cara paused in Lynn's office to stare at the biggest of the television screens on the office wall.

"In a fascinating twist that's seen the president's popularity drop even further," the pretty, blond female announcer cooed from the center of a small crowd at the front gate of the White House, "Madeline Schulenburg, a forty-six-year-old woman who grew up in Doublecreek, Montana, some two hours away from the president's hometown of Fields, is claiming her twenty-eight-year-old son was fathered by Ted Morrow."

Cara set the draft report from the Los Angeles trip on Lynn's desk. "I guess it was only a matter of time."

"Until the crazies came out?" Lynn swiveled in her high-backed desk chair to face Cara.

"There's no chance this is true, right?"

"I don't know what's true anymore," Lynn admitted, twisting her ring.

"It can't be." Though Cara supposed it was possible. Maybe there were two illegitimate children. Then again, why not three or four?

"Have you spoken to the president?" she asked her boss.

"That's what I get to do right now," Lynn rose to her feet, gathering a couple of files from her desktop. "Mr. President," she mumbled in a mocking tone. "On the Madeline Schulenburg situation. Can we talk about your sex life? Again?"

"So the White House is taking this seriously" came a deep voice from Lynn's open doorway.

Lynn's head whipped up, and Cara whirled to come face-to-face with Max.

"Who let you in here?" Lynn demanded.

Cara couldn't find her voice. She'd been working sixteen-hour days since Los Angeles, and it was still a fight to keep

Max from her mind. She missed him. And she was desperately confused and worried about the future.

"I have an appointment," said Max.

"Sandy was supposed to cancel," said Lynn.

"Is it true?" asked Max. "Is there another illegitimate child? Is the White House expecting more of them to surface?"

"Go away," said Lynn.

"Shall I put you down for a no comment?" asked Max.

Lynn squared her shoulders, glaring hard at Max. "Cara, would you please show the nice reporter out of the building?"

The request shook Cara back to life. "Yes." She moved toward Max. "Of course. Come with me, please." She gestured to the hallway.

"What's going on?" he muttered in her ear.

"Go," she ordered in a low growl.

She and Max headed straight down the hallway, while Lynn took a right toward the Oval Office.

Before she could stop him, Max ducked into her own office.

"Max," she called, quickly following to protect the information that sat exposed on her desk.

She crossed the small room, flipping over reports and closing file folders.

"Talk to me, Cara."

She turned. "I have nothing to say."

"If there are more children…"

"There are not," she told him with conviction.

"You're lying." He cocked his head, watching her intently.

She felt her pulse jump, and a funny buzz formed in the pit of the stomach that had nothing to do with the president.

Max took a step forward.

The buzz turned to genuine fear, and she sharply held up a hand. "Don't."

"So," he mused, coming to a stop far too close to her for comfort. "Either you're lying because the president has more secret children or because you don't know one way or the other."

"You have to leave, Max." She meant that on many different levels.

They couldn't discuss the president, and she didn't dare spend time in Max's company. Even now, even in the middle of the West Wing, in the midst of a crisis, she wanted to throw herself into his arms.

He lowered his voice. "I need to see you."

She shook her head. "That can't happen."

"Not here," he clarified. "Later. Tonight. At your place."

"No."

"We have to talk."

"I'm working tonight. And tomorrow night." And every night into the foreseeable future.

"You have to sleep sometime."

"Not with—" She snapped her jaw shut.

A twinkle came into his green eyes. "With me would definitely be my preference."

She tried to back away, but she was blocked by her desk. "This isn't a joke."

"I'm not joking. I miss you, Cara." He eased even closer.

She steeled herself, trying desperately to quash her feelings. She couldn't want Max. She couldn't touch him or talk to him, or even see him.

"You promised, Max," she told him in a pleading voice, looking straight into his eyes.

"I just want to talk."

"You're lying."

"You're right."

Voices sounded outside in the hall, and Cara quickly slipped sideways, putting some distance between them.

Max's glance dropped to her desktop. His blatant curiosity gave her a last burst of emotional strength.

"You're here investigating the story," she stated.

"I am," he admitted.

"Get out of my office, Max. Or I'll call security."

This time, he did take a step back. "Okay. I'll call you later."

"I won't answer."

"I'll try anyway."

And then he was gone.

Cara gripped the lip of the desk to steady herself. She took a few bracing breaths. It was obvious she couldn't be trusted around Max. It was just as obvious that he wasn't going to stay away from her.

She made her way around the desk, sitting down to face her computer terminal. There she brought up the human resources page. She entered a search, checking to see what public relations jobs were currently available in foreign embassies.

To her surprise, there was an opening in Australia.

The optimism that had stayed with Max since he'd made love to Cara in Los Angeles evaporated as he walked off the White House grounds. She was never going to listen to reason. She was never going to give the two of them a chance. She'd decided their relationship was impossible, and she wasn't going to explore any evidence to the contrary.

His only choices were to move on with his own life or to settle in for a long wait and spend the next four years campaigning against the president so that Cara would be free after the next election. Problem was, he didn't think he could wait four years, never mind eight.

He made his way to his Mustang, hit the remote to unlock the door, climbed into the driver's seat and extracted his phone from his pocket. He quashed the feelings for Cara that were messing with his reporter's instincts and entered the Georgetown address he'd seen scrawled across the yellow pad of paper on her desktop. She was meeting with someone in less than an hour.

He started his car, cranking up the heat against the gray,

blowing January day. He scrolled through the search results, discovering the address was in a medical building. More specifically, it was an obstetrics practice. Another quick search told Max the practice had been there for at least thirty years.

It struck him as odd that an obstetrician in D.C. would be involved in babies from Montana. But maybe the doctor had moved. Or maybe one of the mothers had ended up in D.C. They knew for certain in Eleanor's case that she'd hightailed it out of Fields while she was newly pregnant.

He pressed the speed dial button for Jake.

"Yeah?" came Jake's short greeting.

"I've got something," said Max.

"Eleanor?"

"No. Maybe something on her. But don't discount that the rumors of other children might be true. Lynn Larson's pretty rattled by the latest story."

"What do you need?" asked Jake.

"I'm heading for Georgetown. An obstetrics practice. I don't want to spook anyone by showing up with a camera, but can you be on standby in the neighborhood in case there's a doctor there who'll talk?"

"Sure. I'm with Liam, but we're just finishing up. Text me the address."

"Coming at you," Max promised.

He ended the call, sent Jake the address, then exited the parking lot. It took a while to negotiate the slushy, crowded streets, but he managed to find the medical building. He then searched out a parking spot and found one several blocks away.

Partway back to the front entrance of the six-story, brownstone, he spotted Cara exiting a taxi. He glanced at his watch. She was a good fifteen minutes early for her meeting. Too bad. He'd hoped to beat her inside and figure out which doctor or nurse or whoever she'd found who might know something.

Instead, he hung back. He gave her enough time to make it

through the halls and hopefully clear the waiting room. Then he followed.

The suite was on the sixth floor. The directory sign at the top of the elevator took him to the far end of the hallway to a set of double, frosted glass doors. He opened them slowly and glanced around a brightly lit, cheerfully decorated waiting room.

Three very pregnant women sat in the padded chairs, leafing through parenting magazines. Two other women held babies in their laps; one of them kept a sharp eye on a toddler playing with toys in a corner.

Max slipped inside, drawing the interest of the nurse behind the counter. The sign above her listed four doctors.

Trying to look like he belonged, Max moved toward the nurse's smiling face.

"How can I help you?" She peered at him above her reading glasses. Happily, there was no recognition in her eyes. She obviously wasn't an *After Dark* viewer.

Max hesitated, not knowing what to ask. There was absolutely no way to know which doctor to approach. It could be another staff member. It seemed unlikely that it was the nurse herself, or Cara would be out here talking.

Then inspiration struck him. "I'm here with Caroline Cranshaw." He pretended to search his pockets. "It's been a really busy day, and I'm afraid I've lost the name—"

"Oh, you're the *father*." The woman grinned as if she'd seen it all before.

Max's brain skipped a beat.

"She's talking with Dr. Murdoch in his office right now. You can feel free to join them." The nurse pointed. "Straight down the blue hallway. Dr. Murdoch's name is on the office door."

Max blinked in shock. Would Cara have actually lied about being pregnant to get in to see an obstetrician?

What was she, under deep cover? Good grief, she was a public relations specialist, not a private investigator.

"Right that way," the nurse reiterated. "The blue hallway."

"Thanks," Max told her, turning to go.

Cara was going to be ticked off, but he had to follow this lead. She'd made it more than clear that a relationship between them wasn't happening, and he had his professional integrity to think about. He couldn't let his feelings for her cloud his judgment any longer.

Cara had far too much power over his actions, and that was about to stop.

He made his way down the hall.

He gave a cursory knock on the doctor's office door, then opened it up.

The fiftysomething doctor looked up in surprise, and Cara turned her head at the sound.

She froze for a long second. Then her face blanched white, and her blue eyes grew to nearly twice their usual size.

"Hello, darling," he drawled, closing the door behind her. If she could lie, then so could he. If he pretended to be the father, she could hardly call him on it without exposing her own dishonesty.

The doctor looked at Cara for a second, then refocused his attention on Max.

Max strode forward as if he had every right to be there. He held out his hand to the doctor. "Max Gray. I'm sorry I'm late."

For good measure, he planted a quick kiss on the top of Cara's head before taking the chair beside her.

"Max," she rasped, swallowing. "How did you know?"

He smiled broadly and patted her hand. "You told me about the appointment. I know I forget things sometimes, but this is important, darling."

She blinked in what was obviously complete and utter confusion.

"Max Gray? From *After Dark?*" the doctor asked.

"Yes," Max responded easily.

"Nice to meet you." The doctor got back down to business.

"I was just saying to Caroline that I don't anticipate any complications. She's at a great age for a first child. There are no underlying health concerns. I've prescribed a prenatal vitamin, and we'll do the usual blood work. But otherwise, there's nothing special she needs to worry about for the next couple of months."

The doctor fell silent.

Max glanced back at Cara, wondering how long she was going to keep this up. How did she expect to segue from a fake pregnancy into questions about the president's illegitimate children?

She was still staring at him, completely still and obviously dumbfounded.

"Cara?" He waved a hand in front of her face.

She didn't react.

"Caroline?" The doctor rose to come around the desk. He took her hand. "Is something wrong?"

"How did you know?" she whispered to Max.

Something in her eyes turned Max's stomach to stone.

*Wait.*

*No.*

*No, it couldn't be.*

But he'd been an investigative reporter too long to ignore what his gut instinct was telling him.

He looked to the doctor, framing a slow, carefully worded question. "You did a pregnancy test here in the office?"

"Of course," the man responded. "We always confirm the home pregnancy test results. Our best estimate is seven weeks."

Cara was pregnant.

And she hadn't slept with anyone else. She had made that perfectly clear.

She was pregnant with Max's child.

The floor beneath him shifted, and he nearly fell out of his chair. He managed to stand on shaky legs, motioning vaguely to the door.

"I'm going to…" he managed. "I'll meet you…" He flicked a glance at Cara's stricken expression and swiftly left the office.

He walked through the waiting room, his mind a crush of conflicting emotions. He'd invaded Cara's privacy in an absolutely unforgivable way. But she'd lied to him. She'd kept him completely in the dark. And he was going to be a father.

As he pressed the elevator button, the world around him grew fuzzy and indistinct. He was in no way, shape or form in a position to become a father. He'd made that more than abundantly clear.

Cara opened the door of her apartment to greet her sister, trying valiantly to put on a brave face. "You can't just jump in your jet every time my life has a hiccup."

"This is more than a hiccup." Gillian pulled Cara into a tight hug. "This is a catastrophe."

Cara pointedly looked up the spiral staircase. "Ariella and Scarlet are here."

"Do they know?"

Cara started to shake her head.

"Do we know what?" came Ariella's voice from above.

The two women appeared at the top of the stairs, peering down. Scarlet was Cara's close friend, a D.C. party planner she had known for years.

Neither Cara nor Gillian answered the question.

"What don't we know?" asked Ariella.

"You might as well tell them." Gillian shut the door and shrugged out of her black coat. "They're your friends, and they love you."

"Whatever it is, you'd better tell us," Ariella said as she descended the stairs.

"I've applied for an embassy job in Australia," said Cara with a warning look at Gillian not to share more.

"You're doing what?" Scarlet gasped from up-top.

"What on earth?" Ariella asked. "Why would you do that?"

Gillian folded her arms across her chest, arching a brow in Cara's direction.

"Fine," Cara capitulated, deciding it was time to face up to the reality of her future.

"Because she's pregnant," Gillian put in.

*"What?"* Ariella shrieked.

"Well, that was blunt," Cara told her sister.

"There's no point in beating around the bush," Gillian returned. "It'll be obvious in a few weeks. And even if you leave the country, they're going to notice next Christmas when you show up with a baby."

"Who says I'm coming to D.C. for Christmas?"

"Back up, back up," Ariella insisted.

"Are we going to stand here and talk about this in the entry hall?" asked Gillian.

"We're not." Scarlet motioned to them. "Get up here and tell us what's going on."

Ariella pivoted to head back up the stairs. Cara followed, and Gillian brought up the rear.

"Has he called yet?" asked Gillian.

"Who?" Ariella and Scarlet asked in unison.

Cara turned on her sister. "Are you going to lay my entire life bare here?"

"We want to help you," said Ariella.

"And we sure don't want you to leave D.C.," Scarlet added.

There was a note of sincerity in each of their voices that tugged at Cara's heart. She knew she could trust her friends. Maybe their support was exactly what she needed right now.

"I am pregnant," Cara admitted as the women made their way to the living room and settled onto the sofas and into armchairs.

"How far along?" asked Ariella.

"Seven weeks," Cara answered Ariella.

"What does being pregnant have to do with leaving town?" asked Scarlet.

"She needs to get away from the father," Gillian said.

"Is he nasty?" asked Scarlet.

"Who is he?" asked Ariella.

"Max Gray," Cara admitted, deciding it was time to get everything out on the table. She was going to have to make some significant changes in her life. Keeping any of this a secret was no longer a viable option. "It's Max Gray."

"Seriously?" asked Scarlet, a note of awe in her voice. Cara realized Scarlet saw Max only as a television personality and one of the top ten hottest men in D.C.

"He's not nasty," Ariella put in staunchly. "Max is a great guy."

"The biggest problem is that he doesn't want children," Gillian explained.

"So what?" said Ariella. "He's getting one anyway."

"The biggest problem is the conflict of interest," Cara corrected her sister.

"The baby is a conflict of interest?" asked Scarlet in obvious confusion.

"I can't have a relationship with Max. He's a reporter. I work at the White House."

Ariella sat up straighter on the sofa. "I don't understand. You're not in a relationship with him already?"

"I'm not," Cara affirmed.

"Then how did it happen?" Scarlet seemed to search for an explanation. "Are you his groupie?"

Cara couldn't help but laugh a little hysterically at that suggestion. It might have been easier if it was a one-night stand.

"They dated a while ago," Gillian put in. "Before the election."

Cara sobered. "But it's over."

Scarlet glanced around the circle of friends. "That doesn't matter. He has to step up and take responsibility."

Cara subconsciously moved her hand to her stomach. "I'm

not about to foist an innocent baby onto an unwilling father. I'm not even sure how he found out."

"I am," said Gillian.

Cara turned to her sister in surprise.

"I talked to Jake. Max went to the doctor's office because he thought you were following up on a lead about the president."

Cara's mind went back to Max's odd behavior. "He didn't know?" she ventured.

"Not when he arrived. He was going along with what he thought was your ruse."

"Until he asked about the test." Cara remembered Max's reaction to the doctor's words.

Her heart sank. He'd found out she was pregnant right there in the doctor's office, and he had immediately walked away. It confirmed everything she'd ever feared.

"He feels guilty for invading your privacy," said Gillian.

Cara came to her feet, struggling against an unexpected surge of hurt and anger. "Invading my privacy? *That's* what he feels guilty about? Not because I'm pregnant? Not because he's abandoning his child? Not because he doesn't care one whit about either of us?"

"I don't know how clearly he's thinking right now," said Gillian.

"Max can stuff it." Cara paced across the room, trying to bring her emotions back under control. Forget Max. She was going to deal with this on her own, far away, where she wouldn't be tempted by him or hurt by him ever again. "I'm out of here."

"You can't leave us," cried Scarlet.

"Well, I can't stay here." Cara returned to the armchair and plunked back down, feeling exhausted. "He's never going to change."

"He feels bad about that, too," said Gillian.

"Good for him," Cara snapped.

"If you're not hiding the pregnancy," Ariella offered reasonably, "then get another job in D.C."

"What other job?" asked Cara. "Any job in the White House is going to have the same problem."

"Work for me," said Gillian. "You can do whatever you want if you work for me."

"Very charitable of you, big sister. But you're not in D.C. And I'm not taking your handout."

"Then work for us," said Scarlet.

"Public relations for a party planner?" Cara scoffed.

"Not full-time," Scarlet continued. "And you wouldn't have to be in the office very often. You could work from home. Be a mom." She snapped her fingers. "Open a public relations consulting firm."

"We'd hire you in a heartbeat," said Ariella. "You could set your own hours, do a ton of the work right here in the apartment."

"I don't know." But Cara could see that it would solve one of her problems. Well, two of her problems really. It would get her out of the White House and it would give her more time with her baby.

But Max would still be in D.C. She'd still be hopelessly attracted to him. And it would hurt her to see him and know he didn't want them.

"Are you in love with him?" Scarlet asked softly.

"No," said Cara.

"Yes," said Gillian.

Cara glared at her sister, but Gillian just spread her hands palms facing the ceiling. "What exactly do you think this is?"

"I am not in love with Max," Cara stated with authority. "I'm simply carrying his baby and fighting some kind of physical obsession over having sex with him."

"Everybody wants to sleep with him," said Scarlet.

Three gazes swung toward her.

"I'm not saying me personally," she hastily put in. "I'm

saying most of the females across the country have the hots for him."

"She's not wrong," said Ariella. Then Ariella turned to Cara. "You can't leave me. Not now. Not with all of this going on. You know more about politics than any of us, and I am absolutely going to need your help and advice."

Her words helped to put Cara's own problems into perspective.

"You're the president's daughter, aren't you?" Scarlet asked Ariella.

"I'm afraid I might be," said Ariella.

Cara's heart went out to her friend. While she might be able to quit the White House, Ariella had been about to be involuntarily swept up in a whirlwind.

Cara realized it was true. Ariella needed her. She also realized her friends were in Washington. Her life was in Washington. Australia might have been a nice fantasy, but it wasn't a good reality.

"I'll stay and help," Cara found herself promising.

Somehow, she'd summon the strength to stay away from Max. Who knew, maybe her feelings would fade and everything would be all right. Maybe Gillian was wrong about Cara being in love. Gillian might be a genius, but there were a few times when she was wrong.

There was a chance this could be one of them.

# Eleven

Max sat across from Jake at O'Donovan's, an Irish tavern in Georgetown about a mile from the NCN studios.

"I can't believe you haven't spoken to her yet," Jake said, spinning his heavy beer mug in a circle on the polished wood table.

Max shifted in his red leather armchair. "I don't know what to say to her."

"It's been three days."

"She knows it's been three days." Max took a swig of his half-full mug of Irish stout.

"You think you're a comedian?" Jake demanded.

"I think this is none of your damn business."

"I'm your friend."

"Then you should know when to butt out."

A group of college-aged girls giggled as they made their way past the table toward the high stools at the brass-railed bar. Sconce lights and shelves of exotic whisky and leather-bound books decorated the dark wood walls. A picture of the establishment's founder, Angus O'Donovan, flanked by gold-flecked mirrors, hung in prominence behind the two bartenders.

"A good friend never butts out," Jake said.

"What do you think I should say? Do you want me to offer her money?" Max would do that, of course. Financially, his child would never want for a thing.

"You could start with, 'We're having a baby. Let's talk about what we should do.'"

"And open myself up to virtually anything she might ask?" Max couldn't stand the thought of having to say no to anything, of letting Cara down, of seeing the hurt and disappointment in her eyes. "I'd make a terrible father," he repeated for about the hundredth time.

"Why?" Jake reached for a handful of peanuts. "Seriously, why?"

"I don't like kids," Max opened with the obvious.

Jake seemed to ponder that.

"I have a dangerous job that might kill me at any moment," Max continued. "Cara would spend half her life waiting to become a widow. I had zero in the way of paternal role models. I haven't a clue how to even go about talking to a kid. I'm genetically unsuited to fatherhood. When the going gets tough, the Gray men get gone."

"All true," Jake unexpectedly agreed.

"You see my point?"

"I do."

Max rested his hand on his beer mug. "So this conversation is over."

"You still have to talk to her."

Max's stomach clenched, and his jaw hardened in frustration. "And say *what?*"

"She knows all that other stuff, right?"

Max gave a sharp nod. Then he drained his glass.

"Then offer her money." Jake's tone was flat with condemnation. "If that's all you've got, offer to pay her to raise your kid all by herself."

Something stabbed in Max's chest.

Jake wasn't finished. "But look her in the eye, Max. Be a man about it, and tell her in person exactly what you will and won't do for this baby. She didn't get pregnant all by herself, but it sure sounds like that's the way she'll be coping with it."

Max pushed his beer mug away, his stomach going sour.

He caught a movement in his peripheral vision, and Gillian suddenly appeared at the table. Max nearly gave himself whiplash looking around to see if Cara was with her.

She wasn't.

"Did you talk to him?" Gillian asked Jake.

Jake rose, placing a hand loosely at the small of her back. "I did."

Max pushed back his chair and came to his feet. "That was all for her?" he demanded.

"Yeah," said Jake. "That was all for her. Doesn't make it any less true."

"You took me out to the woodshed to get in good with Gillian?"

"No," Gillian responded for Jake. "He's in good with Gillian, and that's why he took you out to the woodshed." She leaned a little closer to Max. "You going to hurt my baby sister?"

"I already did," Max admitted.

"Undo it," said Gillian.

Max shook his head. He couldn't undo it. It was out of his control.

"She applied for an embassy communications job in Australia," Gillian told him.

Max's heart slammed into the side of his chest. "What? Why?"

"So you wouldn't have to be bothered with your baby. She thought it was a good idea to get far, far away."

Max recoiled. But it was a good thing, right? He wouldn't be nearby to mess anything up. The baby would be well cared for, and he could carry on with his life as normal.

Gillian pointed her index finger at Max's chest. "I can see what you're thinking. Don't you dare try to stop her. Don't you dare mess it up."

"Why would I mess it up?" Stopping Cara from leaving D.C. would be foolish. She was separating them. That was a smart move. He'd always known she was smart.

"You messed it up before," Gillian continued. "She wanted you to think there was another guy. You do realize that was the plan, right? If you thought there was another guy, you could tell yourself it wasn't your baby, and you could walk away without worrying about her."

"You lied on purpose?" Max demanded.

"I was your patsy?" Jake asked in obvious surprise.

"Sorry," Gillian said to Jake.

"Here I felt guilty for betraying your secret."

"I knew you would," said Gillian.

"You knew I'd feel guilty?" asked Jake.

"I knew you'd blab to Max. I was counting on it. It was part of the master plan."

"Really?" asked Jake in obvious admiration.

"Really," Gillian answered.

"You're amazing," Jake responded with a sappy grin.

"When does Cara leave?" asked Max.

Not that he needed to know. Or maybe he did. Was Jake right? Did Max owe it to Cara to at least have a conversation? Even if he had nothing but money to offer, should he do it in person? And would she even listen to him if he tried?

Expecting Gillian, Cara was shocked to open her apartment door to Max. Determined as she was, after talking with Gillian, Ariella and Scarlet, to move forward in her new life, she'd cried into her pillow most of last night. Morning hadn't looked much brighter.

He was the last person she wanted to cope with. But standing in the hallway, he looked as tired and hollow as she felt. And she couldn't quite quash a rush of sympathy.

"We need to talk, Cara." He looked like a man headed for the gallows.

She braced herself, determined to get this over with quickly. "No, we don't have to talk. It's fine, Max. There's nothing left to say and nothing left for you to do."

"You're pregnant," he rasped, looking every bit as frightened as he had in Fields when the avalanche hit.

"Yes, I am," Cara confirmed, proud of her matter-of-fact tone. "And I'm fine with that. I truly am. I've made plans."

"So I heard."

"You did?" That surprised Cara.

"From Gillian."

"Oh."

Dear sister Gillian yet again. She'd obviously called Jake last night, thereby sending every word down the überefficient communications pipeline to Max.

"Can I come in?" he asked.

Cara couldn't hold back a frustrated sigh. "Really, Max, I'd rather you—"

But he stepped inside, causing her to step backward to avoid touching him.

"Well, okay, fine," she capitulated. "Come on in."

He closed the door, pressing his back up against it.

"I'm sorry," he began, his glance flicking to her stomach.

"I'm not," she told him with determination.

Amid all the uncertainty and chaos, Cara had come to understand at least one thing. She wasn't sorry about this baby. She was going to be a good mother.

"I meant I was sorry for barging into the doctor's office. I thought you were talking about the president."

"Gillian told me."

"It was a horrible invasion of your privacy, and I don't know what I was thinking." Then some of the fear and defensiveness left his eyes. "But you should have told me you were pregnant."

"Really?" She honestly wasn't sure about that. "Don't you think you'd be better off not knowing? All it's done is make you feel guilty. Knowing the truth hasn't changed your opinion about being a father. It's not going to change your behavior toward the baby."

"Were you really planning to keep it from me? Forever?"

Cara gave a small shrug. That had seemed like her most reasonable plan.

"By leaving the country?" he asked.

"Yes."

"You'd just up and leave me?" he asked, a funny tone coming into his voice.

"*Leave* you? How could I leave you, Max? We were never together. You and me were a nonstarter from minute one."

She could quit work at the White House, getting rid of the conflict of interest. But Max didn't want to be a father. And since she was definitely going to be a mother, the gulf between them was as wide as ever.

He lifted his hand. For a minute, she expected him to touch her face, the way he'd done a hundred times. Stroke his broad palm gently across her cheek, cup her face, draw her in for a kiss.

She could almost feel his fingertips, his full lips coming down on hers.

But he didn't do it. He dropped his hand instead, and her chest tightened in disappointment.

"What do you want, Max?"

"I have money," he told her.

"Really? Being a television star pays well, does it?"

"I meant you and the baby will never want for anything. You'll never have to worry."

Cara swallowed against her tightening throat. She swore to herself that she wouldn't break down. She needed to get this over with as quickly as possible without losing her dignity.

"Thank you, Max," she offered simply.

He frowned. "I might not be able to be with you, but I'll make sure…"

She waited, but he didn't finish the sentence.

"Thank you," she forced out again.

He raised his hand again. This time, it was to rake his fingers through his hair. "Seriously?" he asked her.

Cara didn't understand.

He pivoted on one foot, taking two paces across the small foyer, his voice growing stronger. "That's your reaction?"

"My reaction to what?"

He turned. "Some stupid jerk stands here in front of you and offers you nothing but money to raise his baby all on your own, and you thank him?"

"Are you mad at me?"

"Yes!"

*"Why?"*

He had no right to be angry. She was making this as easy as possible on him. If anyone deserved to be mad, it was her.

He moved back in front of her. "Tell me no, Cara. Tell me off. Tell me that's not good enough. Hit me or something." His tone rose. "Tell me what you want from me."

"Nothing," she assured him with conviction. "I don't want a single thing from you, Max. We don't need your money. I don't want your charity. The baby and I are going to be perfectly fine, thank you very much."

"Without me?"

"Yes, without you."

Wasn't that the entire point of the conversation?

"In Australia?" Max drawled sarcastically.

Cara was confused. "Who said we were going to Australia?"

"It just occurred to me this very second that this is exactly what you want."

"Huh?"

"For me to go away quietly, to leave you alone, to stay out of your and the baby's life."

Cara stepped closer. "Max, you are losing your mind."

He glared at her for a long moment. His eyes went from glittering emeralds to a stormy sea to dull jade.

"Don't let me do it," he finally said.

"Have you been drinking?"

"Don't let me walk away."

"I'm not *letting* you do anything."

Max was making his own choices. They had nothing to do with her. She couldn't force him one way or another, even if she'd wanted to.

His tone went dull with disgust. "If I walk away from you, I'm no better than my old man."

All the fight went out of Cara. Her entire body congealed into one big ache, and her tone went dead flat. "That's not a reason to stay."

She wouldn't want him under those circumstances.

They stared at each other in charged silence. Then he reached for her hand. She glanced down, hating the way his touch brought her whole body to life.

"I love you, Cara," he whispered in what sounded like amazement. "Do you suppose that's a reason to stay?"

Her stunned gaze flew back to his.

He coughed out a brief, confused laugh. "How about that? I love you so much I can't even think straight. And I am so sorry I didn't realize it until now."

His words weren't computing in her brain.

"Max, what are you saying?"

"I'm saying that I'm not letting you go. I can't let you go. I could never let you go." His free hand went to her stomach. "And I'm not leaving our baby."

Her mind flew into a whirl.

Before she could clear it, he'd moved closer still.

"You can't leave the country," he told her.

"I'm not leaving the country. Max, what is going on here?" She was trying desperately not to hope. But it sounded like he was talking about a future together.

"I'm having an epiphany," he told her. "And it feels great."

"But you don't want a baby."

"Theoretically, no. And there are a lot of logical reasons for that. But you're not theoretical, and neither is our baby. So I've changed my mind."

"Just like that?" she challenged.

"Yes."

"In the past two minutes?"

"Yes. Try to keep up, Cara. I'm in love with you. Did I mention that? Let me say it again. I love you very, very much."

"But—"

He brushed his thumb across her lips to silence her. "I was an idiot. But I'm over it now. Maybe it was Jake's lecture. Maybe it was seeing you. Maybe the thought of you leaving D.C."

"I'm not leaving D.C.," she repeated.

"Gillian said you were moving to Australia."

"Gillian lies quite a lot." Cara was going to have to talk to her sister about that.

Max smiled. "I'm going to kiss you now."

Cara scrambled to wrap her mind around his words. "Are you saying what I think you're saying?"

"If you think I'm saying that I love you, I'm not leaving you, I want to have a baby with you and I'm about to kiss you, then yes, I'm saying what you think I'm saying."

Cara couldn't stop a smile from forming on her face. The aches and pains evaporated from her body, her heart beginning to hope. "Kiss me, Max."

He dipped his head, voice dropping to a whisper. "When I'm finished, you better be ready to tell me that you love me back."

His lips touched hers, and she felt his unabashed love spread through every corner of her body. One of his arms went around her waist, drawing her close, while the other hand stayed protectively cupped around her stomach.

His mouth opened, lips parting hers, his tongue teasing her senses, while his warmth and strength engulfed her from head to toe.

Her arms wound around his neck, and she clung to him as the kiss went on and on.

He finally drew back.

"I love you," burst from a place deep in her chest.

Max smiled. "Thank goodness." He smoothed back her hair. "That'll make it so much easier for you to marry me."

Cara's jaw dropped open.

"I don't have a ring. But I can get one in the next ten minutes if that's a deal breaker. I don't know how we'll make this work with our jobs, but we will. You're my number one priority." He glanced down. "You and the baby."

"You don't like babies," she couldn't help pointing out.

"I'll like your baby. I'll love our baby. I promise, Cara, I will love our baby every second of every day. And I won't die and leave the two of you alone. War-torn cities and crocodiles are in my past."

"You can't uproot your entire life on a whim, Max." Cara was starting to get nervous. This was too much, too fast. It was too perfect.

"It's not a whim. It's a long-overdue brick to the side of my head. I love you so much, Cara. I'm not my father. I promise I won't make his mistakes. Nothing matters to me but you."

Cara began to believe him.

"I quit my job," she told him softly. "I no longer work for the White House. So we don't have a conflict of interest anymore."

He drew her close once again, hugging her tight. "No conflict?"

"No conflict."

"So, I can stay here?"

"Tonight?" Cara would love nothing better than to spend the night in Max's arms.

"Forever."

Three nights later, Cara and Max were back at the Worthington Hotel ballroom. It was a fundraiser for the local school district and Gillian's last night in Washington. She'd made a sizable donation to the computer technology program, while Max had been invited as a local celebrity.

It would be one of Max's last appearances as the host of *After Dark*. He'd told Nadine that he was happy to stay on with the network in another capacity, but he wouldn't be traveling to dangerous parts of the world to capture the stories that had become *After Dark's* trademark.

Happily, Nadine had asked him to take an advisory role. He was going to continue to work on both the Eleanor Albert and the ANS angles. Nadine also told him she had her eye on two up-and-coming investigative reporters as rising stars for the network. The young men were handsome, energetic and fearless.

Max would also advise on the updated version of *After Dark*. The young men were beside themselves with excitement. Max had confessed to Cara that his biggest worry was keeping them from taking too many chances. Then he told her they reminded him of himself when he was younger.

Lynn had been disappointed to lose Cara's communications skills. But, luckily, she was a closet romantic who believed strongly in family. She was thrilled by the prospect of both a wedding and a new baby.

The school fundraiser speeches were over, the dinner dishes cleared away and the waitstaff was now serving individual, three-layered, triple chocolate mousse. Each of the beautiful desserts were topped with berries, spun sugar and a spiral straw of white and dark chocolate.

Cara's appetite was still healthy, and her mouth watered shamelessly in anticipation of such decadence. So, when her dessert was put down in front of her, she immediately scooped up her fork.

Max was watching her, a smug little smile on his face. She also realized she had Gillian's and Jake's attention, as well as the attention of the other four people at the round table.

Was it that surprising for a woman to want dessert?

She frowned at Max.

He simply grinned in return.

Deciding to ignore them, she sliced her dessert fork into the edge of the creamy concoction.

Then something caught her eye, something shiny and sparkling glinting in the light from the overhead chandeliers.

Cara squinted, tilting her head to find a gorgeous diamond ring had been dropped over the chocolate straw and was resting against a plump strawberry. The band was woven white-and-yellow gold, inset with tiny white diamonds, all topped with a spectacular pink solitaire, the same shade as the earrings Max had given to her for Christmas.

She stilled, then smiled, raising her loving gaze to his. "How did you get the stones to match?"

"I called in a favor. A guy I met at the Argyle Mine. They expressed it up."

The entire table breathed a collective "Aw."

He deftly removed the ring from the dessert.

"I'm still eating that," she informed him through her wide grin.

"Eat as many as you like. But give me your hand first."

She held out her left hand, and he slipped the ring onto her finger, sealing it with a kiss.

The table erupted in applause, and Cara could feel her cheeks heat in self-consciousness.

She held out her hand to admire the subtle color, loving the way it sparkled against her finger.

"Like it?" asked Max.

"I love it." She leaned toward him, and he met her kiss halfway.

"I love you," he whispered in her ear.

"Me, too," she whispered back.

When she straightened in her seat, conversation had resumed around the table. Next to her, Gillian was waiting to see the ring.

"Nice," she said to Max with a nod of approval.

"Thank you." Then he paused. "Not that I'm going to believe a word you say ever again."

"All the lies were for your own good," she offered.

"Australia?" he asked, capturing Cara's hand once more to hold it in his.

"She *did* apply for a new job," Gillian assured him. "At least until Ariella, Scarlet and I talked her out of it."

"So I should thank you?"

Gillian shrugged her slim shoulders, bare beneath the spaghetti straps of her ivory gown. "Considering how each of my lies ended, I'd say you should thank me very much."

Max laughed out loud.

"I'm eating my dessert now," Cara announced, lifting her fork to dig in. The mousse was sweet and creamy on her tongue, and she moaned in appreciation.

"Is it time for us to leave?" asked Max, glancing at his watch.

"You're contractually obligated to stay until nine," Cara reminded him. Not that she had any objection to returning to her apartment. The pregnancy was still making her tired early, and sleeping in Max's arms was more of an indulgence than the triple chocolate mousse.

"Since this is my last celebrity gig, I'm perfectly willing to break the contractual terms."

"When's your final show?" Gillian asked.

"Next Friday. After that, I go back to ordinary, anonymous life. Not that life will ever be ordinary with Cara."

"Nice save," Cara told him between bites.

"Would you like to know what I'm going to do?" Jake asked Gillian. His arm was stretched out across the back of her chair, his fingers brushing her bare shoulder.

The band launched into its first song, and the other two couples at the table left for the dance floor.

"Are you doing something new?" Gillian asked Jake.

"Max doesn't need a cameraman anymore."

"What about the new guys?" Cara asked. It hadn't occurred to her that Jake would be out of a job.

"They can find their own cameramen. I've got things to do, places to go."

"What things?" Gillian seemed genuinely curious.

"I've been saving money for a while now," he told her.

"For?" she prompted.

"To start my own production company. Documentaries mostly, but maybe a little drama."

"Really?"

"Really."

While Cara watched the interplay, Max absently toyed with her diamond ring.

"It's nearly nine," he whispered in her ear.

"I'm not finished dessert yet," she whispered back.

"And what places?" Gillian's attention was fully on Jake.

"I'm looking for a good home base for the company." His fingers trailed along the tip of her shoulder. "I was thinking maybe Seattle."

"What a coincidence." Gillian smiled playfully, fluttering her fingers across the low cut of her dress. "*I* live in Seattle."

"What a coincidence," Jake echoed.

Cara leaned toward Max. "Should we give them some privacy?"

"We could go home," he suggested brightly.

"If you like, you could stay with me," Gillian offered.

Now Cara was more than a little curious.

"I could stay with you," Jake agreed, eyes warm.

Gillian's smile grew even more mischievous. "I have a nice little apartment above my garage."

"I'm not staying above your garage."

"It's got a view of the ocean, a pool, a lovely rose garden."

"I'm not staying above your garage," Jake repeated with certainty.

Gillian pouted. "You have other plans?"

Jake touched his index finger to her chin. "I definitely have other plans."

Cara pushed back her chair, turning to Max. "Dance, sweetheart?"

He laughingly and swiftly came to his feet, offering her his arm as they took their exit from the table.

Cara allowed herself one quick glance back and saw Jake lean in to kiss Gillian.

She looked up at Max. "Do you think they're…"

"If they're not," he answered, spinning her onto the floor and pulling her smoothly into his arms, "they're about to."

Cara easily matched her steps to Max's, smiling at the sight of her new ring.

"Thank you," she told him. "It's absolutely beautiful."

"I'm sorry I didn't have it when I proposed." He kissed her ring finger one more time.

"I got the feeling that was spontaneous," she told him.

"It was. Once I realized what a buffoon I'd been, I couldn't wait a second longer to make it better."

"I'm glad you didn't wait." Cara wouldn't have given up a moment of the past three days.

"I'm done with waiting. I want to be your husband as soon

as humanly possible." He paused. "Unless, of course, you want a big, fancy wedding."

"Do you want a fancy wedding?"

"I'll marry you in the National Cathedral or at a drive-through in Vegas. Just so long as you become my wife."

"No to the drive-through," she told him with a laugh.

"The National Cathedral?"

"Why don't we let Scarlet decide? She's the expert."

"Can we ask her to hurry?"

"Absolutely. Your baby needs a daddy, the sooner the better."

Max's hand gently cradled her stomach, intense, unvarnished love in his tone. "I'm going to try my best, Cara. I promise you. I'll read books. I'll take classes."

"You don't need classes," she told him, struggling not to tear up. "You're going to be a great father, Max. All you have to do is love our baby."

He gathered her close, a catch in his own voice. "Then it's going to be easy. Because I already do."

\* \* \* \* \*

*A sneaky peek at next month...*

# Desire™

**PASSIONATE AND DRAMATIC LOVE STORIES**

## My wish list for next month's titles...

In stores from 15th March 2013:

*2 stories in each book - only £5.49!*

☐ The King Next Door – Maureen Child

& Bedroom Diplomacy – Michelle Celmer

☐ A Real Cowboy – Sarah M. Anderson

& Marriage with Benefits – Kat Cantrell

☐ All He Really Needs – Emily McKay

& A Tricky Proposition – Cat Schield

**Available at WHSmith, Tesco, Asda, Eason, Amazon and Apple**

## Just can't wait?

0313/5

# *Special Offers*

Every month we put together collections and longer reads written by your favourite authors.

Here are some of next month's highlights— and don't miss our fabulous discount online!

On sale 5th April

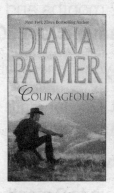

On sale 15th March

On sale 5th April

## The World of Mills & Boon®

There's a Mills & Boon® series that's perfect for you. We publish ten series and, with new titles every month, you never have to wait long for your favourite to come along.

***Blaze®***
*Scorching hot, sexy reads*
4 new stories every month

**By Request**
*Relive the romance with the best of the best*
9 new stories every month

***Cherish™***
*Romance to melt the heart every time*
12 new stories every month

***Desire™***
*Passionate and dramatic love stories*
8 new stories every month